ENJOY A

GW01326643

?-00

Geoff
Raw

03-0)

The Mark

The *'Jack Mawgan'* Trilogy

Book 3

GEOFF NEWMAN

Copyright © 2014 Geoffrey Newman.

All rights reserved. No part of this book may be reproduced, stored, or transmitted by any means—whether auditory, graphic, mechanical, or electronic—without written permission of both publisher and author, except in the case of brief excerpts used in critical articles and reviews. Unauthorized reproduction of any part of this work is illegal and is punishable by law.

ISBN: 978-1-4834-2224-4 (sc)
ISBN: 978-1-4834-2225-1 (e)

Because of the dynamic nature of the Internet, any web addresses or links contained in this book may have changed since publication and may no longer be valid. The views expressed in this work are solely those of the author and do not necessarily reflect the views of the publisher, and the publisher hereby disclaims any responsibility for them.

Any people depicted in stock imagery provided by Thinkstock are models, and such images are being used for illustrative purposes only. Certain stock imagery © Thinkstock.

Lulu Publishing Services rev. date: 12/05/2014

AUTHOR'S NOTE

To SUGGEST THAT THOSE generous souls who put themselves forward as trustees of the many Air Ambulance Trusts around the country are uniformly evil is of course hyperbole. I am sure that the vast majority are entirely without blemish but unfortunately if that were true it would not provide an interesting plot for my story so I beg them not to take my aspersions seriously. That said we know from our newspapers that corruption is everywhere and our government, our charities and our public services are particularly vulnerable to the few who break our bond of trust. Occasionally it is our elected politicians that let us down. Lord Acton, a prominent historian of the Victorian era, once said in a letter to Mary Gladstone (daughter of the Prime Minister, William Gladstone, and his confidante and advisor)…

"I cannot accept your canon that we are to judge Pope and King unlike other men, with a favourable presumption that they did no wrong. If there is any presumption it is the other way against holders of power, increasing as the power increases. Historic responsibility has to make up for the want of legal responsibility. Power tends to corrupt and absolute power corrupts absolutely. Great men are almost always bad men, even when they exercise influence and not authority: still more when you add the tendency or the certainty of corruption by authority. There is no worse heresy than that the office sanctifies the holder of it."(Wikipedia)

Whether you agree with Lord Acton or not we must always be prepared to take our leaders to task when they overstep the mark.

(This story is built around real places, real people and real events, but the plot and characters in the book are entirely fictional.)

DEDICATION

To THE POLICE AIR Support, Rescue and Air Ambulance communities who do a sterling job providing and maintaining the nation's vital aviation-based rapid response services.

ACKNOWLEDGEMENTS

I OWE MY SANITY to the forbearance of my darling wife who has always provided encouragement and a cup of tea whenever either was needed.

Others who contributed to my efforts in some way, shape or form include my two daughters, Tabetha and Milly, Tony Ridley, Nigel Penton Tilbury, Chris Howard, Lynne Hacking and Paul Knight. A special thanks to my editor Hannah Brandley and to Milly for her cover design. Thanks also to all those readers of the first two books who gave me the encouragement necessary to embark on a sequel to complete the trilogy and for suggestions that have resulted in a plan to look at novels that cover Jacks early career as well as that of Dan Barclay.

PROLOGUE

January 2002, Westminster Abbey
Funeral of Sir Gerald Lummis

THE PRIME MINISTER SAT in the front row along with members of the Lummis family and dignitaries from the aviation community including representatives from the military and the police.

Sir Gerry had, in his lifetime, managed to grow the world of public service aviation, and particularly helicopters, into a sizeable business and those who had benefited from his support were gathered to pay homage.

In 1986 there were no air ambulances and just two police helicopters in the UK. By the time he died in 2001 there were close to twenty air ambulances and every one of the forty-three police forces had access to a helicopter or fixed wing aircraft. The nation's search and rescue forces were changed out of all recognition in that time and now the military's undoubted expertise was complimented by equipment that was as good as anything else in the world.

The late Sir Gerald Anthony Lummis KCB was the government minister widely credited with the idea that helicopters were an underutilised resource and he had done everything in his power to promote their use. His crusade to increase the scope of government involvement in search and rescue, police and emergency medical services stemmed from a love of all things aviation and was accelerated by personally witnessing the dramatic air ambulance mission that saved the life of a close friend's young son. From that day to his last he fought the 'nay-sayers' in the National Health Service to promote the interests of air ambulances in particular but was never able to convince the Treasury to fund them in the way he wanted. The financial burden fell for the most part on the charities set up to fund air ambulances county by county.

He had greater success when he held the levers of power at the Home Office. During his lengthy service as Home Secretary he was able to grow police aviation considerably. The battles he fought with the Ministry of Defence were complicated by the kind of inter-service turf wars that characterised life in the military. Eventually though he won his case and moved Search and Rescue helicopters from the military to the commercial sector thus confounding his enemies in the MoD and ensuring his financial future was assured. After all, we live in a world where every good turn deserves another and nothing is for nothing.

In doing these 'good works' he crushed opposition to his ideas and put several young and up and coming politicians' noses out of joint. His death gave two of his victims who had subsequently risen to high office a chance for revenge. Between them Toby Stewart and Freddie McLaren would show the world that Lummis' ideas were out-dated, unnecessary and unaffordable.

CHAPTER 1

19.00 – Monday 17th April, 2006
The Prime Minister's Private Office
Downing Street, London

"I GOT THE ESTIMATES you asked me for yesterday." It was Freddie McLaren's opening gambit. He had been waiting for twenty minutes for the Prime Minister to finish the call to his wife. The PM was sitting in an armchair with his feet up on the coffee table. His wife was apparently buying furniture for their son's new flat in Sheffield. Toby Stewart was the kind of guy who liked to be in control and his wife Marie knew that. They had a twenty-minute conversation about the curtains for a flat he was never likely to see the inside of. When the minutiae were sorted Toby turned to Freddie.

"So how much do we need?" said the Prime Minister, responding to Freddie's arrival.

"About two hundred and fifty million."

"Each?"

"Nope. The whole shooting match."

They were discussing the cost estimates for a couple of would-be government projects for which no budget authority currently existed. The PM had decided that it would be appropriate to build a new teaching hospital in his constituency and to get maximum PR benefit he wanted it to start as soon as possible. Unfortunately the keeper of the nation's piggy bank, the Chancellor of the Exchequer, Montgomery Green, refused to allow the project to go forward unless his own pet project was also funded. He wanted to build a new runway at his local airport to assist with its development.

1

The PM had sent his attack dog, Freddie McLaren, to bargain with the Chancellor on his behalf.

"I spoke with Monty's winger, Gordon Mulligan, and told him that Monty's idea was bonkers but he insists that you have to come up with two hundred and fifty million pounds of savings before he would release the funds for your hospital."

"Where the fuck am I going to squeeze that kind of money out of the current account budget with that megalomaniac Monty holding on to every bloody penny?"

"You are the PM Toby, just tell him to do as he is told." They exchanged looks. Freddie didn't need to go there. They both knew that was impossible. The PM may hold the levers of power but unfortunately for him they were not connected to The Right Honourable Montgomery Green MP, Chancellor of the Exchequer.

"I gave you the bad news, now I'll give you the good news." It was Freddie's turn to take a seat by the coffee table, loosen his tie and adopt the same pose as the PM, feet up on the table.

"Go on then, make my day. What mad-arse scheme have you dreamt up now?" He was wearing a conspiratorial grin.

"You whinged like hell when you heard that yet another of our illustrious constabulary were getting themselves an expensive new toy for the Chief Constable to play with so I looked into it and did a bit of homework."

"Are you referring to their helicopters?"

"And aircraft, it's not just helicopters." He waved a thick wad of A4 pages at him.

"What's that?"

"It's a report, by a well-respected think-tank."

"Christ Freddie for God's sake don't ask me to read it, I'm bushed and I've ploughed my way through enough today."

"Then I'll read part of the synopsis for you."

'The creation of a National Police Aviation Service would, at current prices, save the Home Office three hundred million pounds over five years by operating more efficiently and by centralising the contracts for equipment and personnel.'

"Did we commission that?"

"No, that's what's so amusing, the other lot did."

"So if we did what that report suggests the opposition will more than likely go along with it?"

"I think they will, but they are not the problem."

"Who is the problem?"

"Who do you think? We announce that we are going to take control of their toys and every bloody Chief Constable in the land will backpedal the project and you will find your wonderful money-saving scheme will get a completion date in the next century. That's the reason the other lot were unable to convert an excellent idea into a firm plan. The big wheels inside the Association of Chief Police Officers just kick it around until it ends up in the long grass where nothing ever escapes."

"But I detect from your tone that you have found a way round that problem."

Freddie smiled, "You know me too well Toby, not only will I find a way to save the country money but we can make sure that our pension funds receive a boost in the process."

"Go on then, but remember my name mustn't appear in any dialogue that refers to our little nest-egg."

"Of course Prime Minister, that goes without saying. First we do our homework on setting up a National Police Aviation Service and carefully lay out the plans, in secret of course. Then we get in a suitably qualified muppet from outside the Police to set it up and act as the focal point. We then move him on in say, six months; he takes all that pain and heat when we kick-off and hopefully takes it all with him when he leaves. We will then have a nice new set up with ACPO left wondering what hit them."

"A suitably qualified 'patsy', does one exist?"

"You want to see the list?"

"Sounds good, very good but you would need to choose someone credible otherwise parliament will cry 'foul' and the Home Affairs Committee would give us a hard time. The bitch that runs it doesn't take any bloody prisoners."

"We have someone in mind, don't worry. Just think on this, there's a bonus Toby, a great big bonus."

"Which is?"

"Control of the entire police aviation service will return to the Home Office which means that you can gradually cut their funding and claim that new technologies mean we can do more with fewer, faster helicopters that can cover more ground in less time. If you wanted to you could even wean them off aviation altogether, after all there was a time when we didn't need the damn things. Just think how many bobbies can be hired if you get rid of all the helicopters, you would be 'Mr Popular' all round, no more noisy clattering machines waking up the voters and more uniforms on the streets."

"Can you make it happen?"

"Which 'it' do you mean?"

"The national aviation thing, save us enough in the budget so that I can build the new St Margaret's Teaching Hospital?"

"Sure. My preliminary study indicates that one of the European helicopter manufacturers is very keen to take over as 'preferred supplier' with a number of incentives available in the shape of bulk-buy prices, total support packages and of course the usual commission payments."

"That sounds very tasty Freddie. When I retire at the next election I want to enjoy the same kind of lifestyle that being Prime Minister delivers."

"Without the hassles of course."

"Exactly and no bloody Monty to drive me round the bend."

"Our man in The City has done us proud thus far but now that we are getting into the big league we need to step up the quality of our financial management."

"Are you absolutely sure that the commissions cannot be traced? I don't feel like fighting another bloody battle with the media."

"The City of London pretty well invented the modern version of the ancient art of money laundering but they have proven to be a bit fragile when it comes to security. In that respect alone I believe we have found a better connection, reputedly one of the best in the business in our new Armenian friend. In future we will use him to handle our 'investments'."

"Then get cracking but keep it to a small circle of trusted staffers."

"Shall I tell Monty that we have found a way to save enough money to pay for his runway and your hospital?"

"No, leave that to me, why should you have all the fun? You can leave that think-tank report on my desk, I'll make it my bedtime reading for the week, I promise. Freddie you and your Machiavellian ideas never cease to amaze me. Thank God you are on our side."

CHAPTER 2
- -

10.00 – Wednesday May 17th 2006
Ding Dong Mine, Boskednan, St Just

THE CAMPAIGN TO CAP the thousands of mineshafts dotted all over Cornwall had yet to reach the small village of Boskednan. The moorland hills north of the village still bore the scars of tin mining, an ancient industry that began thousands of years ago and now left one of England's most beautiful counties with a legacy of dangerous open shafts that were defended by nothing more than a fence at best or a simple sign at worst.

The fence defending the infamous Ding Dong Mine had been vandalised too many times to count so the shaft had become a convenient dumping ground for some local inhabitants who, for one reason or another, felt that the journey to the council waste recycling centre was inconvenient. Today, however, the activity around the gaping hole was more about taking something out of the mine than adding to the debris already accumulated.

"Come over here Tommy, look, look down there. I'm telling you I nicked a Honda just like yours last month and chucked it down this mine-shaft and if you take a gander down there you can just make it out… see, that blue one."

"I don't know Ged, it's a long way down."

"Ah you're just chicken. Give me that bloody rope and bring your car up here. I'll go down."

Small-time crook and general layabout Gerald Tregonning and his sidekick Tommy Uren had come to Ding Dong Mine because Ged knew that it was a good source of motorcycle spares. How did he know this? He had been throwing stolen bikes down the shaft for the last six months and now that Tommy was in need of a new engine for his Honda, Ged knew just the place to get one. They had arrived at the mineshaft with some ropes and a plan. Tommy would shin down a rope, secured to the back of his Mini Clubman. He would tie a second rope to the bike and Ged would haul it up before using the first rope to haul Tommy up courtesy of the pulling power of the Mini.

The master plan fell apart when Tommy decided that he didn't realise how deep the shaft was and wouldn't go down. Anxious to prove he was made of sterner stuff, Ged stepped in, calling Tommy a variety of unflattering epithets. He would go down the rope instead.

It would be possible to imagine that Cornishmen are borne with innate knot-tying skills but Ged and Tommy would have problems tying their shoelaces. They were not too brilliant in the knot department.

Tommy was more than happy to leave Ged to tie his own rope to the suspension at the rear of the Mini and then, when that rope was found not to reach the bottom of the shaft, tie the second rope to the first using a knot that was closer to a 'granny' than a 'figure of eight' or a 'double fisherman's bend'.

It was no surprise to anyone other than Ged that once the second rope was taking his weight the knot joining the two ropes started to unravel.

"Tommy, help, the bloody knot's coming undone," cried Ged from the depths.

"You'd better get to the bottom fast then," said Tommy, doing his best to help. Ged duly obliged as the two ropes parted company and he plummeted thirty feet to land flat on his back on top of an assortment of debris that included one Honda motorcycle.

"Are you all right?" yelled Tommy.

There was a lengthy pause and Tommy thought Ged had been killed by the fall.

"No I am bloody well NOT all right. I think I've broken my back. Can't move me legs."

"Look, Ged, I'll go get help."

Without thinking Tommy untied the rope from the Mini whereupon it fell back into the mine, landing on his ailing colleague thus prompting a stream of obscenities from the deep. He then jumped into the driver's seat and set off to find help. At 10.24 the call went out to the Air Ambulance at its base at Newquay Airport.

The duty dispatcher caught the disbelieving tone in the response from the air ambulance paramedic, "Yes Jack, you heard, a man has fallen down Ding Dong Mine. It's at Boskednan, north of Penzance, possible spinal injuries."

"Roger, mobilising to Ding Dong Mine, Boskednan."

Peter Norman, the duty pilot was already out at the aircraft getting the engines started and the rotors turning. Jack scribbled a few notes then grabbed his helmet and trotted through the hangar door to the bright red EC135 helicopter sitting on the helipad. Trudy was already in her side-facing seat behind the pilot when Jack slid into his seat next to Peter, fastened his harness and picked up the take-off checklist. The crew protocols required a challenge and reply checklist to be used prior to take-off to ensure that everything was in order before taking to the skies.

They were soon in the air and heading southwest on what they expected to be a ten-minute journey. The flight across the verdant green countryside told of land that had seen a warm and wet winter and an early spring.

Jack Mawgan was the senior paramedic on duty that day. He had been in charge of the Air Ambulance Unit for the last year and under his management it had become a finely tuned and very professional operation.

When they arrived at the mineshaft they could see a lone figure frantically waving his arms. On the road that led to the waving figure Jack could see a Fire and Rescue tender winding its way up the rough track towards the deep dark hole that marked Ding Dong Mine. The shaft itself was located on top of a moorland hill at the centre of a small area clear of gorse and bracken.

Peter landed the helicopter on a patch clear of vegetation and Jack immediately left his seat and made his way to the waiting figure now kneeling beside the shaft, apparently talking to someone down below.

The fire engine pulled up twenty metres away and disgorged a sizeable crew. The Fire Chief sauntered across to Jack and introduced himself. Apparently the fire crew were familiar with the Ding Dong shaft having pulled a stray sheep from it the previous year. They soon had their mine rescue equipment arranged beside the eight-foot wide hole and in what seemed a trice the lifting gear was assembled over it: a tripod of beams with a block and tackle and a long rope flaked alongside.

Jack established voice contact with Ged and told him that he must be checked over by a paramedic. Jack was chosen from a large cast of one as

Trudy suffered from claustrophobia and declined Jack's invitation to explore the insides of a Cornish tin mine. Jack, now dressed in a safety helmet and wearing a harness system, prepared for the descent. He and Trudy collected the equipment Jack would need then hooked this to his harness.

In one frightening second he went from terra firma to dangling over the one hundred-foot drop. It took just a few minutes to descend to Ged together with a cumbersome backboard slung horizontally from the same hook.

The confines of the shaft made it difficult for Jack to check and prep Ged for the journey to the surface. It was vital that all his injuries were understood. Before he could be moved Jack fitted Ged with a cervical collar then dressed him in a safety helmet and firmly secured him to the board with a four-point harness. The journey to the surface was tedious and somewhat painful. A sling system was provided to support each corner of the backboard. Jack had to keep Ged horizontal to minimise the spinal damage but the shaft was so narrow that the stretcher bumped and banged the walls all the way up. Falling stones pelted them all the way and the odd sizeable rock would bounce off Jack's green safety helmet.

He was exhausted by the time he returned to his seat in the Air Ambulance. Trudy informed him that she found out from the fire crew that the debris the patient was lying on was resting on a farm gate that was thrown down the shaft a couple of years ago. It was jammed in the shaft at the one hundred foot level but the shaft was actually over five hundred feet deep. Jack shuddered at the thought, for what nobody on the surface knew was that he had had to unhook his safety harness in order to deal with Ged's injuries. Peter took them back to Treliske Hospital and landed at the helipad. A short transfer by ambulance and Ged was in safe hands.

Jack was busy completing the paperwork back at their Newquay Airport base when a message came through from Control. As soon as possible he was to ring a number that he recognised had a London dialling code. He wondered 'what now?' Even he wouldn't believe what was about to unfold.

Ged was in hospital for six weeks whilst his spinal fractures were immobilised. He left in a wheelchair and then spent two weeks rattling a tin around the pubs and clubs of West Penwith collecting money for the Cornwall Air Ambulance charity amidst a plethora of self-publicity. He collected enough to finance a drunken weekend in Plymouth but in the end the publicity was his downfall for when the charity representative turned up to collect the £2,500 he had raised he did a runner. When the police eventually caught up with him he had blown the lot and spent a twenty-eight day stretch in Exeter jail for his trouble.

CHAPTER 3

10.00 – Thursday 18th May, 2006
Office of Josephine Mallard, Senior Advisor
The Home Office, Whitehall, London

JACK ARRIVED IN WHITEHALL still unaware of why he was there. The receptionist at The Home Office was expecting him and his ID was already prepared and waiting. He was escorted to the offices of Mrs Josephine Mallard, the Senior Advisor at the Home Office. Her secretary greeted him at the door to a suite of offices and meeting rooms that were furnished with an impressive array of modern and expensive looking furniture. As he entered the main office the other two gentlemen in the room stood up.

"Please sit down Mr Mawgan, I can imagine that you have no idea why we have asked you to visit us today, if you do then I will have to find the leak and make sure we plug it." She laughed to make light of this curious introduction.

"No, none at all" said Jack. The other two men sat back down in their seats.

The woman sitting at the large modern oak-veneered desk was in her fifties, hair up, designer spectacles and an immaculate blue-skirted suit with a small pink rose buttonhole. Her features were angular and her demeanour confident and focussed.

"Let me introduce myself, I am Josephine Mallard and I am the Home Secretary's Senior Advisor. I work closely with the Home Secretary and help him to develop policy and to plan for the future needs of the department. With me today I have Assistant Chief Commissioner Ed Hastings who has been looking after the development of aviation policies within the police service and Captain Max Penworth who is the Home Office Aviation Advisor."

The ACC was a small man, wiry and wore rimless spectacles that made him look professorial in his civilian dark grey three-piece suit. Max Penworth had the bearing of an ex-military man and sported a black beard and a heavily receding hairline. Life at the Home Office was obviously having an expansive effect on his waistline, which had adversely changed the way his otherwise well-made blue suit fitted.

There were nods exchanged and Jack wondered why he found himself amongst such august company. The answer would both surprise and amaze him.

"Mr Mawgan we have been struggling for some years with the rising costs of aviation within the nation's forty-three police authorities and have decided on a future policy that will see the service become more efficient and more effective. To cut to the quick we are planning a national aviation unit. This will be achieved by amalgamating the majority of Air Support Units into one single unit with a single home base that will provide the necessary administration and maintenance support."

"Ma'am I haven't had anything to do with the police force for more than five years now. How can I possibly be of assistance to your project. Are you are considering making police helicopters into part time air ambulances?" There was something about Jack's suggestion that caused an exchange of looks and raising of eyebrows. "If not," he continued, "I don't see how my skill set will be of use."

"No Mr Mawgan we have rejected the idea of police helicopters having an air ambulance capability although of course they remain available for that role in extremis. You have to understand our situation Mr Mawgan. This decision is a highly political initiative. You have served with Devon and Cornwall Constabulary I understand so you will be aware how fiercely each force guards its independence. The concept of sharing, cooperation and working together is alien to most. The notion that they should lose control of their favourite toy sends most into a muck sweat. You can be sure, Mr Mawgan, that if we put the establishment of a national air support unit on the agenda that ACPO would fight us all the way and if we used existing ASU personnel to organise it then they would slow the changes to a walking pace when we need a quick and decisive programme of change."

"I see," said Jack, failing to see anything at all that he could help with.

"The advice we received, Mr Mawgan, was to find a credible outsider who could build us the foundation of a functioning National Air Support Unit then return to his home base without any residual baggage to trouble his own future development. We did our homework and established that you had the required track record with the police service and your management of the Cornwall Air Ambulance helicopter unit has been exceptional. We would like you to consider a short term posting as the officer in charge."

Jack could hardly take it all in. "Wow! That's a lot to consider, I'll need time to think."

"We understand Mr Mawgan so I am going to suggest that you spend some time with my colleagues to discuss the practical elements of our proposal and then you can think about it over lunch and then give us your answer."

"So soon? I need to mull it over and discuss it with my wife."

"We need an answer today Mr Mawgan and may I remind you that as a signatory of the Official Secrets Act any discussion of this project is prohibited until such time as a public announcement has been made. I'm afraid that includes your wife." That news did nothing to encourage Jack's interest and his body language probably betrayed his feelings.

"Don't worry Mr Mawgan, I'm sure you will find what we have to offer you very persuasive. I have to go to a meeting at Number Ten so I'll leave you in the capable hands of Ed and Max and meet with you again after lunch at, let's say, two thirty." With that they all stood and Mrs Mallard left. There was a silence for a short while as the three of them adjusted to the sudden loss of energy in the room. It seemed to leave along with Mrs Mallard and in a parody of Boyle's Law the atmosphere cooled as the air pressure fell.

"Well Jack," Ed Hastings attempted to provide some impetus to the meeting, "let's get down to business." They sat and Jack was given a pen and paper with which to make notes. "Any notes you make must not leave the building Jack, OK."

"OK."

"We would like to propose that you take up your position next week and attend to your duties here at the Home Office where you will be allocated your own office and two secretarial staff. Max, here, will also be working closely with you." More nods.

"The new base for the National Air Support Unit will be at Halfpenny Green Airfield in the Midlands. Each of the current ASUs currently has its own contract with suppliers of helicopters and pilots, some even own their helicopters or fixed wing aircraft and some pilots are directly employed by the parent police force. These units need to be brought together under one roof and the administration rationalised, in other words stripped of the current ground staff who will either be redeployed or made redundant. You would be wielding the axe under our guidance but in six months you can withdraw and avoid the kind of repercussions that a member of any existing Air Support Unit may have faced. We expect you to work here in London for a month and develop a plan for the wholesale movement of all units with the exception of London, which is a special case, and Devon and Cornwall which for logistical reasons will, for the time being continue as is. We will help you to develop a strategy for the deployment of assets around the country but you will need to work with the regional coordinators to agree the details."

"Halfpenny Green?"

"Yes it's here, west of Birmingham." He had a map of UK and pointed out the location.

"Your appointment would require you to work Monday to Friday for the next six months. You will then be granted three months paid leave."

"Salary?" enquired Jack, his mind still whirling and trying to take it all in.

"You will be paid according to Civil Service Grade 6 with maximum seniority, £62,150 per annum. A taxi will collect you each Monday morning at six a.m. at your home in Cornwall and deliver you to Newquay Airport where you will catch the morning Air Southwest flight to Birmingham. A hire car will be booked that you can use for the journey to the office at Halfpenny Green and will be available for your use whilst working on the project. You may leave your office at midday Friday subject to clearing your desk and reverse the route. Accommodation will be provided at the Dunsley Hall four-star hotel, a double room, your wife would be welcome at any time. In addition you will receive a generous meal allowance, payment of all running costs for the hire car and all reasonable expenses."

"Crikey!" exclaimed Jack.

"I think we have thought of everything, but if not please ask."

"I don't know what to say. You are making it very hard to say no."

"When you complete the task you will be appointed to head up a new qango created to oversee the welfare of the UK Air Ambulance fleet. The office will be in Truro and you will be provided with the necessary staff and infrastructure to help you deliver quality and efficiency nationwide."

"Why Truro?"

"Why not Truro, didn't Cornwall create the concept of an air ambulance in the UK? Let's say that Cornwall has earned the right to be the home of the National Air Ambulance Quality & Development Agency or NAAQDA."

"Sounds too good to be true."

"Let's just say that the government have got long memories and one way and another we think you have earned this opportunity." Was that a reference to the Cameroon adventure of 2003? Maybe, if so he was very surprised to find that governments did indeed have such long memories. He wasn't a great fan of politicians and doubted they had sufficient moral strength to do much good. Maybe he was wrong.

Jack was taken off to the executive dining room and allowed to sit quietly with his notes and his thoughts. He was up for the challenge and he believed he could manage the disruption to family life for just six months and the extra cash would come in handy. The whole thing stank of politics but he couldn't see any holes that meant that it was in any way a perilous step. Little did he know what difficulty and danger lay ahead.

CHAPTER 4

09.00 – Thursday 17th August 2006
Office of Mr 'Jack' Mawgan, Head of the
National Police Aviation Service

THE OCCASION WAS THE second monthly management progress meeting of the newly created National Police Aviation Service. Present at the meeting was of course its chairman, John, known to all as Jack, Mawgan; The Chief Pilot, Eric 'Lofty' Anderson, all five foot five of him; Ian 'Robbie' Robertson, Chief Training Pilot; Cliff Barman, Chief Engineer and Chief Inspector 'Dusty' Miller, the Unit Executive Officer.

"Gentlemen can I quickly go around the table and ask you to run through the open left items from the minutes of last month's meeting and update us on any progress. Let's start with you Cliff, I think you had the longest list."

"Right, yes, the biggest problem is still the hangar. We have had the quotes for the new security system, building the six separate bonded stores, one for each type, the new clean workshop and a battery bay but I cannot get the bean counters to sign off on them to get the work started."

"I'll get on it Cliff, I'll lean on my man in the Home Office for you."

"OK well the next thing is the spares inventory. We spent three weeks auditing the spares holdings for twenty-three existing units and whilst some are in good shape others are running on thin air. Either they can't afford them or they can't get them. Currently there are three units AOG and grounded for lack of spares."

"Can we help?"

"We need some reserve aircraft so that we can plug the gaps but we can't get any short term leases on the MD902s. We can get half a dozen Twin Squirrels but only one of the existing pilots has an appropriate type rating."

"Can you help with pilots Robbie?"

"If we had the crews we could train them up in three or four weeks."

"Why don't we train up the existing lot?"

Lofty decided to answer. "The pilots sitting on their bums have been sent on leave so that the time is not wasted when the aircraft comes back on line. It's not a perfect solution but it's too late to do much about it."

"Where do we stand with the pool pilots we planned to hire?"

"You gave me a master plan for the year ahead in which we were expecting to get rid of twenty per cent of the existing units. That means that we will make redundant between fifteen and twenty pilots. I don't see that we need to push hard on the idea of pool pilots."

"Twenty per cent was a rough guide based on your calculations for re-equipping with a single type of helicopter that was fifteen per cent faster."

"It may actually be faster than that but conservatively the fastest machine currently in service would enable the radius of action for each unit to be extended such that we only need fifteen Air Support Units to cover the same territory."

Jack spent a moment consulting his notes, "Dusty, how did you get on with the lawyers and the contract negotiations?"

"Not as well as I hoped Jack, those who hold existing leases are playing hard ball and early termination will undoubtedly cost the government a pretty penny. Naturally if they get to be the sole supplier then their attitude changes but they won't cooperate if they are frozen out."

"But we haven't announced our decision yet so I don't see how they can get upset. We have prepared carefully and technically we have a watertight case but I have no intention of going public until we are certain of our ground."

"That's academic Jack," Cliff interjected, "we have kept things absolutely quiet and haven't spoken to a soul as you requested at our very first meeting but you can bet your life the police aviation world will be alive with rumours."

"Can I confirm that please gentlemen, none of you have spoken of our plans outside the unit except to those I have authorised. Robbie?"

"No."

"Dusty?"

"Nope."

"Lofty?"

"Only the lawyers and I think those talks were authorised."

"Cliff?"

"Same, Lofty and I were at the same meetings with the lawyers sent by the Home Office. I think you should know Jack that what we are planning to do is tantamount to visiting an earthquake on the light twin-turbine helicopter market in this country. The winners are likely to be the Italians, National Helicopters. They stand to gain more than one hundred and fifty million pounds worth of business but the single biggest loser will be the Franco-Swiss outfit, West European Aviation. They will lose one hundred million pounds worth of business. We are not talking chicken feed. There are some very worried people out there and as Lofty and I have been hearing when we visit the various Air Support Units your name is mud. You are not exactly Mr Popular out there."

"But surely they realise I'm only doing what the Home Office have instructed me to do."

"No Jack, we know that, but the word circulating on the street is that this is all your idea and that you've been imported into the air support world specifically because you proposed the idea that costs could be cut by going for fewer aircraft covering larger areas."

"Didn't you tell them otherwise?"

"We're not supposed to discuss it, remember?"

"Yes, all right, I get the message. Sounds like someone is spreading false rumours to put the heat on me."

"Ah! Don't worry Jack the helicopter world runs on rumours. I shouldn't get too worked up about it."

"Thanks Robbie, I'll try to remember that. Look, why don't we take a thirty-minute break. I need to check on a couple of things."

When the room was clear Jack left his seat at the conference table and stood by the entrance door looking carefully at the contents of his office. A conference table with a dozen seats, his desk, two steel filing cabinets, a steel cupboard, bookcase, sideboard with coffee makings. Two large framed photographs of Air Support Unit helicopters and a year planner decorated the wall.

He stood in contemplation for a moment. It was a good job that he had said nothing about the Home Secretary's ultimate plan to replace all helicopters outside London with just six cheaper fixed wing aircraft equipped with some very impressive and sophisticated equipment.

He stepped forward and carefully lifted the first photograph from the wall and inspected the back of it and the wall behind. Nothing, the other picture was the same. He felt embarrassed by his own paranoia but continued the search. He checked beneath his desk and the conference table, still nothing. He looked up at the light fitting and used a chair to get a close look. Removing the glass dome he saw it. 'Bingo,' he said to himself. He inspected the small round capsule stuck to the inside of the mounting plate with a two-inch aerial wire. He recognised it as a continuously transmitting bug. Somewhere close by was a receiver that may even be manned. He would check that out later. Replacing the cover he stepped back to terra firma. The question that immediately went through his suspicious mind was 'who the hell put it there?' Was it the opposition or was it his own people checking up on him. He didn't know but he was determined to find out.

That evening he lay on his bed back at the hotel and reflected on what had occurred that day. The management meeting had gone pretty well and they were homing in on their objective, to create a framework capable of acting as the support structure to a national service. The plan had always been to leave the distribution of helicopters and the two fixed wing operations in place until D-Day, the day when all the contracts were resolved and they had legal control over all the assets. Once that had been accomplished his job would largely be over and he could return to Cornwall and enjoy the life of an administrator for the new qango.

He contemplated the way ahead and reasoned that the existing relationships between the commercial suppliers had, for some, been in place for many years. Plenty of time at least for loyalties to become misplaced. He had discussed this possibility with his team and they gave him a list of likely suspects if problems were to materialise. He found the notebook containing the details, read through it and considered the name at the top of the list: the South Sussex Air Support Unit. They had a long history of operating with West European Aviation and rumours were rife that members of the local force had enjoyed considerable hospitality at their facilities in Switzerland. The feedback that Cliff and Lofty had picked up included an outright threat to bring down the national project, come what may. Someone in Sussex apparently thought they had enough clout in Whitehall to make the whole idea go away. What disturbed Jack most of all was the feeling that those in the establishment who were spoiling for a fight had targeted him personally.

The first indication of this came when the Civil Aviation Authority summoned him to a meeting at their Gatwick HQ and told him that they had received a letter of complaint from the South Sussex ASU that he was not a fit and proper person to command the National Police Aviation Service. Fortunately the CAA inspectors had done their homework and realised that he was more than qualified given that he had the support of aviation staff with a great deal of credibility in the aviation business. Nonetheless it was an unnerving experience to be told that some people were so much against what you had been asked to do that they would stoop that low.

CHAPTER 5

19.00 – Saturday 19th August 2006
The Napoleon Suite, Hotel Europe, Zurich, Switzerland

"CLAUDE, THIS GUY MAWGAN is the problem. Even the guys who are working for him don't believe in what he is doing."

"Why are you so certain Murray? Surely the mandate for this whole bloody idea came from the top?"

"Sure, the top of the Home Office, like your Ministry of the Interior, but not from the top of the Police Service. The Association of Chief Police Officers is spitting bullets, they are not happy."

"So how can we get rid of this Mr Mawgan and if we do how can we be sure it will end it?"

"It may not end it but it will derail it long enough for us to get a foot in the door in London and then we can kill it. They caught us on the hop because our man with the muscle was out of the country and we've been playing catch-up ever since."

"So what do we do, take him out?"

"That would be a bit over the top but we could probably put him in hospital for a while. Maybe even scare him off."

"Can we find an operative to make that happen?"

"Leave it to me Claude, 'nous avons un homme', as we say, we have a man, but he will need paying."

"Combien? How much?"

"Ten thousand pounds."

"Cash?"

"Nothing else will do."

"Does it have to be Sterling?"

"Preferably, anything else would make it a little messy at my end."

"What's your room number?"

"Three twenty-two."

"Tonight I will come with the money."

18.00 – Sunday 20th August 2006
The Prime Minister's Private Residence
Chequers, Ellesborough, Buckinghamshire

"Come on in Freddie, what's been eating you up all day? You look like the cat who just found the cream."

"You once complimented me on my Machiavellian tendencies didn't you?"

"I may have said something along those lines."

"Well hold on to your hat and let me run this beauty past you."

"I'm all ears."

"Once upon a time there was a Health Secretary."

"Christ Freddie this is the weekend, can we leave work until Monday?"

"No, this is important."

"OK, what's so damn important and what has Marian Herd got to do with this?"

"Marian is pissed off. She has a Health Committee banging on her door about the fact that now we have more than twenty air ambulances in the UK every fucking doctor in the A & E world and a few more besides want us to turn a select number of hospitals into Trauma Centres."

"Sounds cool."

"It's not cool, it's definitely not cool."

"How come?"

"Because to make it happen we would have to close dozens of smaller hospitals, most of which turn out to be in our marginal seats. It would kill us at the next election."

"So don't do it."

"The problem is Trauma Centres are apparently the right way to go and to argue against the clinicians will put us in a bind as much as closing hospitals." The PM sat thinking for a moment and tapped the ends of his fingers together.

"Freddie you wouldn't have brought this up if you hadn't already thought up a way round it would you?"

"No."

"Well get on with it then."

"Imagine if we made all the air ambulances in the country go away and at the same time gave the treasury an extra twenty-five million pounds."

"I thought you were serious Freddie."

"I'm bloody serious Toby, I've never been more serious in my life."

"But aren't these air ambulances funded by charities?"

"Yes, most of them."

"And don't these charities have a mind of their own?"

"Yes."

"So how the hell do I persuade them to close their doors and give me their cash."

"That's where my Machiavellian skills come to the rescue."

"You have a serious problem Freddie. I went along with the plan to introduce a National Police Aviation Unit because all along it made financial and operational sense but this sounds like one step too far."

"Not forgetting a good deal of pocket money for us along the way."

"That's irrelevant Freddie, this just sounds like blood on the carpet for the sake of being part of a gory mess."

"Listen Toby, my father was the only one with enough guts to stand up to that prig Lummis when he championed the state purchase of police helicopters and then stamped all over those in the NHS who tried to fight off the bloody do-gooders whose only aim in life was to use the whole idea of air ambulances for self-promotion. He may have been just a back-bencher but he fought Lummis day and night. Don't forget he died of a heart attack brought on by the stress of all that media fuss over his mistress."

"Well you can't blame Lummis for that surely?"

"It was Lummis who hired the private detective who found out about Clementine and then blasted it all over the front pages of every newspaper his poxy brother-in-law owned. He was determined to silence my old man and in the end he won; he killed my father and put my mother in an early grave with a broken heart. Now Lummis is departed and I have been handed the opportunity to finish what my father started and put an end to the huge waste of money that state sponsored aviation in the emergency services represents."

The Prime Minister walked over to the window and contemplated the tranquillity of the view outside where manicured lawns and dancing blackbirds provided a reassuring picture of normality and continuity. Freddie's wrath and bile subsided and all was calm.

The Prime Minister had made it his business to know everything about his Press Officer before he was appointed. He knew the truth behind the death of Freddie's father who was on the take from those lobbying for one particularly aggressive member of the helicopter industry. Unfortunately his propensity to overindulge in the finest malt whisky made him unreliable so it was no surprise that Lummis took the juicy slice of income away from him. McLaren senior decided to repay this treachery by going up against him. This was Freddie settling old scores and about the only thing Toby Stewart could see in his crazy plan was that it would be one more way to piss off his old enemy – The Chancellor of the Exchequer.

"Supposing I gave the go ahead," he said after a long pause in the conversation, "what do we do next?"

"The first step is to make all the units state owned and fully funded. Then once we have done that we do exactly what we did to police aviation. First cut it down to size then rationalise and standardise the fleet and pocket the commission payments."

"How the hell do we persuade them to do that? There was enough of a kerfuffle when that Tory think-tank suggested that all blue-light helicopters be run as a single entity."

"Well that's all very interesting but then they don't have what we have."

"Which is?"

"MI5." Hearing the name of the domestic security service made the PM sit up straight.

"Where the hell do you imagine they fit in to your scheme?"

"They are uniquely placed to do a little research for us. As you know every charity has trustees and so each of the air ambulance charities has a board of trusties. Minimum number four, most have between four and six.

23

Each board has a leader who drives the meetings and sets policy with his or her colleagues.

"We ran checks on all the trustees in the UK, many of whom, as you would expect are the great and the good of our society and as I am sure you have come to realise, the great and the good have a habit of keeping skeletons in their upper class closets. Most of them have enough to provide a guarantee that they will do what we ask."

"And what will you do about those you cannot manipulate?"

"That's where MI5's special skills come in handy but they won't act without your authority."

"So you want me to sign off on a campaign to neuter a bunch of trustees so that they will do as we want?"

"That's about the size of it."

"On what pretext pray?"

"Suspicion of fraud and corruption."

"Will it work?"

"We've done that kind of thing before so why not.

"We're not talking about a fortune but we could certainly find a use for the money that's for sure. Let me sleep on it Freddie and I'll get back to you on Monday."

15.00 – Wednesday 23rd August 2006
Offices of Advanced Vehicle Technologies
Brighton, West Sussex

Murray Burton arrived outside the offices of Advanced Vehicle Technologies wearing a conspiratorial smile. He didn't make a habit of calling in favours in the way he planned but this was a situation in which needs must.

"Sit down Mr Sergeant Murray Sir and I'll run through it in detail for you, I know you'll appreciate our handiwork."

Murray was visiting Darvesh Singh at his small but well-appointed facility on the outskirts of Britain's popular seaside city. In his hand he held a small black box with a short lead and a plug. Murray Burton used to work as a traffic officer in Brighton before being assigned to his local Air Support Unit. His promotion to Sergeant required a posting and he moved to south

Sussex as their ASU Sergeant. During his service with the elite cabal of drivers qualified to conduct high-speed pursuits he stopped many members of the public for every imaginable offence. A common transgression was DUI, drunk driving. Darvesh had one too many DUI convictions and by rights should have been banned twice over but Murray had taken pity on him and let him go after one marginal breathalyser reading gave him just enough slack to use his discretion. Now it was payback time and Darvesh had designed a special little black box that would enable Murray to give Jack Mawgan a nasty moment and send a message that he wasn't welcome.

"Inside this unit is a cell phone and a switch that will send a signal to the Anti-Lock Braking system of a Volkswagen Passat, provided it is the current model – you said a Passat, right?" Murray nodded. "Current model, right?" Again a nod.

"He gets a Passat every Monday morning from the Hertz depot at Birmingham International Airport."

"Good, then there will be no interface problems. When you have access to the vehicle you should plug this unit into the diagnostic socket located under the steering wheel, there is sufficient cable to enable you to hide it amongst the cable looms under the dash. As soon as your target switches on the ignition the software inside here will reprogram the ABS system to enable the calliper on the front left wheel to be operated by the cell phone switch. You follow the target discretely and when you see the right opportunity you dial this number," he pointed to a label on the box, "and the front brake will come on fully and send the car into a spin. When you go to assist the casualty you discretely remove the black box and turn off the ignition. This will replace the original software and nobody will ever know the cause of the accident."

"Perfect." said Murray.

"When you can please bring it back to me, I need to be sure it does not find its way into the wrong hands."

"You mean the cops?" There was a moment of silence then they both laughed.

"So now my slate is clean Mr Sergeant Murray?"

"Slates are never entirely clean, Darvesh, you have a record but I can help to ensure yours doesn't get any dirtier. OK?"

"OK Mr Sergeant Murray, a nod is as good as a blink as you English say."

"Wink, Darvesh, the word is 'wink'."

"Thank you Mr Sergeant Murray." With that the two parted, each happy with the transaction but a little nervous about how this 'dial-a-crash' accessory would perform.

Murray Burton smiled at his own deviousness. Now he had the means to frighten off Jack Mawgan without having to part with the £10,000 he had acquired from WEH. His holiday fund was looking healthier by the day.

21.00 – Thursday 24th August, 2006
The Prime Minister's Private Office
Downing Street, London

"I know what you are going to say Freddie but I've had a lot on my mind so give me a break."

"You promised me an answer on Monday Toby and this project is time-critical."

"What you are asking Freddie is more than 'off the wall' it's bloody crazy."

"But think of what we can do with all that cash. We'll be a shoe-in at the next election. We can spin it really well, tell them we are buying more ambulances, hiring more doctors and give them a few Trauma Centres to keep them happy *and* keep all the local hospitals."

"I didn't say I wouldn't do it Freddie, I just said it was a crazy idea."

"So you will go for it?"

The PM picked up a pink folder that Freddie recognised as the one used for MI5 material. "I spoke with the Deputy Director and asked him to run some names through his system and the Police National Computer. The names I gave him were these," he handed Freddie a list on one page of A4. "Each name has a sequence number, one to eighteen, and they are not in alphabetical order. Henceforth we will only refer to those on this list by their sequence number. You have a copy, I have a copy and the DD has a copy."

"Who are they?"

"These are the names of the Chairmen and Chairwomen of the Trustees for each of the charities running the eighteen air ambulances that are not under our Health Service control. There are two that we have effective control over and when the time comes we may decide to leave as is."

"How did it turn out, your check of these names?"

"Ten were either ex MPs, ex MEPs or ex County Councillors. They all have a record of fraud, fiddling expenses, graft, cronyism or nepotism. Five others were on the MI5 list of 'persons of interest', which could mean anything from subversive activities to benefit fraud. The other three were in need of more detailed research. Number nine is a particular problem for she was a previous head of MI6. You can imagine that she will be a challenge."

"She would have signed the Official Secrets Act so we have leverage."

"Quite, but she was also involved when we took down Doctor Skellie so you might say that she has the gear on us."

"She wouldn't dare go public with that, if she even hinted at it she would find herself with a concrete overcoat. We would be dead meat along with some very senior people across government and the security services, let alone the execution team that did the job."

"Calm down Freddie. You were the one that opened this Pandora's box. Still want to do it?" Freddie took a moment, ran his fingers through his ginger crew-cut and said, "Why not, nothing ventured nothing gained."

"Right, then we do it my way. You start by picking off the low hanging fruit, those that have most to lose if we go public with their transgressions. Your script will be this." He handed another sheet of A4 to Freddie. On it was the following:

'The campaign to create Trauma Centres is a worthy one that runs parallel to the effort to extend the nation's air ambulance population. The government has decided to buy into that concept but we realise that this will put the trustees of those charities supporting the air ambulances in a difficult situation for they have large accumulations of funds that will need to find an appropriate outlet. The government will provide central funding for your unit on condition that you do not discuss this proposal in public until the project is complete. There is no doubt that excessive debate about the whys and the wherefores of this project will delay things unreasonably. You will therefore arrange for the passage of the necessary motions to wind up the charity and transfer the funds to a central fund called 'The National Emergency Service Charitable Trust.'

"You can tell the Chairmen and women that their contribution will be recognised in the next New Year's Honours List. If there are difficulties then we can provide a list of misdemeanours that the Chairmen can use to ensure the compliance of those trustees that kick up a fuss. He or she will only need a simple majority when the time comes to vote. The central charitable fund will have terms of reference that will permit us to have a wide ranging list of acceptable expenditures."

"Can we do that?"

"The Charity Commissioners are a pushover these days, we've made sure of that."

"You've been busy Toby, I'm impressed. How much do you reckon they are worth, these charities?"

"Not that much really, probably a million each on average but that revenue stream is very handy. The trick is that by carefully manipulating the numbers and only telling half the truth we could probably turn that twenty odd million into a paper half billion."

"What about financing these units during the period when we allow them to flourish, won't Monty get on his high horse?"

"I've taken care of that angle but you don't need to know the 'whys and wherefores' of that arrangement. Suffice it to say that our Monty has his own skeletons. We will sell off all the assets and then negotiate a deal with one supplier then pay for a new smaller, faster fleet from the proceeds. Use a bit of credit if we come up short. Compared with what they are spending now we should be able to get a huge economy of scale. As you pointed out Freddie, this is all about moving funds from a place where we have to account to our illustrious Chancellor for every penny into a pot where you and I can do as we please."

"He won't be a happy Scotsman when he finds out."

"He mustn't find out the detail until we have it sewn up so your strategy is to isolate every unit working on the project into 'silent silos' on pain of … well, if necessary the MI5 induced financial disaster package complete with credit cards that don't work, terminated overdrafts … do I need to go on?"

"I got the message. I will need to use a couple of my usual assistants in these difficult evolutions but they won't be aware of the whole story."

"Fine, now get to work and keep me in the loop."

11.00 – Tuesday 29ᵗʰ August 2006
Birmingham International Airport

The summer bank holiday brought with it a shortened working week for those lucky enough to be working office hours. Jack was mindful that there was no such luxury for the nation's Air Support Units as he drove the fifty-five minute trip from the airport to his office. He was just past Stourton on the A458 coming up to a sharp right hand bend when unaccountably the brakes locked and the car slewed off the road and took out a telegraph pole.

The hire car was wrecked and Jack was lucky to survive. The telegraph pole entered the driver's side just behind the front door. A passer-by was first to lend a hand as Jack struggled to free himself from the tangle of seat belts and air bag. He was kind enough to turn off the ignition and make sure the car was safe. He was just a faceless man in a crowd but that was what Murray Burton was counting on. The ambulance arrived a little while later followed by a police car whose crew administered the usual breath test. The test proved negative and the paramedic pronounced Jack fit but for a good dose of shock. His day at the office was going to end prematurely but he was to leave the scene with the comments of the traffic policemen going round and round in his head. He had told Jack that from the marks in the road he was convinced his car had suffered a front nearside blow-out but when he checked the tyre it was perfect save for a curious flat spot. Something had jammed that wheel and sent him off the road.

Lofty came out to take Jack to his hotel and promised to organise a replacement hire car for the morning. The evening was spent dealing with a body that ached with the delayed effects of the impact. It was a constant reminder to solve the question of how the accident happened.

Later that evening he phoned Pam to tell her all about his less than perfect day then he checked his e-mail. Waiting for him in his inbox was a sinister message that really took him by surprise.

'Today was just a gentle hint. Go back to Cornwall and don't come back'.

Whoever wrote that didn't know Jack very well. Now convinced that his attempt to make love to a telegraph pole was no accident at all he was ready to think the unthinkable and to at least discuss the situation with his old friend Dan Barclay.

Dan was once a colleague in the Devon and Cornwall Constabulary. A long time ago the two young policemen were seconded to work under cover in a special anti-drugs squad based in London. It was many months into that operation that they nearly met a nasty end but despite being wounded they managed to pull off a remarkable collar that saw some heavyweight villains put away in the UK, Europe and the USA. Unfortunately for them both a few of the bad guys were not detained and their faces were well known to those individuals. The subsequent award of the George Medal was never gazetted for fear of the villains tracking them down and taking their revenge.

Dan left the police force after a year-long recovery from his wounds and became the owner of a private investigation business based in Exeter. This was no ordinary PI business however, for the Security Services recognised in Dan a special quality and skill-set that they were to find very useful. There were many tasks, large and small, that he had undertaken over the intervening years. He was one of the few they trusted with the task of taking out people who needed to be removed from the scene. If you met him in normal surroundings you would find yourself enjoying a conversation with a tall, dapper, very fit man in his forties who was quiet, reserved and enjoyed intelligent conversation. A lady's man for many years, Dan finally met his match when he and Jack were involved in an operation in Africa and he was now married to Doctor Monique Barclay, an orthopaedic surgeon at the Royal Devon and Exeter Hospital. Their last joint activity had resulted in Dan collecting a couple more bullet wounds but he was made of stern stuff and was back in business after three months convalescence in the South of France.

Jack needed to see Dan and talk through one or two things. He gave him a call.

"Hi Dan, long time no see, how the devil are you?"

CHAPTER 6

19.30 – Wednesday 30th August 2006
Owens Restaurant, Tewkesbury

JACK ARRANGED TO MEET Dan at a restaurant that was halfway between Birmingham and Exeter. The choice was Dan's and his 'foodie' instincts led him to a small restaurant in the old Saxon town of Tewkesbury.

Dining early to ensure they would miss the crowd and be able to talk freely, Jack and Dan exchanged the normal pleasantries and small talk before getting down to the serious stuff. Jack perused the interesting menu and chose the Noggin Hill Farm pork belly, Dan went for the braised Longhorn beef.

The long and troubling conversation sapped their appetites and the lack of any wine to jolly things along meant that the delectable dessert menu was bypassed in favour of coffee.

Jack had described his situation, including the episode with the car crash and the e-mail. Dan took a note of Jack's e-mail accounts and passwords and promised he would look into it and get back to Jack if he found anything concrete.

09.00 – Thursday 31st August 2006
Office of the Deputy Director, MI5 HQ, London

The Deputy Director of the domestic security service is very much the hands-on part of the management team and his office has a finger on the pulse of every major operation in the UK and dozens of on-going low level monitoring operations. One such low level long term monitoring operation is the placing of 'sleepers' within the many arms of government that affect the stability of the nations. The armed forces, the prison service and the nation's forty-three police forces plus the transport police all contain specially trained personnel whose job is to work normally but report back any signs of systemic corruption or extremism within these critical organisations.

The government of the day, the 'executive', would come and go with each turn of the political clock but a nation's stability sprung not from the skill of the team in power at any one time but from the wise heads who controlled the pace of change and whose constant involvement ensured that extremism would never get any traction where it really mattered.

The BBC, some years ago, produced a remarkable TV series called 'Yes Minister' and another, a sequel, called 'Yes Prime Minister'. This was such an effective recreation of life in Whitehall that it was used as a training aid by organisations inside and outside the world of politics and amazingly in countries trying to understand the British system of government.

The main message this programme conveyed was that the 'executive' has to live with the illusion of power; the illusion that the 'levers of power' are in their hands. The reality of course is that this would never be allowed to happen. To ensure this is the case the British Civil Service has been schooled in a myriad of different techniques designed to surround the 'levers of power' with a polite and tasteful 'treacle' that ensures that rapid changes in policy are circumvented by the simple process of controlling the rate of implementation by fair means and foul.

Committees, working groups, surveys, investigations, analysis of data, and a multitude of other tools help to keep Britain 'Great'. It is the job of the domestic security service to monitor these activities alongside the monitoring of the police service to keep at bay the forces of evil.

Justin Wood, the DD at MI5, sat at his desk engrossed in a report he had received from a field operative in the South Sussex Constabulary. The report indicated that a member of the Air Support Unit was overheard discussing the plans to centralise the nations police air support and boasted that he had 'taken care' of the man in charge of the project, Jack Mawgan. Alongside this report Justin had another from another field operative, Dan Barclay, reporting an attempt to murder his old friend Jack Mawgan.

This wasn't the first time that Justin had come across these two names for his first encounter was that same notable international drug related operation back in the 1980s when he was a case officer and these two remarkable young men had featured in its successful conclusion. Their bravery had been suitably acknowledged but some aspects of the case were still active so no publicity of the personnel involved was permitted.

Justin was worried by the report on the process by which the National Police Aviation Service was being created. There had been little consultation within the police service and feathers were being ruffled up and down the country. Now it seemed that one area of militancy had surfaced – in South Sussex. The prima facie evidence pointed to an individual who may harbour extreme views but what if there was an organisation behind that individual. Removing the 'cancer' would be a lot more difficult. Like a loving parent Justin felt a modicum of concern for both Jack and Dan so decided that he would keep things in the 'family' and send Dan to South Sussex to find out what was going on there.

02.00 – Saturday 2nd September 2006
Bowbridge-on-Sea, South Sussex

Sergeant Murray Burton's Ford Focus was parked on his driveway outside the tidy, spacious seaside bungalow and was an easy target for the darkly clothed figure that in the space of fifteen seconds placed a GPS tracker on its magnetic base in a carefully selected location under the bodywork. Dan had practised on a similar Ford Focus at his local second hand car dealer under the guise of a 'thorough inspection' on behalf of a lady who was interested in a purchase.

The tracker would not have been required for the average 'target' for they would have a cell phone so, courtesy of the telecoms company could be tracked all the time. Mr Burton was not proving to be such an easy target to manage. He appeared to own two cell phones. One was a pay-as-you-go unit that, when switched on, indicated that it was co-located with the monthly contracted Nokia that was on record. The pay-as-you-go number had been allocated to a retailer in Crawley who was known to supply sim cards without observing the correct procedures.

The practice of switching a cell phone off may, of course, be a battery saving measure but quite often experience had shown that it was either a sign of paranoia or that the owner was involved in something irregular, an affair maybe, or some other kind of inappropriate activity. Either way it seemed that Sergeant Burton needed two ways to deal with communications and Dan needed to monitor both of them.

Sergeant Burton had the weekend off and decided it would be a good time to get rid of Darvesh Singh's little toy and return it to him personally. On this occasion Murray left the Nokia switched on and was stationary long enough for Dan to get a triangulation from the three cell phone masts nearby. From this data he was able to generate a GPS position for the stop-off point.

Once Dan had worked out the address visited by the target he could easily put two and two together. Advanced Vehicle Technologies was a potential link in the strange behaviour of Jack's car and would neatly connect Murray Burton to the threatening e-mail. At least it would were in not for the fact that the IT specialists at MI5 have tracked the e-mail back to a URL in Switzerland. Further investigations revealed that it came from The Melody Internet Café, Saatlenstasse, Zurich.

Dan's efforts to understand Sergeant Murray Burton led him to look into the history of the West Sussex and the South Sussex Air Support Units. The West Sussex Constabulary website had a photograph of the crew of their helicopter dating back to the late 1990s. It showed Constable Burton being presented with the West European Aviation 'Meritorious Action' award. He used his skill as a FLIR[1] operator to locate a lost child in wooded terrain north of Brighton, the child would have died of hypothermia, the legend read, if Constable Burton had missed the tiny signal the child presented on his equipment. The man presenting the trophy was Claude Deschamps, European Sales Manager for WEA.

The final link in the chain came when Dan checked the website of the South Sussex Constabulary. On the Community Service page was a photograph of a group of schoolchildren visiting a winter sports centre in the Swiss Alps and who should he see standing in the background? Claude Deschamps. It was then a simple matter to check on the locations of the

---

1   Forward Looking Infra Red (night vision)

WEA offices in Switzerland and there he had it. European Sales Office 128 Saatlenstasse, Zurich.

So it looked for all the world as if WEA were using Murray Burton to get at Jack to frighten him off. Maybe Jack could explain why?

14.30 – Tuesday 5ᵗʰ September 2006
Owens Restaurant, Tewkesbury

A hurried lunchtime meeting was no excuse for stinting on a good quality, healthy meal. Jack favoured the Monkfish loin with curried potatoes and spinach with a chickpea fritter. Dan, the poached halibut fillet with a smoked haddock and sweetcorn chowder. After an hour of chewing over both a good meal and Dan's news they tried to get to grips with the reasons why Jack had become the focus of such an apparently unprovoked attack.

"So you reckon that whoever has it in mind to get rid of you has somehow got the wrong end of the stick," said Dan

"I can't believe they honestly think that I am the hinge-pin of this project. I am just a functionary brought in to do their dirty work until the central service contracts are in place. I'm 'Mr. Faceless Incomer'."

"You can't escape the fact that Burton was acting on behalf of WEA and that we could have him for attempted murder and this Claude Deschamps for conspiracy."

"Yes and WEA's name would be mud. Just tell me that you are not going to do anything about Burton and Deschamps until I have all my central contracts in place so I can wrap this thing up. Any scandal right now and the tendering process would go to pot."

"Supposing they don't stop at one murder attempt?" An exchange of looks said it all … 'Let's not go there'.

"What are your plans when this lot is over?" Dan broke the silence.

"Looks like this qango thing won't get off the ground until the beginning of next year so it will be back to the Air Ambulance for a few months."

"Are you still nominally in charge back there?"

"God no! This is a bloody full time job. I need my weekends with Pam or we would both go round the bend. I handed over to Patricia Wellborn, she's been there a while and knows the ropes plus she's got her private pilot's license so she's clued up aviation wise."

"So you will enjoy shedding all this responsibility and getting back to work at the sharp end."

"Something like that." The atmosphere chilled slightly as Dan changed the subject to the elephant in the room.

"Do you want me to watch your back?"

"Do you have much on right now?"

"Not enough to worry about."

"What about Monique?"

"She knows the score ... we both know the score. An orthopaedic surgeon doesn't work nine to five you know."

"I need to keep the lid on this for a few more months but I guess the next few weeks are likely to be the danger period. Let's allow them to think we don't know what's going on and see if the players we have identified are the only ones to worry about. Already I feel better just knowing who it is that's out there but there may be others we have yet to identify. Someone has bugged my office don't forget, but as I told you earlier that could easily be one of my own side just monitoring my activities."

"If that bug is indeed a short range transmitter then I'll bring up one of my gadgets and see if we can find the receiver for you. May even be able to get a handle on who's behind it."

"OK, it's a deal."

21.00 – Tuesday 5ᵗʰ September, 2006
The Prime Minister's Private Office
Downing Street, London

"Shoot, Freddie, what have you got? You'll need to be quick I have to see the Foreign Secretary at nine thirty."

"Right, we have started the ..." he hesitated, "let's call it 'pre-conditioning' process with selected chairmen and women of six of the eighteen target air ambulance trusts. Numbers three, seven, eight, thirteen, fifteen, sixteen and eighteen on your list."

"And..."

"Number three and number thirteen were simple pushovers, knew exactly what the score was, didn't question what we had on them and said they could deliver the rest of the trustees or at least enough of them to get the motion approved."

"The rest?"

"Number seven said he was happy, well unhappy really but you know what I mean, and would try to persuade his fellow trustees but he doubted that he would be able to get the motion through."

"Your next move?"

"I provided some compromising evidence on two of the trustees who are having an affair unknown to their spouses of course. Honestly I could spend all day reading other people's text messages. They make me blush."

"Freddie I can't imagine anything that two human beings would say to each other that would make you blush."

"Thank you for that, I'll continue. Number eight was a spectacular blow up and threatened all sorts of fire and damnation as, being a man of the cloth, he considered himself to be above criticism. I went to see him personally but he believed himself to be way above being told what to do by an oik like me."

"I know how he feels ... joking Freddie, joking."

"Anyway I explained that the images stored on his office PC were enough to get him three years inside so he changed his tune and is now onside and on message."

"Were there any such images on his computer?"

"Let's just say it was an educated guess based on other evidence we had about his unsavoury relationship with kids at his Sunday School."

"You mean he's a known paedophile?"

"Probably."

"Well you can't let him get away with it. You have to arrest him."

"He's marked down for further investigation but I need him in place for the next few months."

"OK, next."

"Number fifteen needed to be reminded that the arrangements he had made for the payment of his elder son's accommodation at Southampton University and the payment of his younger son's school fees by a gentleman who had just received a very large council contract without going to tender were not within the bounds of acceptable behaviour for the leader of such a prestigious body. He too is now on message."

"It gets better, there is no room for such corruption in local government."

"Certainly not ..." Freddie chuckled.

"Number sixteen didn't want to play ball and was convinced we weren't who we said we were so we taught him a short sharp lesson to get his attention."

"Which was?"

"Blocked all his credit cards, made his e-mail address invisible, blocked both his cell phones, then topped it off with a traffic stop that led to a drugs search of his vehicle and a strip search down the local police station."

"Result?"

"His last comment was, 'how high?'"

"Last but not least number eighteen, has a fleet of very expensive cars and runs them all on red diesel. One word from us and he will get a very expensive visit from HMRC that will bring to an end his hopes of being nominated as an MEP candidate."

"Quod Erat Demonstrandum. Good job, keep going, give me an update on the rest next week."

15.00 – Friday 8th September 2006
Abbey Hotel Golf and Spa
Quarterly Conference of the Association
of Chief Police Officers

"Gentlemen, we will move on to the next item on the agenda then we will break for tea. May I remind you to fill out your entry forms for tomorrow's four-ball and place them with the receptionist before eight o'clock tonight.

"The next item is the 'National Police Aviation Service'. The Aviation Sub Committee reports that until they have met with the Home Secretary they have nothing further to report. The statement they made after their last meeting remains valid and I'll read it to you just to refresh your memory."

"The Association of Chief Police Officers wishes to convey to the Home Secretary their disappointment at being excluded from the process of reorganising

the aviation resources of the nation's police services. ACPO will take appropriate action to restore their right to contribute to this vital process."

One member of ACPO was busy with what he personally considered to be appropriate action. That man was Assistant Chief Constable Norman Bennett from South Sussex. His close relationship with WEA's Claude Deschamps went back to the dawn of police aviation in the county when, as a young Inspector he had written the definitive report that led to WEA's product being selected as their first helicopter. Nobody seemed to notice that it coincided with the arrival of his wife's very nice new Peugeot. When he left the unit on his promotion to Chief Inspector he needed to keep the close working relationship warm and selected Murray Burton to take on the mantle of spokesperson for his favourite helicopter. Burton may have benefitted from the crumbs but it was Bennett who earned the serious money. Not cash of course for that would have been too easy to spot. No, ACC Bennett enjoyed a holiday home on Lake Annecy. Wonderful lakeside summer holidays complete with a beautiful boat and close enough to the Alpine resorts for idyllic skiing holidays in the winter. Neither ever cost him a penny.

Of course the proposed acquisition of a brand new machine for the South Sussex ASU was largely down to him but if the NPAS project prevented delivery then his new Riva 33 Aquariva speedboat would disappear down the Suwanee. He had promised his wife, Eleanor, that the most beautiful motor launch in the world would be hers by next spring.

CHAPTER 7

- -

22.00 – Saturday 9th September 2006
Halfpenny Green Airfield

THE ADVANTAGES OF MAGNETIC signs over conventional signwriting is perhaps most apparent if you are the owner of a discrete grey-coloured omni-purpose van and need, from time to time, to assume a number of different guises. Dan Barclay's multifarious activities were a perfect example of how the magnetic sign wins hands down. At that particular moment Dan was apparently working for British Telecomm. The signage was perfect, the personnel ID correct and the gadgetry on board told a story of communications expertise.

Dan closed in on the airfield hoping to pick up the output from the bug in Jack's office. His scanner was capable of receiving signals from every known type of bugging device and it wasn't long before the tell-tale peak on the oscilloscope appeared. It grew until the full strength signal was received. Dan plotted his position on the map he was using to record the reception envelope within which the bug's receiver would be located. The range achieved by the bug was larger than he expected and when Dan examined the area he found that there were too many possible hiding places to be confident of a quick outcome.

Bugs were Dan's speciality and when he was planting one like that used in Jack's office he would try to place the receiver within the circle defined by half the maximum that was possible. This margin for error was one that would protect against any attenuation of the signal. On that basis there were only a few locations on the airfield that might hide the receiver. Most receivers would be unmanned recorders but occasionally they would be manned. Jack's office was closed for the weekend so it was unlikely that anyone would be listening in.

Dan was about to wrap up his initial survey when the flash of a red light in front of the hangar betrayed the presence of a car. It was a brake light. The vehicle was moving but without lights. There was only one reason the driver of that vehicle would be running around without lights. He didn't want to be seen. Dan was immediately very curious about what was going on and moved to a location where he could monitor the entrance to the NPAS complex.

The vehicle that eventually emerged was a Citroen estate car. To his amazement the driver stopped and replaced the padlock on the eight-foot high gates then drove off towards Birmingham. Dan made a note of the registration then punched a text message into his cell phone. The text message arrived on the Duty Officer's phone at MI5 HQ and within five minutes Dan had a reply. The car belonged to a Mrs Eleanor Bennett who lived at an address in South Sussex. The return message from Dan requested a full follow up. Before long the MI5 wheels would be churning out everything the system could locate on the vehicle's registered keeper, links to 'people of interest' and any overseas relationships that emerged.

By the time Dan arrived back at his office in Exeter it was gone midnight. He went straight to his computer and downloaded the 'story so far' on his PC. After the first few pages he stopped reading and dialled Jack's cell phone. A very sleepy and slightly aggrieved voice responded.

"Jack, I was out at your offices earlier this evening and spotted some nefarious activities going on. I'm not going to say any more over an insecure line but be sure you have a bloody good look around when you go in. Whoever it was, and I have a possible name, they had keys to your premises. The curious thing is the individual we have identified has no apparent connection with your unit"

"OK Dan, I'm on it, we'll need to meet, any possibility of you coming up here tomorrow?"

"I'll let you know, by the look of things it will be a while before I get to bed. I'm getting new pages added every minute."

15.00 – Sunday 10th September 2006
Halfpenny Green Airfield

Jack sat alongside Dan in his now anonymous, signless van. They steered clear of using Jack's hire car. There had not been time to sweep it for bugs. Dan ran through the essentials of the deep search that had been carried out in London. It had turned up a web of people whose links astonished Jack and said a hell of a lot about how effective the security services in Europe can be.

The car was registered to the wife of a Mr Norman Bennett, Mr Norman Bennett turned out to be an ACC with South Sussex Constabulary. Dan continued…

"Mrs Bennett has an account with Farmer's Bank in Lewes and she receives an allowance each month from her husband, nothing untoward there but she also has a joint account with her sister, Mrs Bridget Wilson, who in turn has an account with Banc D'Annecy in France. Funds apparently originate at the sister's French account but then flow from that into the joint account she holds with Mrs Bennet. The sums involved are moderate and not enough to draw undue attention. Early indications from France are that the inflow of funds into Mrs Wilson's Banc D'Annecy account originate from a company in Geneva called 'La Vente du Change SA'. They are a marketing company and owned by 'Global Support Services SA', which handles customer support for West European Aviation customers located outside Europe.

"Local police records show that Mrs Wilson is the registered owner of a lakeside house in the village of Les Mongets and a Skiing lodge in Chamonix. Both properties were previously owned by La Vente du Change SA."

"Wow."

"There's a lot more but we don't have time right now."

"Are you sure that the driver of the Citroen estate car was male?"

"Pretty sure, the walk was a male walk and the stature appeared to be larger than I would expect to see in a woman."

"So the likelihood is that we are dealing with Mr Bennett."

"ACC Bennett," added Dan.

"Quite. Where the hell does he fit in the picture?"

"I reckon it's too much of a coincidence that our friend Sergeant Burton also hails from the South Sussex Force. There is something very rotten in that part of the world."

"So what would a senior police officer want to do out of normal working hours in a unit for which he has no responsibility?" Jack wondered.

"He certainly didn't stop by for a coffee."

"No but if mischief was his aim we have to find out what he's been up to. We have a security system of sorts but it's not complete yet. Work in progress I'm afraid."

"CCTV?"

"The cameras are in place but I don't think they are connected."

"Shall we go and see?"

The Security Office was behind the reception area. A bank of video recorders was draped with loose cables indicating work was still incomplete. Only one appeared to have been connected. Dan seemed to be familiar enough with the equipment and soon had the monitor fired up and the recorder running. It turned out to be connected to four cameras covering the office complex. The hangar cameras were not yet functioning. Dan ran the time code back to ten o'clock the previous evening and they both sat watching for action.

The shape of a man appeared by the main entrance. The figure wore a flat cap pulled down low over his eyes. He moved straight to the hangar access door. The unit had what would become the two back-up helicopters inside, held in reserve in case of the breakdown of one of the national fleet. They were the latest, fastest and newest police helicopters in the country but unfortunately only Robbie had completed the type-rating course and was licensed to fly them. He was busy training Lofty so that they would both be qualified to train crews when the new type took over from the assortment of helicopters currently in use around the country.

The time code indicated that the visitor was inside the hangar for fifteen minutes but they had no idea what he had been up to. Was he stealing something or leaving something? Did he interfere with anything or was he just admiring the opposition's shiny new product.

"You know the really worrying thing Dan?"

"What's that?"

"He had a set of keys and by the way he moved around he obviously knew the layout of our premises."

"That would seem to indicate that he has someone on the inside."

"We need to have a quick scout around the hangar, see if there is anything obvious." The two moved through into the hangar and surveyed the £10 million worth of shiny new helicopters neatly arranged at the back of the hangar.

"Trouble is I'm not sure what I'm looking at, or looking for."

"I know, it's the same for me, we need the maintainers in here to give the place a clean bill of health."

"I know it's Sunday but we have a full training programme tomorrow. I'm not sure which one they plan to use but we should get one of them ready at least. I'll call Cliff."

"If you are going to do that, I'd better make myself scarce. I'll keep the ferreting going and be in touch."

"Thanks Dan, I'll let you know if we find anything."

It took Cliff an hour to get in and for Jack to explain what had happened.

Cliff had only been in the hangar five minutes before he came to Jack's office holding a small cellophane packet.

"Look what I found."

"What's that?"

"It's a sugar sachet and if what I think happened did happen we may have a shit load of work ahead."

"Why, what do you think happened?"

"I found this under 'Yankee Papa', it certainly wasn't there when we finished on Friday. We don't have anything like this on the premises. In fact I have never seen sugar in a cellophane sachet before, normally they are paper."

"Is that significant?"

"Yes, it's the difference between wilful damage and maybe murder."

"What? What on earth are you on about? If it really is sugar then it's not exactly poisonous."

"Not in your tea Jack but if I put sugar in your fuel tank it will fuck up the engines big time."

"Shit, is that what you think he did?"

"No, worse than that. He put the cellophane packs in the tank."

"How is that worse for Christ's sake?"

"Put sugar in the tank and the engines wouldn't last long enough to get you off the ground. The reaction between hydrocarbons and sugar is profound, put enough in and it turns to a gel. The fuel control systems on our engines are minutely sensitive to the specific gravity of the fuel and when they get a sniff of that sugar they wrap their hands in and say 'no more', then everything goes very quiet. Put the sachets in and what you have is a time bomb. The cellophane protects the sugar but the Jet A1 fuel will eat away the wrapper and release the sugar, maybe when the machine is in the air. The chance that both engines would go at roughly the same time is very high."

"Would a policeman know about that kind of thing? About the sugar in the fuel?"

"A policeman of a certain age would. In the days before locking fuel caps it was the way you got back at your enemies. The damage to the engine and the fuel system of your enemy's car was out of all proportion to the price of a bag of sugar. The more expensive the car the tastier the result."

"Bloody hell Cliff if that's what happened then we need to do something."

"Yes, the sooner the better."

"What exactly do we have to do?"

"Drain the bloody fuel tank now. At least we can be sure that the engines will be OK."

"Is that a big job?"

"Draining the fuel will be no problem but cleaning the tank will be. You won't be doing any training tomorrow that's for sure."

"We could be wrong." Cliff raised an eyebrow and was off to his desk to phone for help. Jack needed some help too. He went out to the car park and called Dan.

"Hi Dan, are you home yet?"

"Just got in."

"My Chief Engineer suspects sabotage, sugar in the fuel tank, we're about to check."

"Where are you now?"

"Don't worry I'm outside."

"We now have two people in the frame for some very serious crimes, what do you want to do?"

"I want to take them out of circulation but I don't want to involve my unit in the process. Do you think we have enough to start anti-corruption proceedings?"

"Slam dunk."

"Can you give the Serious Fraud Squad the necessary and leave me out of it?"

"Should be possible, I'll get on it in the morning."

"Thanks Dan. Speak tomorrow."

21.00 – Tuesday 12th September, 2006
The Prime Minister's Private Office
Downing Street, London

"Grab a seat Freddie, G and T?"

"Thanks."

"How's your pet project progressing?"

"I had a briefing with Justin Wood at MI5 yesterday and he tells me that the troops are muttering."

"Which particular troops and what are they muttering?"

"Those jumped up bastards at ACPO."

"You shouldn't speak so ill of those that keep us safe at night. When you take their toys away you should expect a few tears."

"It's more than tears, they are trying to delay the new National Police Aviation Service by sabotaging equipment and attacking the management."

"Is everything under control Freddie? We can't afford any scandals right now, not with this air ambulance project on the go. If we are going to win this one we must first gain control of all these expensive assets and then rationalise the fleet. Which reminds me, we have managed to get the rest of the trusts on-side save for number nine, Baroness Parker."

"There must be something you can use to bring her to heal, surely?"

"I'm working on it but Justin is already muttering about being more than a little unhappy about what we are up to and has his spies at work. He forewarned me that there will be resistance to any attempt to sniff out any dirt on someone they see as one of their own."

"Keep looking Freddie or everything we have invested in this will explode in our faces. Deal with her."

09.00 – Wednesday 18th October 2006
Halfpenny Green Airfield

"Good morning Mr Mawgan, there's a message from a Mrs Mallard, from the Home Office. She's in the area and will stop by at eleven o'clock and requests an hour of your time for a meeting."

"Thank you Emily, can we get the posh coffee cups out and make a fresh pot when she comes and if we don't have any biscuits then pop down the village and get some please."

"Sounds like she's important."

"Yes, she's effectively my boss."

"OK leave it to me."

Jack's eyes rose to the ceiling. They had been unable to find the receiver for the bug in the light fitting so Jack was careful not to get involved in sensitive conversations in his own office. He reasoned that the Home Secretary's assistant would almost certainly want to discuss very sensitive issues so he resorted to Plan B. He climbed up on a chair, unclipped the light cover, plucked the bug from its position, took it to the toilet and flushed it down the pan. Dan had suggested that course of action a while back but Jack reasoned that whoever wanted to bug his office would then be alerted and would redouble their efforts. Better to live with what they had and work around it.

Mrs Mallard swept into the building with a flourish, followed by a neatly dressed gentleman wearing a three-piece suit. He was introduced as Peter Falconer and when coats and coffee orders were taken he was further introduced as Jack's replacement, the future head of NPAS.

"The reasons for calling in on you today Mr Mawgan are twofold. To take the opportunity for you to meet Peter and to give you an update on your own future." The arrival of the coffee created a lull in the conversation. Peter sat quietly whilst the cups were distributed and the plate of Hobnobs circulated. "Peter was the ASU Inspector in London in a former life and has progressed to the position of Chief Superintendent Operations. We have managed to persuade him that the head of NPAS should be a civilian, like you. We have found that this works very well when it comes to dealing with the variety of entities encountered in this role. He has therefore transferred to a Civil Service position and will take over from you on the first of November."

"That's fine by me," was Jack's only response, "but we have a way to go to complete the takeover of the central contracts. There's a lot of backpedalling going on in Whitehall. The lawyers are making a real meal of things."

"We shouldn't be surprised at that, Jack, but the last six months have been cathartic for the aviation community within the police service and your contribution should not be underestimated. When the rock-chucking started it was our ace-in-the-hole that you were not involved."

Jack was more than a little taken aback by that, for he personally and the unit as a whole had been the subject of two very serious attacks. He could only imagine that Mrs Mallard wasn't a member of the inner circle that got to see reports from the Security Services.

"The National Air Ambulance Quality and Development Agency has still to pass through the formalities associated with its creation and the responsible Parliamentary Committee is insisting that the Chief Executive is appointed following a formal recruitment process. Don't worry Mr Mawgan, we will get you there but a little smoke and mirrors will need to be applied in the meantime."

"But I finish here at the end of the month?"

"Yes, but you will need to return to your former position in Cornwall in the meantime."

"They gave me a heads up that this may happen a few weeks back so I'm all set. I won't be going back as the Unit Manager but I'll resume duties as one of the clinical team."

"Peter will be staying at the same hotel that you are using until he has arranged his own property and will be available for the hand-over process as from tomorrow, if that fits in OK with your own schedule."

"I can handle that. We have meetings this week with the manufacturers to discuss the spares inventory and the delivery schedule for the new helicopters."

"I'm going to leave Peter with our hire car and would appreciate it if you could arrange a taxi to Birmingham Airport. I have to be up in Edinburgh by this evening so I need to get on the road pretty soon."

"Leave it with me." Jack said as he left the room to speak with Emily.

14.00 – Wednesday 8th November 2006
NSS Corp HQ, Cardinal House, Heathrow Airport

There are times when those in power find the official security services unwilling or unable to deliver some of the solutions required by the executive. For these special tasks a small but capable group of willing helpers had been assembled and were at that very moment attempting to deal with one problem by the name of Baroness Parker. The 'field agent', for want of a better word, carrying out surveillance at Parker's town house called his HQ for instructions. His call was passed to the man in charge of the project.

"This is Freddie, go ahead."

"The old buzzard has left for her cottage in Cornwall, what do you want us to do?"

"Find out where it is, give a late night knock and tell her that the future of her son's career in the Civil Service is in her hands, not to mention the future of her grandchildren. If she doesn't respond then I want her taken care off, permanently. You understand."

"Do you have any preference as to how?"

"Nothing too gory, we don't want any headlines in the nationals. Make it look like suicide, make it neat and tidy. The natural shock and sympathy generated should see the whole thing played down in the media. I'll have the rest of the team on hand to give you cover."

CHAPTER 8

06.00 – Thursday 9th November 2006
St Just-in-Roseland, Cornwall

HAVING FOUND THE COTTAGE Baroness Parker used as her country retreat their plan was to gain access and then silence the old bird, tie her up, tape her mouth then explain the options available to her.

All went well until she presented them with a verbal assault that would make a sailor blush. Replacing the duct tape over her mouth seemed to enrage her even more. This old dear was not going to go without a fight. To ensure she wasn't going to be difficult to handle they decided a little sedative would be the order of the day and carefully placing the hypodermic needle in the crevice behind her ear, administered a belt of ketamine.

Her two assailants adjourned to the kitchen for a conference and decided that the best way to comply with the orders from above was to string her up from the bedroom ceiling where a convenient wooden beam would provide an ideal strongpoint.

A key in the lock startled them and they were forced to retreat upstairs and into the nearest bedroom, across the hall from the Baroness. There were footsteps, then their door slammed as the back door was opened and a sudden gust blew it shut.

It seemed like an age before the person downstairs was heard to leave by the front door and once again all was quiet.

They were shocked to find that the Baroness had passed away whilst they were hiding upstairs. There was an argument about the size of the dose of ketamine they had given her but that was all pointless. She was dead and

50

her body was already getting stiff. They had better string her up before the rigour became unmanageable.

With the job done they left in a hurry.

14.05 – Thursday 9ᵗʰ November 2006
Cornwall Air Ambulance Unit, Newquay Airport

The callout signal sounded. In a well-rehearsed drill the pilot walked quickly to his helicopter and the lead paramedic picked up the phone link to the dispatcher in Exeter. Jack had deferred to his more experienced colleague, Nigel Harris, and chosen to act as the number two. By the time Nigel arrived at the helicopter Jack was strapped into the sideways facing seat behind the pilot, helmet on and ready to go. He took the slip of paper from Nigel and read it out on the intercom so that 'Griff' Griffin, their pilot, could get an idea of the general direction they were expected to go in.

"Person injured, serious, Roseland Farm Cottage, St Just in Roseland."

Taking off into the westerly wind Griff swung the EC135 on to a southerly heading and increased to the very maximum speed permitted. The vibration increased and the undulating patchwork of green and yellow fields passed quickly underneath them. The city of Truro came and went and the Fal estuary stretched before them.

"Helimed this is control, update on the position, the cottage is at the end of Church Lane near Pasco's Boatyard. A suitable landing site could be a farmer's field next to the lane. Difficult to get anything more from the caller as she's in a hysterical state."

"Roger all copied," said Griff, "I'll take a swing over the end of the peninsular and see if I can make out the right field."

The clatter of rotor blades heralded the arrival of vital help for the lone, tearful figure that stood beside the field gate. Nigel and Jack collected their equipment bags and the defibrillator and trotted across to the entrance. The woman turned and led them to Roseland Farm Cottage, pausing at the front step she stood to one side, "She's in the bedroom, upstairs, the one on the right." Nigel took the steps two at a time and turned to the right.

He entered a large bedroom with open beam ceiling and there hung the lifeless corpse of an elderly woman.

Jack wrapped his arms around her legs and took the weight whilst Nigel got his TuffCut scissors from his flight suit pocket and cut the rope holding her to the overhead beam. Jack lowered the frail body gently onto the bed. Nigel was already checking her vital signs when Jack loosened the rope around her neck. Nigel put his stethoscope down and shook his head.

"Rigor mortis is already well established. She's been dead for a while," said Nigel.

"Look at her arms Nige, they should be alongside her body but they're almost out front as if her wrists were tied when she died. There's something fishy here."

They surveyed the scene and realised they were in the presence of someone of some standing. On the chest of drawers, surrounded by ointments and potions was a silver-framed photo of a handsome gentleman with an ermined and robed woman who was clearly the lady now lying on the bed. The two paramedics shared a puzzled look. "Who do you think she is?" said Jack.

"No idea," Nigel replied, "reckon she's down here on holiday." Nigel pointed to the empty suitcase on a stand in the far corner of the room. "Bloody shame. I hate these suicide jobs." Jack stood pensively peering at the body. The sound of gentle sobbing could be heard below. Nigel disappeared down the stairs to tend to the woman's companion. Jack took a pace towards the body and peered closely at the marks left by the cord. A red mark for sure but no bruising. If she had hanged herself there would be bruising caused by the ligature, not just a red mark on the skin. If there was no bruising then no blood was circulating when she met the noose. She was dead before she was hanged. He checked for signs of a disabling blow but none could be seen. He checked the nasal passages and opened her mouth.

"What are you doing Jack?" Nigel had reappeared and stood questioningly by the door. Suicide was not a crime but the police were sure to be involved for until the coroner pronounced 'suicide' the possibility of a crime was ever present.

"She wasn't just hanged Nige, she was murdered."

"You're joking, don't tell me you are going all bloody detective on me Jack. Not again."

Jack's previous career sought to complicate his life in situations like this and his colleagues invariably mocked him for it. Today he was deadly serious.

"It's true, look, no haematoma under the ligature and I have just found this, look here, behind her right ear." Nigel stepped forward and looked closely.

"What, that little red mark?"

"Yes, when someone wants to ensure that an injection site is not identified there is a short list of useful sites that the regular pathologist wouldn't normally check."

"And behind the ear is one of them? Are you serious?"

"Between the toes is a good one or in between the fingers."

"You had best pass this on to the cops when they get here, they'll want to know what you've found. Where the hell are they, they should be here by now? Have you got the radio with you, I need to speak with control?"

"Sure, it's here," Jack handed him the radio.

"I'll give control a call and pass a sitrep then I'll give the housekeeper a sedative. I won't say anything about suicide or murder. I think we'll keep our options open on that score." Nigel went back downstairs to tend to the housekeeper.

Having done as he was asked Jack turned to leave but he felt something under his foot and bent down to see what was there. He picked up a small plastic cap and recognised it immediately. It was the kind of cap that you found on a pre-prepared syringe when you took it from the wrapper. The cap would be removed just prior to the injection. He put it back where he found it, the forensic boys will find it when they go over the place.

Nigel yelled up at him from the foot of the stairs, "Jack! Come on, we have another shout, RTC on the A30, one serious. The cops are on their way here but they are stuck on the King Harry Ferry. Apparently it's thrown a chain, it's stuck in the middle of the river so they're sending another unit the long way round. We'll have to leave it to them, there's nothing we can do for her. Come on, let's go."

Jack went to leave but only got as far as the doorway before returning to take one more look at the deceased. He pulled his cell phone from his pocket and snapped a picture of the marks on her neck and the small blemish behind her left ear. He also snapped a picture of the small plastic cover on the bedroom floor. Before leaving he pulled the bedcover over her, then went below to join Nigel. His policeman's juices were once again flowing, always suspicious, always distrustful. There was nothing quite like a murder to stir Jack's basic instincts.

19.00 – Thursday 9th November 2006
Downing Street, London

Freddie McLaren's early evening call to the PM was brief and to the point.

"It's done, we are in the clear. The Baroness unfortunately succumbed to the pressures that dominated her life as a senior member of the security services and committed suicide."

"Do what you need to do on the protocol side and make sure suitable messages of appreciation and condolences are sent to the family."

"Certainly, it's in hand. Her replacement as an air ambulance charity trustee had to be reminded about the possibility of an investigation into the manipulation of postal votes at the last election, she's a county councillor, but she's now tucked up in our pocket and 'on message'."

"Thank you Freddie, I can't thank you enough. Now I'm afraid I'll have to love you and leave you, affairs of state are calling, I'm late for a reception at the US Ambassador's residence. Just make sure that the loose ends are tidied up as we agreed."

Later that evening at the US ambassador's residence

The melee in the main reception area featured representatives from around the world. Many languages contributed to oiling the diplomatic wheels. Toby recognised Richard Shakespeare, the head of MI5, in the crowd, busy chatting with who he guessed were the CIA's London station chief and his assistant. He nodded, and Richard gave a respectful nod in return.

The G & Ts were excellent, made to his liking with a glass full of ice, Tanqueray gin, Schweppes tonic, a slice of lemon and a good squeeze of lemon juice. Julie was away with the ladies in the far corner laughing and joking and enjoying being the centre of attention. There was a moment when he was standing quite alone and a gentleman he did not recognise approached him with a note. "The Ambassador has asked me to pass you this note sir." Toby took the note and unfolded it with his free hand. It simply said…

CH10 00230 00A109822346 - + SFr 10,000,000, 11/10/06
Turbomeca – no, P & W – yes, make it so.

He stood rooted to the spot trying to take it in. To the uninitiated it was gobbledygook but to Toby it was scary gobbledygook. It was his Swiss numbered account and mentioned the payment recently received from Italy. The rest he would need time to decipher.

08.00 – Friday 10th November 2006
Lower Spargo Cottage, Perranarworthal, Cornwall

Jack propped the newspaper against the cornflakes packet and chomped away at a bowl of the cereal. He was looking for the report of the murder out in Roseland. No such report could be found. He guessed that the news must have missed the early editions. Pam arrived and made herself a boiled egg.

"That murder we dealt with yesterday obviously missed the early editions."

"Yes that was a nasty thing to come across, what did you tell the police?"

"I didn't, we didn't get a chance but I put a written report in as usual. To be honest I would have expected them to call by now. Maybe they spoke to Nigel. I'll give him a call later, he's on a day off too."

As if by divine intervention the telephone rang. It was Nigel calling. "Hi Jack, I had a weird call from the cops this morning, they want to see us in Truro to make statements about the suicide yesterday."

"Suicide, didn't you tell them it was definitely murder not suicide?"

"That's why they want to see us, eleven o'clock this morning."

"OK, we'll get this sorted when we give our statements. Bloody typical, we get a day off and they still manage to screw us around. I'll see you there at eleven." Jack finished his breakfast and set about catching up with the bills and getting his accounts in order. He was about to leave when he had another call from Nigel.

"They've cancelled the meeting. Said they will be in touch."

"Bloody hell!" was Jack's only contribution.

10.00 – Saturday 11th November 2006
The Prime Minister's Private Residence
Chequers, Ellesborough, Buckinghamshire

Toby and Julie were breakfasting alone. Julie wanted to discuss the menu for the evening's dinner party but Toby had more pressing things on his mind. He passed the note he received last night to Julie. She read it, her facial expression communicated confusion.

"This is our bloody Swiss Bank Account number, and by the look of it they have just clocked the payment we received last month. The bastards must have a spy in the bank."

"I thought you said that this new financial wizard was as safe as houses."

"I did, but even he can't dictate what goes on inside the bank."

"Or inside your office," she added with a good measure of venom.

"Whatever. The damn CIA are everywhere. You simply don't know who to trust these days."

"What's the cryptic bit at the bottom?"

"Something to do with the engines on the new police machines, we've ordered French engines and they are twisting my arm to change to the American made version."

"Can you do that?"

"It'll cause some heartache but I'll just have to go along with it or who knows what the buggers will do with the fact that we have an offshore account. If they poke their noses in there too deeply then it will get very sticky for us."

"It would appear to be sticky already." Toby didn't have an answer. He knew the game was well and truly up and that could have only one consequence. If the CIA knew about his illegal account then he would be in the American's pocket from now on. He must talk to Freddie about finding the leak.

08.00 – Monday 13th November 2006
Lower Spargo Cottage, Perranarworthal, Cornwall

Another day went by, another issue of the newspaper with no mention of the murder in Roseland. It was too much for Jack so he called Brian Curnow, an old journalist chum at the West Briton.

"Hi Brian, how's the world treating you?"

"Good heavens, Jack Mawgan, it's been years since we last talked. Where have you been?"

"Had a bit of a career change, I'm driving an ambulance these days or at least flying around in the air ambulance."

"Sounds like an interesting story, I'd like to do a feature on you one day."

"Yes Brian one day, right now I have a quick question for you."

"Go ahead, I'm all ears."

"What happened to the story of the lady that died out on Roseland last Thursday?"

"Baroness Parker you mean? Died of a heart attack, cremated on Saturday."

"Cremated on Saturday? They must have done the autopsy pretty bloody quick."

"Autopsy, I don't think so old chum, apparently she was under the doctor for a heart condition so they probably just signed her off."

"Is that what they told you?"

"Yep."

"But there was no mention of it in the papers."

"What do you mean, we ran it on the front page, two column inches?"

"I meant the nationals Brian, all due respect and that."

"Not surprised. She was down from the Midlands I think, she was staying at her country cottage for a week. Her son runs a boatyard a bit further down, by the church."

"Thanks, you've answered my question, I'll let you get on."

"I'm serious about that feature, `I'll give you a call later this year."

"OK, you're on, cheers."

That call set Jack's mind racing. Once upon a time he would have been straight down the local police station and banged the desk demanding to know what was happening. Recent experience taught him to be more cautious. He decided he would find out a little more about Baroness Parker before raising his head above the parapet.

Work summoned, he would have to do it the following day.

18.00 – Tuesday 14th November 2006
St Just-in-Roseland, Cornwall

Jack made a speculative trip across the King Harry Ferry to St Just-in-Roseland and quickly located the boatyard at the end of Church Lane. Darkness was closing in but Jack found two men working under floodlights on the hull of a splendid looking traditional Falmouth Workboat. He introduced himself and asked if Mr Parker was available. The younger of the two stopped what he was doing and joined Jack on the slipway.

"How can I help you?" he said with an unexpectedly cultured accent.

"Hi, my name is Jack Mawgan, I was one of the paramedics that arrived with the air ambulance last week when your mother died."

"Oh. I'm afraid I don't know much about what happened that day, I was busy collecting the Pegasus, this working boat," he nodded towards the pale blue hull that stood elegantly on wooden bulks and propped by hefty timbers. "Mother was down for a few days to get away from it all and her sudden death rather caught the family off guard. She didn't tell us she had a heart condition."

"I was there Mr Parker, you don't have to be embarrassed about the hanging, it was me that cut her down."

"Yes, yes of course. I'm sorry but it was hard to take. To be honest we are still in shock over the whole thing. We've all agreed not to mention the suicide and the authorities have been very understanding, they haven't mentioned it either."

"Was that your suggestion or theirs?"

After a moment's thought he said, "Actually it was theirs come to think of it."

"Who did you talk to?" There was no response at first.

"Tell me Mr Mawgan, do you have any ID, only mother was with the Security Services so we were always warned about talking to strangers."

Jack produced his ID card issued by the South West Ambulance Trust. Mr Parker studied it but by his body language he knew that his question and answer session was over.

"Thank you Mr Mawgan, if you need anything more please feel free to speak to the Special Branch office in Truro."

"It was very kind of you to see me this evening Mr Parker. I appreciate your help and I understand your situation. You can rely on my discretion."

"Good bye Mr Mawgan."

Jack turned to return to his car. The one thing that Jack was sure of was that he did not understand Mr Parker's situation and he certainly wasn't disposed to going away quietly. There was something funny going on here and when it involved the spooks he knew that meant trouble could come from any direction. Expect the unexpected would be the order of the day.

Returning home he explained to Pam that he was convinced that there was a conspiracy to cover up the fact that a very distinguished member of the establishment had apparently committed suicide. In one respect he could understand that but when the whole thing is looked at in the context of murder it takes on a much more serious and sinister form. It worried him that the lady had a history with the security services. He had prior experience of working for them but also experience of just how uncomfortable it can get when they chose to work against you.

22.00 – Tuesday 14th November 2006
Lower Spargo Cottage, Perranarworthal, Cornwall

Pam was startled by the doorbell, it was so late in the evening. She left the door chain on and held the door ajar. There were two gentlemen waiting for the bell to be answered, both wore dark raincoats, white starched shirt collars shone brightly with discrete patterned ties giving the impression that the two were quite probably Jehova's Witnesses.

"Good evening Mrs Mawgan, my name is Smythe, this is Mr Jordan. We are with the police." He held an ID card that looked impressive enough but Pam couldn't read the detail, her reading glasses were in the kitchen.

"We wish to speak with Mr Mawgan if we may?" Taking them at face value Pam took the door off the chain and invited them in.

"Please go into the lounge, take a seat. I'll fetch my husband."

Jack arrived from outside with an armful of logs and dumped them beside the fire. "Good evening gentlemen, my wife tells me you are from the police. Can I see your warrant cards?" The two exchanged a look and once more produced their ID Cards.

"These say that you are working for an organisation called NATIONAL SECURITY SERVICES corp., how enticingly ambiguous. So you are not police after all."

The visitor doing all the talking responded, "With respect Mr Mawgan I didn't say that we *were* the police, I said that we were *with* the police, and that I can assure you is very much the case."

"And if I chose not to believe you?"

"I can give you a number in Downing Street to call if you really want reassurance but I don't think that will be necessary. We have just come to deliver a message and then we'll be on our way."

"Which is?"

"Baroness Parker, leave well alone. There you have it. We'll say good night Mr Mawgan, I trust we will *not* meet again."

Something about the way he said that riled Jack so that he slammed the door behind them as they left with a firmness that spoke volumes. "Don't worry Mr bloody Smartarse we will meet again, of that I am certain."

"What was that all about?" asked Pam, concern and worry in her tone.

"The Baroness Parker murder. Now I am sure it was murder."

"But if everyone else agrees it was natural causes then maybe you are wrong."

"I'm not wrong Pam and those two have confirmed my suspicions."

"What on earth are you saying, that it was murder and the police are covering it up?"

"Not necessarily the police, let's just say that organs of the state are covering it up."

"But that's not right Jack, that's not how it should be and surely they can't hide the fact that it was suicide. I mean the 999 call must have mentioned that it was a hanging?"

"Funnily enough the caller was too hysterical to explain, just told the dispatcher that she was dying and to hurry."

"What about the police report?"

"By the time they got there she would have been found lying on the bed with the remains of the cord still in place."

"But they would have taken your statement surely?"

"They did arrange a meeting but then cancelled it."

"How weird."

"What about your patient notes for the mission, you must have filed them?"

"You are right my lovely, I'd forgotten all about those. They'll be in this week's pending file waiting for the clerks to enter the data in the computer."

Pam came close to Jack and put her arms around him and gave him a hug, then looked up into his eyes and saw a twinkle that made her shudder. The last time he had that look in his eye it had brought a lot of trouble with it. She hugged him tight. "Promise me no funny stuff, no sticking your neck out again."

"I'll have to do what's necessary Pam but I'll do my best to stay low profile. If the State is complicit in the murder of its citizens then it's not the kind of state I wish to be part of."

"What are you going to do?"

"Method, opportunity and motive, are the three steps to working the whole thing out. I think I understand the method but who was the opportunist and why did they do it. I think we need to get a good night's sleep my darling. We're going to be busy burning the candle at both ends for a while."

The records from the flight would be filed in Exeter. How the hell was Jack going to get there? No chance for a week or so, not with the work schedule he had on.

CHAPTER 9

‒ ‒

10.00 ‒ Thursday 16ᵗʰ November 2006
NSS Corp HQ, Cardinal House, Hanworth
Lane, Heathrow Airport

THE RAIN FELL STEADILY as it had been for the whole of the previous night. Freddie McLaren's taxi dropped him on the main road and he had to scurry to the entrance through deep puddles. By the time he reached the glass doors of the building he was soaked. The lobby seemed brightly lit against a dark and dismal grey morning. For most it was a depressing start to the day but to Freddie it was just another day at the office with problems to solve and people to organise. Today was all about damage limitation.

His appointment was with Sir William Salisbury, the President and CEO of NSS and the problem of the day was a certain Mr Mawgan. Formalities over, Freddie made himself comfortable in a deliciously welcoming leather armchair.

"Our Mr Mawgan has quite a history Freddie, did you know that?"

"He has a history with us Sir William, we chose him as our Mr dumbass 'nice guy' to handle a little project for us. Which I must say he has done very well."

"Don't underestimate him Freddie, our Mr Mawgan is the recipient of the George Medal in the UK and in a certain part of Africa holds the status of Knight of the Realm. Our Mr Mawgan has the potential to be a complete pain in the neck."

"What do you intend to do about it? We have to keep the lid on this."

"He's been given a personal warning by one of our teams so we wait and see if he takes their advice and backs off."

"And if he doesn't?"

"Then we have a range of options that it's better you don't know about. What *must* happen is that when we ask for some action or some information you have to convince Richard Shakespeare and Justin Wood to go along with it."

"They've delivered so far. Not a murmur. They haven't even required a detailed briefing. We just feed the requests through the Home Office and tell them it's related to ongoing police enquiries and they deliver."

"This time it may be different, Mawgan was one of their own and has friends who may get in the way. I think we will have to fall back on our own resources to remove Mr Mawgan from the equation. Let's keep the spooks out of it."

"Can you cope?"

"We always cope Freddie. That's why we exist. Prime Ministers need to feel they are in control and whilst we may be unconventional we do give them that security."

"That's reassuring Sir William, I can get a bit more sleep in future."

Sir William smiled.

"Are you lunching with us?"

"No time I'm afraid, I'll hop a cab into town and catch a bite to eat at Number Ten."

"No, no, I'll have my driver run you in, I'll be driving myself this afternoon so I won't need him."

"That's kind of you, I would appreciate that."

Sir William summoned his secretary who led Freddie away to his free ride into town. When he was well on his way Sir William gathered up his coat and briefcase and made his way to the underground car park to collect his Bentley sports coupe. The luxury of the Bentley was enough to make the miserable drive in pouring rain thoroughly bearable. The M40 at midday on a very dark and damp Monday is only improved by the knowledge that you are heading out of town rather than into the vehicular morass that is life inside the M25.

At junction five he headed off through Stokenchurch and into the wooded countryside. An un-signposted country lane led to an impressive entrance with two large gateposts and two large metal gates. Stretching as far as the eye could see in either direction was an eight-foot high wall topped with neatly layered strings of razor wire.

A transponder in the Bentley signalled its arrival and an invisible operator swung the gates open. Ahead in the gathering gloom was a gravel driveway leading to one of England's minor stately homes. The Georgian house with its Palladian frontage owed much to Inigo Jones' influence and this particular house had been well cared for and now formed the base for NSS operatives. This was where they lived, where they trained and where they planned.

Operatives came in different shapes and sizes and from different backgrounds but all had one thing in common, at one time or another they had been trained operatives for the special forces or the security services. For reasons best not subjected to too much scrutiny they had no longer met the standards required by their former employers and had been 'let go'. This meant that they knew the correct procedures and techniques for their role as 'alternative' operators and even had a few tricks of their own to help convince where convincing was necessary.

Sir William parked out front and scurried in the front door as the heavens delivered a burst of horizontal rain to welcome him in. Greeting him in the entrance hall was his Operations Director Damien Porter.

"Good afternoon Sir William."

"We have to talk Damien, I'm not happy with this Mawgan affair."

"What about lunch?"

"Yes we can talk over lunch, where are we?"

"The Main Board Room."

"Right, I must just make myself comfortable then I'll join you upstairs." Sir William disappeared through a heavy oak panelled door to reappear minus the paraphernalia of management and now wearing a pair of designer jeans and a mohair roll neck, the brogues replaced by deck shoes. Breezing into the Main Board Room he took his place opposite Damien, plucked his serviette from its silver ring, flapped it open and spread the rich damask cotton over his knees. A waiter produced bowls of steaming French onion soup and the two settled into a silent period of contemplation whilst enjoying the exquisite flavour of the classic dish. When the soup was finished it signalled the end of the meditation and the start of business.

"Mawgan is going to come back and bite us, I can feel it in my bones," began Sir William.

"We sent a team to speak with him and warned him off."

"That may be but Mawgan is a certain type. They get on their high horse at being told to butt out. Trust me we need to get our act together and head him off."

"I have just the thing for that kind of troublemaker. I'll show you after lunch."

"I don't want another corpse if we can help it, they tend to be more troublesome that they are worth."

"Don't worry. I think that we can teach him a lesson without making too many waves."

18.00 – Thursday 16th November 2006
Lower Spargo Cottage, Perranarworthal, Cornwall

Jack looked through the photos he had taken of Baroness Parker's body. They were now stored on his PC and he printed copies to show Pam. She agreed with his hypothesis that the injuries looked very much like murder and the plastic cap and hypodermic needle marks only added to their suspicions. Pam offered to show the pictures to her colleagues at work but Jack told her that to widen the circle of sceptics might not be such a good idea just at that moment. He reasoned that the evidence was so convincing that he wanted to keep the photos a secret until such time as he could use them to best effect.

Gripped by what he thought was a justifiable paranoia he copied them on to a couple of SD cards and then recorded a video in which he gave a short speech explaining what happened on that day and what had happened to him since. He took one set of the prints plus an SD card and put them in an A5 envelope, scribbled a note on the outside telling the recipient to keep it safe then put the note and envelope in a larger A4 version with the address of his brother, Robert, already written on it. Doing the same with the other set of prints and memory card he addressed this second envelope to Dan Barclay. The envelopes were sent on their way by registered mail the following morning.

10.00 – Friday 17ᵗʰ November 2006
Newquay Airport

Life at work was dominated by the bad weather. Day after day they were forced to ground the helicopter due to the low cloud in the east and the fog in the west. When the weather was too bad for flight operations the paramedic crew would use one of the spare road ambulances to provide coverage in the area around Newquay.

Jack and Nigel had not discussed the events of the previous Thursday since that day. Jack knew that Nigel was one of those that thought that he was obsessed with looking for crimes where none existed. He could sympathise with that view but then Nigel was no policeman. He was one of the world's nice guys and for the most part saw good in everyone unless and until they crossed him. Jack was sitting in the driving seat of their Mercedes sipping a cup of coffee parked up at Carland Cross on the busy A30 when he was taken by surprise by a clearly upset Nigel.

"Jack, my old matey," somehow his lilting Cornish accent strengthened whenever he had something serious to say.

"Yes Nige, what can I do for you?"

"I got a visit yesterday, at my home ... at my home mind, from a couple of heavies who said they were from the Security Services and wanted to talk to me about that old lady we found hanging last week."

"What did they say?"

"That it wouldn't be in the interests of national security for the world at large to know that Baroness Parker committed suicide. It would however be in order for the death to be recorded as a heart attack and that's how it would be and did I fully understand?"

"What did you say?"

"What do you think I said? I told them I fully understood, Baroness Parker had a myocardial infarction."

"Bloody Hell Nigel, this isn't right you know. She was jolly well murdered and then strung up to make it look like a hanging."

"Just think about it Jack, you're supposed to be the bloody detective. Why would they dress it all up to look like a hanging if they could have just made it look like a heart attack?"

Jack had to think about that for a moment. "Maybe the housekeeper disturbed them. I don't know, I haven't worked that out yet but all I know is that there is something going on here which is not right and I intend to find out what it is."

"I suggest you do what I'm going to do and leave well alone. When I retire I don't want any baggage to worry about. Whenever I've been foolish enough to tangle with authority I've always lost out. I once had a fight with my old dad and told him he was wrong and I was right and I was going to do what I wanted to do because it was a matter of principle. Do you know what he told me?"

"Let me guess, you can't afford to have principles my son because you don't have enough money."

"Well, it was something like that. I did it anyway and guess what, he was right. I lost my job and was unemployed for six months. I'm not going there again Jack so let's play the game and let those buggers in London play their silly games."

For the first time since he joined the Ambulance Service he realised that he was facing tension in the crew. Nigel was not to be humoured; he was thoroughly pissed off with Jack. It made for a miserable day on what was already a miserable day. He spent the rest of it sitting in the cab waiting for a shout. They were listening to the ambulance radio as it burst into life at regular intervals with instructions to crews around the county to attend call after call but nothing for them. For once the A30 'idiots' had stayed at home.

Jack planned ahead to work out a way of moving his murder enquiry forward. He would avoid any and all formal approaches to authority of any kind but he some very clever friends who had previously come to his aid in times of trouble. One was an IT specialist based in Bristol. He may also need to rattle Dan Barclay's cage again.

10.00 – Saturday 18th November, 2006
St Just-in-Roseland

Jack's police experience comes to the fore when ferreting out information. He headed for the one remaining Post Office in the area at St Mawes with the intention of tapping into the wealth of gossip and local information that the Postmistress in a small village tends to accumulate. The purchase of a couple of post cards provided the opportunity to begin a casual conversation and by the time he had finished he knew that Baroness Parker's housekeeper was a Mrs Mitchell and that the Mitchell family occupied a terraced cottage between St Just and St Mawes.

He knocked on the door and the woman he recognised from that memorable day opened the door. She took about five seconds to size him up and down, put a time and place to the face and attempt to close the door before Jack could finish the first sentence.

"Mrs Mitchell, can I ask a couple of questions about last week only I need to complete my paperwork and forgot to collect some answers before we disappeared in the helicopter?"

"They said you'll be round and I was to say nothing. But 'twasn't suicide like they say, she wasn't that kind of person. I did love her like a sister and we were close even if I do say so myself."

"I agree Mrs Mitchell, she was murdered, of that I'm sure."

"Murdered! Who on earth would want to do that, she was such a lovely lady."

"I guess she had enemies Mrs Mitchell. Tell me, were you expected up at the cottage on that day?"

"Of course, I had word she'd be down as usual but she weren't supposed to be there that day. My message said the next day. Strange, she do normally call I when she leaves London."

"Did you see anyone else in the area when you arrived?"

"There was a van parked outside when I arrived. I was going to set the bed and turn the heating on so she had a nice warm cottage to come down to. I normally do that for her."

"What colour and size was the van?"

"Was white and the same size as Billy the plumber, I thought it were him at first but it had no writing on the side. The boiler's been playing up so I called Billy and asked him to sort it out. He knows where we leave the key."

"Did you see anyone while you were there?"

"Not exactly, see I went to the utility room first off to get the washing machine ready and set up the drying rack. When I went through the kitchen I heard a door slam but I didn't see nobody and just thought it was 'cos I 'ad the back door open. Gust of wind you see."

"Is that when you found her, the Baroness?"

"No, 't were later on. I forgot see, forgot to turn the bed. I'd got all the way home for me dinner and 'ad to come all the way back."

"So how long were you working at the house the first time?"

"Maybe a couple hours. I wanted to get one lot of washing out on the rack, see and that old washing machine isn't the fastest one I've ever seen. Put it on a hot wash and you won't get much change out of two hours I'll tell ee."

"So what did you do while you were waiting?"

"What I always do, put the radio on and do a bit of knitting."

"So what time did you get to the house at the start of the day."

"Usual time."

"What's that?"

"'Bout ten, did the washing and went home for my dinner at around twelve thirty and came back around an hour later. Told you, I forgot to turn the bed."

"Was the van still parked outside when you came back later?"

"No 't were gone."

"That's when you found the Baroness?"

"Yes, 't was a hell of a shock I can tell you. I was shaking all the time till you and your friend arrived and gave me a bit of something to calm me down."

"That's very interesting. Did you tell the police when they arrived?"

"They did come, eventually but two other men were here. Security Services they said. They told me they would take care of the situation and make sure the police were properly informed."

"What car did they have?"

"It was a white van with Police signs on the side."

"Was it the same type of van that you saw leaving earlier on?"

Mrs Mitchell had to think for a few minutes. "It was the same type but it had 'police' sign in big blue letters on the side. I'd better go now, I'm not supposed to be talking to you."

"Alright but don't say anything about me mentioning murder, there are people out there who'll get cross if they hear that word, know what I mean?" She smiled and slammed the door shut.

When he got home he told Pam about the conversation with Mrs Mitchell.

"I'll tell you what else," he said, "I reckon that I now know what happened on the day we found her."

"What happened then?"

"I think she was actually attacked and sedated, but she probably had an adverse reaction to the sedative and died. The murderers were intent on making it look like suicide and hung her up to the beam. Their problem appears to be one of timing. Mrs Mitchell was sitting downstairs whilst they were upstairs. They were obviously unable to string the old girl up with the housekeeper wandering around downstairs and had to wait for her to leave."

"By which time the rigour would have set in and it would be plain as day to any clinician that the hanging was post mortem."

"You've got it, bang on."

"Why were they so incompetent? I thought you portrayed these guys as professionals."

"My guess is that they thought a quiet suicide in a far away part of the UK would be easy to stage manage but it all went wrong on the day. They may have been forensically aware in their planning but not so good at the execution."

"Meaning?"

"They sedated her using injections. They made those injections in the junction between the ear and the scalp. Not easy for any pathologist to spot. If you are planning to make it look like suicide then you need to be sure there are no other signs of foul play."

"But you said there was no autopsy."

"No, they played that part very well. No one wanted the illustrious retired head of one of the country's security services to be found to have committed suicide."

"My God, can you imagine the rumours that would circulate if the press found out?"

"Absolutely. Whoever organised this murder definitely wanted Baroness Parker to go quietly."

"Whoever it was must have had some influence because the police have been made to look the other way."

"Yes, and if my hunch is correct I bet the people who did her in were the same ones that came back half an hour later pretending to Mrs Mitchell that they were the police. By the time the real cops got there they would have had everything nicely tidied away."

"Hell Jack, I don't like the way this is going. The last time you got involved with some nasty people we had to move house. Let's not go there again."

"This time I'm not dealing with criminals from the underworld but criminals from our own government."

"Can Dan help?"

"Not a bad idea. I'll set up a meet and we can talk it through as soon as he has seen the material I sent in the mail."

13.00 – Sunday 19th November, 2006
Exeter Services M6

Dan climbed into Jack's Jaguar and made himself comfortable.

"Thanks Dan, good of you to spare the time."

"That's OK mate, I only have an hour or so as I've got another job starting up in Bristol this evening. I've had a look through the stuff you sent me. Looks pretty fishy to me."

"This is the story behind those pictures. I was working on the air ambulance back on the ninth of November and attended a callout at St Just-in-Roseland. When we got there we found an elderly lady hanging from a beam in an upstairs bedroom."

"Did you know who she was?"

"Not at the time but it turned out to be Baroness Parker. I went back later and spoke with her son but he was tight-lipped. I also got to have a few words with the housekeeper, Mrs Mitchell."

"Baroness Parker eh! Probably better known by her maiden name as Helena Baker-Knowles, used to be head of MI5 in the days before their names were made public."

"It's beginning to add up, she had a photograph on her chest of drawers when she was elevated to the peerage and I recognised the gentleman with her – George Parker, the shipping magnate, died of cancer a while back and left enough money to fund a hospital in Liverpool."

"And a bit more besides, he was loaded, but yes, you've got it."

"Anyway, I cut her down and we checked her over."

"So what made you think it was murder?"

"I loosened the ligature and instinctively checked the neck markings."

"What do they tell you?"

"If someone is hanged whilst they are alive then the ligature will cause massive localised bruising as the heart is still pumping and the blood flows into the damaged area of tissue. If the person is already dead when hanged then there is no blood-flow so no bruising."

"But surely the killers must have known that."

"You would have thought so but for whatever reason they screwed up. They used an injected sedative to keep her under control but misjudged the dosage. I suspect that their plan involved the old lady being found the following day but the housekeeper turned up to prepare the cottage for her arrival and disturbed them before they could tidy the place up. I found the tip cover for a standard hypodermic syringe on the floor."

"Did the housekeeper see them at all?"

"Apparently not."

"So what happened then?"

"The police were stuck on the King Harry Ferry and guess what?"

"What?"

"I think the people we are dealing with are somehow getting inside information. Either that or they are working for the security services. They must have known that the coast was going to be clear long enough for them to tidy up the crime scene. The same white van or one very similar turns up with two ersatz cops inside now miraculously wearing large police signs. What does that tell you?"

"They came prepared."

"Exactly."

"Which means that you are dealing with professionals, although maybe not quite so professional as they would like when it comes to faking a suicide."

"Just like your lot."

"What do you mean?"

"We have never actually sat down and formally discussed it before Dan but from what I do know you work for the security services as a kind of independent contractor."

"I can neither confirm nor deny your assertions." He was trying to keep a straight face but after all they had gone through together Jack knew damn well who and what Dan really was.

"So you're not going to confirm that we have assassins that indirectly work for the Security Services?" There was a long pause during which both said nothing. Eventually it was Dan that broke the ice.

"This goes no further. I mean it Jack, not even your nearest and dearest."

"I'm all ears."

"I hope that means you are not recording this conversation."

"No Dan, no recordings."

"Good, because my life could depend on what I am about to share with you. You are right, the Security Services use people like me to do the kind of work that needs to be … well … un-attributable. But we are controlled by the Security Services and we don't freelance … and we are disciplined."

"And you are paid."

"Of course."

"There are complications these days however for whilst the Security Services are responsible to Parliament and we are part of that chain of command we believe that there is another branch that … let's say, live in a parallel universe. These 'other' professionals work directly for the executive and bypass Parliament."

"Hell Dan, you mean that there is a bunch of tooled-up independents out there that nobody officially knows about?"

"Probably."

"What do you mean probably, don't you know?"

"Not yet but we are getting close. We call them 'The Moneymen', on account of their motives appear to focus on increasing the wealth of their patrons but we also refer to them by a nickname, 'The Men in Black'."

"So much for any illusions of 'principle' then."

"The only principle we can observe is greed. Unfortunately one of our other freelancers who was hot on their trail has gone missing whilst checking out what we believe is their HQ, a big house in the countryside just off the M40. We fear the worst. We are not dealing with faint-hearted amateurs Jack, these people, whoever they may be, are hardened professionals and some were even trained by us."

"I'm trying to get my head around this. What use could these people be to the Executive?"

"Keeping people in line, on message and helping to ensure that when necessary people do what you want them to do."

"Do you think that's what they wanted with the Baroness, they wanted her to do something and when she didn't play they topped her?"

"Maybe."

"Bloody Hell, who are these people?"

"The truth is we don't know for sure. They are good Jack; good at their job of mimicking the Security Services and they know that for security reasons we work in 'silos'. I don't know who else is doing what I do. I come across people that I think might be involved but these days I don't know if they are legit and working for Justin or 'Moneymen' working for whoever runs the Executive's version of the same thing."

"How do they recruit their operatives?"

"They are almost certainly 'discards', people we let go for one reason or another. They have had the training, speak the language and know how we work. They just do the same thing only they dance to a different tune."

"What is the establishment doing about it? How far up the tree does it go? Is the Prime Minister involved?"

"Probably not directly, but we suspect that it's coming out of Downing Street via his aides, one in particular is top of the list … Freddie McLaren."

"How do you know all this Dan, you're not even on the official payroll?"

"I was given a briefing by Justin a few weeks back. We are on the lookout for any leads that might allow us to find their operating bases and their management then we'll need to put a stop to what they are up to."

"Rather you than me."

"You may well be involved yourself you know. These people could well be behind the Baroness Parker murder."

"Which reminds me, we think we know the 'how', we think we now have a handle on the 'who' but we don't have a 'why'. What could the motive be?"

"Hey, buddy, not so much of the 'we', this is your fight, you picked it so you have to deal with it. I'm up to my neck already."

"What if the people I'm on to are 'Moneymen'?"

"Food for thought I guess. Let me see if I can get a response from management. I'll let you know."

CHAPTER 10

17.15 – Sunday 19th November, 2006
On the A30 Highway to Cornwall

DAYLIGHT WAS ALL BUT extinguished by the dark overcast that every now and then threw bucketfuls of rain against Jack's windscreen. The wipers were on 'max', the lights of oncoming cars were a strain, the taillights of the traffic ahead formed a hypnotic array of dancing red spots on a smeared view of the darkening world.

The long and tense day had taken its toll. Jack was already feeling tired and had another hour or so to go before the prospect of a nice hot supper and an evening in front of the box. As he approached Kennard's House a small hatchback pulled alongside. He quickly glanced across at the woman in the passenger seat. She was waving frantically and pointing towards the rear of Jack's car. Ahead was the steep downhill to the Polyphant junction where he knew there was a layby and parking area.

The van ahead of Jack obviously had the same plan for both indicated to turn into the parking area and the hatchback followed them both in. Jack found his umbrella on the floor behind him and opened his door. He stepped out into the steadily falling rain and moved to the back of his car to see what was amiss. He didn't see the four men leave the rear doors of the van but as he bent forward to examine his exhaust pipe the lights went out.

08.00 – Monday 20th November, 2006
Lower Spargo Cottage, Perranarworthal

"Hello, Dan?"

"Yes."

"It's Pam, Pam Mawgan."

"Oh, hi Pam, how's things?"

"Not so good Dan, Jack didn't come home last night and I'm going crazy trying to find out where he's gone."

"Well he left here around five o'clock last night so he should have been with you by seven."

"I've checked with the police and they told me to check the hospitals but they say they have no record of any accidents between Exeter and our place."

"Any sign?"

"No, none. I'm going crazy Dan and don't know which way to turn. Can you help?"

"I'll do what I can Pam. Can you give me details of the registration of Jack's car and the clothes he was wearing. I know it was the Jag and I know what he was wearing when we met but I guess he had a topcoat in the car so I need a description of that. I'll make a few calls then head for the office."

10 o'clock that morning
Dan's Office in Exeter

"Pam, Dan here."

"Any luck?"

"No, not so far. The police are checking the A30 for any sign of the Jag but nothing so far. Did you get any sleep last night?"

"No, none at all."

"Then get some sleep, I'm on the case."

5 o'clock that afternoon
Dan's Office in Exeter

"Hi Pam, we've had a lucky break but it's not all good news, it looks like Jack has been kidnapped."

"What? How? Who would do that?"

"We have a few ideas thanks to Jack's visit. I don't know if you were aware but he was working on some contentious stuff and he has unwittingly trodden on a few toes in the process."

"Oh Dan! What does this mean? Is his life in danger?"

"It's undoubtedly serious Pam but we both know that Jack can take care of himself. We have to keep believing that." There was a sound of weeping and Pam was obviously distressed.

"How do you know he's been kidnapped?"

"A truck driver was taking a nap in a layby on the A30 and was woken by sounds of a scuffle. He peeked out of his cab to see a man being bundled into the back of a van and another man climbing into a silver Jaguar. They drove off in convoy with a small hatchback. That's all we know. We are doing a check on all the CCTV cameras in the area and as soon as I have any news I'll let you know."

"Thanks Dan,"

"Fingers crossed that we get a break."

"All right, I have to get hold of Nathan. I've told Josh and he's going to try and get home as soon as he can."

"Speak later, bye for now."

08.00 – Tuesday 21ˢᵗ November, 2006
Mzala, East of Tangier, Morocco

When Jack opened his eyes he had to blink three or four times to convince himself that he hadn't gone blind. The light level with his eyes open was only marginally more than with them firmly shut. He lifted his head just an inch and smartly put it back down again. He grimaced, his head hurt like hell. He tried again then gave up. He was breathing heavily and sweating profusely, his mind addled by weird dreams and illusions. Life was almost pain free when he left his head where it was and his eyes shut. Still, it was life. He struggled with the scrambled memories of what seemed to be another, previous existence.

The sound of a sliding door was accompanied by a shaft of light. When Jack next opened his eyes he was staring at a leather sandal. The next sense to penetrate the fog was his hearing. Someone was talking but it was an unintelligible scribble of noise. His sense of touch was called into service when the sandal delivered a blow to his gut. The owner of the sandal turned out to be a man, a stranger, a strange man. He wore strange clothes, a strange hat and looked for all the world as if he had escaped from the 'Casablanca' movie set.

Slowly Jack began to realise the man was talking to him but he didn't understand. Another kick and he figured that lying down was not such a smart idea and that standing up was the order of the day. Unfortunately whilst his mind was willing, his body had other ideas. He stumbled against a wall and despite his wobbly knees eventually achieved the vertical, or near vertical. This wasn't good enough for his protagonist who put one hand on his shoulder, turned him around, moved the hand to the middle of his back and propelled him through a door and out into a blisteringly bright new world that made his head ache even more.

The man continued to yell at him and threw some clothes on the floor in front of him. He gestured at Jack to put them on which prompted him to look down at what he was wearing. He was stunned to realise that he had on a dirty old bomber jacket that was about two sizes too small over a grubby 'T' shirt that was once white. He had no underwear on, just a pair of old pyjama bottoms. How did he get like this? Where was his wallet, his car keys, his car for Christ sake! The realisation that he was in a parallel universe and somehow not in Cornwall strained his powers of comprehension to bursting point. No matter how many times he sent his mind into 'reboot' it still kept coming up with the notion that he had gone to sleep in Cornwall and woken up in some far off Bedouin fairyland.

The burly Arab who had so inconsiderately woken him from his slumbers was still yelling at him to change his clothes. He had a short stick like a riding crop and brought it down on his thigh. It stung like hell but had the desired effect as it prompted him to disrobe in a trice and put on the grey, cotton baggy trousers and the shirt-like top that came down to his knees. It was clean and made Jack feel more presentable, if a trifle odd.

Now that he was dressed he was taken by the arm and led down a track between ramshackle wooden buildings to where he could see nothing but terraced hillsides stretching of into the distance. They arrived at the first field and stepped over an irrigation ditch. The man pointed at the long lines of plants, red and yellow capsicums as far as the eye could see. The series of gestures and jabbering in Arabic were obviously meant to convey Jack's work instructions. He was to pick the peppers and place them in the trays then stack the trays at the end of the line of plants. Then another worker would use a sack barrow and wheel them down to a packing station in amongst the wooden sheds. Another swipe on the thigh meant that he had better start picking.

By midday Jack was struggling for the physical strength to keep going. The weals on his legs from the constant beatings were taking a toll on his stamina as well as his will to live. The temperature was rapidly rising and adding to the discomfort and the fatigue.

As the sun reached its zenith it was the signal for picking and packing to stop and Jack's fellow workers gathered at the far end of the field close to the packing shed to pray. They were all of the Muslim faith with the exception of Jack of course who had little choice but to stand by and watch. Prayers began with a queue at the standpipe outside the main building where each man washed his hands and feet under the running water. Most produced a scrap of prayer mat to kneel on during their devotions. They were rolled up and stacked together in one corner of the shed.

After prayers it was time for lunch. It was served by two of the group from large blackened saucepans. One contained couscous and the other what looked and smelled like boiled fish with onions and spices. A worker received a ladle from each on a cheap tin plate. It was eaten with the fingers. Jack stood at the end of the line, as hungry as hell and keen to get his share.

His co-workers were exclusively black men who formed small groups and chatted amongst themselves in languages he couldn't fathom. He guessed they were migrants from other parts of Africa. Some may have been trafficked into the farm as slaves by criminal gangs and others at the end of their tether after a debilitating trek across the Sahara and now desperate for any way of staying alive. The occasional glance in his direction conveyed a mixture of surprise and distrust. The realisation that he was isolated suddenly brought on a fit of depression. Where was he, why was he here, what had happened to him? He caught sight of the cardboard cartons being used to pack the peppers. Written on the side were the words "Produit en Maroc" alongside which was the logo of a well-known European supermarket. So, it appeared that he was in Morocco. How the hell did he get there?

The lunch break was over so the never-ending task of picking peppers began once more. The overseer yelled and banged his stick on an empty packing case. The eagerness with which his colleagues went back to work spoke volumes about their fear of incurring his wrath.

His first working day eventually came to an end. He followed the other pickers as they gathered for evening prayers. Afterwards they returned for their evening meal. More food arrived in the same large blackened saucepans, couscous was obviously a staple but this time the other saucepan contained pieces of meat of indeterminate variety, probably goat as they were the only farm animals he could see in the nearby fields. The meal over, Jack was anxious to find the lavatory but didn't know who to ask or how to ask. He had seen men visiting an area behind an adjacent poly-tunnel so assuming that was where the toilet facilities were he set off in search of relief.

It was the smell that guided him to a concrete slab on the side of the hill with a row of round holes in it. When he stood above one of the holes he found that the slab was constructed over a human slurry collecting point. The product of the communal latrines appeared to flow down the hill to a pit where animal and human waste was 'matured'. He had never had to use a 'squatter' before, it proved to be an interesting experience and one that would ensure that he would in future eat his meals with one hand.

During the walk back to the shed he had an opportunity to take in his surroundings. The farm was situated on the side of a hill on the outskirts of a village. It was probably built around the spring that gushed clear fresh water into a small reservoir before tumbling down the side of a rocky ravine and into a river that met with the Mediterranean several kilometres later. The night was young but the stars were already plastering the heavens from horizon to horizon. Identifying the North Star was a simple process when the Plough constellation is so obviously recognizable. Facing north he studied the distant lights and realised that he was staring across the Straits of Gibraltar at the sparkling, flickering lights on the Spanish coast. He was overcome by a feeling of utter despair. He was standing far away in a foreign land with absolutely no way of telling the world that he was alive. What was Pam thinking? Did she realise that he had been kidnapped? It was all he could do not to burst into tears in frustration at his hopelessness. With gritted teeth he turned and returned to his work colleagues. He would get back home, he promised himself, one day.

The whole of that working day he had dreamt up a dozen different plans to get away from that hellhole. Every plan he came up with stumbled at the first hurdle, no money, no clothes, no phone, no passport. How the hell could he even take a step outside the hillside farm when he knew nothing about the terrain, the language or the people? What chance would a white face have in such a strange place? Like the would-be migrants alongside him he was a virtual prisoner.

08.00 – Sunday 26th November, 2006
Mzala, Morocco

Four days of mindless fruit picking was driving him mad. The five a.m. starts for morning prayers, the same food every day, the isolation and loneliness were getting him down. He was a prisoner yet he was not locked away in a prison, he was fed and watered each day but had no future. He needed a bit of luck and on that day, the fifth day, his luck changed.

At around ten o'clock a big Mercedes swung into the main yard where trucks were loaded by forklift. The routine rattle of the clapped out diesel forklift truck suddenly stopped and a man screamed. There was a rush of people to the side of a truck. The forklift driver hadn't seen the Mercedes until the last second and when he swerved to avoid it he pinned the overseer up against the side of a truck. Jack arrived in time to see the forklift back off. The overseer, the man who had made his life a misery all week flopped to the ground seemingly lifeless.

There was no hesitation, no pause for thought, no measured response. Just an instinctive need to save a life in danger of being snuffed out right before his eyes. Stepping from the crowd Jack knelt beside the unconscious figure whose face was already turning blue. Rolling him on his back and without the protection latex gloves would provide Jack fished inside the man's mouth to clear his airway. He had swallowed his tongue but the speed with which Jack had intervened meant that as soon as it was removed from the trachea the victim spluttered into life and Jack was rewarded by a nasty bite on his finger.

The murmuring crowd that had gathered to watch suddenly began to shout and applaud. Jack was patted on the back by a dozen or so fellow pickers who had no real reason to be enthusiastic about the slave driver's survival but nonetheless were impressed by this unprecedented act of charity.

One observer, however, knew that he had witnessed an act of skill and knowledge. The large, well-dressed man who stepped from the rear of the Mercedes spoke to Jack in French and asked if his wound needed attention. Jack's halting French drew the realisation that he was not a natural Francophone and the man in a lightweight powder blue suit, switched to English. His question was answered with an element of surprise.

"Thank you sir, I just need some disinfectant and maybe a sticking plaster."

"Then we will take care of it, get in." He opened the door of his car and ushered Jack inside. The burbling crowd were busy helping the overseer to his feet and helping him to his office nearby. The occupant of the Mercedes spoke briefly to his chauffeur and the car set off down the hill towards the town.

"My name is Doctor Assad Helu. You probably don't realise it but you are working for me." Jack didn't know how to reply. What do you say to a slave master? Sensing the tension Doctor Helu felt the need to expand on this simple statement.

"We have many people from all over Africa working here."

"Not so many from England," Jack replied apprehensively.

"What do they call you?" He was surprised that his employer didn't appear to know who he was. He thought about giving his real name but figured it would be wise to remain anonymous for the time being.

"Don't you know who I am?"

"No, we don't stand on ceremony on my farm and I have learnt not to ask too many questions. We have had a few English, they come for the unique Moroccan experience and get involved in the drug scene like you I guess." Jack was about to protest but bit his tongue. He wasn't sure that an explanation of his professional career and his lack of drug-taking experience would sit so well with this enigmatic Arab dressed as a western businessman. He sensed that events were flowing in a positive direction for the first time since he woke up in that god-forsaken place. He kept his own council, deciding that this was an occasion to do more listening than talking. His instincts were to prove in good shape.

They drove in silence, at first through open countryside then through coastal towns until they came to the town of Fnideq. Jack tried to observe this enigmatic medico without causing offence.

He had a very smooth complexion and his dark closely trimmed beard was in contrast to his silvery locks that were dosed with an aromatic oil that didn't entirely compliment his aftershave. He was slightly overweight but his tailor had done a very good job of disguising the belly that fought with his snakeskin belt for control of his waistline. Jack guessed he was in his sixties but looked younger. His chubby fingers would tend to rule him out as a surgeon and the chunky gold rings looked like they were pretty immoveable. Not good for anyone needing to remove them on a daily basis for 'scrubbing-up'.

Entering a walled compound through electronically controlled gates at the rear of an impressive four-story residence clad in marble, they stopped under a large palm tree. Doctor Helu led Jack from the compound through the Arabesque furnishings that adorned the ground floor. The marble terrazzo and ornate marble walls gave the residence a coolness that was a welcome change from the heat outside. As they wafted through the corridors Jack caught a fleeting glimpse of staff members. They ducked away from their master, seeking refuge in doorways as he strode purposefully past the main entrance lobby and into an office complex. Through the outer office they entered his surgery with all the accoutrements of the medical practitioner.

With hat and jacket removed the doctor donned a white coat and went to a large white cabinet. He unlocked the door removed a bottle of disinfectant and a plaster and dressed Jack's wound. All this happened in a dignified silence but in the end Doctor Helu felt the need to use a name.

"Have you had a tetanus booster, recently Mister … er … Smith?"
Jack smiled, "Mawgan, Jack Mawgan."
"Hepatitis?"
"Yes."

"Tell me Mr Mawgan, do you know what this is?" He took an instrument from the cupboard.

"It's a laryngoscope."

"And this?"

"It's an intubation tube, a child's size at a guess."

"You are correct." Doctor Helu moved back to his desk and sat down in his swivel chair. "I don't believe you are a doctor Mr Mawgan but you have some medical skills. Tell me about your training."

"I am ... was ... a qualified paramedic."

"Trained in the UK?"

"Yes."

"What hospital?"

"Does it matter?"

"I spent some time as an anaesthetics registrar at The Royal London."

"A fine hospital I believe."

"Yes, one of the best."

Jack looked longingly at the telephone on the desk. If he could just make one quick call to Pam she would know he was alive and send someone to set him free. Doctor Helu saw him looking at the phone and understood what must be going through his mind.

"No, Mr Mawgan, no telephone calls for you, not just yet. I have a job for you and when you have completed this task then maybe you will have earned your freedom."

"A job? What kind of job?"

"Something to your liking I would guess. Certainly an improvement on your current circumstances." He looked Jack up and down and scowled at the state of his clothes.

"We need to do something about your dress." He pressed a button on his desk and a distant buzzer sounded. The door opened and a nurse appeared.

"Miriam kindly ask Haitham to come here as soon as he can spare a moment."

"Yes, Doctor."

"We need to get you looking the part Mr Mawgan, you are going to sea and you need to acquire some suitable apparel."

"Going to sea? What on earth are you talking about?" At that moment the chauffeur arrived.

"Haitham I want you to go down to my tailors with Mr Mawgan and have him fitted out with some appropriate clothing. I will call them and tell them what is required." He turned to Jack, "Mr Mawgan, you have been placed in my charge. If you try to do anything other than those things you have been explicitly told to do then your life will become a misery. If you think that picking fruit and vegetables is miserable then think again. I also own a sulphur mine and if you end up there it will probably be your last job anywhere. Don't even think about running away, you have no papers and no money and I own every policeman for fifty kilometres. You won't last long. Do as you are told, serve me well on this assignment then you will get your life back."

"What assignment?"

"One that will be to your liking I have no doubt, given your present situation. We will talk when you return, now go with Haitham. I will make some calls while you are in town and if you are acceptable to my client then you will have the chance to return to the world of medicine."

They left together and set off in the Mercedes for the souk in the town centre.

CHAPTER 11

10.00 – Sunday 26th November, 2006
Lower Spargo Cottage, Perranarworthal

WITH NATHAN AND JOSH now home and able to offer their mother some support the Mawgan household had established a kind of routine that enabled them to get through the day.

Pam wanted to persuade every newspaper in the country to run headlines that called for a global search for her husband but Dan had cautioned against it. She had taken his advice but in return demanded he call her every morning with a progress report.

That morning there was some positive news at last. Dan was coming to visit. He planned to explain personally then he could be sure that the whole family got the story first hand. He was worried that Pam was beginning to lose it and the boys were as worried about her as they were about their missing father.

Dan arrived in time for a simple salad lunch. Pam was looking a shadow of her former self. She had lost weight and her eyes seemed to recede into their sockets as the weight loss told on her features. Nevertheless the atmosphere at Lower Spargo had brightened at the prospect of news and they sat around the dining table waiting for Dan to deliver.

"We have spent days going through a wide assortment of CCTV footage and think we have a breakthrough. We couldn't work out why we had no hits for Jack's car registration on our ANPR system."

"What's that?" asked Pam.

"Automatic Number Plate Recognition system," said Josh, keen to be in on the conversation. "It can recognise and track cars as they move around the country and the police store it all on a computer."

"That's about the size of it Josh. I can tell you've been watching a lot of cops and robbers on the TV," said Dan. Josh blushed, suddenly realising he was the focus of attention.

"We had a bit of luck though, a local Community Service Officer was at a scrap yard twenty miles from where Jack was last seen and found the Jag. He was buying a new wheel for his own 'S'-Type Jag and couldn't believe they were dismantling what looked to him like a perfectly good car. He made a note of the VIN and when he was next on duty he gave the details to the desk sergeant. There's a note on the computer to call one of my numbers if any news relating to the Jag turns up.

"I got a call last night and had the local bobbies check it out. The yard owner was spooked when he saw the CSO making notes and tried to crush it. Fortunately we were able to get there in time and in the boot we found the medical kit that Jack carries around with him. It had his name on it. We are busy interrogating the yard owner now but it looks like it was a one-off sale by a guy who paid him a thousand pounds to get rid of it. He was supposed to crush it right away but his greed got the better of him and he decided to strip it for parts before sending it to the crusher. The rest you know."

"So what now?" enquired Pam.

"We have a description of the man the yard owner did the deal with and his own CCTV has given us a glimpse of the hatchback the kidnappers left in. The video experts are trying to get a registration from the tape by enhancing what was quite a low quality image. They promised to get back by the end of the day. If we are in luck then we once again go through the ANPR data and see if we can get a hit and a trace."

"Will you promise to ring me as soon as you know anything?"

"Don't worry you'll be the first person I call."

15.00 – Monday 27th November, 2006
Tangier Harbour

The drive to Tangier took just over one hour. The freshly washed and shaved Jack Mawgan now stood on the dockside staring with a certain amount of disbelief at the beautiful mega-yacht moored alongside the harbour wall. She was called 'La Reine Bleu', 'The Blue Queen', and she was registered in the Bahamas and must have cost a fortune. She was a hundred and fifteen metres long and seventeen metres wide and displaced nearly three thousand tonnes. She was built for range rather than speed and could take the owner to almost any hiding place between Cape Horn and Tasmania without the need for a refuel. The crew of thirty could support the same number of guests and deliver a level of service that was second to none. Supplies on board could keep crew and passengers fed and watered for three months and this could be stretched to six months if circumstances required. Doctor Helu finished his brief description of Jack's future workplace wearing a broad smile. He knew that Jack was impressed.

Jack was dressed in an outfit that ensured his role on board would be immediately understood. The doctor's white trousers and white 'chemise' were the extent of his new clothes although his patron had been kind enough to ensure he had two more sets and some underwear, socks and a pair of white Crocs. He was assured that his predecessor had left enough 'civilian' clothes should he ever need them. Jack was reminded that his predecessor had vacated his position with singular lack of formality.

Jack had stayed the previous night at the doctor's mansion and there had the best night's sleep since his ordeal began. In the morning he shared a pleasant breakfast with his employer who filled in some of the missing details about his immediate future. He had learnt for the first time that he would be serving on a luxury yacht and hold the position of medical officer. The owner of the vessel in question was a Russian speaking Armenian 'oligarch' based in Beirut.

His predecessor was 'let go' for committing what the owner considered to be a heinous crime. Apparently he didn't take kindly to men who didn't do as they were told and 'letting one go' entailed slitting their throats and throwing them overboard. A nod was as good as a wink as they say.

Dr Helu had explained to Jack that one of his moneymaking enterprises was to supply the owners of expensive gin palaces with suitably qualified medics. Jack was about to assume the role of ship's medic but had little idea what lay ahead. All he did know was that one way or another he would find a way to let Pam know that he was still alive.

He followed Dr Helu up the narrow gangway carrying a small tote containing his few possessions. Arriving on the ships helideck he was introduced to the ship's Captain as Doctor Smith. Dr Helu advised him to use a false name during the voyage to guard against any unforeseen consequences. The Captain was an almost comedic character sporting a black eye-patch and burn-scars up his left arm. His crisp white uniform and gold bars gave this larger than life character a clinical appearance. Before he was led inside he had a chance to cast an eye over the shiny helicopter parked on the stern. He recognised it as the same as the type he had been told to buy for the NPAS back home. The shock of remembering his previous life stunned him. How could so much change in so short a time?

The medical centre was located amidships, two decks below the bridge and at the same level as the helideck. The facilities included a small cabin and a bunk that sat on top of the drawers used for clothing and personal effects. Space was at a premium and the small area set aside as his treatment room had a desk, a surgical operating table and a glass-fronted cabinet apparently stocked with medications. Lockers and drawers covered the walls. Looking around he could see that it may have been tight on space but it was extremely well equipped and no expense had been spared.

With introductions complete the captain told him that he should report to the bridge before dinner for a safety briefing by the Duty Officer. He was to dine with the crew in their mess located in the area under the fo'c's'le at the forward end of the ship. Dinner for the crew started at 18.00 and finished at 19.00, watch-keepers could order a late meal if required.

Suddenly left to his own devices Jack took stock. First things first, he needed to know what he had by way of equipment and medication. He wished his predecessor had hung around long enough to give him a handover. The medical centre had been fitted out like a top class A & E with no expense spared. Despite the confined space Jack found that there was enough in the way of facilities to handle complex surgical procedures but handling more than a couple of patients would be difficult. There simply wasn't the room to work on more than two people.

When he had finished he sat down at the desk and pondered his next move. There was a shudder through the hull of the ship as the huge diesel engines were fired up. The ship was preparing for sea. He checked his watch. He had better go up to the bridge to receive his safety briefing before it became too busy for the Officer of the Watch to deal with him.

He found his way to the beautifully veneered staircase with its chromed handrails and thick woollen carpet. The bridge was already busy when Jack introduced himself to the senior officer present. He turned out to be the Third Officer and was Portuguese but spoke enough English to take Jack through the protocols for abandoning the ship or dealing with a fire on board. His duty station in the event of an emergency would be his surgery and he was to remain there unless the signal for abandoning ship was sounded. Jack signed the log entry confirming his briefing and returned to his office.

The ship vibrated heavily and the engine noise increased as it reversed away from the dock. After a while Jack sensed that everything up top was calm and ventured back to the bridge to see what was going on. He gingerly stepped from the rich deep pile carpet on to the beautiful teak deck and caught the eye of the Captain who was overseeing their departure from Tangier. Jack had yet to learn the names of the other ship's officers but he certainly remembered the name of the captain from their earlier introduction, Diego Dellamorte. In his native Spanish it was just a name but in Italian it could be translated as 'James of the Death'. He didn't consider it to be a wonderful omen.

Seeking permission to venture on to the bridge wing the third officer consulted the captain who nodded and returned to peering ahead with his huge binoculars. The ship was moving quickly through the azure sea and the foaming wake stretched behind them into the distance. Ahead lay the Straits of Gibraltar and the Officer of the Watch was talking to the Moroccan Coastguard about positioning the vessel in the shipping lanes. It was important to be in the right place in this part of the ocean as hundreds of ships, large and small, converged on this natural choke point in the sea-lanes, 'The Pillars of Hercules', The Rock of Gibraltar to the north and Monte Hacho in Ceuta, to the south.

Jack stood, spellbound, the warm evening breeze gently caressing his body and calming his inner, tormented soul. The sun began to set and he realised that he was heading east, away from home. The British Overseas Territory of Gibraltar was getting closer by the hour and would pass tantalisingly close to their left. A helicopter flew overhead shuttling rich businessmen and tourists from the airport at Malaga to the Spanish enclave of Ceuta. Their day would soon be over and the passengers would be settling in their homes or checking into their hotels whilst Jack would be spending his first night in a place that he could never imagine in all his wildest nightmares.

As the sun began to set the orange and powder blue sky turned darker by the minute. The wake, stirring up the microorganisms in the sea, began to give off a phosphorescent glow. It was surreal. He thought of Pam and the kids and his heart felt heavy with the worry. He knew they would be fretting and didn't want them to give up on him. He desperately needed to tell them he was OK and that one day, soon he hoped, he would be home.

18.00 – Monday 27th November, 2006
The Offices of Dan Barclay – Private Investigator, Exeter

Dan waited patiently for a call from his contact in the Metropolitan Police Special Branch. When it came it brought some good news but not as good as he had hoped. The hatchback involved in Jack's kidnapping had been identified thanks to a partial registration taken from a blow up of the CCTV images from the scrap yard. It had been traced to an area of Kent just east of the town of Ashford. Images from the four ANPR cameras on the M3, M25 and M20 were on their way to Dan's computer via the E-mail.

When they arrived Dan printed them out and sat back to study them carefully. He needed to see if anyone inside the car could be identified. The little hatchback turned out to be one believed stolen from a house in Bristol. The real owner had left her car behind when she set off on holiday. Somehow the villains had known that she would be away for at least two weeks. Dan was already beginning to suspect that they were not ordinary car-thieves.

The photos were all taken from the front of the vehicle as it passed under the gantry supporting the ANPR cameras and showed that there were two front seat occupants. They were almost certainly male but their faces were indistinct and partially covered by the top of the windscreen. Dan checked the time code at the bottom of the photos, 23.13 on the 19th November, at Junction 10 on the M20, about six hours after the time Jack was reported to have been kidnapped.

That reminded him about the van, he checked the photos again. Bingo! There in each of them, sometimes in the distance, was a dark coloured van, the same van in each picture. He figured that for this to be coincidence was too much to believe. There was one picture that showed the van clearly, three occupants, maybe two males and one female and a readable number plate. The last in the sequence clearly showed both vehicles signalling their intention to leave the motorway. He called London, gave his contact the registration and waited for a call back.

The van turned out to be one stolen from a van dealer in Swindon who apparently had so many vans in his yard he didn't even know it had gone missing until the police called him to tell him it had been found burnt out on a track near the Medway marshes on the 20th of November.

Turning to the satellite images available on Google Earth he found the location of the burnt out wreck on the Medway Marshes and ran his eye back to Junction 10. There was one huge complex that stood out in the satellite image and thanks to the Streetview facility he was able to identify it as a supermarket warehouse and distribution centre.

Further research showed it was primarily used to store fruit and vegetables imported by truck from the EU or brought in through the docks in that part of Kent. That news sent Dan's mind racing. If the intention was to do away with Jack he was sure they would have found his body in the burnt out van or somewhere nearby. His gut instinct was to believe the intention was to either teach Jack a lesson or to ship him as far away as possible, maybe both.

Hope for a happy ending to this saga rested with him being right about Jack's fate and he dare not dwell on the alternatives. He set his mind to working out the possible ways in which Jack could have been smuggled out of the country. The warehouse complex had to be a clue; either he went by boat or by truck.

He rang his contact in London and explained his analysis and the team there set to work on following up the lead.

Dan decided to tell Pam the news, as he had promised. For the first time in a while there was, at least for her, a chink of hope and that night she slept well for the first time since Jack disappeared.

CHAPTER 12

07.00 – Tuesday 28ᵗʰ November, 2006
At Sea – The Western Mediterranean

THE HUM OF THE mighty diesel engines was now more subdued. The vessel had settled into a long legged cruise, eastward, across the Mediterranean. The gentle motion told a tale of friendly seas with only a small pitching motion to inform those aboard that they were at sea. The stabilisers were working well and the vibrations from the steady beat of the propellers hardly noticeable. Jack reasoned that it was a ship ideal for those who actually didn't enjoy a life at sea and his own apprehension about seasickness faded as his confidence grew.

Dinner the previous evening had been a fairly solitary affair for it seemed the majority of the crew were very busy at their stations and the first hours after leaving port required them to take care of a lot of important tasks. Some of the shift workers were in their beds trying to catch up with their sleep. Only three diners joined him that evening. The menu consisted of a delicious gazpacho followed by paella cooked as only a Spanish chef can. His fellow diners were the two girls that looked after the spa facilities, who chatted and giggled endlessly, and the helicopter pilot.

The girls were both in their twenties and very attractive and were friendly enough although not very communicative. Jack was to find out later that his predecessor had become 'involved' with one of them and they were very much aware of his fate. Misinterpreting their reluctance to engage in conversation he thought their English was limited. In fact their English was very good but they were nervous about encouraging the smallest amount of over familiarity. He managed to glean their names, Sonya and Maria and little more. He was desperate to borrow a mobile phone but so far from land he doubted he would get a signal. When he asked the girls if they had cell phones they seemed at first not to understand but then they just looked at each other and giggled.

The helicopter pilot was a little more communicative but the atmosphere between them was one of nervous apprehension and he soon found out why. The helicopter would leave the following morning to pick up members of the owner's family. He guessed that when they were aboard he would be somewhat fearful of their presence and tensions aboard were set to rise. To Jack's surprise the pilot turned out to be Croatian and his name was Marko.

At first Marko had been quite chatty but soon tired of answering all Jack's questions and had hurried away to his cabin before Jack could raise the possibility of him sending a text message for him.

After an early night Jack awoke refreshed and felt strangely positive about the days ahead. His new surroundings had infused him with a sense of purpose. He checked his watch and decided it was time for breakfast. This time the dining area was a little busier with some of the Spanish deck crew tucking into chunks of freshly baked bread, slices of cheese, tomatoes and cold meats dosed with peppery green olive oil and washed down with strong black coffee. It wasn't what he preferred at that time of day but being grateful that it was good quality food he took his fill from the self-service counter and watched as the crew busied themselves and chatted in rapid fire bursts of Spanish. There wasn't much laughter in their conversation.

When Jack returned to his bunk he began to go through the drawers containing his predecessor's belongings.

He found a drawer full of shirts and tried one on. It was a reasonable fit although the neck size was too small to do the top button up and the sleeves were just a little too short. Another one was an even better fit and the Polo shirts in the next drawer were all useable but emphasised the fact that he had lost a bit of weight since his enforced departure from home shores.

The underwear drawer contained some crisply laundered underpants and vests and an unopened three-pack of Dolce and Gabbana boxer shorts that he put to one side with the Polo shirts. The sock drawer contained more than he expected for as he gathered up the many assorted pairs of socks he came across one with a hard centre and carefully removed a small Beretta semi-automatic pistol from its home inside a pair of white Reebok sports stockings. He checked the magazine and quickly hid it out of sight inside another pair of socks. He gave an audible sigh of astonishment. Should he need it he had a weapon but even with a full magazine he had at best just nine bullets. Fine, maybe, for an assassination but not so handy in an all-out fire-fight.

The next drawer was full of expensive sweaters from Paul and Shark and these fitted Jack perfectly and he made a note to find a store in Cornwall that stocked that brand when he returned home. He chuckled at his own optimism. Under the pile of half dozen sweaters he got another surprise for there was a passport and inside it a driving license. Both had been issued in Italy and the owner was apparently a dark haired gentleman sporting a goatee beard. He contemplated the likeness but without the facial hair it would be hard to convince anyone but the most casual observer that the passport and license were his. He resolved to rectify the situation and grow his own goatee. He smiled at his good fortune. Suddenly he went from having nothing to having the means to get home.

Flicking through the passport he found several stamps from Israel. He hoped that he never had to cross the borders of an Arab state for if he tried to travel using that document he would find himself in trouble. Those tell-tale stamps were reminders that those that visit the Jewish State are treated like enemies of the Arab world.

He looked at the name – Giancarlo Andretti – and said it out loud a couple of times. His blood ran cold as he suddenly realised he couldn't speak a work of Italian. He checked his place of birth – Sydney, Australia. A lucky break he could get away with the pretence that he was born and raised in Sydney of Italian stock. It had been issued in Naples in 2001 and was valid until 2011. There was no Australian passport. Maybe Giancarlo had taken it with him when he visited the fishes. He shuddered at the thought and carefully replaced the passport under the sweaters.

In the wardrobe he found a couple of smart two-piece suits and a white dinner jacket in a cellophane cover. He would try them on one day. The various trousers hanging from wooden hangars looked promising but with the exception of one pair of chinos they were all tailored to be a tight fit and Jack found the crutch on these to be unbearably tight. If he bent down he feared a traumatic amputation of the wedding tackle or a split up the rear of the trousers.

He was surprised to find a nice looking Barbour jacket and it fitted him well enough. He judged that a good proportion of his predecessor's clothes would set him up well for most eventualities. He then peered at his white Crocs and realised that he had forgotten one important contribution to his master plan to put together an outfit fit for an escapee in cosmopolitan Europe.

Rooting through the collection of Italian styled footwear at the bottom of the wardrobe Jack had great difficulty finding anything that would fit his size eleven feet. Giancarlo must have had tiny feet. The best he could come up with was a pair of deck shoes that he could tolerate if he didn't wear any socks but walking any distance would cause some difficulty.

Searching through the desk his heart jumped when he found a small cigar box and inside was a cheap cell phone. He tried to switch it on but nothing happened. The battery was flat. Where was the charger? He looked everywhere but there was no charger. He checked the sim-card but the slot was empty. His heart sank, so near and yet so far.

He was startled by a knock on the door and quickly replaced the cigar box at the back of the drawer and slid it closed.

"Come in," said Jack adopting the appropriate position at his desk. The door opened and the Third Officer poked his head round the door.

"Hey, Doc, the skipper wants to see you on the bridge soon as you can."

"I'll be right up."

"OK." Jack looked around his cabin and made sure there was nothing to give away the fact that he had found a veritable treasure trove of tools to aid any bid for freedom.

Captain Dellamorte greeted Jack with a gruff hello and took him out to the bridge wing. He wanted a private conversation and used the opportunity to smoke his way through an evil looking cheroot. The aroma was tantalisingly pleasing but somehow he thought that the same experience in a confined space would not have been so pleasant.

"Mister Smith," his Spanish accent made Jack's adopted name sound slightly comedic, "soon we will have a visitor and we have some rules when we have important visitors, especially when they are from the owner's family. All crew personnel are to ensure their behaviour is always polite and you will not wander around or frequent the weather decks unless you are properly dressed."

"OK sir, all understood." The Captain turned to face the bow, blew smoke into the breeze and inspected the end of his cheroot. Jack thought the interview was over and stepped towards the bridge doorway.

"Mister Smith, something you need to be aware of." Jack stopped and retraced his steps but the Captain remained staring out ahead, watching the bows carve their way through the sparkling blue sea. "The man arriving today is the owner's son. His name is Boris, Boris Mikoyan. He's an animal, he always brings trouble. I want you to be careful. If you want to live to see out this voyage then you need to be very careful. This man doesn't believe in taking prisoners." He turned to face Jack, squeezed the tip of his cheroot between his seemingly fireproof finger and thumb and tossed it over the side. "Don't get in his way."

"Thanks for the tip," said Jack and judging the interview to be over he stepped away and this time there was no recall.

09.00 – Tuesday 28th November, 2006
Prideco Supermarket's Warehouse, Kent

Dan flashed a warrant card at the warehouse manager and told him they were investigating the illegal importation of a variety of smuggled goods. Of course the ID was a false one but good enough for the job in hand. He asked for the records of all deliveries that arrived at the warehouse between midday on the 19th November and midday on the 20th November. The timings were based on Dan's hunch that the villains would have disposed of Jack before getting rid of the van so probably did the deed in the early hours of the 20th.

The manager was a bit of a 'jobsworth' and insisted on contacting his boss before digging through his files and giving Dan the information he wanted.

There were twenty-three trucks unloaded that night during the period in question. They ranged from potatoes from Belgium and France to Oranges from Spain and tomatoes from Holland. He made notes of the suppliers and the trucking companies and left after three hours of tedious plying through mountains of shipping forms and customs documents.

Dan reasoned that the villains would have bound and gagged their victim and packaged him for the trip, probably with the aid of a sedative of some kind. They wouldn't want him waking up before he was well away from the country. Given the opportunity to choose which truck to put Jack in it was likely that it would be one that didn't have a backload, as anyone loading anything into the trailer would have seen Jack's body and maybe made a fuss.

By the time he arrived at Dover Dan had formed a basic plan in his head. He stayed the night at the Ramada Hotel to work out the details and study the options.

09.00 – Wednesday 29th November, 2006
Ramada Hotel, Kent

The following morning Dan made some calls and tracked down each of the trucking companies and spoke to them about their activities in the early morning of the 20th. Eleven of the companies had backloads organised. Eight others had no backloads but were heading for UK destinations after the drop off at Prideco's warehouse. There would be no point trekking all the way across England if the objective was to simply dump Jack in Kent. He reasoned that Kent was chosen because the aim was to ship Jack off to the continent and because he knew that he was dealing with some clever people he figured that Jack Mawgan alive was worth more to someone out there than a Jack Mawgan dead. In the world of international crime Jack may have even have had a value, he may have been sold to an unknown bidder. He didn't realise how close to the truth he was.

Of the four remaining trucks, two were refrigerated and Dan had his doubts that they would use that kind of trailer for their 'export' plan unless they really did plan for Jack to die en route. He shuddered at the thought of dying in that way. He hoped his buddy enjoyed a bit more luck and was hauled away in a nice warm potato truck and was sunning himself on a beach in the south of France.

Turning to his notes he considered the two remaining options. One truck had delivered a load of Capsicum Peppers from Holland and the other a mixed load of apples and pears from Poland. He called Pam and told her about the progress he had made during the day. He planned to cross the

Channel and check out the Scandes Trucking Company at Alkmaar in the north of The Netherlands.

Pam was heartened by the fact that some progress was being made but she was having problems with Nathan, her eldest son. The twenty-four year old was all set to get in his mum's car and join Dan in the hunt for his father. Restraining him was proving to be tough and poor Pam was running out of arguments as to why he shouldn't go.

10.00 – Wednesday 29th November, 2006
La Reine Bleu, off the coast of Menorca

The previous afternoon had seen the arrival of a small party of guests led by the now infamous Boris. He brought a male friend and two girls. The helicopter came in from the north having picked up the new arrivals from a helipad in the grounds of the owners' estate. The island of Menorca was just visible on the distant horizon.

The trouble didn't start until after the crew had finished their evening meal. It began with simple hi-jinx and loud music but then the sound of breaking glass and loud giggling spilled over into the corridors close to the crew's quarters.

In the early hours the inevitable happened and Jack was woken by loud banging on his door. When he opened it he was confronted by a young man in his twenties in a rather dishevelled state burbling in Russian and dressed only in a towelling dressing gown. Jack didn't understand a word and could tell that this youth had been dabbling in more than just alcohol. Jack explained that he didn't understand.

"Oh no," the youth burbled in heavily accented English, "don't tell me we've got a fucking English doctor?"

"I'm afraid so," replied Jack, trying to sound calm and in charge of the situation.

"Well I hope you're fucking good doc because I've got a big problem for you. You'd better come with me."

"Well, sir I may need some equipment so please give me some information about the problem you want me to solve."

"It's one of the girls, she been a bit too friendly with a coke bottle and

99

now Lars can't get the bloody thing out. Silly fucker I told him not to do it but he got his girlfriend rockin' and rolling with this dam bottle man and when she came she yelled like a bear and the fucking thing got stuck. Now she's screaming that she wants to pee and can't stop crying."

Jack put his whites back on, slipped his feet into the Crocs and picked up his doctor's bag. He went over to the medical cabinets to fetch a few bits and pieces. He closed the bag and turned to follow the young man.

"This way Doc." They went down one deck and then forward to the guest quarters. The opulent surroundings were a blur as Jack focussed on the prospect of a difficult task ahead. He entered a large cabin with a super-king-size bed. Another youth with blonde hair sat nursing a glass of amber looking fluid. A woman lay on the bed completely naked whimpering gently. Another woman was trying to help by mopping the brow of the patient with a wet towel. She swore at the man that had brought Jack and he replied in kind. Jack understood not a word but was quick to pick up the tension and anger. The 'foursome' party had gone terribly wrong and now they were rapidly coming down from the highs they had enjoyed only hours before.

Jack could see the neck of the coke bottle protruding from her vagina. He put on a pair of latex gloves then took a stethoscope and two small containers from his bag then grasped her wrist to check her pulse. She had a pulse of nearly 100 and Jack guessed that she had taken some 'uppers'.

"She going to be alright Doc?" It was Lars, the Nordic looking guy, "I didn't mean to hurt her, last time we did it she enjoyed it so I was just showing Boris how to give your girl a good time."

"Somehow I don't think she's seeing the funny side," replied Jack, removing the stethoscope and setting a small blood pressure monitor on her wrist and an Oximeter peg on the end of a finger.

He replaced the stethoscope and listened to her heart. It was racing. He turned her face towards his and peered at her pupils.

"What's your name?" he asked in a gentle sympathetic tone. When she didn't answer Lars said, "It's Sandra, she's French, I don't know if she speaks any English."

"Sandra, est-ce que tu peux m'entendre?" she turned to look at him, tear-stained eyes begged for help. Mascara ran down her face. She wasn't in a happy place.

"Oui, je peux."

"Vous parlez un peu Anglais peutêtre?"

"Yes, just a little," why does English spoken by a French woman sound so sexy thought Jack. In her plight she was blissfully unaware of her nakedness but her bronzed body and fulsome breasts were difficult to ignore. She was a handsome lass thought Jack, about the same age as his older son, Nathan. He pushed the thought to one side and looked at the readings from the monitors, nothing unexpected there. Pulse high, blood pressure high, oxygen levels down just a little.

"Do you have any pain?" he asked.

"Comment?"

"Pain, douleur."

"Yes I need to pee but I can't, it hurts, can you help me?"

"I'm sure I can but I think we need some peace around here first." He turned to Boris.

"Do you mind moving to another cabin guys, perhaps your girlfriend should stay to help me but the fewer people around the easier this will be."

"Come on Lars, let's go to my cabin, I'll get you another slug of rye."

They left Jack to deal with a tricky extraction. He had never performed this process with a coke bottle before but had come across several other similar shaped objects that had been used by enthusiastic sexual athletes in search of bigger thrills and higher highs. Funnily enough a lot of them enter the 'tunnel of love' OK but then that's when the problems start. Jack had been asked to remove an assortment of 'toys' before, fruit, vegetables, dildos and vibrators and even once a nun with a Barbie Doll that had become an uncomfortable addition to her anatomy.

"My name is JoJo said the other young lady. I would like to help."

"All right JoJo, you can start by keeping your friend nice and calm. I'm going to give her a sedative then we will insert a tube into the vagina to release the vacuum then we should be able to remove the bottle with the minimum of fuss. Did they use a lubricant do you know?"

"Just this body lotion." She picked up a jar of expensive looking cream. The perfume in that sort of cream is just the kind of thing that could cause an allergic reaction and prevent her from urinating. Then again the use of amphetamines can have the same effect.

He prepared a syringe with some ketamine but decided that on second thoughts it might be ill advised as he was unsure about mixing what is essentially an anaesthetic with the 'uppers' she appeared to have taken earlier.

He took a rubber tube from his bag and improvised a rigid tube by inserting an aluminium rod that is normally part of a display stand. Not exactly the regular way to go about things but needs must. Having satisfied himself that the walls of the rubber tube would be rigid enough and that the rod was the right size he carefully washed both in surgical spirit then wiped them with Vaseline.

The tube slipped into the space between vulva and bottle and when Jack judged it had passed the base of the bottle he withdrew the rod. There was a sound of air being released and as Jack eased the bottle from her she pissed all over him. She let out a cry of relief and he muttered under his breath. Two problems solved in one go. She was lucky for that's not always the case and 'acute urinary retention' as the ailment is called, can persist even after the cause for the allergic reaction has been removed. He took the now infamous coke bottle to the bathroom and washed it, then took off his latex gloves and washed his hands, dried the bottle on a towel then and put it on a shelf beside the bed. Sandra had fallen asleep and Jack checked to be sure she was OK.

He held the bottle up to JoJo, "I want you to give that to Boris. A souvenir of a memorable night." JoJo looked suitably embarrassed and turned away. Jack packed up his kit and prepared to leave them to think about their recklessness.

He would check on her in the morning. She was to call him if there were any problems. His number was on the wall beside the phone. He advised them all to stop taking recreational drugs. He was about to leave when he had an idea.

"Do you have a cell phone?"

"Yes," she replied.

"Do you mind if I borrow it?"

"No, but I don't have it. We had to give our phones to the helicopter pilot when we left the house. Boris said there is a strict rule about phones on board. There is some kind of detector that sounds an alarm if it picks up the signal from a phone as soon as you switch it on. Boris says his father is very strict about his security and if you break the rules you can be thrown off the ship." Jack nodded his understanding but with what he knew about

102

his predecessor he had a more graphic idea about what being *'thrown off the ship'* actually meant.

Jack returned to his quarters and took a shower. He tossed his soiled clothes in the linen basket and contemplated going back to bed.

He lay on his bunk and studied the ceiling above his head. There was a row of colourful dots on the trim rail that ran along the joint between ceiling and wall. The raised bunk meant that the ceiling panels were just an arm's length away from where he lay.

He sat up and inspected them more carefully, then chuckled as he realised that he was looking at a long row of supermarket fruit stickers neatly placed in a long row. His predecessor was obviously a fruit eater and the ship clearly bought its supplies from a prominent supermarket chain. Counting them he found that if his predecessor consumed one fruit per day then had been on board for one hundred and five days.

Lying back on his pillow he wondered what had happened to bring the former ship's doctor's reign to an end. It was a bad move for depression descended. He craved the warmth of his wife's body and the comfort of his own bed.

11.00 – Thursday 30th November, 2006
En Route to Alkmaar

Dan checked the data on his navigation system and made a note that he had better stop for fuel before he arrived at his destination. The trucking industry is a vital organ of distribution and an important element in the economic survival of the continent but it was also the means by which a whole host of illicit goods were moved around.

Dan was reminded of the story of the Austrian farm worker who every day crossed into Switzerland to tend a neighbour's fields. In the morning he would wheel a wheelbarrow across the border and the Swiss border guards carefully inspected the contents. They were suspicious that this scruffy and dubious looking farmhand was up to no good but all they ever found were the tools of his trade, hoes, rakes, spades and forks.

It wasn't until one of the guards who worked the morning shift moved to the evening shift and caught sight of the farmhand returning to Austria empty handed. They then discovered that for the best part of a year he had been smuggling wheelbarrows and gardening tools across the border and selling them at a local market. Trucking was a vast and complicated version of that apocryphal story.

He pulled into a service station, filled up the fuel tank and grabbed a cup of coffee and a ham and cheese baguette. He also took the opportunity to make sure he would find the Scandes Trucking Company's management at home and called their office pretending to be a potential customer. He was reassured that the boss would be around until late and not to worry if he was delayed by the rush-hour traffic.

An hour later he wound his way around the new bypass and eventually managed to locate the depot on the northern outskirts in the part of town called 'Sint Pancras'. He pulled up outside the offices and studied the ranks of trucks and trailers. The site included warehouses and clearly the firm was involved in transhipment as well as offering haulage services. He saw trailers from Spain and Portugal, Greece and Hungary, even one from Morocco although the tractor unit on the Moroccan trailer carried Spanish plates. He wondered just how much of what was going on right before his eyes was actually legal. His policeman's nose was twitching wildly.

He went into the offices and asked to see the manager. The receptionist spoke good English and explained that Mr van Damm was busy right now but should be free in five or ten minutes. She gave him a coffee and sat him down in the waiting area.

After a short while a very large man-mountain appeared and walked towards Dan with his dinner plate sized hand outstretched. His handshake crushed the life out of his guest's own sizeable hand leaving Dan wondering what they fed these enormous Dutchmen.

"Gerard van Damm."

"Dan Barclay."

"What can we do for you Mister Barclay?"

"I need some information."

"What kind of information?"

"I need to find out what happened to your truck after it left the Prideco warehouse near Ashford in the UK."

"We have lots of trucks delivering to that warehouse, which one are you interested in."

"On the 20th November it delivered a consignment of Dutch Capsicums. I need to know where it went after it left the warehouse. I believe it had an unofficial cargo – my friend Jack Mawgan. He was kidnapped the night before and we believe he was shipped out of the UK. I need to find him."

"We will need to look into that for you but my scheduler is away today. Perhaps you come back in the morning." Dan tried not to let the disappointment sound in his voice.

"Thank you Mr van Damm, I'll do that. What time do you suggest?"

"Let's say ten o'clock."

"I'll be here at ten."

"Good bye," Dan took a chance and held his hand out for a farewell handshake. This time he was prepared and gave as good as he received.

"See you tomorrow." The boss man returned to his office and watched from his window as Dan drove out of his yard. When he was out of sight he picked up his phone and dialled a number from memory.

"Hercule, we have a problem. I want you to come to my place tonight. We have to discuss a few things. Do you still have the Gordini boys staying with you ... good, bring them with you."

Later that day
The van Damm Residence

"Come in Hercule, where are the boys?"

"They will be here in an hour, they're collecting a tractor unit from Haarlem."

"One of our rentals?"

"Yes, three months behind with the payments but they had no problems once they showed the driver who was the boss." Gerard could imagine the tact and diplomacy that wasn't on display in Haarlem that day. More likely it was a knuckleduster and a baseball bat. Once you show you are serious about repossessing the truck they usually back off.

"What kind of problem do we have?"

"There's an Englishman sniffing around our capsicum supplies."

"You mean our Dutch capsicums that just happen to come from an unregistered farm in Morocco?"

"Well yes, if you want to put it like that."

"I sometimes wonder if it's worth all the hassle doing these back-door deals."

"You're joking, we make over a thousand Euro a ton extra profit doing it that way. The supermarket don't know any different and the farm owner gets double what the Moroccan market pays."

"That's as maybe, but remember they use slave labour and their methods are rather suspect."

"Human shit is just as good as cow shit. I don't know what the fuss is about. It's giving life to their pathetic mountain soils."

"We won't mention the hepatitis risks and all sorts of other ailments that come with that kind of farming."

"Bullshit, the produce is perfectly safe. I even give it to my kids. Anyway we don't have time to go into all that. We have this British guy looking into the disappearance of his friend. He thinks he was taken away in our truck."

"Who was the driver."

"I'm pretty sure it was the Romanian."

"Petre?"

"I think so, I need to check."

"If it's Petre then you can bet that he would grab any opportunity to make an extra Euro."

"But he would have come back here to change trailers, we always take the Moroccan stuff in on one of ours."

"Where did he go after us?"

"Probably back to Morocco."

"Our problem is that this guy Barclay can stir up trouble with Prideco and if he does he will fuck us up good time."

"Maybe he will just go away when you tell him you can't help."

"Then we will all give a cheer and thank our lucky stars."

"If he doesn't go away?"

"Then you tell your boys to deal with him."

"You want him dead or just moved abroad?"

"Christ Hercule, we don't do murder, for fuck's sake, ship him out, long distance. I don't want the bloody police sniffing around. We've got a good thing going here and I don't want a greedy Romanian and a nosey Englishman spoiling our operation." Gerard poured his guest a cold beer and they sat around waiting for the Gordini brothers.

CHAPTER 13

10.00 – Friday 1st December, 2006
Scandes Trucking, Alkmaar

"Good morning Mister van Damm, I trust you slept well." Dan had been up for hours and was champing at the bit.

"Good morning, yes I slept like a baby thank you." Dan could see that there was only one car in the office car park so the office staff obviously didn't work weekends.

"Were you able to check the route of the truck you sent to Ashford on the 19th?"

"Yes, Mister Barclay, and we know that the driver came back to the depot here in Alkmaar. There were no stowaways I'm afraid."

"Can I speak with the driver please?"

"I'm afraid not, we don't give out the contact details of our staff." Dan sensed that he had run into a brick wall and reasoned that he had better find another way of getting the information he wanted.

"Thank you Mister van Damm, I'll have to try elsewhere."

"Have a good trip home Mister Barclay."

Dan turned to leave only to find his way barred by two burly gentlemen wielding baseball bats. The first took a low swing trying to break Dan's leg and thus rendering him easy prey. The problem with amateurs is they don't know about 'balance'. Taking a two-handed swing like that sets you up for a fall as soon as the victim hops over the bat, grabs an arm and dumps you on your backside leaving the bat behind. Dan, now armed with that bat brought it down, end first into the assailant's solar plexus. Whoever the guy was he was out for the count and would be doing nothing for the next twenty minutes except trying his best to acquire enough oxygen to stay alive.

That was the first thirty seconds of the encounter. Batsman number two allowed his anger about seeing his brother dumped on his arse to get the better of him and came in with a wild swing. Dan used his bat to parry the blow but the open stance of his attacker was just begging for the simplest hack in the gonads. That was the two heavies sorted. Mister van Damm was in the early stages of shock, he may have been a big guy but he was also in his sixties and was in no fit state to argue with Dan.

"Inside," said Dan, "I don't have long so I want all the papers for the load you took to Ashford on the 19th."

Just to be sure the old man got the message he waggled the bat in his direction. They went inside and van Damm decided he could talk his way out of it and stay clear of the cops. He blurted out the whole story including the probability that the Romanian had taken any 'passengers' with him after he left the depot and switched back to his original trailer. He could have dropped them off anywhere between Alkmaar and Morocco. Dan turned to leave and met the one of the brothers, bent double and nursing a pair of crushed sweetbreads and staggering into the office. He was past doing any damage so Dan left with a file full of forms and a shit-load of worry. There's an awful lot of territory between Alkmaar and Morocco. The only solution was to find the driver and make him talk.

13.00 – Friday 1st December, 2006
At Sea, The Western Mediterranean

Jack sat in his office chair with his legs crossed, feet up on the edge of the desk. He was studying the stamps in the newly acquired passport. They were scattered through the whole document in random fashion. If he was going to get past the first encounter with an immigration official he needed to know where he had been and when he had been there. There were stamps from the UAE as well as Israel but that was explained by the fact that Israel was the last place he had visited. Before the UAE there was Tunisia, before that Jamaica and before that Mexico. There were no Moroccan stamps so if he joined the ship in Tangier he hadn't used his Italian passport.

There was a knock at the door. A gentle knock, a female type of knock. He slid the passport into the desk drawer, took his feet off the desk and said, "Come in". It was JoJo.

"Hi Doc, how're you doing?"

"Fine thanks, how about you guys?"

"Boris is still asleep. I haven't seen the other two."

"Can I get you anything?"

"No, I just came by to say thanks for last night and to say I'm sorry I can't help you with the cell phone. Is it important?"

"I need to get a message to my wife."

"We are all going to fly ashore when we get close to Malta. Boris's father is coming on board with his guests in a few days so we have to leave. If you write a message and give me a number I can send it for you when we get ashore."

"Thank you, that would be kind. I'll let you have something before you go."

She waved a cheery salute and closed the door. Jack's mind was suddenly racing. His policeman's instincts were at work and he thought carefully about what to say. If he told the whole story it would bring Pam to find him. She could be in danger. In the end he decided he was confident that he would find a way to get free so the most important thing was to let Pam know that he was well.

He wrote out a brief note to that effect and put Pam's cell phone number on it. He would ask JoJo to send a text message rather than call and he would tell her not to answer any return calls. He would explain that they were surrounded by evil people and not to trust anyone and he didn't want his wife to know what he was doing in case it upset her.

He picked up a piece of paper lying on the desk. The ship had a daily newsletter for the crew that was designed to keep everyone informed. It wasn't very forthcoming, apart from the weather data and the menus for lunch and dinner there was precious little information. The menu for dinner included the usual range of salads and cold meats. The hot meal was usually a pasta dish and sometimes a chicken. According to the senior steward the weekends were the most interesting and Saturday would be a tagine and Sunday a roast joint of beef. Jack was looking forward to that and hoped it would be cooked so that it was pink on the inside with a rim of tasty cream fat. He wondered if they had any horseradish sauce or some English mustard.

The *'location at 06.00 and next port of call'* section of the newsletter merely stated *'Mediterranean'*. The next destination was only known to the captain and Jack reasoned that with the owner about to arrive even that knowledge may be out of date.

18.00 – Friday 1st December, 2006
Lower Spargo Cottage, Perranarworthal

Nathan was adamant, he was going whether his mother agreed or not. He argued that young men his age fought in every war we have ever had and he was damn sure that he could take care of himself. It was impossible to refute this assertion.

Pam looked him up and down and realised perhaps for the first time that the years at university and working in the wilds of Canada as a research scientist had transformed her son into a strapping young man who was physically capable and mentally prepared. He was his father's son; there was no doubt about that. He was her baby but now she was going to have to let go. She wanted to go too but there were other demands on her time that she couldn't ignore. Her youngest son, Josh, would be back from university after his first term, her mother was dealing with the early stages of Parkinson's and her father needed help now that he had lost his driving licence. He was waiting for a cataract operation but in the meantime his eyesight wasn't good enough to pass the driving test.

The call from Dan earlier that day had given them hope. They were hanging on to the notion that Jack had been transported away from Alkmaar in a truck driven by a Romanian. The man was out there somewhere on the roads of Europe and held the key to where Jack had been offloaded. Dan had fed the information back to his contacts in the Special Branch and they were on the case. A description of the Romanian and his tractor unit came from Gerard van Damm but he could be hauling almost any trailer unit as he was a freelance. It was a black Mercedes six-wheeler with a sleeper cab and a row of spotlights on the cab roof. The registration was Spanish and his speciality was hauling fruit and veg for the Spanish and Portuguese farmers.

Dan said he needed some help to track down the Romanian and Nathan had immediately volunteered. Dan's agents at Scotland Yard were working to get information through their Interpol contacts but in the meantime he planned to ply the roads between Alkmaar and Spain in the hope of finding their target.

Nathan took his mother's car and set off to find Dan. When he heard that help was on the way Dan arranged to meet Nathan at Calais and then make plans. In the meantime he spent a tedious night watching a trickle of heavy goods vehicles entering the ferry terminal. It was a reminder that in France the trucks have to park up and wait until midnight to re-start their journeys. There is a ban on nearly all HGVs at the weekends. It was pretty much the same deal in Spain, Germany, Switzerland, Austria and Hungary. Wherever he was, Mr Iliescu was unlikely to be going any further until the early hours of Monday morning. It wasn't much in the way of comfort but did nothing to cheer him up. He would await Nathan's arrival and work out a plan.

07.00 – Sunday 3rd December, 2006
Calais Ferry Port, Pas de Calais, France

On Sunday Dan moped around Calais then checked into the local Campanile Hotel and tried to console himself with a bottle of red wine.

At six o'clock on Monday morning, refreshed by a good night's sleep, he was watching the trucks streaming out of the ferry-port gates. He had used the time on Sunday to research his quarry. The port of Calais saw two million trucks pass through its gates in the previous year. He calculated that it was roughly ten thousand a day, five thousand in and five thousand out. That's approximately three every minute of every weekday. Calais is one tiny pimple on the world of heavy good vehicles so the veritable ocean of trucks milling around European roads was truly mind-boggling. It was depressing.

By the time Nathan drove off the P & O cross-channel ferry Dan had exchanged text messages with him and arranged a meeting place outside the port gates.

When Nathan pulled up at the rendezvous and stepped out of his mother's Renault Clio Dan could hardly believe his eyes. The last time he had seen Nat he was about to go off to university. That spindly youth had turned into a man and what was more, a man who looked hardened by a life outdoors. His chiselled features were accentuated by the dark shadow of two days growth on a deeply sun tanned face.

They shook hands and Dan slapped him on the shoulder and embarrassed him by reminding him how much he had changed. He responded in typically subdued tones. Nat was *'Mr Tough Guy'* to the casual observer but by nature he was quiet and reserved.

They went to the nearby sea front and sat sipping coffee and snacking on French pastries. Dan gave Nat an update and told him that searching for a single truck in a sea of trucks would be like trying to find one piece of plankton in the Pacific Ocean. They would have to wait for the researchers to come up with a lead. Unfortunately the rest of Europe had been slow to take up ANPR technologies and although they did exist here and there the cameras were generally located at border posts and some toll plazas. The Spanish registration was being circulated and agencies associated with traffic management asked to look out for it. There was no guarantee that the dragnet was complete or even comprehensive. Interpol worked well at one level but chasing trucks was not one of the roles they were famous for.

The driver, Petre Iliescu, was also being sought of course and that hunt focussed on borders and hotel registrations. Petre had a sleeper cab so it was unlikely that he would waste money on a hotel but you never knew what would happen and his police experience told him not to take anything for granted and never leave a stone unturned.

They sat chewing the fat for hours and were beginning to feel that they were on a fool's errand when they were jerked back into the real world by Dan's phone. It was London. They had a break. Iliescu and his truck were at the Spanish border.

"They had crossed into Spain on the Autoroute de la Cote Basque at 07.03 yesterday," said the voice in London.

"Yesterday!" exclaimed Dan, "at seven-oh-three, Christ are we running a history department or a police department?"

"Look Dan it was the weekend remember, we are doing our best here but we have to rely on the folk at Interpol to get back to us."

"Don't tell me, Interpol don't work weekends. OK, but see if you can chivvy them up a bit will you. I'll head for the South West of France and by the way, Jacks eldest, Nathan, is with me." He turned to Nat, "Not much point in taking two cars, we can take one and share the driving."

"Ok, but let's be serious, your old wreck might not make it, let's take mum's Clio."

"My 'wreck' as you call is actually in better nick than you realise and it comes with a few extras that are not in the brochure, so we'll leave your Clio in the Campanile car park and collect it when we come back."

They set off on the long haul to the South West and mentally prepared themselves for a long drive.

CHAPTER 14

08.00 – Sunday 3rd December, 2006
Shayetet 13 Headquarters, Atlit Naval Base, Israel

"IN MY OPINION THIS is not something we should be involved in. If the Prime Minister gets caught with his hand in the till then we should not be asked to risk our necks to bail him out."

"Amil, they are all the same, this is business as usual for the political class. If you are going to succeed in your political career then you will have to get used to this kind of crap."

"My political career, when it comes, will be based on honest dealing and not this endless corruption I see every damn day."

"So you say my friend but trust me when you put your head into the lion's den you will find a different world. You will need more than honesty to survive, you will need allies and allies cost money whether you like it or not."

"But how can I stand before my men and brief them on a dangerous mission to sink a ship in the open sea just because the owner holds credit slips the PM cannot pay."

"You will do it nevertheless and you will say nothing about the Prime Minister. You will do it because you have no choice, the executive order is clear and direct. The nation's premier naval Special Forces unit will devise a plan to sink the target vessel and ensure there are no survivors."

"No survivors? You said we had an agent on board, the doctor. What about him?"

The General was silent. He pressed his lips together and said nothing. When the moment of tension passed he said in lowered tones, "No survivors.

How the hell can we get him off if the objective is to sink the ship. We have been unable to communicate with him for the last two weeks. We have to do what we have to do and he must …"

"… be sacrificed? Another good man dies for the cause. What bloody cause eh? The bloody Prime Minister's Swiss Bank Account?"

"Amil, if you can get him off then do it but the objective must be achieved. Aram Mikoyan must die."

"Why didn't our man take care of him before?"

"You can ask him when you see him."

"So as long as we take this guy Mikoyan down I have the freedom to decide how we attack the ship?"

"Yes. But you must ensure he dies. We know he will be aboard very soon and he must go down with his ship. Be sure you leave no evidence of our participation in the passing of Aram Mikoyan and never speak about what we did and why we did it ever again."

"I don't like it. No officer should be asked to do this kind of thing."

"Just get on with making plans and let me know when you are ready. You have access to all the necessary resources."

With that parting shot the head of Shayetet 13 left the office of his deputy and set off for 9 Smolenskin Street, the Prime Minister's official residence in Jerusalem.

10.00 – Sunday 3rd December, 2006
At Sea, La Reine Bleu, Central Mediterranean

The ship passed south of Sardinia and increased speed. Jack guessed that the rendezvous at Malta had been brought forward. The guests were all on the upper sun deck enjoying the fine weather behind plate glass windbreaks. The sky was clear and away from the breeze the temperature was over twenty-two degrees. Jack was perched on a stool on the edge of the helideck. His chosen spot was also out of the wind. He was busy reading an Andrea Camilleri novel, 'The Terracotta Dog'. He had found it in the crew 'library' – two shelves in a corner of the dining area. The Italian equivalent of Inspector Morse, the main character was a Sicilian police inspector who spawned a series of detective stories. The irony of the scene of the crime being a matter of a few hundred kilometres away was not lost on Jack and he considered the possibility that some supernatural force had guided his hand to the shelf in the library.

The wind suddenly began to flick at the pages of his book. The ship had turned to the southeast and the northerly breeze was now finding its way around the edge of the ship's superstructure and over the helideck.

"Doctor Smith." It was a voice from above, a woman's voice. He turned and looked up but the sun was right in his eyes.

"It's me, JoJo."

"Hi there, everything all right?" There, above him, was the enticing sight of JoJo and he could just make out that she was in a tiny bikini that made the most of her figure. Her blonde hair was up in a bun.

"We're fine thank you, it's a lovely day." There was a voice behind her yelling then Boris arrived. "Go back to the others," he told her.

"Just a moment Boris, I'm talking to the Doc." He appeared at her side and grabbed her arm.

"When I tell you to do something you damn well do it." He grabbed her arm.

"I'm not your slave Boris. Let go…" She wriggled free and slapped his face. He didn't even hesitate and with clenched fist smacked her full in the face. She went down like a stone and her head smacked on the steel deck edge with a sickening thud. There was a moment of stunned silence after Boris's brutal attack.

"What happened, is she OK?" yelled Jack. He was looking up against the sun and couldn't clearly see what had happened.

"Stay out of this English," said Boris, leaning over the rail and thrusting an accusing finger in Jack's direction, "or you will end up feeding the fishes like your colleague."

Jack didn't understand, where was JoJo? From his position on the helideck he didn't see Boris's punch on his girlfriend. He stood staring up at where Boris had been standing a moment before. Lars appeared and waved at him to come up to the sundeck. He ran to the stairway and leapt up them two at a time. He found Sandra and Lars bending over JoJo's lifeless body. Boris had left and was nowhere to be seen.

Kneeling beside JoJo Jack checked her pupils. One was blown, wide open. Her pulse was erratic and her skin clammy. She was unresponsive and Jack assessed her as GCS 3. Her breathing was low and faltering. He turned to Lars.

"Do you know where my office is?"

"Yes, I think so."

"Beside my desk is a black doctor's bag and on the wall is a defibrillator, bring them here as soon as you can." Lars disappeared below.

"What's this, what is happening?" It was Captain Dellamorte.

"Boris hit her, she fell down," volunteered Sandra.

"She's got a serious head injury, her life is in danger."

"Is it serious?" said Dellamorte.

"As bad as it gets Captain."

"Just what I don't need, that bastard Boris is always causing trouble." Lars arrived with Jack's bag and he set about fitting his little blood pressure monitor and Oximeter. He took his stethoscope and listened to her heart. Then he took the defibrillator paddles, switched the machine on, selected 'quick look' and placed the paddles on her chest. He sighed and sat back on his haunches.

"What is it Doc?"

"She's showing all the signs of a sub arachnoid haematoma."

"What the hell is that?"

"A very serious condition, she needs brain surgery, now."

"But we are sea. Can you perform the operation?"

"No I'm not trained to do complex neurosurgical operations and anyway you don't have the facilities and equipment for surgery, not to mention the support staff."

"So what do we need to do?"

"Fly her to the nearest hospital capable of doing the operation."

"But I would need the owner's authority to do that, it will delay our arrival off the Maltese coast."

"Then get it … quick. I'll get her packaged for the journey. Where is the nearest hospital do you know?"

"I'll have to contact the Italian Coast Guard and give them our position. Shall I ask them to send one of their helicopters?"

"There won't be time Captain, she needs to go now."

"I'll call the pilot." Captain Dellamorte left and hurried towards the access to the bridge. He used the quickest way to find the helicopter pilot.

The peace and quiet was shattered by a loud hailer broadcast, first in Spanish, then in English. Boris appeared on the bridge now dressed in designer jacket and a crisp white shirt and demanded to speak with the Captain.

"Can I help you Mister Mikoyan?" Dellamorte appeared from the bridge wing.

"What the fuck is going on with the helicopter? We're nowhere near Malta."

"It is your girlfriend, she is very sick we need to fly her to a hospital in Palermo."

"But you will need authority for that from my father, if you tell him then he will know that it was my fault the girl is hurt. I will be in big trouble again and I can't afford that."

"But the doctor says she will die."

"Then let her die. My father will make a big deal out of this you can be sure. My future is more important that the life of a slag like that." He left the bridge and hurried off to the sundeck, the captain followed. Boris arrived beside Jack and pushed him aside. He tried to pick JoJo up. Jack put his hand on Boris's arm.

"What do you think you are doing?" asked Jack.

"Get your hand off me or it will be the last thing you do."

"I said, what are you doing?" Boris stood back and reached inside his jacket. His hand reappeared holding a small semi-automatic pistol. He cocked it and pointed it directly at Jack and squeezed the trigger. Before the hammer came down the captain lunged at his outstretched arm and when the gun fired the bullet missed Jack and ricocheted off the deck and flew harmlessly into the sea with a wailing wine. Jack turned pale and then regained his composure. The captain was struggling to disarm Boris who cursed and finally dropped the gun on the deck.

"Look she's as good as dead, just throw her over the side like we did the last fucking troublemaker we had on board."

"Please, Mister Mikoyan, calm yourself, don't talk about such things." The captain picked up the neat little Sig P-290, removed the clip, eased the slide forward, caught the ejected bullet and returned it to its owner.

"You can shut up as well Captain, I'll have my father deal with you when he comes aboard."

"As you wish sir." Jack could see why Dellamorte had survived in what must be a difficult job. He had tact, diplomacy, a wise head and quick reflexes. Jack owed him a big favour.

"Captain, you were looking for me?" It was Marko, the chopper pilot.

"Marko we have to take this girl to hospital in Palermo."

"Oh no," exclaimed Jack, "she's stopped breathing." He grabbed the paddles again, turned a switch on the machine and placed both paddles on her chest once more. He could tell from the trace on the screen that she had no output and announced to those around to 'stand clear'. The shock and the subsequent attempts at resuscitation were to no avail and after twenty minutes Jack gave up the struggle.

Sandra burst into tears and Lars tried to comfort her.

"I told you it was a waste of time," said Boris.

"You murderer," yelled Sandra, "I saw you punch her in the face."

"Watch your mouth or you'll follow her over the side," replied Boris waving his pistol in her direction. "Take all that stuff off her Doc and chuck her overboard."

"You can't do that, there needs to be an autopsy and a police investigation."

"The hell there does," and with that he tore Jacks equipment free, scooped up JoJo's body and hurled it over the side rail.

They all knew there was no point in remonstrating. It was too late. Jack was aghast and could hardly believe what he had just witnessed.

"Nobody say anything about today. If my father finds out about this there will be trouble for each of you. I've got friends who can deal with you if you ignore my warning." He turned to Jack, "You are already history Mister Smith, you're a dead man walking." With the threat still ringing in Jack's ears Boris went below.

"Don't worry Doc, he's all mouth. His father knows exactly what he is like and I will make sure he gets to understand what happened today."

"What about the murder, what about calling in the police?"

"No police I'm afraid. What we saw him do was wrong but that young man is fireproof. I could call the police in Sicily and have him arrested and two things will happen. The first is that he will walk free as soon as the police are paid off, the second is that you and I will lose our jobs and we'll probably, in Mafia parlance, be *swimming with the fishes wearing a pair of concrete boots*."

15.20 – Sunday 3rd December, 2006
A10 Motorway, Tours, France

Nat was driving and Dan dozing when Dan's cell phone sprang into life. It was a text message from London.

'Iliescu crossed the Franco-Spanish border A9 northbound with cargo of oranges this morning 0500. Destination unknown.'

"That was rather timely," observed Nat, "another few hours and we would have to turn around and head north. My guess is that we head east now."

Dan was head down and checking the map.

"South to Poitiers then east towards Lyon. We know that the toll plazas on the Lyon to Paris Autoroute have ANPR cameras. If he's heading in that direction then we should get a hit."

Nat prodded the radio button in the hope of finding a decent music channel. "Doesn't work," said Dan.

"Like I said, this old thing is a wreck."

"It's not a wreck, it doesn't work because that's not a radio." Nat looked puzzled. "I guess you need to know one or two things about my old car."

"Like what?" asked Nat. Dan put his hands on both the tuning and the volume knobs and simultaneously pushed them inwards. There was a click and Dan removed the front panel. From the interior he produced a black plastic packet. Inside was a Glock 17 semi-automatic pistol. Further delving into the radio's interior produced another black plastic packet. Inside were four magazines.

"Have you fired a gun like this before?" asked Dan.

"I did a spell in the OTC at uni so I've fired the Browning but that doesn't look like a Browning 9mm to me."

"No this is a Glock 9mm but the essentials are very similar. The Glock is a far superior weapon though and you need to know how to use it just in case. We are not dealing with pussycats Nat. These are serious crooks and they won't take kindly to our attentions."

"Can you give me some lessons on how it works?"

"Sure, but we'll have to wait for an opportune moment. The French are a bit fussy about who carries a gun like this." He replaced the gun and magazines and then closed the front panel of the radio.

"Tell me something Dan, my Dad always described you, and I quote, 'as a very special kind of Private Eye'. I can see what he meant but how come you have such good contacts in the Police, at Scotland Yard?"

"Nat I won't lie to you, I don't just do marital disputes and trace runaways. Let's just say that once a policeman always a policeman and leave it at that." Nat let the comment sink in and tried to decipher the coded message. He thought he understood but all he really cared about was that Dan was trying to help his Dad and between them they might have a chance of finding him.

10.15 – Monday 4th December, 2006
At Sea, La Reine Bleu, Off The Coast of Malta

The trauma of the previous day resonated around the ship. News of what had occurred had rapidly spread around the ship's crew of thirty odd men and women. The atmosphere was chilled, the crew silent and uncommunicative. They all knew what they wanted to say but were all very mindful of what would happen to them if they said a single word outside their own circle.

Jack stood beside the helideck waiting for the three remaining guests to board the helicopter. With the death of JoJo he had lost the chance to send a message to Pam but he was going to gamble on Lars being on his side. There was a good chance that he would send it for him so he had a scrap of paper in his hand with a brief message scribbled on it along with Pam's mobile number.

Boris strode out on to the helideck carrying a briefcase. Marko was holding the door open allowing Boris to take his place on board the sleek and highly polished Italian made executive helicopter. Lars and Sandra appeared loaded down with luggage, Jack stepped forward to help them. A deck hand loaded the bags into a compartment at the rear of the helicopter and Jack had an opportunity to slip the note into Lars' hand and whispered in his ear as he did so. "My wife is desperate for some news from me, please send a text message for me when you get ashore."

Lars said nothing but smiled and nodded leaving Jack hopeful that Pam would soon know he was safe and well. He contemplated the word 'safe' and wondered just how safe he would be when the owner arrived and was given chapter and verse about the previous day's events.

Jack was a man familiar with death, and indeed had actually killed people in the line of duty, but the casual way in which Boris treated death had shocked him. Here was a man, maybe a family, which had scant regard for human life and considered it their prerogative to take it any time they felt inclined.

He watched as the helicopter engines started up and the rotor blades began to turn. With a clatter and a whine the beast rose from deck, strangling the lift from the surrounding air and simultaneously defying all the laws of aerodynamics and gravity. With uncharacteristic grace the noisy creature floated away into the distance and with it went Jack's hope of delivering some relief to his family.

10.15 – Monday 4th December, 2006
The Paris to Lyons Autoroute

After a long cross-country haul Dan and Nat finally settled for a small hostelry close to Macon, north of Lyons. At breakfast they discussed a plan.

"I can't believe that our target has not appeared on one of those damn cameras," contemplated Dan.

"Maybe it just takes time for the information to filter through," responded Nat.

"Bloody French bureaucracy," grumbled Dan. They had agreed before turning in for the night that they would await another call from London otherwise they could be chasing their tails. A long late breakfast had done nothing to ease the tension but when the phone rang it was good news. Iliescu's truck was southbound again on the A6. Every camera between Lyons and Paris had recorded hits but the information had been held up by a supervisor at the Gendarmerie HQ who wanted permission to pass the data on. Dan cursed but Nat pointed out that the whole mess had turned to their advantage for they could have been chasing him all night. Now Iliescu was heading their way.

15.15 – Monday 4th December, 2006
At Sea, La Reine Bleu, Off The Coast of Malta

The returning helicopter could be heard before it could be seen as it raced in from the North. Marko set it down on the gently heaving deck and the crew immediately set about securing it to the ring bolts in the helideck and once all the lashings were in place the Third Officer, acting as helideck controller, signalled to Marko that he could stop the engines and rotor.

The sudden silence accentuated their isolation out in the sea-lanes with only the sound of the wind to accompany them. The hum from the ship's engines grew slightly and The Blue Queen accelerated to maximum cruise speed. Their course was east, into the Ionian Sea.

The crew were confined to quarters during the arrival of the owner and his guests and only those actually on watch saw Mr Mikoyan and three male guests leave the helideck and make their way to the main lounge.

Jack was busy cleaning his equipment and re-stocking his doctor's bag. He couldn't get the aroma of JoJo's perfume out of his mind. The image of her limp form in Boris's arms as he tossed her over the side like a worthless rag doll haunted him. He was ashamed on behalf of the human race that such deviant personalities were allowed to exist.

To cheer himself up he contemplated that with any luck Pam would soon get a message to say he was alive and well.

There was a knock at the door.

"Come in." The door opened and Captain Dellamorte stood in the doorway, cast an eye around the surgery then beckoned Jack to follow him.

They went down one deck and entered the main lounge. Mr Mikoyan was in close conference with his guests. Two rather large gentlemen were hovering in the background and Jack guessed that they were probably bodyguards. Upon seeing the captain arrive with Jack alongside him he broke away and led the threesome into a side office and closed the door. The two bodyguards stood like sentries outside the door.

"Doctor Smith, welcome aboard La Reine Bleu. I understand there was an unfortunate incident involving my son Boris earlier today."

"You mean the murder of a young girl and the illegal disposal of her body?"

Mr Mikoyan took a stroll around the office before speaking again. Jack got the impression that he had just spoken out of turn and the boss man was quietly boiling inside.

"The captain tells me you did a good job, let's focus on the positive shall we? I will deal with Boris in my own way and believe me it will be a lot more effective than trying to interest a policeman in his activities." He decided that the conversation would benefit from some fresh air and slid the weather deck door open and stepped out into the sunshine. He put on his sunglasses and appeared to be studying the sea. The others followed, somewhat perplexed by his behaviour.

In many respects Aram Mikoyan was an unremarkable man. Small in stature and quietly spoken he would not attract any attention walking down any high street in Europe but to underestimate him, as many had made the mistake of doing in the past, would be fatal.

Aram Mikoyan was born in 1931 in the Armenian-Soviet Union borderlands, of parents who had survived the Ottoman genocide by the skin of their teeth. He was named for Armenia's ancient founder, Armenak but Armenia was not a very pleasant place to be during that Stalinist era and by the time the Germans invaded Russia during the Second World War the young Aram had seen things that no young man should ever see.

The case-hardened youth had lost his father some years earlier during the Spanish Civil War when he was serving as a Soviet Military Advisor to the Republican Army. He had been drafted into the People's Army and sent to Spain to fight with the Republicans in their struggle against Franco's Nationalists.

Aram was no soldier, he didn't have the physicality to survive as that kind of fighter but he had the mind of a genius when it came to managing 'deals' and manipulating money.

He grew to prominence working at the elbow of some of the emerging businessmen during the industrialisation of the Soviet Union and when the revolution came in 1990 he saw his chance. His home was now in Beirut where he lived in a virtual fortress on a hill outside the city on the slopes of Mount Lebanon.

La Reine Bleu was not a 'gin palace' in the normal sense. It was not used just to impress clients but was his mobile office where he could entertain the rich and the powerful away from prying eyes. His guests could meet people that they could never meet in public, do deals that were scandalous and arrange to move funds to and from accounts organised and managed by Aram Mikoyan. His sophisticated communications allowed him to control an empire worth countless billions of dollars through his global banking hub in the City of London.

There was nowhere else in the world where a man who has illicit funds can make more profit than London. The City may once have been a community with a proud past but it had become the home of a new kind of socially acceptable criminal who moved money here and there and used outstations like Jersey, Guernsey, Gibraltar, Cayman Islands, Bermuda, Isle of Man, the British Virgin Islands and more and more lately, the Emirate of Dubai. The latest addition to the world's corrupt bankers was the jewel in the Middle East's financial crown. Whatever the Islamic world says about making money from money it doesn't appear to inhibit those in Dubai who launder millions every day.

Aram was ill but he had no intention of retiring. He was a man who appeared on the surface to be comfortable with his past but all was not as it seemed.

"Doctor Smith, or should I say Doctor Mawgan, John Mawgan although I believe those that know you well call you 'Jack'."

Jack was taken aback. "If you know my name Mr Mikoyan then you will probably know that I am not a doctor."

"Yes, of course but you are, I see from my briefing file, an accomplished paramedic and so you will no doubt appreciate what I have to say more than most." Captain Dellamorte handed Aram a glass of water and he sipped at it before continuing his address.

"I will share a closely guarded secret with you and the good captain here. I am dying. I have a heart condition which lately has been getting worse. My doctors wanted me to stay at home but I needed to make this trip and meet some important guests. They fuss over me and so I have escaped to my island of peace and tranquillity on board La Reine. I would prefer not to die until I have made certain arrangements so I need a good doctor to help me if I should fall ill."

"What exactly is wrong with you?" asked Jack.

"I can never remember the technical word but it's a valve that is failing."

"You appear well enough at the moment, is the condition under control?"

"I have good days and bad days, today is a good day."

"The condition may well be operable sir, why not fix it?"

"Jack, if I may be so familiar, I have had three operations already and I am not going through that again. I now put my trust in God and when my time has come ..." he gave a shrug and a smile.

"What can I possibly do, I am not even a doctor let alone a cardiologist and there are no facilities for surgery?"

"I wanted to talk to you because it is possible that I will collapse if I have another attack. If that happens then you will be expected to resuscitate me and keep me alive. I have a morbid fear of being alive inside a dead body. My mind functioning but unable to communicate, unable to move. I am not a vegetable Jack, if I collapse then you will let nature take its course. No resuscitation, do you understand?"

"Perfectly."

"The captain will support you if you come under pressure from anyone else on board. Only you and the captain will know about this decision of mine and you will not tell anyone else about it or there could be severe repercussions. Do you both understand?" They both nodded. "Then please go about your duties."

Jack led the way back to the deck above where the captain told him, "Be careful around the old man, doc. He can sound like a sweet old bird but I can assure you he has a wicked temper."

"Thank you, Captain, I'll try to remember that."

09.00 – Monday 4th December, 2006
Israel

The officer commanding the attack group brought the briefing to order. "Gentlemen, your attention please." The twenty-three men and four women stopped talking amongst themselves and focussed their attention on the new arrival.

"Our agents in Malta report that the target has left the island by helicopter and is now on board La Reine Bleu. Her position is confirmed here," he used a laser pointer to indicate a point south east of Malta. "She is heading east and we believe she will take aboard more visitors when they are close to Cyprus in approximately four days."

"More visitors sir, do we know who they might be? If they are additions to his security detail then it could complicate the job a good deal."

"No news yet, Sergeant, but we have agents in Cyprus who will give us ample warning. So far the only additions to the passenger list are two Italian businessmen. Now, we have an update on the plan of attack. We will arrive by boat. The two primary boats and one back-up boat will be acquired by Section Four from the harbour at Paphos during the previous night. On the night we execute the attack we will assemble the three boats together directly in the path of the target vessel so as to appear on radar to be one contact. The objective is to make like a single fishing boat. When the target passes by, Sections One and Two will proceed alongside the vessel and use the standard Somali pirate tactics we have been practicing the last few weeks. I want you all to wear your old civilian clothes and look like the ill disciplined mob that I know you are not. The boarding parties will be armed with Kalashnikovs and carry both anti personnel and stun grenades. The support teams will carry our normal equipment.

"I'm going to divide you up into your Sections now and your Section Leaders will continue with the detailed briefing. Remember that amongst the imperatives for this mission, the one that is most important is to preserve our anonymity. We do not under any circumstances give away our nationality so we have to avoid voice communication and if absolutely necessary then use English or Arabic. Terminating the prime target remains essential for mission success. As long as we are not compromised then all the personnel we find on board will be set free in the ship's lifeboats then we will scuttle the ship leaving any deceased persons in place. When mission complete is announced we will proceed to the north at speed and rendezvous with the submarine 'Dolphin' before dawn. The attack boats will be torched and sunk as soon as we are safely aboard. Nothing and nobody will be left behind to indicate who carried out this mission. Do I make myself clear?"

The men and women nodded silently as the gravitas of their mission descended upon them. No one thought to ask for clarification about the fate of the crew and guests on board La Reine Bleu if their cover was blown. They all knew that it would mean everyone on board going down with the ship.

16.00 – Monday 4th December, 2006
Paris to Lyon Autoroute

"That was him I'm sure, Black Mercedes six wheeled tractor unit with sleeper cab and lights on the roof," cried Nat, suddenly excited and running towards the car where Dan sat waiting to roar off up the slip road from the Autoroute Service Centre. The last message they had from London was that their target was fifty kilometres north of their location and apparently heading back to Spain.

It took them ten minutes to catch up with the truck and to pull alongside. It was impossible for Dan to check the cab out safely from his position behind the wheel and Nat couldn't see anything from the passenger seat. Dan dropped back again and studied the trailer. It carried a set of Spanish plates but there was no indication as to what load he was carrying if any. By the way the rig was rolling and the loosely flapping side curtains Dan guessed it was empty.

They followed for hour after hour and eventually the truck pulled into an overnight truck park. Dan parked the car outside and watched as it parked beside a long line of similar HGVs. The driver's door opened and a figure dropped down from the cab and began to wander around his rig, checking the wheels and feeling temperature of the tyres. It was probably a routine ritual for his truck didn't appear to be under any strain.

Nat said, "Do you think that's him?" He turned to find Dan peering through the fading daylight with a very expensive looking pair of binoculars.

"That's him, I recognise him from the CCTV coverage at Prideco's. Well Petre Iliescu, it's time for a wee chat."

"What are you going to do?" asked Nat. Dan didn't reply but instead he returned to the car and removed the Glock from its hiding place, put a clip in place in the handgrip then put the weapon on the dashboard. To Nat's astonishment he then began to unscrew the gear stick.

"What are you doing?" asked Nat puzzled by Dan's antics. Dan looked up and smiled.

"My old wreck still has some secrets Nat. Never underestimate the ingenuity of the British." With that he held up the short stubby gear stick and then screwed it into the barrel of the Glock.

"Blimey!" said Nat, "it's a bloody silencer."

"Correct, more correctly a 'suppressor'. I don't plan to use it but we need information from our Mr Iliescu and he may be a little reluctant to comply with our request."

"Do you want me to come with you?"

"No, you stay here and watch from a distance. If it all goes pear-shaped and you see me go down and not get up then call the police. The café over there will have a phone and I'm sure the barman will help you." With that Dan cocked the weapon, put the safety to 'on' and tucked it into his waistband in the middle of his back.

Dan made his way across the tarmac towards Iliescu's truck and arrived at the passenger door. With a nimbleness that defied his age he hopped up the step, simultaneously swung open the door and climbed on to the passenger seat. Unfortunately it was suppertime and Iliescu was using the seat as a dining table. It was covered in cold cuts and assorted cardboard plates of salad items he had acquired en route. It went everywhere and a furious Iliescu swore at Dan, or at least did the best he could with a mouthful of salami. His fists were full of baguette and he could not have been in a more vulnerable state unless he had been stark naked.

"Who the fuck are you?" Iliescu dropped the fork from his left hand and Dan saw him reach down below his seat. His hand reappeared holding a steel bar but before he could raise it Dan had the business end of the Glock's silencer massaging the end of his nose. The change in Iliescu's demeanour was palpable and the anger drained from his face as terror overtook his enthusiasm for a fight.

"Don't worry Mr Iliescu, we are here for information, nothing more."

"What sort of information?"

"Last month you visited the Prideco Warehouse in England, you were paid to take an unconscious man and send him a long way away. I need you to tell me where you took him."

"It wasn't me, I don't know what you are talking about."

"I hope you have medical insurance, Petre? Because if you don't give the right answers to my questions you will have some expensive repair bills." He theatrically moved the safety catch to 'fire' and the loud click seemed to persuade Iliescu to come clean.

"OK, I was paid one thousand five hundred Euro to backload a prisoner to Morocco."

"Morocco!" said Dan, "why the hell take him to Morocco?"

"They asked where I was going next and I said Morocco. They made a phone call and then said that would be cool."

"Was the prisoner conscious?"

"He was when they loaded him into my bed-space but they knocked him out and said I had about 24 hours before he would wake up and gave me one of those injection things and said I was to give it to him in his backside when he started to wake up."

"Was he OK when you delivered him?"

"He was alive anyway."

"Where did you leave him?"

"It's a farm, in the hills south of Ceuta, the details are on that clipboard. It's a regular stop. I take vegetables labelled for the French and British supermarkets to Alkmaar and they send them on as Dutch produce. It's good money."

"Do you often carry people around Europe like that?"

"Once or twice, it's pocket money and the guards are only interested in stopping people coming into UK not out of UK. There are no risks, not really. The farm paid me for him. They use all sorts of slaves there. The place is crawling with blacks trying to get into Ceuta and across the Straits."

"So this man was going to be used as a labourer on a farm?"

"I guess so."

Dan picked up the clipboard and put the pistol down by his side.

"What will you do with me now?" He was suddenly very scared that he would be executed on the spot now that he had given away all the information that Dan required.

"Nothing, you have been very helpful. That man is my friend and I am going to find him and return him to his family. You had better hope that he's alive and well because if he isn't then I will come looking for you and I won't be delivering early Christmas presents. Do you understand?"

"Yes, sir."

"You don't tell anyone about our conversation or the same fate will await you, got it?"

"Got it."

Dan slipped backwards out of the passenger door and into the night, gun and clipboard in hand. He ran at a trot to where Nat was watching through Dan's binoculars.

"Any luck?" said Nat.

"Yep, jump in we're heading south, for Morocco."

"Morocco? You're kidding."

"No, I'm deadly serious." He spent the next fifteen minutes heading south on the motorway and fine-tuning their route to Algeciras where they would catch a ferry to Ceuta and then cross into Morocco.

"Can I tell Mum?"

"Sure, she will be relieved to know he was last seen alive and ... well alive. Let's leave it at that and not tempt fate."

Nat dialled home but there was no reply.

"Mum must be out, I'll try her mobile. No reply there either, I wonder what she's up to."

"Are you up for driving through the night?"

"Sure thing."

Despite their enthusiasm for non-stop motoring Dan eventually ran out of steam passing south of Barcelona. He looked at Nat who was fast asleep and decided that some common sense was required so he pulled over at a hotel sign and checked them in for the night.

CHAPTER 15

09.00 – Tuesday 5th December, 2006
Copenhagen Airport

"NAT ... HELLO NAT, it's Mum."

"Where've you been Mum, I've been trying to call you."

"I'm in Copenhagen."

"Where? What are you doing in bloody Copenhagen?"

"Listen, I had a text message in the middle of the night, it was a message from Dad."

"What did he say?"

"Safe and well and hopes to be home soon."

"Well we tracked down the guy who took Dad away in his truck and he told us where he is now, in bloody Morocco."

"But he can't be, the people in London traced the text message, it came from here, Copenhagen."

"Hang on, I'll explain to Dan then you talk to him." He turned to Dan who was busy with a piece of bread and cheese. "She's in Copenhagen, she's had a message from Dad. You talk to her."

"Hi Pam, what's this about a message from Jack?"

"I had a text message in the middle of the night, it was from Jack so I called that number in London you gave me. The chap who answered was very helpful. I told him what the message said and gave him my number. He called me back about half an hour later and said that the message came from a Danish mobile and had been sent from a location in the centre of Copenhagen. I got a taxi to Newquay Airport straight away and caught the first flight to Gatwick and then on to Copenhagen. I arrived about half an hour ago."

"So it was a message that appeared to come from Jack but it was sent using someone else's phone."

"Yes, hang on someone is calling me. I'll come back in a minute."

The minute turned out to be five. "That was your man in London, he says the Danish Police are on the way to interview someone called Lars something and I am to go to the Central Police HQ and wait for information."

"That sounds like a good idea. Listen Pam, I don't want to burst your bubble but do me a favour and don't get your hopes up. I don't know how the sender of that message got to be in Denmark but our information is that Jack is almost certainly in Morocco. It may be his message but it could well have come from someone he met who sent the message on his behalf."

"Oh Dan! What should I do?"

"Go to Police HQ and find out what this guy Lars has to say. We will stay here until we know what he says."

"Well where are you?"

"We're just south of Barcelona."

"Can you get to Morocco today?"

"Maybe not today, certainly tomorrow, but I'm not moving from here until we know more."

"Can we send someone to this place in Morocco, the place where Jack might be?"

"Maybe, but we are not dealing with regular situations in a place like Morocco. It may be safer to let me check out the place first then we can be sure that we do the best by Jack."

"Thanks Dan, you've been a rock. I'll call as soon as I hear anything."

10.00 – Tuesday 5th December, 2006
At Sea, La Reine Bleu, Ionian Sea

Aram Mikoyan sat with his guests and enjoyed some pleasant chit chat and some excellent pastries with their cappuccinos, and espressos.

"I think it is time for us to get down to business gentlemen." He was addressing the CEO of the Italian nationalised giant Malmeccanica, the

Finance Officer of the same corporation and the CEO of its helicopter-manufacturing subsidiary.

"Can you be sure the British will buy all these helicopters Aram?"

"You can ask them yourselves for they will be here on board in a day or so. At least one member of the Prime Minister's inner circle will be arriving. I'm sure they wish to discuss some serious issues including, of course, money."

Down below Jack was reading one of the medical reference books his predecessor had left behind. There were a lot but only a few in English. He was reading up on heart valve failures when there came a knock at his door.

When he opened the door he found one of the bodyguards with a bloodied hand wrapped in a handkerchief.

"Doc, please, my hand," his eastern European accent was apparent. Jack waved him in.

"What happened to you?"

"The wind came, it blew door shut and my hand was in door."

"Ouch, I bet that hurt."

"Yes, hurt." His voice was impassive, as if pain was an alien concept. This brute could probably dish it up as well as take it.

"Let's have a look." Jack looked carefully at the large but well-manicured hand. It was the hand of a fighter and Jack could tell that the damage was going to give its owner a big problem. The unambiguous bulge in the gentleman's jacket was on the right hand side. Jack was about to strap up a hand with at least two broken fingers and two that were badly bruised. His thumb had escaped damage but that was largely irrelevant. This was one left handed bodyguard who wouldn't be using his pistol for quite a while, not unless he was ambidextrous.

Jack cleaned the wound and was binding the hand with a dressing when another knock came at his door.

"Come in," he called. A rather timid Maria appeared with a tearful Sonja close behind.

"Oh you are busy," there was an interesting exchange of looks between the bodyguard and Maria which suggested a hint of a relationship that was perhaps a little more than just work.

"No, come in Maria, I'm just finishing here." Maria cast a worried look at the bandaged hand and said, "Sergey you are hurt."

"No, nothing, just door bangs on hand, some fingers are broken the doctor says."

"That is sad. Maybe you will need some help?" she added.

"Help?"

"Yes, help with ..." Jack could sense Maria was mentally running through a list of possible activities that Sergey would now require some assistance to perform. The girls giggled.

"Yes Sergey, help with eating your food or maybe taking off your clothes." Jack was taken aback to see the great lump of a man blush and the girls giggled again.

"Thank you doc, I must go back to work now."

"Go to the galley and ask chef for some ice then wrap the ice in a towel and keep it on your hand for as long as you can. It will control the swelling. Come and see me tomorrow and I'll change the dressing. If you have any pain take some of these, the instructions are on the pack." He handed Sergey a pack of Paracetamol.

"OK, tomorrow, thanks." The girls stood aside as Sergey moved past them and into the corridor.

"So what can I do for you two charming young ladies?"

"It is nothing really Doctor, Sonja and I were cleaning the gymnasium and we disturbed a hornet. When Sonja tried to brush it away it stung her on the arm. Look her arm is swelling." Jack inspected Sonja's right arm and sure enough there was a mark where she had been stung. The area was hard to the touch and she was in a certain amount of pain despite her stoic attempts to pretend otherwise. Close examination with a lens confirmed that the red mark was hiding the tip of the hornet's stinger. Hornet stingers are not barbed so it is unusual for the insect to leave it behind. Using the edge of a knife and with Maria holding the lens he carefully removed the sting without causing any more poison to enter the wound.

Using a tube of antihistamine ointment he covered the area around the sting and then suggested that maybe an ice pack would help with additional pain relief.

Jack waved them goodbye and pondered how long it would take to get to know all of the thirty crew members on board La Reine if he waited for them to visit his office as patients. His rather limited number of acquaintances made at meal-times was gradually expanding courtesy of accidents and incidents. His work mates were proving to be an interesting bunch.

11.15 – Tuesday 5th December, 2006
Central Police HQ, Copenhagen

Pam sat patiently in the public waiting room, sipping a cup of machine coffee that was struggling to impress. The Police Headquarters building was a fine piece of neoclassical architecture and from her position beside a window she could admire the fine circular courtyard that lay at its heart. Unfortunately Pam was not in any mood to pay attention to the fine qualities of the building and its interior décor for she was anxious to learn about the curious events that led to her receiving a message that purported to come from Jack but originated in Copenhagen.

The door opened and a uniformed officer called her name. She was escorted to a room on the second floor where a small group of plain-clothes policemen sat chatting. They stopped talking when Pam appeared and invited her to sit down. Instead of telling her what was going on and explaining how the text message came to be sent from Copenhagen they began to question her about Jack's whereabouts and what she knew about his movements.

All she could tell them was that he was kidnapped on the 19th November and nothing more had been heard from him until the text message last night. Pam began to feel uneasy. It was if they suspected Jack of doing something wrong.

Eventually they took her back to the waiting room and she called Dan to tell him what had happened. Dan called London right away and an hour later he received some very worrying news. The bodies of Lars Jontvedt and Sandra Deschamps had been found in a luxury apartment in Copenhagen. The murder weapon was a jagged bottle and the murderer had left a bloody mess that was by all accounts a scene of depravity and mindless mutilation.

If it wasn't bad enough that their hopes of finding out how and why Lars came by the message from Jack the police say that the remains of the bottle have Jack's fingerprints on it. They have put two and two together and believe he was the murderer. The message to Pam undoubtedly came from Lars' phone and that was found at the scene with the outgoing message recorded on it.

Dan sat Nat down and told him what had happened. He was desperate to be with his mother but Dan had other ideas. He told Nat that they would hire a car for him and he was to continue down to Morocco and find out if Jack was still there. If he was then he could not be in two places at the same time and he would then be in the clear.

"We know he didn't do it so it's up to me to find out who did and keep our Jack in the clear. I'll drive straight to Copenhagen and get on the case."

"Why not fly there? You'll be there a lot quicker."

"Remember Nat, that's a special type of old car sitting out there. I want it with me."

Leaving Nat to pick up the hire car Dan set off for Denmark. He was passing Lyons northbound when he had a call from his contact in London.

"The scenes of crime guys in Copenhagen have turned up another set of prints at the murder scene. It was on the handle of the toilet cistern and on one of the sink taps. A partial set but it was good enough to get a hit on the Interpol computers. They belong to a 'Boris Mikoyan'. He apparently lives in Zurich and was arrested last year by the local police for GBH after a fight in a bar. It's the only record of any kind if you search under 'convictions' but if you search under 'narrative' you find that he is the son of a very powerful Armenian 'oligarch' and has seen the inside of many cells around Europe but somehow, and we can guess how, he never seems to be charged with an offence. Clearly a nasty piece of work who's well connected."

"Mikoyan? I can't say I have ever heard of him."

"No he is a very shy gentleman. There is a file a couple of inches thick on him but no one has ever managed to pin a single crime on him."

"What I can't figure is this curious triangle, Morocco, Zurich and Copenhagen. Where the hell does Jack fit into that little lot?"

"Might I suggest an interview with Mr Boris Mikoyan is in order?"

"Where the hell is he though? If the Danish police have his prints at the scene then you can bet your life they are after him. Let's see if they come up with anything, in the meantime I'm going to head east to Zurich, it's not too far out of the way but if he is at home I would love to have a quiet word with him."

"You can forget that idea Dan, my orders are to keep you out of the spotlight. You are meant to be under cover remember."

"OK, well keep me in the picture, I'm off." In the back of Dan's mind was the notion that, whether the establishment liked it or not, he would love to have a one to one with Mr Boris Mikoyan.

12.15 – Thursday 7th December, 2006
Zurich, Switzerland

One little known aspect of life in Switzerland is that the government publish a list of all number plates along with the name and address of the owner. If you know where to look you can find the owner by searching the internet.

Dan knew exactly where to look and in just a few minutes found the entry for Boris Levon Mikoyan. He apparently was the owner of a veritable fleet of flashy motors: two Ferraris, a Maserati, a McLaren, a Range Rover and an original Mini Cooper. The address for most was given as a condominium complex in the city but one stood out. The newest Ferrari was registered at an address in the mountain village of Les Diablerets, east of Lake Geneva.

He checked the route and the weather forecast. Given its location it was almost certainly a ski lodge and Dan was pleased he had the foresight to have winter tyres fitted when he arrived in Switzerland. The Swiss can be a bit funny about things like that. To be allowed up in the mountains in the middle of winter they are a legally required essential. The blessing was that snow had so far been a rare visitor to the Alps so the roads were passable without difficulty.

The feeling he had in his water was that he would find a character like Boris Mikoyan skulking in his mountain hideaway. Having committed a crime in Copenhagen hoping he had gotten clean away he would disappear from view until the dust settled. He looked at his watch. It was close to forty-eight hours since the murders so there was plenty of time for Mikoyan junior to get back to his ski lodge especially when you may have a superfast car at your disposal and the journey was almost entirely through Germany, a nation famous for its lack of speed restrictions.

Les Diablerets was a three-hour drive away so with luck he could be there before dark.

16.15 – Thursday 7th December, 2006
Malaga Airport

Nat stood in the queue at the Avis car hire desk anxiously checking his watch. He had used his initiative and decided to fly to Malaga rather than take on another ten-hour drive down to Algeciras. By 8pm Nat was sitting in the restaurant of the Ceuta Parador and contemplating the tasty Moorish cuisine and a challenging day ahead. He had established that he did not need a visa and that he would be able to take his hire car across the frontier in the morning. It would be an intimidating journey to take on his own for he spoke little French and no Arabic. After dinner he went to the business centre to download and print out a photograph that he had of his dad on his mobile phone. In the morning he would drive to the farm in the hills to the south.

21.30 – Thursday 7th December, 2006
Rue La Coutaz, Les Diablerets, Switzerland

Dan drove slowly up the steep and windy road at the edge of the small resort town. The steep sided mountains stole away the tiny bit of starlight that offered some understanding of the severe terrain that dominated Les Diablerets. The ski lodge owned by Boris Mikoyan was at the end of a road that had taken Dan half an hour to find in the darkness. It was perched high above on a rocky ledge that only a Swiss builder would say was worthy of the toil involved to construct it. In fact, mused Dan, only a Swiss citizen could have afforded the sack of gold it must have cost to build. Along with extreme wealth comes the ability to buy a new homeland.

Dan approached the house slowly with lights out. There was no way of driving a car up to the front door. A small car park about fifty metres below served the house and there Dan found a Ferrari with plates that matched a car listed in the register under the name 'Mikoyan'. He believed he had found his man. Parking his car well away from the Ferrari he went to the boot of his car and removed a tin of Red Bull from the overnight bag in the boot and rolled it under the rear of the sports car.

The last thing he took from the car was his pistol and silencer. Making his way up the rocky terrain by the light of a moon was tricky but he needed to find out who was in the house.

From a vantage point above the rear of the lodge he could see right into the living area. There appeared to be one person sat in a lounger watching something on T.V. The man was drinking from a glass that was rested on a small table when not actually in hand.

After an hour of careful observation it became clear that the man was alone. Dan made his move.

He climbed down and around to the front of the lodge where a sizeable balcony provided a relatively easy access. Having reached the balcony he was able to stand to one side of the large sliding windows and assess his next step. When he saw the man disappear towards the kitchen he tried the door, it moved easily and he stepped inside. Holding the pistol in his right hand and leaning into the room he peered around the corner, looking for his prey.

Boris was waiting. He was a street fighter whose father forced him to fight for survival on the streets and in the bars of a homeland that wasn't famous for its charity. He carried the tools of a street fighter and aimed a blow at Dan's head with a wicked brass knuckle-duster. Dan wasn't quite quick enough to sidestep the incoming brain-masher and the glancing blow made him stagger off into the centre of the room, his pistol clattering on the pinewood floor. Boris was in pursuit, looking to finish him off.

Dan fell back on an old trick he learnt as a young copper, "He's in here," he yelled, as if there was an accomplice outside. Boris looked at Dan's pistol, now lying where it fell. Dan saw him eying the gun. He could almost see the thought process going on in Boris's head, 'can I get to the gun before him?' He must have decided it was too risky for he took off at run and scampered down the steps to his shiny red Ferrari.

Boris was not such an easy mark as Dan had thought. His network of security cameras were so well hidden that Dan did not see any of them in the darkness. The motion sensors had alerted Boris to Dan's approach but he did not know for sure that Dan was alone.

Boris made it down to the car park and was about to start his sports car when Dan appeared on the balcony nursing a headache the size of Africa. He could just see Boris getting into his car and quickly took his mobile phone and dialled a number.

There was a loud explosion from under the Ferrari. Boris leapt from the driver's seat and ran off down the hill towards the town. Dan followed and soon his superior fitness showed. With chest aching and gasping for air he fell on Boris like a panther and found him to be more exhausted than he was. He tied his hands with his own trouser belt and pushed him back up the hill to the house. The flames had consumed much of the side of the Ferrari and Dan's entire car. His precious 'special' had been sacrificed to capture Boris. The improvised explosive device that Dan planted under his car was activated by his phone call. The explosive charge was detonated by another handset attached to just fifty grams of C4 and stuffed into a tin can that to the casual observer looked like just another soft drink. Now Dan planned to find out why Mr Boris Mikoyan was involved with two murders that had implicated his old friend Jack Mawgan.

Dan tied Boris's limbs to the arms and legs of a heavy wooden 'carver' chair using an assortment of ties he had found in the closet. When Boris had recovered enough to be able to speak Dan began.

"Why did you murder those two in Copenhagen, Mr Mikoyan?"

"Fuck off."

"Now now, a little more cooperation would be appreciated and may even be rewarded. No cooperation will result in some pain, which option do you want?"

"I said fuck off."

Dan picked up his pistol and made a show of screwing the silencer on the end of the barrel. He moved the slide back and let the spring cock the weapon. Boris remained impassive, arrogant to the last. He knew that a slightest sign of fear and his enemy would have won.

To his surprise Dan bent down and removed Boris's shoe, then his sock. He took a velvet coloured cushion from a nearby sofa and placed it over Boris's naked foot. For the first time Boris began to show signs of nervous apprehension.

"What game are you playing, you want to wash my feet? Go ahead."

"No Mr Mikoyan, I have always wondered why we have five toes on each foot when maybe four would do just as well. Let's have an experiment shall we? I'll remove the little toe with my 9mm scalpel." He waved the pistol to emphasise the point. "The problem is I don't like the sight of blood so I'm going to aim through the cushion, I'm sure I'll hit the toe I'm aiming at ... probably." Dan took aim at the cushion and fired. The cushion leapt in the air and a flurry of feathers joined a plume of gun smoke filling the room with the curious and unpleasant aroma of burnt feathers and gunpowder. Boris yelped involuntarily and tried to peer down at his foot unaware where the bullet had gone. He knew that feeling no pain was no guarantee that he wasn't minus one toe. What Dan could see and Boris couldn't was the neat round hole in the floor beside the naked foot.

"Dear me, I missed, I had better try again. Let's see how many toes I can get with one bullet."

"They were witnesses, they had to go. My father was looking for them. There was an incident on the boat, a girl was killed. If my father found them they would tell all and my life would be hell."

"What girl, what boat, where does my friend Jack Mawgan fit into this?"

"The girl was just a girl. I don't know your friend. The only Englishman on board was Doctor Smith."

"Doctor Smith? 1 metre 85, 100 kilos, dark hair, blue eyes."

"Yes, sounds like him."

"Tell me all about Doctor Smith and this boat."

10.15 – Friday 8th December, 2006
The Moroccan Border with Ceuta

The concierge at the Parador was alarmed when he heard that Nat was planning to take a hire car to Morocco. He told him that if he parked somewhere where he could not see the car for more than five minutes he would return to find a shell with no wheels and every conceivable part that could be removed, gone. Instead he recommended hiring a car with an experienced driver who knew how to deal with local issues.

Nat was gullible enough to believe all that bullshit and so he found himself in the back of a reasonably intact and only slightly dented Mercedes of 80's vintage heading for the border.

There was a queue at the frontier post but Ahmed, the driver, drove down the side of the queue and imposed himself upon the Spanish guard who was not the slightest bit interested in seeing the papers of someone foolish enough to leave the safety and security of this small island of Europe in North Africa. The hooting and shouts from the others in the queue were meaningless as Ahmed paid the border guards to give him free passage. Perhaps dents that adorned the side of the Merc were a tribute to the regular use of this bully-boy tactic.

The Moroccan guards were more punctilious and checked his papers and the car's papers and lastly Nat's passport.

"Business or pleasure?" the customs officer asked in a thick accent.

"Pleasure," said Nat instinctively, believing, correctly, that to answer 'business' would bring forth more questions, some of which he may not have been able to answer.

They were waved on and in a cloud of dust and black diesel smoke the Merc shot forward and headed for the town of Fnideq.

At first the road followed the coast then Ahmed took a rougher road west into the hills. The mercurial Ahmed was relying a little too much on Allah's good offices for their survival as far as Nat was concerned. The rough track and lack of any kind of shock absorber function on the suspension made for an exciting, if at times unpredictable, progress. He occasionally caught sight of a sign saying 'Mzala' and checked his notes. That was the place where the Farm was located. The docket found in the truck referred to the farm as 'Mzala Market Gardens'.

He thought carefully about what might lay ahead. He was by trade a scientist, a student of Arctic Wildlife. He was no detective but he had inherited many of the analytical thought processes that had made his father one of the best detectives in the country.

If his father had been brought to this place against his will then the chances were that if he was at the farm then he would be a prisoner. He could not expect a straight answer from the people in charge of the farm for they could not be expected to admit Jack's presence as some kind of slave labourer. No, he needed to find someone lower down the food chain who might be expected to be more communicative. Jack's fellow workers for example.

Arriving at the entrance marker to the town of Mzala Jack told Ahmed to head for the nearest café. They dawdled through town with the smell of hot engine oil percolating through the open car windows. Engines must live a tough life out here guessed Nat. He hoped that Ahmed's Mercedes would last the day.

Once installed in the café, he told Ahmed to order any food and drink he needed on his bill but not to leave until he got back. He took his rucksack and set off in the most likely direction, looking for a farm. The surrounding hills were all supporting cultivation of one sort or another but he could just make out what looked like a complex of poly tunnels off to the northwest.

As he approached the stone walled entrance to the loading area associated with the poly tunnel complex he saw a weathered sign that declared it to be the Mzala Market Garden Company.

It was not the kind of place that used sentries or guards of any kind but there were plenty of people engaged in all manner of tasks related to what looked like a tomato, pepper, aubergine and courgette growing business. Forklift trucks darted here and there loading trucks. Some had Spanish plates, some with French. The trailers were all forty tonnes and Nat guessed they were headed across the water and into Europe. From what he could see in Ceuta precious few trucks took that route so those he was watching at that moment would probably be routing to Algeciras via Tangier.

He set about walking the perimeter of the farm and soon found himself on the hillside looking down on the entire complex. He took a pair of binoculars from his bag and studied the layout and the movement of personnel.

After twenty minutes observing he realised that there was a comparatively static element in the workforce who were involved with picking. These all seemed to be exclusively black, immigrants Nat guessed, some of whom he thought would speak some English.

He made the decision to try his luck and walked down the hillside, vaulted the small stone wall with ease and approached the first poly tunnel.

There were three guys working in there picking peppers. Nat walked up to the first one and asked in English, "Can you help me, have you seen this man?"

The worker was quite taken aback at being accosted by a white man and apprehensive he may be seen slacking by the overseer. He clearly understood what Nat had asked and instantly stuck his hand with the palm flat out whilst simultaneously taking a long hard look at the picture Nat was showing him.

Nat took the hint and fished around in his pocket for some of the local currency he had purchased in Ceuta the night before. He gave the man a few Dirhams and he seemed satisfied enough and burst into unfathomable pigeon English. The only words he could catch seemed to indicate that Jack had left the farm. Something dramatic had happened and Jack had left. The man kept pointing towards the end of the tunnel where the yard office was located.

It was time to take a chance and Nat set off for the offices determined to find out what dramatic event had occurred. From the hand signals the man used to describe the incident someone had been crushed by a forklift. Needless to say Nat feared the worst.

The burly man that suddenly emerged from the office carried a large stick and walked with a limp. He whacked a passing black worker with the cane and berated him in a language he did not understand. He saw Nat and yelled at him too. Nat froze for a moment then in his schoolboy Spanish he said, "Habla Inglesi."

"No, I don't speak de fuckin English," he replied in perplexing clarity. They stared at each other for a moment then Nat stole the initiative by thrusting Jack's picture under his nose.

"Do you recognise this man? He is my father. I am trying to find him."

"This man saved my life but I don't know where he is now. He left with my boss and was send away as crewman on a boat."

"On a boat? What boat?"

"I don't know. My boss, he supplies these rich bastards who have big boats with medical persons."

"But I thought your boss is a farmer."

"Yes, farmer too, but he is doctor in Fnideq and has office in Tangier also."

"You don't know what boat?"

"No. but it would have been in Tangier, that's where the big boats come for supplies."

"When did it leave?"

"He left here the day of my accident. That was twelve days ago."

Twelve days, hell, a boat can go a long way in twelve days. "Thank you very much, I'm very grateful."

"If you find your father tell him Allah was kind to send him to me, I too am grateful."

Nat waved a farewell and set off back to the Mercedes and was already planning his next move … to Tangier

10.30 – Friday 8th December, 2006
At Sea, La Reine Bleu, Off The Coast of Cyprus

Captain Dellamorte checked his watch, the message from the agents in Paphos said that the helicopter left on schedule at 09.00. It would be another thirty minutes before he would need to turn into the gentle, and thankfully warm, southerly breeze and prepare to receive the important guests. It was unfortunate that when the wind comes out of the Sahara it brings with it a fine dust that reduces the visibility and makes it difficult for the helicopter pilot to see the ship.

Dellamorte heard the helicopter pilot come up on Channel 16. He picked up the hand mike and responded to Marko's call.

"Roger Alpha Mike we are three miles south west of Point Alpha, turning on to flying course one nine zero."

Point Alpha was the original planned rendezvous point and its use avoided the unnecessary transmissions of their position. Aram Mikoyan did not get to be rich and powerful by underestimating his enemies. The helicopter had departed Paphos heading west and then descended below radar before setting course for Point Alpha.

"Relative wind is red three zero, pitch plus and minus one, roll plus and minus zero point five. You are cleared to land."

Marko responded and set the helicopter on an approach path to the port quarter of the magnificent vessel. Marko's instructions were to show off the ship to his guests by flying slowly past on the port side then come in for a landing.

As he flew beside the ship Marko could hear his two guests oohing and aahing in the rear cabin. Needless to say they were mightily impressed at the sight of this beautiful and luxurious expression of one man's wealth.

Marko finally arrived in a stable hover beside the helideck and assessed the ship's movement before sliding neatly across to the landing area and putting the machine down in exactly the right spot. The helideck crew responded to Marko's signal and ran in under the rotor disc to attach the tie-downs.

With all secure the engines were cut and the rotors coasted to a gentle whirl before the rotor brake brought them to sudden stop. Doors were opened and Captain Dellamorte arrived to greet his guests.

From the rear of the machine stepped a very attractive young lady followed by a gentleman in his early forties. Both were dressed for the holidays rather than for business and both wore broad smiles.

They were led below to meet their host. The time would soon come to deal with important matters, issues for which this voyage had been specifically organised to address.

10.45 – Friday 8th December, 2006
Tangier Harbour, Capitan de Puerto

Nat was lucky enough to find a Capitan de Puerto with not only passable English but also a sense of humour. Asking the man who runs the entire port complex which boats were likely to have sailed away with his father aboard drew a hearty laugh. Nat was fortunate not to be hurled out of the office door with a boot print on his backside. Instead the Capitan thought the earnest young man was worthy of a chance to explain why he would ask such a ridiculous question.

Nat left Tangier armed with some useful information about the vessels that left port around the 27th and 28th of November. He was en route to Ceuta to collect his hire car and would then drive to the nearest international airport, Malaga. Ahmed's driving had not improved any but Nat had adjusted to the heave and sway of the Merc on the well-worn highway to Ceuta. He called Dan.

"Hi Nat, what can I do for you?"

"Where are you?"

"I'm at Montreux Police HQ."

"Montreux, as in Montreux Switzerland?"

"Correct."

"What are you doing there, don't tell me you were caught speeding?"

"No, but I have just delivered a 22 carat arsehole to the local cops and he is singing like a canary. He's coughed to manslaughter and by the sound of things has crossed swords with your old man."

"What? Explain."

"Patience, where are you?"

"I left Tangier half an hour ago and am now en route to Ceuta."

"Where?"

"Ceuta, remember, it's the Spanish enclave in North Africa, across the water from Gibraltar."

"Oh yes, that Ceuta. Obviously there's a lot we need to tell each other and that will best be done face to face. My prisoner tells me that Jack is on a boat and all things being equal is not going to be getting ashore any time soon. I'm heading back to my people in London, there are things they need to know. I'll meet you there."

"London, where in London?"

"Take a train to Marble Arch and then text me."

"What about Mum?"

"She's in the picture and will meet us in London once I've had a chance to catch up with my colleagues."

"OK, see you later."

"Stay safe, bye for now."

CHAPTER 16

- -

19.00 – Friday 8th December, 2006
At Sea, La Reine Bleu, The Levantine Sea

THE PROTOCOL WHEN ARRIVING on board La Reine for the first time
was for guests to acclimatize at their leisure after their arrival, get their
sea legs, enjoy the indoor swimming pool, the spa, sauna, steam room and
gymnasium. There would be ample time for them prepare for a black tie
dinner with the host and other guests.

When Prime Minister Toby Stewart received the invitation to attend
these clandestine meetings it was obvious that he could not attend in
person. Instead it was expected that he would send his close friend and
personal financial advisor, Louis Granger, as well as his spin-doctor Freddie
McLaren. They were his co-conspirators in what they jointly referred to as
their 'Pension Protection Fund'.

Freddie's Machiavellian machinations contrived to arrange for Louis
to be sent on another errand at a banker's conference in Iceland. What he
planned to achieve in the next two days needed absolute secrecy for he had
in mind a coup that would ensure his retirement from the world of politics
would be well funded; very well funded indeed.

The invitation was for two so there was no reason he could see why he
should not take the opportunity to show off and bring along his current
girlfriend, Ariadne Cooper-Smythe. It was a pity he didn't realise just how
much this would annoy his host. Decorous as the lady may be this was one
occasion when such diversions were not welcome. The focus of the nautical
get-together was money. Distractions of any kind were unwelcome.

So as not to sour the important conversations planned for the days ahead Aram asked the Captain to visit the guest's suite and explain that it would be much appreciated if Ariadne would, after dinner, accept an invitation to the Spa where Sonja and Maria would be pleased to demonstrate their skills. This was agreed and arrangements were made for Maria to collect her after dinner. Misogyny was definitely the order of the day given the current guest list so the lady had better like it as there were no alternatives on the menu.

19.00 – Friday 8th December, 2006
NSS HQ, Buckinghamshire

Sir William Salisbury sat down at his desk, picked up the memo and read it through one more time.

"When did you get this?" he asked.

Damien Porter, his Director of Operations stood nervously on the other side of the desk awaiting what must surely be a good bollocking.

"We had a heads-up from our lawyers in Geneva. They were summoned to represent Aram Mikoyan's son, Boris, at a hearing in Montreux this morning. His client made a statement that referred to an Englishman called Daniel Barclay who was behind his arrest."

"That name rings a bell."

"It should, he's a black ops specialist for 'five' but has also been involved with some notable operations for 'six'.

"Yes, I remember now, he was one of those who brought about the demise of Willy Chaloner and that French Legionnaire he lived with."

"Well our Mr Barclay wasn't in Switzerland on a skiing holiday. Our man in 'five' came across that memo and managed to get us a copy."

"According to this," he stabbed a finger at the memo, "Barclay was chasing down our mister Mikoyan junior because he was implicated in a murder in Copenhagen and that another suspect in the case is Jack Mawgan. Now tell me if I am wrong but I gave orders for him to be shipped off to Africa. What the hell is he doing in fucking Copenhagen?"

"Actually Sir William we don't think he was in Copenhagen. We think it must be a mix up. The murder weapon had his fingerprints on it but it seems that this was left at the scene by the real murderer. He was definitely shipped off to Africa but Barclay is busy trying to track him down. Maybe we should have just terminated him and buried him with the others."

The implied criticism of Sir William's decision to teach Jack a lesson rather than kill him and dispose of his body was greeted by a look of distain delivered with a scowl.

"If we start taking out the real government agents, even the ones working for them unofficially, then we will start a war that in the long run can only hurt us. We need to work in the shadows and not, repeat not, attract undue attention. Murdering a man who has friends in important places would make us the number one priority instead of an irritation."

"Yes sir."

"The problem we now face is to find our Mr Mawgan. It may be appropriate to end his exile, one way or another. If someone else takes the blame for his death then I can't think of an organisation more appropriate than the evil empire run by Aram Mikoyan. He makes the Mafia look like Magic Roundabout."

"I'll get on to it right away."

"This is a very sensitive time. Freddie McLaren is meeting with Mikoyan senior as we speak. He's negotiating a very big deal that will help ensure our financial position is strengthened."

"I suggest you go back to Boris's lawyers and try to find out why Mawgan is supposedly involved in the same murder. We may be able to turn the situation to our advantage."

"I'm on it."

"Please tell Wilkinson I'll be a little late for dinner this evening, I have to make one or two important calls."

Damien left his boss to get on with his telephone calls and he thanked his lucky stars that his boss didn't blame him for the apparent reappearance of Mr Mawgan.

19.30 – Friday 8th December, 2006
MI5 HQ, London

Justin Wood and his boss, Sir Richard Shakespeare were standing around a table covered in papers and maps. Sir Richard's Saville Row sartorial elegance set him apart from Justin whose somewhat 'Saturday afternoon' approach to office attire helped him to appear more relaxed in the workplace. They poured over the material with their MI6 counterparts, Dame Alice Montgomery and her Deputy Geoffrey Miller. Both were dressed for their role as guardians of the nation's foreign affairs in dark blue suits that were probably selected from the 'his and hers' MI6 uniform catalogue. Justin pointed to one report written by Barclay just eight hours ago.

"Can I assume that we have all read this report by now?" There were nods of assent. "By the look of it Barclay was hot on the trail of his former colleague Jack Mawgan and on his way to Morocco on the basis of information received from the truck driver responsible for taking him down that way. Mawgan's son Nathan is apparently working with him now. The curved ball we received this morning is that suddenly, out of the blue, the Danish Police are after Mawgan for a gruesome murder in Copenhagen. Either Mawgan is a man able to be in two places at once or we are missing something."

It was Dame Alice who continued the analysis.

"Barclay's report says young Nathan discovered that his father was taken away from Tangier on board a ship on or around the 28th November but he was unable to say exactly which ship."

Miller continued on the same theme, "Don't forget that the trail to the boat began at this farm where Mawgan appears to have been taken as some kind of forced labourer."

"Geoffrey, can we use our connections in Morocco to find out more about this farm?" asked Alice, "it seems a hell of a leap from farm to ship, maybe there is a connection but for the life of me I can't see it. I'm sure that if he can be a slave on a farm then he can no doubt be a 'pressed man' on a ship. The puzzling thing is how did he engineer such a change of career or was it changed for him?"

Sir Richard had remained quiet during this dialogue but now he spoke. He had moved to the window and was peering at the lights of the slow moving London traffic as it fought to escape the surly bonds of the capitals overcrowded road system. The gravity of his contribution was apparent in his tone.

"I believe it is time I shared a little secret with you all." Suddenly the atmosphere changed. Secrets are the stock-in-trade in the world of the spooks but secrets within the intelligence community are those that are likely to matter the most. Returning to the small group, now in rapt attention, he began his explanation.

"I must tell you that we have an on-going operation on board a vessel in the Mediterranean. The name that would appear to join all the events we have been discussing this evening together is, I believe, 'Mikoyan', 'Aram Mikoyan'."

"What are you saying Richard? If you are involved in an operation in the Med then why wasn't I told about it? I believe we are supposed to have an accord…" Sir Richard held up his hand to halt Dame Alice's increasingly irate tirade.

"I know, I know, please allow me to explain. This is an extraordinary operation and one that had to be conducted in the utmost secrecy. It is fair to say that Justin and I, and the agent concerned, are the only people on earth that are aware of its purpose and its importance to our nation's credibility in the world."

"This had better be good, Richard."

"I'll leave you to judge but you, both of you, must understand that if the fact that we ran an operation against our own executive was ever to get out then we would never enjoy their trust again."

"Good God, what are you saying?"

"I'm saying that we have reason to do what we are doing. A very good reason indeed."

"Well what is it that you are doing. What's so important?"

"Right now Freddie McLaren, the PM's attack dog and erstwhile Press Officer, is meeting with a number of European businessmen on board a palatial yacht belonging to one of the world's most successful financial gurus, the aforementioned Aram Mikoyan. One of the things that ties together these events …" he pointed to the reports lying on the desk, "would appear to be his ship, 'La Reine Bleu'."

"You will have to explain Richard, is this man Mawgan your agent on this gin palace you refer to."

"La Reine is a bit more than a gin palace, Alice. At nearly three thousand tonnes it's bigger than one of our frigates … and no, mister Mawgan, if he is on board this ship, and from what we know he may well be, then he is not there on our behalf."

154

"But you do have an agent on board?"

"Of course but I am not at liberty to reveal their identity, at least not until I know they are safe."

Justin came up with an observation that caused them all to pause and re-evaluate the situation.

"If by some remote possibility mister Mawgan is on the same ship then he has brought the whole subject to a head and forced our hand somewhat."

"Why do you think that?" asked Miller.

"I would say the chances are that our agent is on borrowed time. Jack has the nose of a veritable bloodhound and can smell a 'wrong-un' a mile off."

"If they are both working for 'five' then what's the problem?"

"Jack Mawgan is not working for us, you could say that he's there by accident and not be far from the truth," Justin reminded them. "Jack is a detective though, and a good one, a copper through and through and if I am right he will not know when to leave well alone. He told Barclay that he had established that the recent death of Baroness Parker wasn't suicide but murder. What is more the murderers appear to be agents of the state. Or at least agents of the executive. He was pursuing that line of enquiry when he was 'disappeared' by persons unknown."

"And the elephant in the room is...?" Alice was treading on toes but they all knew what she was on about.

"The 'Men in Black'?" she added.

The top men and women in the SIS had awarded this unofficial sobriquet to the agents of the executive who worked as the Prime Minister's personal version of the Security Services.

"Looks like it," said Justin.

"You really must do something about them, Richard, we can't go on like this."

"I'm doing just that, Alice. This bloody operation in the Med is about killing off a major source of funding that is being used by the executive to finance not only the so-called 'Men in Black' but a lot of other nefarious activities besides."

"Tell us more," demanded Alice, "where does Mikoyan fit into our domestic politics for God's sake?"

"Mikoyan is an intermediary. He arranges 'deals' then collects commission payments from each party and shares the proceeds with the top men involved then hides the proceeds away in banks that, well, let's just say they are at the opposite end of the banking spectrum from your high street variety."

"Explain Richard, I still don't get it. What are you up to?" she added in a tone that conveyed her loss of patience.

"We have information that indicates that members of the PM's so called 'kitchen cabinet' have been manipulating government policy to favour certain suppliers of equipment and consultancy services. Mikoyan arranges corrupt 'deals' with the big players behind the scenes. He has such a well-developed chain of bankers all around the world that he can handle the kick-backs on their behalf but keep all the details away from prying eyes. That way all parties appear to have clean hands. He can hide fortunes in one part of the world then make them reappear in another. He's a genius and probably the best there is at that game."

"So where is his ship now, and what is McLaren doing on board it?"

"It is off the coast of Cyprus. McLaren flew to Paphos in a private Jet and was taken offshore by Mikoyan's helicopter. We believe he is meeting executives from Italy. They are negotiating a deal with the government to become the sole suppliers of all public service helicopters in the UK, Police, Air Ambulance and some Search and Rescue operations too."

"Isn't that against the European regulations? Don't they have to go through a tendering process?"

"Alice, please, look around you. The European rules may be followed by some but many members of the EU just ignore those that are inconvenient. Have you ever seen an Italian police car that wasn't made in Italy, a French police car not made in France? Only the muggins Brits play the game and the rest of Europe rams the bat up our arse."

"So what does your agent hope to do?"

"Our agent will collect evidence via a variety of bugging devices. The plan is to place them in strategic locations around the vessel."

"What will you do with the evidence?"

"Well McLaren is really a bit-part player, we are after the top man."

"The PM?"

"Exactly."

"What then? How on earth do you plan to use this evidence when you have it? If you go public it will probably cause a run on the pound, a collapse in confidence and the market will go down the toilet."

"I don't believe we need to go public but we do need the executive to clean house and everyone at the top needs to go."

"You could only do that if you forced the PM to call a general election."

"True but we can control that don't worry. We have enough dirt on the major players to ensure that a different shade of government takes over."

"And then you get more of the same, they're all made from the same mould, you know that."

"Well we can only do our best but don't forget that all the while we have been collecting information on members of Her Majesty's Honourable Opposition so if necessary we will take them to task too."

"Supposing they don't want to play the game?" asked Geoffrey Miller.

Sir Richard decided that it was time to sit and discuss the situation properly and moved behind his capacious mahogany desk and waved his guests into the buttoned leather chairs arranged in a semi-circle in front of him. "They, our esteemed executive, may need to be taught a lesson."

"Oh yes?" said Dame Alice, in sceptical tone, "and how do we do that?"

"They are not the only ones to have people that know their way around the banking system. GCHQ has the capability to do anything they can do only we have never before had to use it in an aggressive way. We have the means, should we so wish, to wash away all trace of every bank account and every credit card these people, and their families and if necessary, their friends, have ever had. They could wake up one day and find all their ill-gotten gains have evaporated."

"But we need evidence," Justin added, "the courts will back us if we have the evidence but we must be careful for there are bad eggs in the judiciary too."

"Are you in touch with your man on the ship? Can you warn him about Mawgan? You can't afford for the operation to be compromised by accident can you. Better that both parties are aware of each other's presence. Mawgan may be able to offer your man some help." Sir Richard and Justin exchanged a look that betrayed their own concern.

Justin responded, "We are not certain about communications. All visitors to the ship are required to hand in their cell phones and any radio devices they carry. Mikoyan is very sensitive about his security and guards his communications integrity closely. He even has sensors that can detect anyone trying to communicate by SMS, or by cell phone. He doesn't treat breaches of security lightly for by controlling who can say what to whom during the deal-making process he can ensure a fair outcome. At least that's how he sees it. No outsiders can interfere with the negotiations."

"So no way of contacting your man?"

"I didn't say that. I am hoping that a satcom device is amongst the equipment we have successfully smuggled on board. We have yet to receive any messages from our agent to confirm that comms have been established."

"What on earth do you imagine you will be able to record that could make the difference. Can't we do something positive with evidence gained on home soil?"

"Maybe we could but to make our plan complete we need to collect some vital data concerning Mikoyan's modus operandi. He has some contacts we have yet to track down. We need them to complete the picture, then we can move. We were handed this opportunity at very short notice and we want to turn it to our advantage if that's possible."

Dame Alice left her seat and touched her deputy lightly on the shoulder, he followed as she moved to the opposite end of Sir Richard's office and they spoke together in hushed tones.

"Geoffrey I'm not sure I can believe what's happening here and whether we should be part of it or not."

"Well ma'am, we have spoken together at length about the rumours surrounding these so called 'Men in Black' but we have not yet seen the same hard evidence that 'Five' say they have."

"But it sounds like they have been trying to get to grips with them for some time, why didn't Richard tell us about what he was doing?"

"Who do you trust? When the executive have a different agenda to the one they display in public their supporters behind the scenes could be almost anyone in Whitehall, even us."

"Surely not." Dame Alice was amazed that anyone would imagine that the head of MI6 could not be trusted. With a moment's thought she had to consider that her world was one where trust was something ephemeral. She turned back to her deputy, "The bloody politicians always have other agendas, truth is a surely a stranger in these parts. What worries me most is the way the executive are indulging in activities that smack of the kind of blatant money grabbing that's more in line with what goes on in Africa, South America or Russia. It's as if they are so sure that they have such a firm grasp on the levers of power that they are beyond the reach of Parliament, beyond the reach of the law."

"If Baroness Parker was indeed murdered by these people then we are not dealing with the faint hearted. If they are prepared to kill anyone who gets in their way then we are getting too close to those nations that are run by a powerful elite that consider themselves to be almost untouchable"

"The so called 'elite' may want to believe that they are untouchable but we have to demonstrate that they cannot get away with it. I suggest we give 'Five' our support and see what we can do to make the operation in the Med a success." They returned to Sir Richard's desk where a map of the Med was spread across it. They were interrupted by a text message on Justin's cell phone.

"We've just had our first satcom message from our agent on the ship. We've pinned her location down to this position here." He pointed to a spot on the map, south of Paphos, a port on the island of Cyprus.

"What do you need from us to make this work Richard? We need to work together on this."

21.30 – Friday 8th December, 2006
At Sea, La Reine Bleu, The Levantine Sea

Jack was taking the night air on the sun deck when he came across a beautiful woman wearing a long black evening dress. She appeared to be sending a text message from a small handset.

"That looks suspiciously like a cell phone."

The woman was startled by his sudden appearance and her guilty look told a story. Who was she, why was she there and what was she doing with a cell phone when they were many miles from shore. They were too far for any phone signal to be available.

"Oh! Who are you? You startled me." She looked at the device clearly visible in her hand and slipped it into the elegant little purse dangling from her wrist.

"No signal here."

"No, we are a long way from land I would guess. You know that cell phones are forbidden on board?"

"Really?"

"Maybe I should introduce myself, Doctor Smith, how do you do." They shook hands, her hand was cold, her grip positive but not overdone. "Please call me Jack."

"Ariadne Cooper-Smythe," They both smiled at each other. It could have been an awkward moment. The silence that followed was telling for it appeared that both were trying to deal with the sudden and unexpected arrival of a stranger who spoke English like a native.

"What are you doing here?" she said at last.

"I'm the ship's medic, they call me 'doctor' but really I'm just a paramedic."

"I must say you certainly look like a doctor but for some reason my antenna are telling me that you don't look like a 'Smith' to me."

"Yes, well it's easy to wear the clothes of a doctor ..." he gestured at his all-white outfit ... "but ..."

"Less easy to wear an alias?"

"What is it about us Brits adopting the handle 'Smith' whenever we want to hide our real identity?"

"Yes, a fascinating trait isn't it."

"You are one of Mr Mikoyan's guests?"

"Yes, but obviously I have been deemed to be surplus to requirements and invited to amuse myself after dinner and banned from the important discussions the men are planning."

"You are with the gentleman who arrived by helicopter earlier today?"

"Yes, Freddie, Freddie McLaren."

"He must be an important man, are you married to him?"

"No, I mean yes, he is an important man but no, I'm not his wife."

There was a pause whilst she removed a small silver cigarette case from her purse, took out a cigarette and lit it.

"He works for the Prime Minister, the British Prime Minister that is. I'm what he calls 'his regular squeeze', girlfriend."

"You don't sound too impressed with your boyfriend." She put the cigarette back to her lips and moved to the railing. The breeze ruffled her auburn hair, neatly piled upon her head in an attractive formal style. She put her hand up to the back of her neck and fiddled with the clips that held the bun in place then shook her head until her hair tumbled down around her shoulders. When she next looked up Jack saw a beautiful woman with dark locks flowing in the light breeze and standing defiantly against the starlit night. The sight would raise the blood pressure of any man and Jack was no exception.

Jack had unconsciously suppressed his sex drive ever since he had been abducted but now he was forced to ignore the stirrings in his loins and think about what was happening here. This was a mature and confident woman and he had caught her with a communication device that she knew she shouldn't have. That meant that she was clever, had come prepared and had a sophisticated way of hiding what he guessed was a satellite communicator. Anyone with that kind of equipment and that degree of training was either a government agent or an enemy agent. The question facing Jack was which was she, friend or foe? Something about her lack of respect for her boyfriend led Jack to think that she was probably a friend. He didn't know if that was a conclusion that he wanted or one that he could justify. Either way the dye was cast, he wanted off that ship, he wanted to be home. He would break the ice and tell her his story.

"Ariadne, may I call you that?" She smiled, then tossed the remains of her cigarette over the side in a shower of sparks.

"Of course."

"I am not what I appear to be either." She raised her eyebrows in a kind of mocking way that said 'you don't say'.

"Are you implying that I may not be what I appear to be?" He ignored her question and continued with his revelations.

"Well, I am at least a paramedic but I am not here of my free will. I was kidnapped in the UK and shipped out to Morocco in the back of a truck. There I worked on a farm as a virtual slave. Then I was assigned to this ship as the medical officer but I am not free to do as I please and I have been unable to inform my family that I am alive and well. I am hoping that you might help me."

"What on earth makes you think that I can do anything to help?"

"My guess is that you are SIS."

"What do you mean? How did you come up with that wild idea?"

"Ordinary folk don't have the knowhow to smuggle a satcom device on board in the way you have. Ordinary folk don't need satcom devices when they are fully aware that to be found with one could compromise what must be an important meeting with Mr Mikoyan. Ordinary folk wouldn't know where to buy such equipment let alone know how to use it."

"So what?"

"So you are either working covertly as an operative for your boyfriend or for some other agency. My guess is the latter."

"Huh, you think I am some kind of Mata Hari?" It was said with just a little too much venom and Jack knew he had her bang to rights.

"My guess is MI5, they would be dealing with persons involved with the UK government and besides, I had the previous model of that communicator when I worked for them a while back."

"What?"

"Yes I was once a policemen but I have worked for 'Five' on and off."

"But you said you are a paramedic."

"It's a long story."

"How can I trust you?"

"Simple, send a message to your handler and ask him for a profile on Jack Mawgan."

"Mawgan! You're Jack Mawgan?"

"Yes, Jack Mawgan, from Cornwall."

"Hell I know the name. Freddie mentioned it when he made a call from the car on the way to the airport."

"Well there you go, my case must be rattling around the corridors of number ten. Fame at last."

"There's only one problem Jack."

"What's that?"

"Our host runs a tight ship, he's got a jamming system on the bridge that prevents any normal radio signals leaving the vessel. We seem to be able to get signals out courtesy of the frequency hopping circuits but they don't work on incoming signals. I can tell them you are here but I can't receive any instructions or sitreps."

"Well at least do that. Prepared is forearmed." She took the device from her purse and began to input a message. When the 'send' button was pushed a red LED came on then turned to green. She turned to Jack

"Well at least they will know that there are two of us here."

"Why are you here?"

"Pardon?"

"Why are you here, what's your mission? You must be here for a reason. Smuggling a satcom device on board means you need to communicate. If this was a social visit I hardly think you would need to take the risk."

"You're right. I'm here to collect data on Mikoyan. We think that McLaren, my 'boyfriend', is on the take and Mikoyan is behind the deal to buy helicopters from Italy. McLaren is meeting them now. The people from Italy were already on board but you probably knew that already."

"Yes they came on board with Mr Mikoyan when we were off Malta. They've been in a huddle ever since I gather."

"I've managed to attach a flash-memory bug under the table to record what they say. I wasn't privileged to be equipped with a penis so I didn't get to attend the meeting."

"Said with feeling."

She walked towards the door leading to the upper lounge. "Coffee?"

"I'm not allowed to fraternise with the guests I'm afraid." Ariadne gave Jack the look and said, "Pity, I could do with a bit of fraternising, all I've got to look forward to is a night fighting off Handy Andy."

"You mean Handy Freddie." They both laughed.

"Business calls Jack, I have to get within Bluetooth range of the bug and download the story-so-far. If the jammer covers the Bluetooth frequencies then I'm not likely to have much luck."

"And then?"

"If I get something worthwhile then I'll send it off to London." She patted the purse.

"Thank God for technology," said Jack.

"Yes, let's thank her too."

The quip wasn't lost on Jack who set off back to his surgery with a spring in his step and the comforting knowledge that he was no longer alone.

Meanwhile – In the Main Dining Room

Mr Mikoyan sat in between the Italians and the Englishman at a round table that had just one vacant space previously occupied by Ariadne. The small talk was fading in line with the length of the after dinner cigars. Eventually the subject turned to money and Aram set out his plans.

"In these circumstances I have decided that we need to make as much of these arrangements invisible as possible. To that end I propose that the headlines of the deal are known to the main board but the funds we hold in reserve in special accounts that are, let's say 'off balance sheet' are used to furnish our English friends with their 'commissions'. That way you can openly discuss the headline figures but keep the under-the-table payments out of sight."

"That sounds fine," said the Head of Malmeccanica, "how much do we have in our 'reserve fund'?"

Aram picked up a folder and studied the papers. He wrote a message down on a notepad and passed it across to him. It said 'at the moment you have a total of $2.5 billion on deposit and earning around 8%.' There was no need for Freddie to know how much the Italians had in their 'slush fund' but if he ever found out he would be stunned. People pay bribes to officials in order to get them to buy their products. These normally take the form of 'commission' payments or agent's fees, often routed through accounts belonging to friends or family or, as in this case, hidden from view in banks with a different code of ethics.

Of course the price of the goods is inflated to allow for a double payment. One set of 'commissions' goes to the agent and the other goes in the company slush fund from which individuals can dip in and out like the proverbial pigs dipping their snouts in the trough. The ebb and flow of illegal cash payments in the 'black' banking system is amazing but it's one of the things that makes the world go round, like it or not.

Aram knew that his life was coming to an end and recently had surprised himself when he found solace in the Church. He met the Eparchy Assistant Bishop, His Excellency Mgr. Hovhannes Teyrouzian almost by accident and found him to have a great deal of simpatico. It was Aram's first experience of the church and its rituals and teachings. His father had apparently been a strict Catholic but Aram saw little benefit in cultivating the notion of heaven and found the worship of Mammon more satisfactory.

It wasn't long after this chance meeting that Aram became an avid student of Catholicism and had read about a catholic doctrine called 'purgatory', something he had not encountered before. He asked his priest about it for 'purgatory' was something that troubled him greatly. The Orthodox version of catholic doctrine excluded the teaching of purgatory but nevertheless Aram become obsessed with the possibility that death would not deliver release from past sins and given the vastness of his misdeeds he would be faced with unbearable torture after death.

It was long held by the western church that the time spent in purgatory, that period after death when all sorts of miseries are endured before the spirit's arrival in heaven, could be reduced by making certain payments to the church and by making restitution for past misdeeds. These payments bought 'indulgences' and they, together with 'restitutions', added to the possibility of a rapid transition to heaven. Aram struggled with the inner turmoil of a man who had come to realise that he had led an evil life and the final judgment lay ahead.

Those thoughts invaded his consciousness at inopportune moments and now, in the middle of these negotiations he felt the need for a break. He wasn't feeling well and asked the steward to summon Jack.

CHAPTER 17

22.30 – Friday 8th December, 2006
At Sea, La Reine Bleu, The Levantine Sea

THE CAPTAIN STARED AT the radar screen and ordered a small change in course. The fishing boat one mile ahead wasn't showing any lights and he cursed the Cypriots who were often too lazy to turn on their navigation lights.

The night vision device showed a strange outline for a fishing boat but at that moment a message from below distracted the captain and he decided to go down to the dining room and find out what was happening. The steward had sent the message to the bridge to inform them that the owner had summoned the doctor. He needed to find out what was going on.

Jack had just received the message from the steward when the first sound of gunfire punctuated the calm on board. The rattle of a machine gun came from the stern area of the ship, then another. He grabbed his doctor's bag and as an afterthought, went to the drawer unit and removed the little Berretta from its hiding place and tucked it into his bag. The gunfire had him worried. Could this be the end? Who could be bold enough to attack a ship the size of La Reine. He decided to take the hidden passport too and shoved it in his trouser pocket. He looked in the mirror. His attempt to grow a goatee beard was quite a success and he wondered what Pam would think of it. He hoped she would get the chance to comment. With a sense of foreboding he set off for the main dining room.

There was chaos with crewmen rushing here and there and the guests looking pale and worried. Two of Aram's bodyguards ran past carrying

AK47's. The First Officer was yelling orders to the crewman and ordered everyone else to return to their cabins until the order to attend their emergency stations was given.

"What's going on?" Jack heard a voice cry.

"Pirates, we're being attacked by pirates."

Jack found Aram in a state of collapse but totally with it and totally coherent. "Jack, so pleased you could come. Can you help me into that room over there?" He pointed at a door decorated with beautiful burr veneers. Helping Aram to his feet Jack took him to the door.

"We will stay in here Jack, we'll be safe here." They entered a room devoid of windows with cupboards and shelves on all four walls. It was about five metres square. When Jack closed the door he could see that it was solid steel and about two inches thick.

"This is the safe room Jack, please be sure to lock it." Jack threw the bolts into their locks with a loud clunk. It looked like it would take a good deal of explosive to open that particular door.

"We can hide in here and the world outside can go to hell – they can't get us." That's all very well so long as the ship doesn't sink, thought Jack. He was uncomfortable not knowing what was going on outside but he could tell from the intensity of the gunfire that the exchanges were not all one sided. The crew obviously had access to weapons and he thought to himself that he shouldn't be surprised by that. Aram Mikoyan must have made many enemies in his time.

"Jack, come here." Aram moved over to a couch set against the shelves on the wall opposite the entrance.

"What is it sir, are you feeling OK?"

"No I am not OK, actually I am dying but I have to do something before I go."

The rattle of gunfire and the sound of muffled explosions punctuated their conversation.

"What are you talking about?"

"Tell me Jack are you a good man?" Jack was stunned and speechless. "I can tell by your response that you *are* a good man. I think someone who was quick to answer that question would somehow worry me." Jack remained silent but nodded an acknowledgement.

"Well Jack you must listen whilst I tell you something very important."

"Go ahead sir."

"Jack I think you are good man so I am going to trust you. Fate has delivered you to me. It is an omen. I have met many bad men in my time and some bad women too. Some I would say could even be described as evil. I know when I meet a good man. It must be said that my own life is not without criticism for I have been at the heart of a system that is corrupt, has corrupted others and then perpetuates corruption amongst the political and business classes. Lately I have come to have many regrets and I have decided that I must …" he paused to take a breath, his strength seemed to be fading "… I must make some restitution."

"What do you mean … restitution?"

"I will make my peace with the church in my own way but you, Jack Mawgan, you can help me make peace with the secular world."

"How can I help you to do that?"

"Take this." Aram removed a gold ring from his right hand and passed it to Jack who took it and studied it.

"Inside you will see a number." Jack looked closely and sure enough a string of numbers was engraved on the inside.

"What do they mean?" A sudden explosion close by and the sound of ricocheting bullets caused the old man to become agitated.

"By themselves they mean nothing but you must go to my church on Menorca, Santa Maria, and you find my priest Father Pedro Guitierez. You ask him a question. He will be expecting someone to come and to ask this question one day." He stopped to take a breath and appeared to Jack to be in need of some oxygen. He bent forward to help and was waved away.

"What question should I ask?"

"When you are alone with Father Pedro you will ask '*can an old sinner go to heaven when he comes from the east?*' now repeat it for me."

Jack asked the question exactly as he had heard it.

"Now memorise it because if you get it wrong Father Pedro will just answer the question. If you get it right then he will give you the brother to that ring. It too will have numbers engraved on the inside. I do this to prevent my family and my friends and yes, my enemies from gaining access to my wealth." Jack sat stunned at what he was hearing.

"What do I do when I have the rings?"

"You must go to Italy, to a town called Arona on the shores of Lake

Maggiore. There you buy a return ticket to Locarno on the hydrofoil ferry. When you get to Locarno you go to the Credit Suisse Bank, it is near the harbour. You ask for the manager and you show him your return ferry ticket and you then give him the two rings. Don't do it the other way around or he will send you away. He will take you to the safe deposit box I have used for many years. In it you will find all you need to destroy all the evil men and women I have been involved with for the last forty years. To make sure that the world changes after my death I have made certain provisions to help whoever carries the rings. It is explained in the papers you find in the box. You Jack, you must make a difference. Do you understand?"

"Yes I understand, I go to Arona, get a return ticket to Locarno. I go to Locarno, to the Credit Suisse Bank and show the manager the ferry ticket and then I show him the two rings.

"Why all the cloak and dagger Mr Mikoyan why don't you just do what you need to do. You are a powerful man. I'm sure you could fix it, whatever it is."

"You are right Jack but you can imagine I have many enemies and my family are just a bunch of crooks who would stop at nothing to get my money. All will be revealed when you open that box. You must promise me that you will follow my instructions. I have made it hard for my enemies and my family to get at the money because I want to use it to do good things. This was to be my last big deal just to be sure that there would be enough."

"Enough? How much is enough for a man who owns all this?" Jack gestured at the La Reine Bleu. Aram chuckled and said, "Enough, yes, how much is enough. I won't need any of it where I am going Jack. Be sure to follow my instructions then you will be remembered as the man who destroyed many evil men and changed the world."

"What is in the deposit box?" Aram laughed a pathetic and sickly laugh then collapsed on the floor before Jack could catch him. Jack could tell the old man was dead. The hammering on the door of the safe room suddenly snapped him out of his dreamy state and back into reality. He looked at the ring and put it on his right hand on the wedding ring finger, it was too small, he moved it to his little finger and it fitted perfectly.

What lay waiting outside? If it were indeed pirates then he would probably be better off staying put. He looked around and checked the cupboards. There was plenty of food and water so staying holed up in the safe room looked like a good bet.

The commotion outside seemed to die down and soon there was no noise at all. The engines had stopped and then the main electrical system failed bringing on the emergency lighting and an eerie silence. A sudden huge explosion broke the peace. It reverberated through the whole ship. The room began to lean and Jack immediately dashed to the main door and unlocked it. He peered into the semi darkness and saw nothing. He dashed out on to the nearest weather deck as the ship tilted further beneath his feet. He set off back to his surgery to get some clothes. He was going to need something warmer if he had to abandon ship.

The ship was a mess, broken glass everywhere and bloodstains on the doors and floor but not a sign of anyone. Could they have abandoned ship already? He went to the deck below and checked the guest cabins. The first was empty, the second was occupied but only by the corpse of a small man in blood-stained dinner jacket. Jack found the same situation in the next cabin but in the large double cabin he found Ariadne and Freddie McLaren trussed up on the bed. They were both still alive.

The deck tilted alarmingly and Jack struggled to climb the now sloping deck to reach the two writhing figures. When he had untied Ariadne she went straight to her purse and began typing a message on her satcom device. Freddie was also freed and sat rubbing his wrists on the edge of the now precariously balanced bed.

"Come on, we have to go. She'll be over on her side in a few minutes."

"Where," said Freddie, "are we abandoning ship? Where are the lifeboats?"

"This way," said Jack, and they set off down the corridor like three runners making their way along the side of a mountain. They managed the stairs and made it to the helideck. The once shiny helicopter was hanging precariously from the last lashing as all the others appeared to have been cut. That was one expensive toy that would never fly again. Soon it would be heading for the bottom of the sea, along with the rest of La Reine Bleu … and if they didn't hurry the three of them would soon be in Davey Jones' Locker too.

Jack led them up to the sun deck where the ship's boats were located. He was surprised to find them all in their place, firmly lashed to the deck and little chance of being used for their escape. The listing was now so severe that they could not launch them. For a moment Jack was confused by the fact that there was no sign that the crew had made use of any of the emergency equipment.

The large white capsules containing the life rafts were located on either side but as the ship was lying on her port side only those life rafts could be launched.

Selecting the launch handle for the upper of the two capsules Jack gave it a hefty pull and the links in the hydrostatic release fell away and the great orange and black whale of a raft inflated alongside the railing. They had little time but made it into the interior of the raft as the boat threatened to capsize on top of them. Jack found the dinghy knife beside the painter and cut them free. The light breeze carried them clear and a chill descended on the poorly clad trio of survivors who were now facing one more challenge to their survival; the cold winter night.

They were not to know that the remainder of the crew, at least those that were not killed by the 'pirates' in the fire fight and thrown overboard, were in the forward galley, locked in the chill room. Even if they had known they would have been too late to save any of them.

The next two hours were an almost unbearable mix of erratic motion, biting cold and miserable seasickness. By the time Jack had found the Emergency Locator Beacon and worked out how to launch it, a helicopter from the RAF base at Akrotiri had arrived in response to the message Ariadne had sent via satellite.

06.30 – Saturday 9th December, 2006
Medical Centre, RAF Akrotiri, Cyprus

Jack was busy chatting with the RAF Police Officer and the crew that had conducted the night hoist rescue of the three survivors from La Reine Bleu. Freddie was on the phone to London and Ariadne was fretting over the loss of all the recoded material on the flash memory card attached to her bug. If the Bluetooth link to her satcom unit was working and she was within range then it may have been transmitted to MI5 via the uplink to GCHQ. All she could do was hope and pray. As soon as he could get away from the questions he was allowed to make a call to UK and sat listening to the continuous ringing from his home phone. Eventually the phone was picked up. A sleepy voice said "Hello".

"Josh? Is that you?"

"Dad? Do you know what time it is?"

"What do you mean, what time is it? It's bloody early and I'm back on dry land, back in your life."

"It's Saturday morning and I was fast asleep."

"'Welcome back Dad, where have you been?' is what you're supposed to say."

"Sorry Dad I'm just a bit tired that's all, it's 5.30 in the morning where the hell are you?"

"I'm in Cyprus, where's your mother?"

"I think she's in Copenhagen or maybe London, not sure."

"Hell, well she hasn't got her mobile phone switched on and I can't get through to her."

"Like I said Dad it's five bloody thirty in the morning."

"A bit less of that kind of language please young man, I'm not one of your prep school chums."

The phone went dead. "Bloody teenagers," he said with feeling to the handset, then plonked it down in the cradle. "Where is my darling wife?" His frustration was building.

12.30 – Saturday 9th December 2006
Officer's Mess, RAF Akrotiri

Jack was having lunch with Ariadne and Freddie, slowly working his way through a chicken salad. The silence was profound, as they had just been told that all the others on board La Reine Bleu had indeed perished during the attack. Ariadne had told them that she had heard one of the attackers ordering his men to take the hostages to the chill room below the galley and lock them up.

Freddie had spent an hour on the phone to the Prime Minister. The PM told him that they had received information, albeit a little too late, that the so-called pirates were actually Israeli Special Forces. For reasons they had yet to fathom the Israelis had an issue with Mikoyan. They both agreed that the Israelis were probably just one of many that had grievances with that man. US satellites had tracked the attackers from their base in the north of Israel and the Americans had then informed MI6. Their spies in Cyprus had done their homework on the passengers heading out on the private helicopter. They then knew there was a UK government official on board the target vessel and did their best to let London know what was going on.

During the conversation Freddie had also been told that the Security Services believed that the man that saved his life and that of his girlfriend was none other than Jack Mawgan, the troublemaker he had exiled to Morocco. Freddie was having trouble dealing with the hand that fate had dealt him. Sitting next to someone you had very nearly sent to his death was not proving to be a comfortable experience.

Unfortunately Freddie's meeting with Aram Mikoyan was a secret known only to the Prime Minister's inner circle. Even Ariadne hadn't known where they were headed and why until the day before the couple left the UK. The nature of her mission meant that MI5 could not share the details with other agencies. When the hot information started coming in from the Americans nobody knew what they were on about until MI5 heard about their rescue by the RAF. It was a big screw up that caused problems for everyone involved. The PM in particular had to do some fast-talking.

Jack managed a private conversation with Ariadne and they discussed the period leading up to their rescue. He was taking the news about the crew of La Reine very badly. He had been on board the ship long enough to know almost everyone in the crew and could not get out of his mind that somehow they had all perished.

What she told him next explained a lot. She said that the attackers were not pirates but were Israelis. They were not interested in anything other than killing Aram Mikoyan and when they found they couldn't get at him they argued amongst themselves. Should they use their explosives to blow up the boat or to blow open the room he was hiding in? Apparently there was not enough for both. While they were arguing they tied them up. The leader then appeared and told them they had run out of time and to scuttle the ship.

When he asked why the two Italians were murdered she said she didn't know for sure but there was a lot of yelling in Italian and in English and then she heard shooting and the yelling suddenly stopped. Maybe they didn't have time to tie them up and took the quickest way out. They didn't have to worry about the implications because as far as they were concerned the whole ship would be at the bottom of the Mediterranean within the hour. Fortune smiled on her that day.

Jack reached into his pocket and showed Ariadne the Italian passport he had found in his cabin.

"I found this on board when I took over from the previous doctor. If you look through the visa pages you'll find that my predecessor had visited Israel on several occasions and probably under cover."

"Why under cover?"

"Let's imagine for one moment that he was an Israeli agent sent to kill Aram but was found out and murdered. That would fit with his sudden disappearance and the stories I have heard since I came aboard. Oh, and you don't stamp the passport of an agent unless he is making like a tourist. It's all beginning to add up."

<h1 style="text-align:center">13.00 – Saturday 9th December, 2006
Office of the Commanding General
Shayetet 13 Headquarters, Atlit Naval Base, Israel</h1>

"One of our men killed and five wounded, they seem to have put up a fight."

"The boarding went well but when the crew realised what was happening they armed themselves pretty quickly."

"Did we really have to sink the ship with all hands?"

"The target had locked himself in an armoured safe room. I decided to use the explosives we had with us to scuttle the ship. I did not have enough to guarantee that I could open the safe room and then scuttle the ship. Either way we achieved the objective."

"Unfortunately one of the people on board was a British government official. The British Prime Minister's press officer."

"Shit!"

"Exactly."

"Why weren't we told?"

"We only got the information after the attack. It was too late to stop you."

"Well there will be hell to pay if the Brits find out that we were responsible."

"I know." There was a knock at the General's door and a sailor delivered an envelope. The General opened it, read the contents and turned a shade of pale. He looked up at his deputy.

"What is it?"

"Good news and bad news."

"The British have rescued three UK nationals from a life raft, they include their government official."

"I don't get it. Is that the good news or the bad news?" The General sat quietly reading through the paper once more and trying to work out if the British man's survival was indeed 'good news'.

"The really bad news is that our intelligence people intercepted a message from the Americans to the British alerting them to our attack."

"Hell! How the fuck did they know what we were planning?"

"That is something we have to look into but in the meantime make arrangements for the dead and wounded, I have to see the Prime Minister."

"Have the press got hold of the story yet?"

"I don't know but tell your men and women that they must remain silent about the operation – no leaks." With that he cleared his desk and followed his deputy out of the office. He had a feeling in his water that the meeting with the Prime Minister would not go well.

16.30 – Saturday 9th December 2006
Officer's Mess, RAF Akrotiri

"Hello, Pam, is that you?"

"Yes, Darling, it's me."

"Where have you been? I've been trying to call you all day."

"I've been at Scotland bloody Yard with Dan and Nat enduring the third degree."

"What for? Didn't they tell you that I'm in Cyprus at the RAF base?"

"I don't really understand it all but you can ask Dan when you see him."

"What's Nat doing there, how come he's involved."

"Darling he's been helping Dan to scour Europe looking for you and he's been roped in to this high pressure questioning by detectives from all over."

"Where's Dan now?"

"He's gone over to Vauxhall for a meeting, he didn't say why but said he will be back tonight and to make reservations at a hotel for all three of us."

"Better make the reservation for four. The RAF are flying us back to Northolt and I expect to be with you late this evening."

"Oh Darling I can't believe I am hearing your voice after everything." she began to cry.

"Sweetheart, hang on in there, I'll be home soon. Love you."

The flight to Northolt was conducted in silence as all three adjusted to the realities of a very close brush with death. As they left the terminal that evening Ariadne kissed Jack on the cheek and thanked him for saving her life. It was a kiss that lingered half a second too long and told Jack that hers was more than a passing expression of appreciation. He smiled and she returned the compliment. Freddie's expression of gratitude was a limp handshake with a distinct lack of eye contact.

CHAPTER 18

10.00 – Sunday 10ᵗʰ December, 2006
Park City Hotel, West Kensington, London

THE PARK CITY HOTEL sits in an elegant Georgian crescent a stone's throw from the busy Cromwell Road that feeds traffic into Central London from the west. It benefits from an air of tranquillity that was very much appreciated by the many tourists taking breakfast before heading to the turmoil of pre-Christmas shopping in the West End.

The emotions of the previous evening's reunion were understandably intense, very personal and very private. At breakfast there were smiles and happiness and a certain amount of relief tinged with sadness now that news of the fate of La Reine Bleu had become widely understood and a major feature in the late editions of the Sunday papers.

Nathan and Dan appeared and joined Jack and Pam at their table beside the window looking out on to the small garden at the rear of the building. The conversation inevitably turned to their experiences over the previous weeks. Jack was humbled by how many people had dedicated their time to trying to find him.

Pam was amused by Jack's new goatee beard but wanted to live with it for a few days before giving it an official approval rating. Eventually the conversation got around to the subject of who had abducted Jack and why. Pam and Nat listened in silence as Dan explained what he knew. He felt that including Pam and Nat in the conversation was justified but explained that the privilege of hearing classified information carried with it the responsibility not to repeat it outside their small circle.

It had always been difficult for Pam to come to terms with Dan's role as 'part-time unofficial' MI5 agent but she found it impossible to understand how the British system of government apparently allowed another parallel group of 'agents' to operate in a way that may have made them accountable to elements of the executive but were not accountable to Parliament in the way that the Security Services were.

Dan was determined to root out the cancer and he told them that all the Security Service heads had agreed to make a concerted effort to destroy the 'Men in Black'. Jack told them the story of Aram Mikoyan and the two gold rings. They sat, spellbound, whilst a tale that would look good in a Harry Potter movie unfolded.

"What will you do now?" asked Pam.

"I have no idea what is waiting for me inside that safe deposit box but if Aram says that he wants me to use it to destroy the evil men that featured in his past then I have to believe him. It would appear that I have been sent on an important mission and I owe it to all of you and to everyone else in this world to follow the trail to the deposit box and open it."

"I'm not letting you out of my sight Jack Mawgan, after the last few weeks I can't stand another of your bloody adventures."

Jack held his hand up, "Listen folks this is no big deal. I go to Menorca, collect ring number two, go to the Swiss bank via a boat trip up Lake Maggiore and then collect the contents of the box and come home. A doddle."

"Wait a minute," interrupted Dan, "what the hell will you find inside the box?"

"Yeah," said Nat, "how big is it?"

"Well of course I have no idea," said a slightly deflated Jack.

"I'm sure you will handle it my friend," offered Dan, "I have too much work to catch up on, so let me know how you get on."

"Are you off?" asked Jack.

"'fraid so, Monique is grumbling, she needs me."

"Give her our love Dan, and thank you for everything." Pam gave Dan a great big hug and a kiss on the cheek and he turned and walked off towards reception. There was an awkwardness about their farewell that told the tale of a long standing mutual attraction. Falling for your best friend's wife was one of the mistakes that Dan had thus far not made but life was full of twists and turns that might one day even surprise him.

Jack left the table and followed him out. He called after him, "Dan, one more thing. Ariadne, McLaren's so called girlfriend, she told me the pirates that sank us were really Israelis," Dan paused, said nothing, nodded his understanding, turned and left.

Pam, Jack and Nat sat around the debris of breakfast in a kind of embarrassed silence. There was just too much each wanted to say, needed to say, but none could find the words to begin the conversation. Eventually Nat broke the impasse, "When do we book the flight to Menorca?" Pam and Jack exchanged looks and both smiled at the blessed relief of admitting to one another that they were all up for a bit of adventure.

"I'll need a new passport first, mine was in my briefcase when my car was stolen, remember?"

"Can you get one tomorrow?"

"If I attend the Passport Office in person I think that will be possible. I'll call Dan and ask him to pull a few strings."

12.30 – Sunday 10th December 2006
Office of the Deputy Head of MI5, Justin Wood

"I had a feeling you would be in the office today," said Dan. A weary and tired looking Justin sat back in his chair and grimaced.

"No peace for the wicked old chap, your chum's adventures off Cyprus have created a storm."

"I don't believe you can lay that at Jack's door, Justin. He was almost a bystander."

"Very true, but I seem to be reading more reports bearing his name than any other agent – and he doesn't even officially work for me."

"He doesn't even 'unofficially' work for you." Justin threw his pen onto the desk as a gesture of frustration.

"Shit, Dan, piles of shit, guano, merde, mist, poo. Yes, poo, I am in the poo."

"Why,"

"Because we missed the heads up from the Americans and let our Prime Ministerial Press Officer walk into a horrible Israeli 'take-down'."

"Well here is something to cheer you up. It may even dig you out of the poo."

"Go on dear fellow, save me!"

Dan went on to explain to Justin the two gold rings, although Jack had skipped some of the details when he related the story so nobody else knew what to say to whom or the names Aram had told him to remember.

"Wow! So this safety deposit box may hold some explosive material," Justin commented after listening patiently.

"Not literally explosive of course, but it may be damaging to a lot of important people."

"What should we do, do you think?"

"If we can put two and two together then you can bet that others can do just the same."

"But do they know about the rings?"

"It's not the rings that are important, it's Jack himself. He was the last person to see Mikoyan alive. If they have the slightest suspicion that he has been given something important, information, a computer disc, a file or a key then they will follow him and see where he leads them. If there is anything to find then they may feel that they need to take it from him before he can use it."

"Does he need some kind of protection?"

"I believe so."

"What do you mean?"

"He needs watching."

"Will he go for that idea?"

"Probably not but it will be better if he is not aware we are there."

"We?"

"Me."

"Don't you think you might be a bit obvious? You know Jack, he'll sniff you out in a trice."

"Not this master of disguise. Anyway I've a feeling that I won't be the only one watching what he gets up to so I also want to watch for the watchers".

"Would you go solo or would you want back up?"

"I'll take a rain check on that until I see what crawls out of the woodwork."

"How are you fixed, stock-wise ... your 'box-of-tricks'?"

"Bugs OK, comms OK, trackers now a bit short, weapons are problematic.

I had to ditch my pistol in Switzerland but a hiding place under a rock doesn't give you a receipt and the quartermaster is giving me a hard time. He keeps complaining that I get through too many weapons and need to learn the art of returning things to stores."

"Oh I'll sort him for you. What would you like for this job?"

"Something lightweight that packs a punch, the usual field agent's dream. If Jack is visiting Menorca and Italy then I need a handy consular office with a secure diplomatic bag on Menorca and I guess one in Milan too."

"I'll see to it. What other jobs do you have on at the moment?"

"Two, both long term surveillance but I can collect the tapes once a week and send them to you for transcription if that's OK?"

"I think we can manage that."

"OK well I'll go straight to stores if you can give them a call."

"Consider it done, good luck. Stay in touch."

Dan left the top floor and went to the stores in the basement. There he received a tongue lashing from the Senior Storeman who failed to understand the difficulties of the front line agent and forecast trouble ahead if he failed to return this latest increment in the long list of equipment entered into his personal records. Dan took this mock deprecation in the spirit in which it was delivered and left wearing a smile. The equipment would be delivered to the British Consul at Es Castell in Menorca via the normal diplomatic bag and the embassy in Madrid.

16.00 – Sunday 10th December 2006
The Prime Minister's Private Office, Jerusalem, Israel.

To the west of the ancient city of Jerusalem lies the newly constructed government campus housing the offices of the Israeli Prime Minister. Sunday being a normal working day the Jewish leader was at his desk and dealing with the latest crisis.

"General you promised me you would take care of Mikoyan and there would be no fallout. I've just spent four hours on the telephone denying all knowledge of the sinking of La Reine Bleu to five different foreign secretaries and two prime ministers. Those damn Americans, why can't they keep their damned noses out of our business?"

"All we can do is keep denying it. I will be surprised if they push the point. There were no Americans on board that I am aware of."

"Have you seen the news on CNN and BBC, there were three survivors, all British. One of them was this fellow Mawgan. They say he was the ship's doctor but I thought you said our man was the ship's doctor?"

"He was the ship's doctor but we lost contact with him last month. It seems he was replaced by the Englishman."

"Your Section Leader wrote in his preliminary report that they were able to account for everybody on the crew and passenger list with the exception of the owner and the doctor. They had apparently taken refuge in the ships armoured safe room and could not be dealt with."

"Yes sir but they did deal with them, they sank the ship."

"In that case how come the ship's doctor was one of those rescued by the RAF and taken to Akrotiri?"

"I don't know sir."

"Find out where this fellow Mawgan is and find out what happened inside that safe room. Mikoyan is a vindictive old bastard he may have handed Mawgan details of my dealings with him. If they get out then I'm done for."

"I'm not sure I can do that sir, you see …"

"Don't tell me you can't do it, you can use MOSSAD. Now get on it."

"Yes sir."

The General left the Prime Minister's office with a big problem on his hands. He had already had a difficult conversation with the Head of MOSSAD following the news about the sinking of La Reine Bleu. He knew that if he were to relay the Prime Minister's instructions to him now then he would be told in no uncertain terms which bodily orifice would accommodate his request. There would be no more organs of the Jewish State sacrificed to the PM's indiscretions.

09.30 – Monday 11th December 2006
Visiting Hall, Bezirksgefangnis Aarau
Telli (Pre Trial Prison), Switzerland

The old District Prison in Aarau stood on the corner of Laurenzenvorstadt not far from the River Aare, a tributary of the Rhine. It was a dismal uninviting building. The grey-suited figure who parked his Mercedes and ambled to the front door had no enthusiasm for the good deed he was about to perform for his unruly, unreasonable and demanding client.

"Mr Boris you're crazy."

"I'm not crazy, now find this guy Mawgan and if necessary beat it out of him."

"I'm your lawyer Mr Boris, not one of your heavies."

"I don't care, the guy in this morning's paper who survived the pirate attack on my old man's ship is the same guy I know was the ship's doctor. He's English and I owe him big time. He's the reason I'm in here."

"But why do you want to know about his meeting with your father?"

"The paper said he was with my father when he died but then escaped when the pirates had left and the ship sank. If he was with my father when he died I want to know what was said and whether he was given anything. The miserable old bastard hasn't left a will has he?"

"Not that we know of."

"And you are the family lawyers, right?"

"Yes, but as I told you, your father told me that he didn't need to make a will and that everything would be taken care of."

"You told me he said it was in the hands of God."

"I did, but I still don't really understand."

"What father doesn't leave his son something when he dies? Mawgan knows something and I intend to find out what happened on that ship. The story in the papers says he was locked up with my father for hours. Something must have been said, he can't just die and take it all with him."

"There's not much I can do about it I'm afraid."

"Get Julio here, he'll find Mawgan for me."

"Julio?"

"Julio Emmiyan, my cousin."

"Ah yes, I think we have his details on file after his last appearance before the courts."

"Get him down here, I need to tell him what to do."

"Is that wise, Mr Boris?"

"Just do it."

The Following Day

"Hello Julio, my dear friend."

"Not so much of the 'dear friend' you arsehole."

"Hey Julio, whatever problems we have had we have to put them behind us."

"Why? You screwed my fiancé and crashed my car. I can't work out which is the worst crime, you horny bastard."

"Come on I bought you a new car didn't I and you would never have survived marrying that bitch. She believed that 'variety is the spice of life'. Trust me, I did you a favour." Julio paused, peering through reflective Ray-Bans that prevented Boris from seeing the expression of hatred he would see in his eyes. They had once been close friends and both had a chequered relationship with police in and around Europe.

Boris enjoyed being in trouble and trouble became his middle name. This seemingly contagious condition had infected those around him so the family law firm was kept busy and the names of the family miscreants a regular feature in the newspapers.

"If you can find this guy Mawgan for me I'll show you my gratitude, big-time."

"Oh yeah? What's the deal?" His sceptical tone betrayed his distrust.

"I'll give you all my cars if you can find him and find out what he knows about Papa's money." Boris knew that he wouldn't be driving anywhere for a while. Now that his father was gone there was no one to pay the bribes.

"What? Including the new Ferrari?"

"What's left of it anyway but there's the other one plus the Maserati, and don't forget the McLaren, that's a beast. There's my Range Rover too."

"OK, so supposing I agree, what do you expect this Mr Mawgan to have that's any use to you?"

"Father told the lawyers that he didn't need to leave a will so that means everything passes to me, I'm his heir but he didn't leave me any papers, nothing. We don't know where he has hidden the money. If anybody knows then I figure the last person to speak to him would be the one that knows something, anything."

"What if he doesn't want to play ball?"

"Make him play ball, you used to be good at that I seem to remember."

"I'll need spending money."

"Stick it on your credit card and I'll get the lawyers to send you some cash."

"Where have I heard that one before?"

"Then sell one of the cars."

"OK," he said after spending a minute or so thinking about the deal, "but you agree to pay me ten per cent of whatever you get as a result of me talking to this guy Mawgan." Boris could tell that Julio was going off the idea so readily agreed. He figured ninety per cent of something was infinitely better than one hundred per cent of nothing.

"Deal." He spat into the palm of his hand and held it out to Julio who copied the gesture and shook his hand.

"Registration documents for the McLaren, I think that will give me the quickest sale and the thought of driving that thing scares me to death."

"See the Company Secretary in Zurich, he keeps all that kind of thing. Tell him to call me and I'll tell him it's OK."

"When are you due in front of the judge?"

"Weeks, months, who knows?"

"I'll get back to you as soon as I have had a chat with Mr Mawgan. See you later."

14.00 – Wednesday 13th December 2006
NSS Corp HQ, Cardinal House, Heathrow Airport

It was a day when the grey cloudy skies outside were echoed by grey clouds of depression inside NSS HQ. Freddie McLaren sat opposite a thoughtful Sir William Salisbury having listened to a briefing on revelations about MI5's activities against their organisation. They were fully aware that they had acquired the sobriquet 'Men in Black' and at first this was amusing, but now that they were being pursued by the full weight of the establishment life was becoming more awkward and a lot less predictable. What they had imagined was a quiet tolerance of their activities was not so much tacit permission as a fear that any interference would result in upsetting the management.

Freddie was especially depressed to find that his relationship with Ariadne lived up to her Greek mythological characterisation – 'Mistress of The Labyrinth'. She was a plant, he had been conned. He tried to think of all the things he had told her during their pillow talking sessions. Had he said too much? Sir William wanted to know and he couldn't remember enough to reassure him. Fortunately she hadn't been present during the negotiations with the Italians otherwise she would have realised that the upper echelons of government were up to no good.

The murderous attack on the ship had, fortunately for them, left no witnesses but at the same time they had lost a potential income stream and that troubled Sir William as much as anything else. Their mole inside MI5 had come up trumps with the inside track on the story behind the sinking but every time they communicated with him it raised the prospect of his discovery. It was a nerve-racking time with little room for optimism.

"When you were together in Akrotiri did Mawgan discuss his time inside the safe room?" asked Sir William at last.

"A little."

"What did he tell you?"

"Just that he had been summoned to see Mikoyan and when the attack started they took refuge in the safe-room."

"How long were they together?"

"How the hell do I know?"

"Well how long did the attack last?"

"At least an hour I guess."

"Did he say when Mikoyan passed away?"

"No."

"But he was definitely the last person to converse with him?"

"Absolutely."

"I would give a lot to know what they talked about."

"Why don't you ask him, Mawgan I mean, not Mikoyan."

Salisbury gave him one of his withering looks that put Freddie firmly where he belonged, in his place.

"Not you personally of course, but one of your hired hands, someone who knows how to get answers?"

"Maybe I will but we have a small problem in that 'Five' have decided to put a tail on him."

"What for, protection ... who from ... us? We're not going after him any more ... are we?"

"No but either they don't trust him and they want to know what he gets up to or, yes, they could be protecting him."

"That's odd."

"Yes. You don't put scarce resources on to a 'follow and protect' unless you think there is something in it for you."

"What will you do, watch the watchers?"

"No, we will let 'Five' get on with it and wait for the feedback from our man. Let them do the legwork, all we need is to know what's happening in case we need to step in."

15.30 – Wednesday 13th December 2006
Lower Spargo Cottage, Perranarworthal

The debate about who should and who could accompany Jack to Menorca had been raging since the Mawgan family were in London together. Nat thought it was his duty to come but suddenly found more pressing tasks when it came to nailing him down. His girlfriend was planning to visit from Canada and stay over for Christmas.

Pam's interest in the trip faded when her boss suggested that she ought to repay her colleagues for their support and understanding during her recent absences when Jack was kidnapped.

In the end Jack made a booking for just himself. He planned to leave the following day and thought that he might find some interesting presents for family members in the Spanish shops.

16.00 – Wednesday 13th December 2006
Dan's Office in Exeter

Dan was busy reading the manual for his latest bugging device when the signal that a text message had arrived on his cell phone chirped away in the background. The phone was plugged into a charger on top of the filing cabinet.

With a sigh of frustration he put down the booklet and got up from his comfortable position in front of the warm air blower. Like many who had travelled the world it seemed to Dan that the British heating engineers based their calculations for heating efficiency on the worst of summer days rather than the worst of winter days. Every time the biting easterly winds brought their vindictive icy blast his heating system fought to keep his meagre office suite at a sensible working temperature.

His secretary basked in the comparative warmth created by two night storage heaters but he found it difficult to justify the same expense in his own office when he spent most of his time away.

He read the message and was immediately galvanised into action by the news. The airline computers had registered a booking for a Mr J. Mawgan on a flight to Madrid then on to Menorca. GCHQ had many useful functions and this was one that Dan found particularly helpful. Eavesdropping on the booking systems threw up some very interesting activities and in this case saved Dan from having to watch and wait for Jack to make a move.

13.00 – Thursday 14th December 2006
Aeropuerto de Menorca

As Jack passed through the crowded baggage area he congratulated himself for having the wisdom to travel with just a carry-on bag as he zoomed past the queues at the baggage carousels and was soon standing in the taxi queue. The twang of German rang around the line of newly arrived tourists and he realised that there were obviously many from that country seeking respite from the north European winter.

His preoccupation with the bright sunshine together with the disorientating effects of strange sights and sounds meant that he didn't observe the otherwise insignificant figure of Dan Barclay dressed like the average ex-pat tourist abroad with his dark glasses and broad rimmed Panama and carry-on flight bag adding to what Dan hoped was an air of anonymity.

When it was Jack's turn to take the next taxi Dan was close enough to hear as Jack yelled through the open passenger window … "Hotel Almirante per favore". He opened the back door, threw his suitcase on the backseat and clambered in. The journey to the hotel went without incident and Jack neither saw nor felt any reason to be nervous, excited maybe but not nervous.

Dan had rudely elbowed his way into taking the very next taxi offering profuse apologies to some surprised oriental tourist who could care less that Dan's brutalised Spanish actually made no sense at all. He arrived at the Almirante Hotel just in time to see Jack walking in through the front door. He waited for half an hour then approached the check in desk and booked himself in. The concierge was a little concerned about Dan's lack of luggage but, as only Dan could, he managed to sweet talk his way into a discounted single room on the top floor.

Checking out the room would have to wait so he found himself a convenient spot in the lobby from which to observe all the normal exits and waited for Jack to appear. The standard trick of hiding behind a newspaper was tedious enough but when you don't understand any Spanish the tedium of make believe reading of El Pais from cover to cover can become enough to drive a man mad. Dan was a professional though and managed to look absorbed in its contents for long enough to catch Jack as he strode out of the lift and out through the front doors.

Jack paused to get his bearings then headed down towards the coast road and followed it all the way round to Puerto Mahon. Dan kept a safe distance and trailed Jack all the way to Iglesia Santa Maria without a single hint that he had spotted his 'tail'.

For Jack it was no great surprise to find that a stranger was tagging along behind. As always the problem is to understand if he was friend or foe. The chances are that it was MI5 keeping a motherly eye on him. He knew how things worked and wasn't too concerned. If it was somehow an enemy then he struggled to understand who that might be. Until that moment he had never considered that he might even have enemies. Could those that kidnapped him be after him? He looked up at the darkening skies as the last vestiges of daylight ebbed away. He picked up the pace and tried to convince himself that he was being paranoid. To be on the safe side he would not risk visiting the priest that day. He was due to fly back the following afternoon so he would recce the church then return for the ring in the morning and go straight on to the airport.

Dan realised that Jack was walking just a little faster and increased his own pace. There was no outward sign that Jack had seen him and he was a long way back. What was the hurry?

Jack walked up to the entrance of the fourteenth century church and found the huge embossed front doors to be unlocked. The cool, dark interior was lit only by flickering candles with just a glow from the streetlights little of the light filtering through the stained glass windows in the far end of the chancel. A few men and women were kneeling in prayer. The priest was collecting the prayer books left by previous worshippers. Having made a mental note of the layout Jack retraced his steps and set off back to the hotel.

The restaurants along the sea front delivered a heady mix of aromas as kitchens cooked up paellas and kebabs, chicken joints, boquerones and a dozen different tapas. The Spaniards dined in the late hours but tourists invariably dined in the early evening. The sights and smells tortured Jack's taste buds until the flow of saliva threatened to turn into a river. The final straw was a charcoal grill bearing great chunks of smouldering beefsteaks. He asked the waiter for a seat and spent the evening with a good meal and a fine bottle of Ribera Del Duero.

Dan cursed as he was unable to find a spot where he too could dine and simultaneously keep an eye on his target. "You owe me a steak dinner Jack Mawgan," he muttered to himself as he leant casually up against a wall munching on a doner kebab bought from a dodgy looking street stall by the sea front. Still, the day had gone well with no sign of anybody else taking an interest in Jack's activities. Maybe he was being over cautious.

CHAPTER 19

11.00 – Thursday 14th December 2006
Stinson Strasse, Zurich, Switzerland

JULIO STRODE OUT OF the front door of Schohl A.G. and into a waiting taxi. He had arrived with Boris's McLaren just two hours earlier, a pristine six month old, low mileage F1. He was now on his way to the local branch of Credit Suisse with a bank draft for one million Swiss Francs. The car was chassis number one hundred and twenty-eight and had been sold to a famous American racing driver before Boris acquired it and imported it from the US. If Julio had been just a little bit more street-wise when dealing with specialist cars he would have known that one million was on the low side for such a collector's car. Never mind, there was no time for wheeling and dealing, Julio wanted money and he wanted it fast. He had people to see and people to bribe. He needed information and that cost money.

A few phone calls later that day led to a liaison with a woman in Milan who had access to the National Police Computers at the Guardia di Finanza. One hundred thousand Euros is a lot to pay for a service but the woman concerned was taking a risk, a big risk. She put Jack's name on a Europe-wide watch list and the next time his passport details were logged at any border in Europe the alarm would be raised.

Unfortunately for Julio the arrangement came too late to catch Jack on his way to Menorca but other opportunities would lie ahead.

11.15 – Thursday 14th December 2006
Hotel del Almirante, Mahon, Menorca

Jack spent the early morning preparing for the day ahead. He had a shower and tidied up his goatee. He had lived with his new image for some time now and wasn't totally convinced it was really 'him'. He peered in the mirror and decided that it had to go, but not that day. He would talk to Pam when he got home.

The plans for the immediate future were simple. Go to church, meet Father Pedro, collect ring, go to airport, fly to Madrid, fly to London, fly to Newquay, go home. A quick analysis of that plan revealed a weakness. Christmas was almost upon them and there were too many things to fit into the calendar and he had not even thought about organising a trip to Locarno.

He went straight down to the hotel business centre and used their computer to check the ferry timetable on Lake Maggiore. His heart sank. At first sight there were no ferries after the 31st of October until the service re-started at the end of March. A more detailed check showed that the hydrofoil that ran between Arona and Locarno did provide a service on Friday, Saturday and Sunday. It left Arona at 09.30 arriving at midday and returned at 14.00 arriving at 16.30.

Another session on the Internet confirmed the fact that the bank would be closed at the weekend. If he didn't visit the bank the very next day then he would have to wait until Friday the 22nd December and that would mean travelling over the weekend just before Christmas. That idea was not one that filled him with glee. With the holidays approaching travel was already becoming a tedious process.

The next port of call was the airline websites where he found an evening flight direct to Milan from Menorca with Easy Jet. He booked it and then called Pam to explain his change of plans. She was disappointed to hear that he wouldn't be home as promised but reconciled to the idea that what she mockingly referred to as the 'quest', would be over and done with.

A tired and impatient Dan sat at his vantage point and cursed as Jack appeared from the Business Centre complete with luggage and headed to the front desk. He quickly scampered up to his room grabbed his things and headed for the checkout desk. By the time he was ready to leave Jack was long gone and he had no choice but to call a cab and try to catch up. The only problem was that Dan, unaware that Jack's business in the town was incomplete, expected his next destination to be the airport. Arriving at the terminal he couldn't find his target anywhere but assumed that he was already waiting in the gate area and continued through to the departure area … still no Jack.

Meanwhile Jack had arrived at the church, left the taxi with the meter running and entered the church through the main door. It turned out to be nearly as dark inside in the middle of the day as it had been the previous evening but his eyes soon adjusted to the low light levels and his anxiety faded a little in the calm and tranquil setting. The beautiful stained glass windows glowed in the sunlight. They surrounded the altar in a semi-circle and bathed the scene in a surreal patchwork of colour. It was an impressive sight that spoke volumes about the designers of this ancient building.

At the centre of the altar stood the priest, he was busy finishing the morning communion service and with the assistance of two altar boys was administering wine to the members of his flock. On an impulse he walked up to the altar rail and knelt as if in prayer. He hadn't taken communion since he was a teenager and a long time ago became a sceptic about the whole religious scene. Nonetheless for what he needed to do he reasoned he must deliver the message from Aram in a way that reflected what it said.

The priest moved along the line and suddenly realised he was looking into the unfamiliar face of a stranger, he hesitated. It gave Jack the moment he wanted.

"Can an old sinner go to heaven when he comes from the east?" For a moment the priest was nonplussed.

"A man who repents can always find his way to heaven even if he comes from the east." Jack nodded, not sure how to respond. He held the ring tightly in his right hand, ready to show his bona fides.

"My friend is dead?" the priest asked, his voice tinged with sadness.

"Yes, he died in my arms."

"If you have the ring you must be a good man. Aram told me he would only send a good man."

Jack placed it into the priest's outstretched hand. The rest of the congregation feigned disinterest but each one was trying to understand why their priest was talking to a stranger. Father Pedro inspected the ring then removed an identical gold band from his chubby little finger. He passed both back to Jack who rose, bowed in respect and left. The emotions he felt were boiling up inside and memories of the moment when Aram passed away were causing some distress.

He passed through the great doors at the entrance and burst into the glare of the midday sun. Despite the time of year the sun still had plenty of heat in it and Jack had a moment to realise why the English found such places so attractive when the time came for retirement. He took a quick look at the two rings and sure enough both were engraved with a series of numbers only now he couldn't tell which one was his and which was the priest's. He would have to wait until he had time to look more carefully for he had written down the numbers on his ring just in case.

Slipping both the rings on to the same finger he climbed back into his taxi and set off for the airport. Had he known that Father Pedro was at that very moment making a phone call that would threaten to end the adventure altogether he would have taken a plane straight home.

CHAPTER 20

January 1939
Puerto Mahon, Menorca

THE SPANISH CIVIL WAR was coming to a head. The island of Menorca was a Republican stronghold and the garrison had remained loyal to the elected government in Madrid. The Nationalist forces on the mainland were inflicting heavy defeats on the disparate collection of communists, anarchists and the famous International Brigade.

On the 8th January the Republicans sent Admiral Luis Gonzalez de Ubieta to Menorca to take charge of the naval base and Republican forces at Puerto Mahon.

On the 7th February the British cruiser HMS Devonshire arrived in Puerto Mahon carrying an emissary from the Nationalists. He told the Admiral that the Nationalists would occupy the island the following day and all Republican soldiers should leave the island on the British cruiser.

The same day three battalions of the Republicans in the western town of Ciudadela de Menorca killed their commander and mutinied. A brigade of loyal Republicans arrived from Puerto Mahon and defeated the mutineers. During this battle their Soviet advisor died saving the life of the loyalist commander. The advisor was the Armenian born soldier Captain Joseph Mikoyan.

On the 8th February Italian and Nationalist bombers attacked Puerto Mahon. The loyal soldiers decided however that despite their victory at Ciudadela de Menorca the fight was no longer worth continuing given the size of the army that would invade later that day. They climbed aboard the British warship and were given safe passage to Marseille. The British delivered 452 refugees from an uncertain fate.

After the war the locals were unable to celebrate the extraordinary heroism of Joseph Mikoyan for the Franco regime ruled with an iron fist until his death in 1975.

As Joseph Mikoyan's son, the young Aram Mikoyan, began his climb up the greasy pole in the world of financial criminality he found out about his father's heroic past and resolved to build a home on the island. The leaders of the Island Council were courted by Aram and persuaded to donate five hectares of land for his private estate. The land chosen was that confiscated from the family of Juan Pigarro, the man who had led the mutiny in Ciudadela de Menorca. Pigarro had survived the war but had to move to the mainland due to the hatred that lingered amongst those that felt he was a traitor. He left his farm to his two daughters, Isabella and Maria. Pigarro died in mysterious circumstances one month after Franco.

The two daughters married local men and took over the farm when their father died. Maria married Miguel Guitierez, whose brother was the priest at Iglesia Santa Maria in Puerto Mahon.

12.05 – Thursday 14th December 2006
Puerto Mahon, Menorca

"He's leaving the church right now," said Pedro the Priest.

"What does he look like?" came the response from his brother.

"About one metre eighty-five, medium build, mid-forties, short dark hair, goatee beard."

"I think I have him. He's just climbed into a taxi. Speak later."

One of the duties of a priest is to hear a man's confession. The extent to which Aram had confided in Father Pedro was in fact fairly minimal but by careful questioning in the confessional he had learnt that he planned to make restitution to both church and the secular world via the contents of a safe deposit box. The only other snippet of Aram's plan that he knew about involved the rings.

The plan the priest and his brother had put together involved following whoever collected the second ring.

The brothers could not believe their luck when Father Pedro was able to convince Aram that the path to righteousness lay with the church. Over the last few years he had coached him into realising that he needed to make restitution. They had vowed, one way or another, to restore the land that rightfully became theirs on the marriage of Maria Pigarro to Miguel Guitierez. By rights they should be wealthy landowners with a farm to pass on to their own children, Francisco and Severiano but thanks to Aram Mikoyan and the crooks who ran the island council they had just one hectare and a fishing boat with which to scrape a living.

Their enthusiasm for the task ahead was not, however, matched by the quality of their preparation. Miguel, a spritely eighty year old, managed to follow Jack to the airport and identified him standing in the queue to check in for the Easy Jet flight to Milan.

"He's going to Milan," he told Father Pedro on the phone.

"Milan, in Italy?"

"How many other bloody 'Milans' do you know?"

"Miguel, please don't swear at me. Remember I am a man of the church."

"So what?"

"So a man of the church has friends, important friends. You find out who he is then get Seve to buy a ticket to Milan. As soon as I have a name I'll use some of my friends to find out where he's staying."

"How can you do that?"

"Just get on with it and call me as soon as you have his name."

Manuel thought about how he might find out the name of the mysterious stranger and decided to play-act the crotchety old man. He moved to a position beside the queue for Jack's flight and immediately found himself on the wrong end of some abuse from one irate Italian. He was accused of queue jumping but pretended to be hard of hearing and simply stepped up to the desk at the same time as Jack. They both attempted to engage the check-in clerk but then Miguel in his best English, which wasn't actually very good, said, "Very sorry Mister... Sorry I didn't catched your name?"

"Mawgan, Jack Mawgan."

"Sorry Mister Jack, please, forgive me you go first."

Miguel stepped aside and moved away from the check-in area and put a call through to his brother.

"His name is Morgan, Jack Morgan."

"OK I'll get on it. Now find Seve and tell him what to do."

"What should he do?" said Miguel with a degree of panic. They had talked of this day endlessly and now that it was here his nerves were beginning to frazzle.

"Tell Seve to go to Milan and follow this guy Morgan to the bank where the safe deposit box is located."

"Then what?"

"What do you think? When he comes out of the bank Seve waits for an opportune moment then hits the guy over the head and leaves with the bag."

"What bag?"

"The bag containing whatever is in the box."

"The money."

"Yes ... no ... I mean it may be papers, deeds, share certificates."

"Jewels?"

"Maybe ... I suppose ... we didn't think about that, did we. It could be anything but if it is in a box it must be something he can take away. He told me that the contents of the box was the key to his reconciliation with the secular world. Whatever it is it must be worth a fortune. He has gone to too much trouble to keep this a secret. All this fuss with rings and secret codes. It must be really important. We have to have it, whatever it is then we can use it for our revenge. All those sanctimonious bastards I hear at confession every week who don't care one little bit that they treated our family in an unforgiveable way. We will right all those past wrongs."

"What if Seve has to kill him?"

"No killing, just a bump on the head then run away."

"Life's not that simple Pedro, sometimes a bump can kill."

"Just get Seve to Milan, I'll put my contacts in Rome to work and soon we will know where he is staying."

Seve was a good looking, well-built retired soldier in his mid-fifties, one metre eighty tall, bald as a coot with a tanned and muscular torso honed by years in the Spanish Legion. Unlike the French Foreign Legion the Spanish equivalent recruited only Spanish nationals and Spanish speaking ex patriots but was similarly introduced to fight foreign colonial wars.

Seve had been a member of the elite parachute brigade and now lived on the remains of a military pension that he shared with his ex-wife. He was tough and capable but never quite had what it took to pass the sergeant's exams so left the military without any useful qualifications apart from being able to fire a gun and dig a trench.

He had married a woman on the mainland but they divorced when he left the Legion. She had wanted to live close by her parents in Madrid but he wanted to return to Menorca. He had two children who lived in Madrid with their mother. The entire family scraped by on his army pension and what he could earn as a farm labourer and part-time fisherman.

Spending his hard earned money on travel was something he wasn't used to but on this occasion he had little choice but to follow his father's orders and get to Milan in Italy as quickly as possible. The travel agent in Mahon managed, after some searching on the Internet to get Seve on an Easy Jet flight that night into London Gatwick then on the first flight in the morning to Milan, arriving at Milan Malpensa at 08.30. It was all she could find at short notice but Seve accepted the plan with a degree of resignation. She booked a hotel at Gatwick for him and a return flight direct to Menorca the following afternoon. He paid for the whole trip in cash using some of the precious savings he kept in a tin box under his bed.

17.00 – Thursday 14th December 2006
Aeropuerto, Menorca

"Pam, it's Dan."

"Hi Dan, where are you?"

"I'm at work. Is Jack around?"

"No, he's on his way to Milan. He's going to the bank in Locarno in the morning."

"Locarno? You're sure?"

"Yes he was supposed to be home tonight but there was some kind of problem with the ferry timetable so he's going straight to Milan from Menorca."

"Do you know where he'll be staying tonight?"

"Yes, hang on I'll just get my note … he's booked into the Hilton Garden Inn at a place called Somma Lombardo."

"OK, got it."

"Anything wrong?"

"No, just needed to have a chat. We'll catch up later, have to go."

"OK, bye."

Dan cursed. Jack had changed his plan and he'd missed him at the terminal because he had gone to the domestic flight area and Jack to International Departures. He went to the huge TV screen inside the main entrance and checked for flights to Milan.

The direct flight had closed and that left just one option, he would have to get a flight to another airport then on to Milan. He already had a ticket to London via Madrid and that flight had, according to the terminal displays, been called. There was no time to try any of the airline ticket desks. He would have to try for a flight to Milan when he got to Madrid.

18.00 – Thursday 14th December 2006
Zurich, Switzerland

"Julio? This is Maddie, A Mr John Robert Mawgan has booked on the 17.10 flight to Milan Malpensa from Menorca in Spain. He used a web-based agency and he's booked a Fiat Panda from Avis and he has a reservation at the Hilton Garden Inn in a nearby town called Somma Lombardo. This is probably the guy you are after although the first name is not the one you gave me but the second is a very rare form of that family name so I'm confident that this is your man."

"Thanks Maddie."

"If it helps he has a flight to London booked tomorrow night from Milan Malpensa."

"Yes, that helps."

"Let me know if you need more, the fee is the same."

"Thanks, I'll remember that."

Julio Emmiyan checked his watch. It was a three hour drive to Milan and he didn't fancy getting up in the middle of the night so it would be better to drive to Milan that evening and stay with an old friend then get out to the hotel to watch for the Jack. He figured that six o'clock in the morning would be a good time to park outside the hotel then accost the man Boris had so carefully described.

21.00 – Thursday 14th December 2006
Hilton Garden Inn, Somma Lombardo

The hotel turned out to be newly built and provided a comfortable resting place. Jack undressed and prepared for bed. He decided to treat his weary bones and take a bath. It had been a long and tiring day. He thought about what might happen at the bank the following day. The sense of anticipation was beginning to grow and the adrenalin beginning to flow.

He had better have some ID ready and picked up his passport. The photograph wasn't him. At least it was him before he grew that goatee. The Passport Office were prevailed upon through MI5 to make Jack's new passport as quickly as possible so had used the digital photograph from his previous passport. That worried him. The people at immigration didn't seem to have a problem but maybe it wasn't such a good idea to breeze into that bank in the morning with a visage that didn't match his passport. It was time for the facial hair to go.

01.05 – Friday 15th December 2006
Travelodge Hotel, London Gatwick

"Hilton Garden Inn."

"What?"

"He's staying at the Hilton Garden Inn in a town called Somma Lombardo."

"Where?"

"Pay attention Seve, Mawgan is staying in Somma Lombardo at the Hilton Garden Inn."

"It's the early hours here, I've only just been able to get to sleep."

"I'm perfectly aware of the time Seve, I have been up all night myself. We're an hour ahead remember? If your father had given me the right name maybe we could have done all this a little earlier in the day."

"What do you mean? He gave you the wrong name?"

"The right name but he gave me the wrong spelling."

"Fuck you."

"Don't speak to me like that. It confused the hell out of the computer systems and we had to get the airline passenger lists before we could check the hotel registrations."

"Let me get a pen … OK say all that again."

"Room 31, Hilton Garden Inn, Somma Lombardo. I've checked on the map and the hotel is five minutes away from the airport. Now be there, in the lobby when breakfast starts and follow him to the bank. I want you to call me on your cell phone whenever you get the chance and keep me informed about what he is up to. We may have to make some quick decisions and quick decisions were never your speciality."

"Uncle Pedro. What are you trying to say?"

"Get some sleep and make sure you set the alarm."

07.00 – Friday 15th December 2006
Hilton Garden Inn, Somma Lombardo

Jack helped himself to the buffet breakfast, the very welcome cappuccino made just how he liked it arrived as he took his seat.

Julio sat in the lobby reading a magazine and Dan was outside waiting in his hire car. Unfortunately for Seve his flight from Gatwick was delayed by an air traffic control strike in France so he was still somewhere over the Alps. Uncle Pedro was not going to be happy. The congregation assembled for Jack's visit to the bank would be incomplete but then Jack was blissfully unaware that there was anyone else on this excursion to Locarno and had no idea that what awaited him in the safe deposit box would surprise them all.

In preparation for carrying whatever was contained in the box Jack had brought with him a sports bag rolled up in his carry-on bag. It was quite capacious but he was still uncomfortable about its suitability. His imagination vaulted between a single sheet of paper to a fortune in banknotes, a dossier a foot thick to a sack of jewels. By the time he was ready to leave it was 07.30. The journey to Arona should be less than an hour so there should be plenty of time.

Dan was watching as Jack arrived at his hire car and put his bag on the back seat. Julio was still sitting in the lobby when he heard the receptionist say, "Goodbye Mr Mawgan," to the beardless figure walking out of the door.

He was almost too slow on the uptake for he had been waiting for a man with a goatee beard.

Dan on the other hand was so familiar with the face of a beardless Jack that at first he didn't even realise that he had shaved it off.

Julio reached his newly acquired Range Rover in time to see Jack departing. He followed as quickly as he could with a screech of tyres. Dan waited before he followed so was then able to observe the Swiss registered Range Rover apparently setting off in pursuit of Jack.

"Bingo," he said to himself, "the worm has crawled out of the woodwork."

The convoy wound its way around the edge of Somma Lombardo and on to the town of Vergiate. From there the Via Sempione wound through the lake side town of Sesto Calende and across the bridge that leads from Lombardia to Piemonte. The commercial districts of Dormaletto crowded either side of the main road and traffic during the early rush hour was heavy enough for long queues to form at the traffic lights.

Range Rovers are a common sight in that part of Italy so Julio blended into the scenery quite well. Even Swiss registrations were common as after all the Swiss border was not very far away. He only caught Jack's attention when he crossed a red light. The Italian style of driving seems to encourage a certain amount of 'brinkmanship' but Julio seemed just a little too eager. Not that Jack thought for one moment that he was being followed. It was just that the Range Rover would stick in his memory. Policeman do that kind of thing, they file away their observations then when they need to understand the bones of a problem they sift through all that accumulated 'rubbish' and occasionally they come across a gem of a clue.

The only gem that Dan wanted at that moment was to know where the hell he was going to park when he got to Arona. In the heavy traffic it was going to be a bun fight. As far as he knew Jack had never been to Arona before so he was pretty sure that one way or another the parking dilemma was going to create a degree of mayhem when they got there. It would be interesting to see how Mr X up ahead in the Range Rover handled the parking problem. At least Dan knew they were heading for the Ferry Terminal.

The rush hour melee was a challenge to those unfamiliar with the Italian driving style. Many of the commuters appeared to be talking on cell phones, doing their make-up, adjusting their hair or smoking a cigarette and sometimes all four, which probably explained the lack of traditional activity on the horn buttons. The Italian motorist had apparently invented a new form of 'motoring-multitasking'.

Jack entered the town on the lakeside road following the signs to the car park. Once there he wound his way up and down looking in vain for a space. Finally he got lucky and found a spot being vacated by a large four by four.

It's not so easy to follow someone in those circumstances and Julio cursed as he watched Jack back into the only vacant space for as far as the eye could see. In a minute or too his target would be off on foot and he was stuck in the middle of a bloody access lane. He made the decision to abandon his car and follow Jack but as soon as he opened his door the driver of a car waiting behind him climbed on to the horn button and started giving him earache. He cursed and drove off hoping to catch up with Jack later.

Dan was a wise bird and followed the sign for a car park on the other side of the main road. Once parked he set off for the Ferry Terminal. It had to be on the lake edge and sure enough he found it just five minutes' walk along the shores of the beautiful Lago Maggiore. Across the lake was the amazingly impressive Rocca Borromeo di Angera. Sitting atop a lakeside hillock the thirteenth century castle dominated the eastern skyline. Taking care not to be observed by Jack he found a seat in the café next door to the terminal. It was 09.00, the hydrofoil would be there in fifteen minutes or so, ready for the 09.30 departure. The mysterious Mr X had disappeared. He closely examined each passer-by unhappy and agitated by the fact that he had lost sight of him.

Jack stood patiently waiting in the queue to buy a ticket. He made sure it was a 'biglietti ritorno' and put it carefully in his inside jacket pocket and left the office to follow the directions of the ticket clerk. He made his way down to the jetty where a large assortment of uniformed ferrymen waited patiently for the arrival of the ferry.

Julio meanwhile was scurrying round town checking out every café figuring that Jack was on his way to meet someone. It was pure chance that he saw Jack standing at the stern of the hydrofoil and hurried down to the jetty to find the ferrymen withdrawing the boarding gantry. Ignoring their yells he vaulted the barrier and made it on board as the ferry captain accelerated away from the quayside. There was an argument with the crew but Julio soon made that go away with a couple of fifty euro notes.

Both Jack, standing on the stern close by, and Dan, up front in the cabin, clocked the commotion and the man that caused it. The December weather in that region was fine and clear but that also meant that it was cold and crisp. None of the three protagonists was really fully equipped for the change in climate. Menorca was comparatively balmy compared with Arona. The warmth of the cabin's interior beckoned and gradually the crowd of latecomers filtered into the seating area.

The twin turbocharged diesels buried deep inside the hull suddenly burst into life, the four hydrofoil legs folded down from their parked position and like an athlete striding out of the starting blocks the ferry surged forward and up onto the plane. Like a rocket she sped across the flat calm lake leaving a trail of foaming water and amazed onlookers.

Jack was about to enter the cabin area when the only person left outside stepped forward. It was the man who had jumped on board at the last minute.

"Can I talk with you for a moment please?"

"I'm sorry," replied Jack, "do I know you?"

"No but I know about you." With that he came close to Jack's side. He felt the unmistakeable prod of a gun barrel in the sensitive part of his ribs.

"Hey, what's going on?"

"I need some answers, you were the last person to speak my uncle, Aram Mikoyan. We want to know what he said, what he did with his will."

"We?"

"His son Boris and me his cousin."

"You surely don't think this is an appropriate place to use a pistol?"

"Why not? Nobody will hear the shot above this noise, I have a silencer. 'Pop', and you go over the side. Oh dear! By the time they get your body ashore I'll be long gone."

Dan could see what was going on and was slowly making his way aft.

"I don't know anything about a will."

"What did Aram tell you? No man goes to his grave without sorting his affairs."

"But I am nothing to the Mikoyan family."

"Then why are you here. We know that a Swiss bank is where he keeps his stuff so tell us which one. We have a right to know." As if to add extra emphasis to his words Julio gave Jack a seriously hard prod. Jack, however, anticipated the move and stepped away, unbalancing his opponent enough to grasp the barrel and deliver a wrist-breaking snap that brought a cry of pain. Julio was completely off balance and with some effort Jack pushed him away and over the stern rail and into the boiling wake.

The resulting commotion involved several members of the crew who were trying to restrain Jack believing that it was he who caused the man to fall overboard. Nobody spoke English and the confusion reigned for several minutes until another passenger offered to translate. Jack was able to explain that he had no idea who the stranger was but that he was trying to steel his wallet and he was merely defending himself when the man fell overboard.

It took some minutes for the Captain to hear about the incident and his first instinct was to return to the scene and search for the survivor but there was no need. The loud chatter on the bridge radio was the skipper of the Arona to Angera shuttle ferry. He had seen the man fall from the hydrofoil and they were about to rescue him. The two captains joked on the radio about the fact that they would both now be involved in paperwork for days but neither could find a way to see the funny side. The accident had a happy ending but it still required reports to be filed and Jack spent much of the voyage north writing out his account of the incident.

Dan patted himself on the back for not intervening. He should have known that Jack was able to take care of himself.

12.20 – Friday 15th December 2006
Credit Suisse Bank, Locarno, Switzerland

Locarno is a pretty lakeside town with typical Alpine architecture and lots of shops stacked with everything a Christmas shopper from Italy needs. The bank was a short walk past the busy stores and cafes.

Jack approached the enquiries desk and asked to speak to the manager. The smartly dressed middle-aged lady smiled and responded in excellent English.

Swiss efficiency was legendary and it took just a few moments before a small, distinguished looking, grey haired man in his late fifties appeared. His stern expression was designed to be a neutral as possible. Not for him the sycophantic smile or the growling sneer. He was enigmatically unreadable.

"Can I help you sir?" Jack handed him the return ferry ticket. The bank manager looked at it carefully, turned it over and looked at the reverse side, held it in both hands and stared at it. Jack could almost hear the gears in his head whirring away merrily. The penny appeared to drop. "Follow me," he said at last. They repaired to his office at the rear of the building. He closed the door and he then introduced himself.

"Claude Lindner, it is a pleasure?" His English carried the Swiss-German lilt.

"Jack Mawgan, pleased to meet you.

"You are English?"

"Yes."

"You have your passport please."

"Yes, here," Jack handed over his passport. Claude inspected it and flicked through each page looking for tell-tale stamps. There were none of course, as it was a brand new passport.

"This is a very new document Mr Mawgan, are you who you say you are?" This completely floored Jack although he understood the man's justifiable suspicions.

"I am Jack Mawgan, John Robert Mawgan, you may not know but in the UK 'Jack' is often used as a nickname for people called 'John'." Claude went through the crisp new document once more.

"The British Prime Minister has a Press Officer by the name of Freddie McLaren. Please call him and ask him to verify my identity."

"Maybe that won't be necessary Mr Mawgan, you have something else for me I believe." Jack took a small Jiffy Bag, from his pocket and handed it to Claude.

12.35 – Friday 15ᵗʰ December 2006
Hilton Garden Inn, Somma Lombardo

By the time Seve's taxi arrived at the hotel Jack was long gone. He called his Uncle and Pedro gave him another tongue lashing although the delay was, of course, nothing to do with him. A brief argument followed before Pedro told Seve to check with the concierge who may know where Jack had gone.

He was in luck. Seve asked if the concierge remembered Mr Mawgan, he had a goatee beard and came from England. The concierge did indeed remember a gentleman by that name, he had indeed arrived with a goatee beard but in the morning it was gone. It stuck in his mind how different Mr Mawgan looked without the beard. Did he know where Mr Mawgan had gone? Yes he did because he had asked for directions to Arona and taken a copy of the ferry timetables.

Armed with that information he gave the taxi driver instructions to head straight to the ferry terminal in Arona. On arrival he thanked the driver and paid him off. Another fifty euros; funds were getting low.

The lady at the ticket office was not quite so forthcoming and only by prevailing on her good nature did he ascertain that there were only two boats running that day, the Angera shuttle and the hydrofoil to Locarno and every person boarding the hydrofoil had purchased a return ticket. The returning hydrofoil would get in at 16.30.

Uncle Pedro was mollified by the news and impressed by his nephew's initiative. Maybe there was some grey matter up there after all. The chances were that Mr Mawgan was visiting a bank in Locarno. Just as they suspected Aram had connections with the clandestine world of Swiss Private Banking. When he arrived back in Arona, Seve could pick his moment and steal the bag with the … his thought processes stumbled at that point for he just couldn't decide what could possibly be so valuable but at the same time capable of achieving reconciliation with the secular world. Maybe soon he could find out.

CHAPTER 21

12.40 – Friday 15th December 2006
Carabinieri Office, Arona

A BEDRAGGLED JULIO LEFT the Carabinieri Office in clothing from the Umana charity store. Normally they collected second hand clothing for the poor but the Lieutenant on duty took pity on Julio and prevailed upon his sister who managed the Umana shop nearby. His smart clothes were still soaking wet and were now the contents of two plastic carrier bags bearing the logo of a local supermarket chain.

Julio had a hard time with the police and only escaped a night in jail by agreeing a fine of five hundred euros for 'creating public disorder and failing to purchase a ferry ticket' just to make the whole thing go away. The Polizia Locale wanted to interview the crew of the hydrofoil but the Captain of the vessel spoke with the Lieutenant on the phone and told him that the man he had assaulted did not wish to press charges.

As Julio left for the shopping centre he wanted nothing more than to get out of his charity ensemble and return to the elegant and confident persona that would dish out an appropriate sanction to the man who had tossed him in the lake like a fly. Inside he was boiling with rage and bent on revenge. To that end he revisited the ferry terminal and enquired about the arrival time of the returning hydrofoil. He resigned to be there at 16.30 and deal with Mr Mawgan once and for all.

12.45 – Friday 15th December 2006
Credit Suisse Bank, Locarno, Switzerland

Claude took the packet and opened it. He poured the contents onto his desk and the two gold rings tumbled out. There was a moment to observe these magical objects and wonder at the power they held.

Claude picked each ring up in turn and examined it carefully then began to transcribe the numbers engraved on the inside. He then went to his magnificent elderly safe bearing the familiar name 'CHUBB'. It was already unlocked and the huge door swung open quite easily. He opened a drawer and removed a pink coloured pocket file. He put the file on his desk and removed a letter from within. He checked some details with the notes he made earlier then stood up, took a deep breath and spoke to Jack in lowered tones.

"I have waited some months for this day Mr Mawgan. I am not sure what I expected but somehow in my imagination I thought it would be an older man and a man from the world of power and influence."

Jack was taken aback at first but then, with a wry smile on his face replied, "Maybe it would make you feel more comfortable if I told you that I work as a paramedic Herr Lindner, and I can assure you I have many times held the balance of someone's life in my hands. I think you will agree that there is no greater power and no greater influence than that." Claude was silent but after a moment he nodded and then handed Jack the rings together with a key and beckoned him to follow.

"Please, come this way." Claude approached a hefty-looking steel door and punched a code into the keypad beside it. The loud click signalled acceptance and he pushed the door inwards revealing a flight of steps.

Below, in the cellar, was a vault with a huge round access door. Claude opened it and they moved into the cool interior where the wall crammed with safe deposit boxes stood before them. He went to a box the size of a microwave oven with two keyholes in the door and put a key into the left hand lock and turned it anticlockwise to unlock it. He gestured to Jack who put down the rolled up sports bag he had been clutching then put a second key in the other lock. "Your key," he said then turned to leave the room. "Ring this bell when you need to come outside."

"Thank you." Jack swung the door open and was stunned at what he found inside. Just a white envelope, an ordinary looking letter size envelope. He tore it open and something fell from the inside. He picked it up; it was a two-gigabyte SD card.

Jack didn't know whether to be disappointed or happy with such an insignificant find. Maybe there would be something more substantial on the card. He carefully put it into a compartment of his wallet and returned it to his jacket pocket.

He closed and locked the box then removed his key. He left the vault to find Claude standing at the bottom of the stairway.

"You have finished Mister Mawgan?"

"Yes Herr Lindner, I believe we are finished." He held out the key to the box.

"No Mister Mawgan, that is your key now. Anytime you wish you can put something into the box or take something out." The nickel-plated key was engraved with the annotation 'CS 48 64 75 92' on one side and the word 'LOCARNO' on the other. "Just remember that you or your delegate must present the return ticket from Arona first, then we will know that the enquiry is genuine. Those are Mr Mikoyan's instructions."

"What happens if I forget the ticket?"

"My instructions are to keep the enquirer inside the bank and notify the police."

"I must be careful not to forget that bit then."

"Yes, please be sure to remember the ticket."

"OK, thanks." Jack said his goodbyes and left the bank in search of somewhere to have lunch. It would be a while before he could investigate the SD card. He had a lot of thinking to do and his mind always worked best after a good meal.

Dan watched as Jack left the bank and strolled towards the waterfront. He crossed the main lakeside road and headed towards the ferry terminal. Opposite the terminal were two restaurants, La Regina and Luigi's. Jack chose the latter and found a table by the window.

This was a critical moment for Dan. He figured that if the guy Jack threw off the ferry had accomplices then they would be here now and watching Jack. As far as he could tell nobody appeared to be paying much attention to the lone figure strolling into Luigi's carrying what appeared to be an empty

211

sports bag. Whatever Jack had collected from the bank Dan realised that it couldn't have amounted to much.

After lunch Jack decided that Christmas shopping was now on the agenda. By the time he had bought some presents for the family and was ready to board the ferry back to Arona he had acquired enough in the way of gifts to comfortably fill the bag.

16.30 – Friday 15th December 2006
Arona Ferry Terminal

The daylight was just beginning to fade as the Captain throttled back the engines and the hydrofoil came off the plane and settled into the flat calm water. With the hull now on the surface the four insect-like legs carrying the wing-shaped foils were raised to the vertical so that the skipper could manoeuvre the vessel alongside the quay.

The hustle and bustle of the departing passengers was accompanied by a lot of loud chitchat. Christmas shoppers loaded down with their tax-free shopping were eagerly trying to leave the area as quickly as possible hoping the Guardia di Finanza had something more important to do than collecting the twenty per cent sales tax from these cheerful bargain-hunters.

Jack stepped into the evening air and felt its chill. He paused to turn up the collar on his topcoat and placed the bag on the quayside. Suddenly the bag was picked up by a complete stranger who produced a wicked looking hunting knife and jabbed Jack in the ribs; he could feel the point digging into his side and knew it had drawn blood.

As soon as the attacker spoke Jack recognised that he was dealing with the same man that had attacked him in the morning but now he was dressed in different clothes. Something in the back of his mind registered that after taking a ducking he could hardly be back in the same clothes. Curiously there were tiny moments of lucidity when his mind's eye pictured a naked man standing in front of a Laundromat drier. Strange what extreme stress does to the subconscious, he mused, now a millisecond later, back in reality with a dark haired stranger yelling at him and causing him to wince at the pain in his side.

"Get going wise-arse. Down there along the quayside." Holding his hands up like a surrendering soldier told at least two observers that all was not well. Fifty metres away Seve was on the phone to Uncle Pedro.

"He's leaving the boat and he's carrying a blue sports bag, looks like it's full."

"Get the bag, but don't forget the key to the bank box."

"Wait! He's been mugged, some guy has grabbed him and is stealing the bag."

"Stop him, don't just stand there. Go stop him. You have to have the bag and find that key."

Seve put the phone back in his pocket and with the kind of adrenalin rush that he remembered from his exploits in Spanish Sahara he took giant steps towards the pair now proceeding in a curious huddle towards the boatyard at the end of the quay.

Julio put his lips close to Jack's ear and in a growling bear-like voice said, "You think you are fucking clever tossing me in the lake you bastard so now I'll take your bag of goodies and it's your turn to take a swim." As he braced himself to force Jack over the steel railing a large hand fell on his shoulder.

"Stop," said Seve, "give me that". He ripped the bag from the astonished Julio and gave him such a shove that he tottered backwards and with a helping hand from Jack disappeared over the rail and into the lake. The commotion was attracting the attention of passers-by and Seve, bag in hand gestured to Jack to move down the quayside, away from the now extremely vocal Julio.

Jack briefly thought that he had been rescued by a stranger but was mortified when his saviour turned on him and holding Jack by both collars demanded that Jack handed over the safe deposit box key. Fumbling in his pocket and with mind racing Jack reasoned that giving up the key to an empty box was preferable to getting a beating. He produced the key and dangled it for Seve to see. He grabbed it, pushed Jack to the ground and ran off with the bag.

Dan was one of the last passengers to leave the ferry and had lost sight of Jack as he walked up the boarding jetty towards the melee of jostling evening shoppers striding along the lakeside concourse and bent on Christmas shopping at the nearby Christmas Market. Arriving at the pavement he struggled to see through the crowds. To get a better view he stepped up on to the entrance stairway leading to the ticket office and peered in the direction of Jack's hire car in time to see Julio frog marching Jack along the quay.

He was about to set off in high dudgeon when he saw the stranger intervene and apparently save the day. Pushing his way towards the scene he could hear the commotion going on as passers-by attempted to rescue the floundering assailant and eventually came upon Jack flat on his backside and apparently in astonishingly good humour.

"Hello Jack, what have you been up to? I can't leave you alone for one minute."

"Dan, Daniel bloody Barclay, what the hell are you doing here?"

"What do you think? Babysitting you, you tearaway."

"Listen, I've just been mugged. Did you see him? That big fella." Dan's expression changed.

"I thought you dealt with him," nodding in the direction of the floundering Julio.

"No not him, the Spanish guy. Anyway it was the big fella that dealt with him, not me." Dan held out a hand and helped Jack to his feet.

"Did he get away with anything?"

"Yes, the bugger's pinched my Christmas shopping."

"Anything of value?"

Jack looked about him; they were surrounded by an increasing number of bystanders, attracted by the commotion over Julio's ducking.

"Let's go back to my car ... over here." Once in the car Jack felt able to relax. "The guy in the lake was the guy who attacked me this morning."

"Yes, I saw it happen, that was a nice move you pulled on him. He was no Judo artist or he'd have seen that one coming."

"No, my improvised 'Tai Otoshi' did seem to surprise him," they both laughed. "So do you mean to tell me you've been tailing me all day?" Dan smiled.

"The last two days me old mucker."

Jack grimaced, "Dammit, I knew there was someone in Puerto Mahon, I could sense it but I couldn't clock you," again the smile. "I had to give up the key to the box."

"Who to?"

"The big fella. He spoke in Spanish so maybe he came from Menorca too."

"So he got the lot, your bag of goodies and the key to vast riches?"

"Not very likely I'd say." Dan raised an eyebrow. "The box was all but empty. Just an envelope with an SD card in it."

"Have you played it?"

"Not yet, I can do it when we get back home."

"Or my office."

"I need to report the theft of my stuff to the cops, before that big fella gets clean away."

"Let's give that idea a miss shall we?" Dan checked his watch, "we'll miss the London flight but we can make the Bristol flight if you hurry ... and we don't get tied up with any police crap."

17.00 – Friday 15th December 2006
Terminal 2, Milan Malpensa Airport

"Hello, Uncle Pedro,"

"Where have you been?"

"I'm at the airport and I have the bag and the key. I don't think that anyone followed me here so I think we are in the clear."

"What's in the bag?".

"I haven't looked yet."

"Well look now." The priest sounded impatient. Seve did as he was told and was surprised to find a collection of gift-wrapped packages, a bottle of blueberry liqueur, boxes of chocolates and two packets of sugar-coated almonds. He ripped open the packages... a pair of ladies leather gloves, a wallet, a digital camera and a jeweller's box containing a silver bracelet.

"There's nothing here but shopping."

"What?"

"Just the kind of stuff you buy at Christmas time." There was silence on the line whilst Father Pedro considered the situation.

"He hasn't taken anything from the box, it's still there."

"What is?"

"Whatever was in the box, it must still be there."

"Maybe it was empty."

"Don't be stupid, do you think that Mawgan would have come all this way and Mikoyan would have used the gold rings and all that fuss to access the box if there was no point? No there was a point and the answers lie in that box. Get back there and find out what's inside."

"But ..."

"No 'buts' Seve, get back there now." Seve signed off, gathered his bags and trudged off to the taxi rank. It was when he came to pay for the taxi that he realised that he didn't have enough money to pay for another night at the hotel. He rather apprehensively put through a call to his uncle.

10.00 – Saturday 16ᵗʰ December 2006
Lower Spargo Cottage, Perranarworthal, Cornwall

Pam was listening to Jack's tale of woe about his trip to Spain, Italy and Switzerland. He was busy at the stove frying eggs and bacon; she was at the kitchen table sipping a cup of instant coffee.

Jack had arrived back home in the early hours of Saturday morning having dropped Dan off in Exeter and then continued on down to Cornwall in the little hire car they had picked up at Bristol airport.

"So after all that you got nothing but a teeny weeny card memory thing. Was it worth all the effort?"

"It's a 'memory card', not a card memory and only time will tell if it was worth an awful lot of effort … and a few bob too. We're going to call Hugh Martin and get him to take a look."

"Why don't you just hand it in to the people that Dan reports to. They must have boffins galore in GCHQ."

"Dan spoke to Justin, his boss, but he told us to keep it quiet and not let any of the security services have access to the files. He didn't exactly spell it out but I guess he doesn't trust the people he works with."

"That's unbelievable. If you can't trust the people in MI5 who can you trust?"

"Nobody."

"Can you still trust Hugh? You haven't seen him for years."

"Let's find out, I'll give him a call. His number's on my phone." He fumbled around looking for the cell phone.

"You left it on charge, your side of the bed."

"Thanks, let's strike whilst the iron is hot. I'll call him now."

CHAPTER 22

12.00 – Saturday 16th December 2006
NSS Corp HQ, Cardinal House, Heathrow Airport

SIR WILLIAM SALISBURY HAD summoned his protégé for a crisis conference at NSS HQ.

"Listen Freddie, we have information to indicate that since his return from Cyprus your friend Mawgan has been on a trip to Spain to collect the key to a safe deposit box in a Swiss Bank. Our man told us he apparently found a computer disc inside and a letter from Aram Mikoyan."

The head of NSS was rattled. The prospect of a computer disc that might contain damaging information floating around Whitehall was a worrying development. He didn't trust the Security Services to be 'on message' when it came to material that might embarrass the executive.

"I want you to have a word with the PM. He has to make sure this computer disc is found and destroyed. Heaven knows what could be on it but it won't be good if the contents are made public."

"Where is it now?"

"Mawgan arrived in Bristol last night. He lives in Cornwall and as far as we know the disc is still with him."

"How come it didn't go straight to MI5?"

"You need to ask them that. He should have been met on arrival and the disc taken to Whitehall. There's somebody playing a game here Freddie and I smell a rat."

"I can't believe that Mikoyan would devote his life to furthering the cause of corruption then decide on his deathbed to burn all the people he

217

has helped over the years by giving away sensitive information. Maybe the disc is harmless and our paranoia is getting the better of us?"

"Maybe it's not," said Sir William.

"Maybe if the disc was in our hands that information would allow us some leverage over the people we do business with ... and a few we don't."

"Are you suggesting that we should remove the disc from Mawgan and determine its contents?"

"Sounds like a plan, but he may have made copies."

"I'm less worried about the copies and more worried about knowing what on earth is on it and what game Mikoyan was playing at."

"Our chap inside Scotland Yard told us they want to interview Mawgan in connection with his kidnapping so we have a pretext for paying him a call."

"Can you get on to that now?"

"First I want to know about the meetings with the Italians. Were you able to finalise anything?"

"We were in the middle of agreeing terms when the balloon went up so the answer is 'no'. We need to find out who's replacing them and if they are OK with our sales agreement."

"Well you get on with sorting the Italians and I'll sort out our Mr Mawgan."

17.00 – Saturday 16th December 2006
Lower Spargo Cottage, Perranarworthal

It was raining the kind of tiny raindrops that gently caress your face but whilst you enjoy the sensation that these heavenly, watery feathers deliver they soak you to the skin in no time.

Driving in those conditions is bad enough in a modern car but Hugh Martin was on his way to Cornwall in his lovingly restored Triumph TR6 and in that kind of rain the 1960s vintage wipers were about as much use as a chocolate fireguard.

The last time Hugh drove down to Cornwall in the TR he was about to embark on an adventure with Jack and Dan that nearly cost him his life, so it was with a measure of trepidation that he pulled into the driveway at Lower Spargo Cottage.

"Come in Hugh, good to see you after all this time and kind of you to come on down to see us at such short notice." They shook hands and they went into the kitchen where Pam was making a pot of tea.

"Hello Hugh, lovely to see you again, how's Marjorie?"

"She's fine but her mother's not so well so she's been up in Norfolk for the last week taking care of her."

"We're in the same boat with my folks. My Mum is in and out of hospital at the moment."

"It's that time of our lives I guess, no sooner you have the kids sorted than you are having to worry about your parents."

Jack handed Hugh a cup of tea, "It's good of you to come all this way without knowing exactly why we need your help."

"You know I'm a sucker for a good mystery and of course I'm always glad to have an excuse to give the old 'TR' a blast. Now, what's this all about?"

Jack explained what had happened to him since he got involved with the death of Baroness Parker. After the best part of an hour Jack had brought Hugh up to date.

"Bloody hell Jack, you've been in the wars. What a tale that is. What do the cops have to say?"

"You know what happens when the high-ups get involved. That Freddie McLaren is a piece of work. I saved his life and he hardly said a word of thanks."

"McLaren, he's the PM's Press Officer isn't he?"

"Officially yes but he seems to do a hell of a lot more than write press releases."

"Such as?"

"He was on board to meet with two Italians from Malmeccanica, a huge conglomerate that runs a lot of the big engineering firms in Italy."

"Yes, I know them from my days at British Aerospace."

They sat sipping tea with the click, clack of kitchen utensils going on in the background. "If you guys want some supper I suggest you clear off and let me get on," Pam said.

The duo adjourned to the lounge and made themselves comfortable in the armchairs. Hugh put his computer bag down beside his chair. Neither said a word but the noise emanating from the whirring wheels inside both their brain boxes was deafening. Eventually it was Hugh who spoke first.

"Baroness Parker, she used to be head of MI5?"

"Correct."

"She retired and took over as head of that air ambulance trust up in the midlands."

"If you say so."

"Don't you know her? I thought you would have come across her given you were in the same business."

"I'm the clinician remember. Those charity types move in different circles. They organise the cash to keep us going and we take care of the wounded."

"As head of IT for one of the nation's premier accounting companies I have to tell you that there are some funny things going on in the half dozen air ambulance trusts that we are involved with."

"Such as?"

"This is not for consumption outside this room but there are some unusually large amounts of cash being moved out of their holding accounts."

"Where's it going?"

"Funny you should ask. We don't know yet but I have one of my best people looking into it."

"You smell something funny?"

"Maybe, time will tell."

"Could the Baroness' death be tied in with these strange financial activities?"

"I can't think how."

The wheels began whirring once more. This time it was Jack that broke the silence.

"You remember I told you about the job I did for the Home Office."

"Yes, up in the Midlands but you glossed over the detail."

"I was apparently hand-picked to head up the new National Police Aviation Service. It was a short term position and in retrospect it was clear that I was a sacrificial lamb."

"How come?"

"It soon became obvious that the government plan was to circumvent the normal protocols and bypass the senior police officers. They knew that the Chief Constables and their sidekicks would block it one way or another."

"So how did you get involved?"

"Someone up there in the upper echelons decided that an ex-copper who could spell the word helicopter was ripe for a bit of abuse."

"You sound bitter."

Jack thought for a moment. "Disappointed rather than bitter I suppose."

"Disappointed?"

"Whilst we are busy sharing secrets I'll share one or two with you. Maybe it will get me over my disappointment."

"Don't blab on my behalf mate."

"It's not blabbing, it will be therapy. During my time at the NPAS we were extremely focussed on setting up a highly effective and highly efficient outfit. To that end we were going to standardise on one type of helicopter and reap all the economies of scale that would go along with that principle."

"Who did the evaluations before you committed to the selection?"

"It was done by an external consultancy called CHOPA."

"You're kidding me, the Consultants for Helicopter Operations and Administration?"

"Yes, how do you know them?"

"We were their auditors. They were put under scrutiny by the Revenue for making and receiving undisclosed payments."

"Do you know who their CEO is?"

"Was!"

"Oh, it's like that."

"It was Derek Salisbury or should I say Colonel Derek Salisbury Army Air Corps, retired. Now he's on Police bail pending a court appearance."

"Interesting ... charged with ... ?"

"Fraud, money laundering, misappropriation of public funds and misconduct in public office. Now be careful, you are in danger of putting two and two together and coming to the conclusion that the disappearing funds were routed through a certain Italian organisation famous for its successful range of utility helicopters."

"And were they?"

"That's the bit that's difficult to nail down. We know that to be the case but we can't prove it ... at the moment."

Pam interrupted their chat to tell them that dinner was served. Hugh was always very complimentary about Pam's cooking and the mealtime chatter was friendly as they reminisced about their adventures back in the year 2000. Whilst the food and company were engaging it didn't prevent both Jack and Hugh from running their brain cells over the seemingly endless connections that brought together the threads of Jack's and Hugh's recent past.

It was inevitable that after dinner the discussions would return to the NPAS theme and that the fruit of their thoughts during dinner would add to the analysis. Back in their armchairs and with the aroma of freshly brewed coffee in the air it was Hugh who began.

"Jack, are you aware of any links between the world of Police Aviation and the world of Air Ambulances?"

"Of course, there are only so many types of helicopter available and they are both dominated by a small group of overseas manufacturers who in turn have UK based agents."

"Would you say that the Italians feature strongly in the market?"

"No, they don't, not yet anyway, just one or two out of maybe fifty or sixty machines."

"So which helicopter did your independent consultants select for NPAS?"

"The Italian one, it was unquestionably the fastest."

"Don't tell me, they used the old argument that a faster machine can cover more territory so you need fewer of them."

"Exactly that."

"Could they be trying that on with the air ambulances?"

"Not possible Hugh. They could maybe do it with the odd one or two that happen to be run by the NHS but the majority are run by fiercely independent charities."

"Fiercely independent charities led by people like Baroness Parker."

"Hell, where are you going with this?"

"Look, it's the same people ultimately running both the Home Office and the NHS. If they are playing games with one why wouldn't they want to play games with the other?"

"But by implication that would mean that I could draw a straight line between the murder of the Baroness and the purchase of helicopters from Italy."

"That's a big hop to connect those two together."

"Not such a big step because I have found a connection between those involved in the murder and organs of the state."

"Organs of the state? You must be joking. More conspiratory stuff, like the Doctor Skellie mystery."

"Suicide."

"Touché. Maybe they weren't official state operatives, more like unofficial agents working outside the normal scheme of things."

"What, you mean like Dan?" Jack was nonplussed momentarily at the mention of Dan but then remembered that Dan had been involved with Hugh during the Chaloner affair back in 2000.

"I mean that people like Dan are involved but they are not sponsored by the Security Services."

"You've lost me."

"Black ops people run directly by the executive not by MI5 or MI6."

"Still lost."

"The executive, the people at No 10, hire, brief and use people that are lookalike agents working off-piste."

"What, and they murdered the Baroness?"

"Probably."

"Hell!"

"And kidnapped me and ran me out of town."

"Do you think this chap McLaren is involved?"

"Up to his neck."

"Blimey, I only came here to chat about a computer disc now I'm privy to a virtual coup d'état."

"Let's not get carried away mate, the armed forces aren't involved and nobody is trying to take over."

"Arguably that's because they already have … taken over I mean."

"No, I don't think so, we still have an elected government in power."

"Maybe but they are not doing things according to the norms of open government."

"What do we know about the norms of open government? We haven't the faintest idea what goes on behind those closed doors. Sometimes it doesn't bear thinking about but what can we do about it?" Hugh stopped to think for a moment.

"Let's check out this disc of yours, shall we. Maybe we can find a crumb of comfort there."

Jack produced the SD card from his wallet.

"Ah, good, a card rather than a disc" Hugh said, bending to remove a laptop from his bag. "That makes my life easier."

"Do you want to use my PC rather than the laptop? You're very welcome."

Hugh looked up and just smiled. "In here there is magic," he pointed to his chunky looking laptop.

"I'll get some more coffee," Jack said disappearing into the kitchen. Pam was working in the office upstairs and appeared at the doorway. "I heard the kettle going on."

"Making some more coffee."

"Can I join you or is it stuff you'd rather I didn't know about. I stuck my nose in earlier but heard those magic words you come out with."

"What magic words?"

"When you say something like 'I could tell you but then I'll have to shoot you'."

"You know the rules love, come and join us but no gossip about what is said in this little forum."

By the time they had prepared and delivered a tray of freshly brewed coffee Hugh had had a chance to assess the data on the SD card.

"Anything of interest?" Jack asked, "I was worried what kind of tricks might be hidden on what looks such a simple and innocent device."

"Very wise of you, I would say more than interesting. Watch this." Hugh turned the laptop for them to see and then hit the 'go' button. A bronzed but haggard and troubled looking Aram Mikoyan came into view, seated in what appeared to be his home office and wearing a blue Polo shirt. The background was a magnificent looking bookcase crammed with impressive leather-bound books. He began hesitantly.

This is my final message to the world. You have been specially chosen to receive a precious gift but first I have to explain why this video is necessary. My health is not good and I may die before I have completed my mission to make restitution to a world that has given me huge riches and allowed me to live a life of privilege.

My life has not been a glorious one. It has in fact been one big lie. I have corrupted many men and women and helped those that were already corrupt. In order that I may go to heaven I must first make my way through Purgatory. I am a serial sinner who might expect a long and miserable time in that place. Thanks to my priest, Father Pedro, I have been reunited with my faith and shown the way to righteousness. The monies that I have stolen and the monies I have helped others to steal will be returned to society but also I must make restitution to those who have been humiliated by my lack of humanity. You will need to use your judgement to decide who to bring down and who to impoverish. Your wisdom must be your guide.

You have been chosen because you are a good person and I trust you to complete my plan.

I have continued my liaisons with many corrupt people from the world of politics, the world of commerce and those that hold military posts and have access to elicit funds. This will allow me to create a tool for you that can change the world, maybe just a little, but it will change the world.

You will find this data card is the key to a remote server containing a collection of bank statements for each of my clients. You may not recognise the names without understanding the positions they hold in their world but that is unimportant for it was my intention and now your responsibility to deprive these corrupt people of their undeserved wealth.

There is a file on the card called 'Choose and decide'. You will need a good Internet connection for the system to operate correctly. When you click on this file you will be presented with access to the list of my clients. Selecting a name will take you to their bank statements held on my private servers. They will show you their nationality and the name that appears on their passport, they may have more than one account so these will be listed on the screen to enable you to choose which one you wish to use for your activity.

Selecting the account you want to manipulate you will be presented with a range of activities. The first is 'Destroy'. This option will do two things, the first is that the funds will be transferred to my personal account and apparently disappear. The second is that the account statement will be e-mailed to The Washington Post in the USA and The Guardian newspaper in England.

If you choose to use the 'destroy' function you must be prepared for the political and other consequences this may bring about. Beware the law of unintended consequences.

The second function is called 'Disappear'. This option will transfer the funds to my personal account and they will apparently disappear.

To access my personal account you should download the instructions that are in the folder entitled 'My Account'. These instructions also contain a guide to disbursements, you should study this carefully.

Please be aware that secreted within the software are a number of features I have asked the designer to include. One will prevent you copying any part of this card or any file on the remote servers. Another will shut down the automatic functions and delete the files that provide access to the system if you attempt to misuse the funds in my personal account. For example, any attempts to move funds to unapproved locations will result in the 'shutdown' function being activated. What is an unapproved function? You will only find out the hard way. The algorithm is a secret.

That is all I have to say. I wish you good fortune and good judgement. May your God go with you?

The video ended as abruptly as it began and they all sat around looking at each other rather stunned by what they had heard. An argument ensued. Pam, to their surprise was all for finding all the villains she could recognise and experimenting with the destroy button. This unexpected megalomaniacal tendency shocked Jack and amused Hugh.

"Listen folks," Hugh put his laptop to one side and got up from the comfort of the armchair. "This is the scariest thing I've heard since the last time you two indulged in cops and bloody robbers."

"Scary," said Jack, now lounging in the other armchair, "it frightens me to death. Can you imagine putting the skids under one of those greasy politicians only to find that you bring the house down too?"

"But the man himself says that he wants us …"

"… me," corrected Jack.

"OK, you … to punish these people. Surely we should take the hint and get on with it?" Hugh moved over to the window and stared into the night. The skies had cleared and in the light of a crescent moon he could see a frost was beginning to form on the lawn outside. They could tell he was about to say something and waited for his words of wisdom.

"From what you tell me this guy Mikoyan wasn't much of a moral leader, not someone fit to dish out a principled view on the world, not someone qualified to guide your hand Jack." Attention moved to Jack who still lounged in his chair and looked ready for bed.

"Food for thought, maybe we can chew it over tomorrow and give it a try."

"Give what a try?" enquired Pam.

"Find a name that we recognise and make his fortune disappear."

"If you are going to do that you should tell the papers too otherwise their evil will go unpunished."

"Like I said, food for thought. Come on, let's go to bed and have another look at things tomorrow. I have to go to work Monday so can't afford too many late nights."

"Me too," said Hugh. "I need to get my bag from the car." Hugh collected his overnight bag from the boot of the TR and hurried back inside without noticing the man sitting in an anonymous dark saloon across the road from Jack's front gate.

06.00 – Sunday 17th December 2006
Lower Spargo Cottage, Perranarworthal

The banging at the front door woke the whole house but it was Jack who bounded down the stairs in his dressing gown and opened the front door. Two men in dark overcoats stood in the doorway.

"Mr Mawgan, Mr John Mawgan?"

"Yes, how can I help you?"

"I'm Detective Inspector Walters and this is Detective Sergeant Anderson." They held their ID up for inspection but quickly put them away again. "We have reason to believe that you have recently returned from abroad and have interacted with persons unknown in connection with illegal activities. We have a warrant for your arrest in connection with those on-going enquiries." The estuarial twang yelled 'Essex'. Anderson held up a pair of handcuffs and indicated he wanted Jack to hold out his arms.

"One moment please, I know most of the guys in CID round here and I don't recall seeing either of you two before. Let's see your warrant cards again, you can't be too careful these days."

"We're not local Mr Mawgan, we're from the Serious Crimes Squad and we're based with The Met at Scotland Yard but we cover the whole UK and a few other places too." He tried an unconvincing smile but Jack was too busy to notice. He found the IDs to be in order.

"I'll need to get dressed."

"We'll wait here."

Pam appeared at Jack's elbow and Hugh was hovering in the background.

"What is it Darling? Who are these people?"

"They are policemen and they have come to arrest me."

"The hell they have. What's this all about?"

"It's OK love, I'll get dressed and we'll get this sorted as soon as we can." Jack disappeared upstairs.

"But where are you going, where are you taking him?"

"We'll be at Camborne Police Station for the time being but we may need to transfer to London." The sound of a motorbike suddenly wrecked the peace and quiet and the taillight of a big Triumph appeared from the side of the house and rapidly disappeared up Cove Hill, the headlight casting an eerie glow in the early morning mist. The startled policemen guessed that it was Jack making a rapid exit. The Sergeant dashed towards their car but the inspector was already on his cell-phone yelling instructions as he trotted down the gravel driveway.

Pam and Hugh looked at each other, both stunned by the sudden turn of events. Hugh was amused by it all but Pam was anything but. She couldn't work out whether Jack's sudden departure was a good thing or a bad thing. Inside she knew that Jack was for the time being a free man and somehow that made her happier than the thought of him being under arrest. It was an irrational proposition for it had all the hallmarks of ending badly.

"What now?" asked Hugh.

"We wait," Pam replied, "Jack will be in touch I'm sure."

16.00 – Sunday 17th December 2006
Lower Spargo Cottage, Perranarworthal

They both jumped at the sound, it was Hugh's cell phone. "It's him, it's Jack," he waved his arm at Pam who was dozing in the other arm chair, beckoning her to come and listen then put the phone on speaker.

"Hi Hugh, sorry to ruin your morning but I figured I was better out of it. I'm guessing that your cell phone is not likely to be monitored whereas mine, Pam's and our landline probably will be."

"Where are you," asked Pam.

"I'm not going into detail but I'll be staying at the house we used when that chap Chaloner was around."

"What, Rose Cottage?" Hugh slapped her wrist and she suddenly realised that she had given away Jack's hiding place.

"Sorry Darling, bit slow on the uptake."

"Well I'm counting on them not listening in on this number but you never know. Let's take sensible precautions. By the way those coppers weren't the real thing, the IDs were real but the photos had been tampered with."

"What can we do to help Jack?" Hugh asked.

"You still have the SD card?"

"Yes."

"Then gather all you need for a long night and meet me at the cottage. Take Hugh's car and make sure you're not followed." Pam and Hugh exchanged looks and both nodded agreement.

"Right, see you there."

18.00 – Sunday 17th December 2006
Rose Cottage, Helford Village, Cornwall

The sky over Cornwall began to shed its overcoat of grey cloud allowing the last rays of the setting sun to turn the long shadows into weird shapes before they disappeared into the greyness of twilight. Fortunately Hugh was able to remember the route along the tortuously narrow lanes that led to a small farm that sits above Helford Village. It provided an alternative roadside parking spot for those that preferred to walk down to the heart of the village rather than take the normal and very conspicuous route to Rose Cottage.

Pam and Hugh finally arrived carrying nothing more than a couple of overnight bags, a rucksack full of computer gear and a flashlight.

"Come in you two, where did you leave the car?"

"Up at Kestle Barton then we walked down the hill."

"Good, we should be safe here for a while." Jack took their winter coats and ushered them into the lounge where a log fire burned brightly.

"How did you get the keys?" Pam asked.

"I went straight round to Auntie May's flat in Falmouth when I left our place and asked if I could borrow the cottage for a week or so."

"Where's your motorbike?"

"In the old garage,"

"At least it's nice and cosy in here," observed Hugh,

"Make yourself at home, I haven't done much except drink tea and eat biscuits but now that you are here we can get started trying to find a way out of this mess."

"What's the communication set up like these days. Has modern technology caught up with Helford Village?"

"Certainly has, Auntie May has had broadband connected but it's not up to much I'm afraid, not as fast as you get at your place. At least you can use a cell phone here now that they put the mast on the hill across the river. However folks," he held up his cell phone, "we can't use them remember, they are going to be monitored. I didn't have much time but I did stop at the Vodafone store and pick up a pay-as-you-go cheapo stand-in handset just in case."

"Something is better than nothing I suppose," Hugh responded.

"I'm afraid there's not much in the way of supplies. I managed to grab some tea bags, a packet of biscuits and a litre of milk at the corner shop but couldn't carry much more on the bike."

"In that case I'll put the kettle on," said Pam, heading for the kitchen.

Reinforced by a tea and Hobnobs the three hunched around the fire, Jack and Hugh in old style stick-back arm chairs and Pam curled up on the floor in between them.

"What's the plan?" Hugh asked. Hugh was head of IT at one of the country's big five accountancy firms and his job required some formal and some informal skills. When it came to all things computer then Hugh was the man to have on your side. His speciality was an unexpected talent for hacking into other people's computers. He excused his criminal behaviour by insisting that he had to be able to see what his corporate charges were really up to when his auditors were busy inspecting the corporate accounts. "The bigger the firm, the bigger the lies so when we sign off on the corporation's accounts I want to know what we are signing up to," he explained.

"Wait," said Pam, "you haven't explained where those bogus policeman came from and why they wanted to arrest you."

Jack put on his pensive expression, "Almost certainly they were the Men in Black again."

"Why would they want to take you away?"

"I can think of a couple of reasons but what worries me, is that they seem to know all about my trip to Switzerland, and the only person I have told about that in detail was Dan."

"Hell you don't think Dan's involved with them do you?"

"No, I would trust Dan with my life. I'm sure he's not involved with the bad guys but he must have told his minders in Whitehall and someone in that office is leaking stuff to the Men in Black."

"That's worrying," Pam said.

"More than worrying, it means that we can't trust anyone in MI5 until we have found the leak. It's probably the reason why Dan's boss told me not to hand the disc in to London but to keep it safe."

"Does Dan know about our situation?"

"When I had the keys to Rose cottage and I knew we would be able to go there I sent him a cryptic text message eluding to our previous adventures in Helford Village. If he gets the message then I'm sure he'll pitch up here eventually. As before, we have to think twice before we communicate with the outside world. Cell phones are a dead giveaway these days."

"We can use the internet without fear of being traced by using my VPN network."

"Good, I was counting on that."

"By the way, the data card has very little actual data on it. All the crucial stuff is kept on servers. I managed to have a quick look at the list of names on one of the servers back at your house but it would take many hours trawling through every one to find one we recognised. I am going to re-jig my little homemade search engine so that you will be able to punch in a key word and it will list all the files that contain that keyword. You will be able to use words like 'police', MP, Doctor, and so on."

"Wow, that's cool," said Jack, "will it work?"

Hugh put on his withering look, "Of course it will work, look I'll show you." Hugh unpacked his laptop and set it up on the dining room table. His voluminous computer bag contained a router that he set up in the hallway and connected to the ADSL outlet. Soon he was clacking away on the keyboard and then pronounced himself ready to experiment with keywords.

Pam was first to proffer a suggestion. "Prime Minister," she said with a certain amount of venom.

"OK, let's see what that throws up." Hugh typed in the words and hit the 'Enter' key. A stream of files aligned themselves on the screen.

"The folder contains one thousand, four hundred and eighty-five names and has found fifty-two that contain the words 'Prime Minister'."

"Let's have a look," said Pam, craning her neck over Hugh's shoulder. Jack joined on the other side and together they silently scanned the names that appeared.

"Look," said Pam, "I know that name."

"Yes look, 'Beg A', that's the prime minister of Israel."

"No, lower down the list, 'Stewart G', that's our own prime minister."

"No that would be 'T. Stewart', he's Toby Stewart," corrected Hugh.

"No he's actually Gordon Toby Stewart but he uses his middle name instead."

"I want to see the 'Beg' file," said Jack, "that man has a connection to Aram Mikoyan and I want to know the details. He may well be behind the sinking of La Reine Bleu and the loss of her crew."

"OK," Pam replied, "but I want to see what that bastard Stewart has been up to."

"Sorry Hugh, she's still fired up about Stewart and the Iraq war."

"Don't apologise for me Jack Mawgan. There's nothing to apologise for anyway, he lied through his teeth and got away with it. Him and that righteous American who spouted fine words and then concocted a pretext for war that Stewart went along with."

"Right, but let's come to him in a moment." Hugh clicked on the name and the screen displayed a number of accounts in different folders. Selecting the first folder there were two files, one called 'Notes' and the second called 'Statement'. Curious about the text file called 'notes' he opened this first.

1/1/06 Loan – $1m passed to account M. Leclerc pending receipt funds ex

US. (probably related to approval to build his new ski lodge in Chamonix. Loan repayment via incoming funds from The Indiana Zionist Association)

The second note simply said:

1/4/06 Late. (IZA does not appear to exist)

The third note said:

1/7/06 Late, first warning.

The last note said:

1/10/06 Late, final warning.

"Crikey," said Pam, "what does it all mean?"

"Looks to me that this guy Beg took a loan from Mikoyan on the promise of incoming payments from the US. Maybe the threat from a final warning was what pushed him over the edge." Hugh speculated.

"I am trying not to have these thoughts guys but you can guess what's going through my mind," said Jack.

"You think a head of state would use the forces of the state to sink a ship, kill thirty odd people for an unpaid debt?"

"Yes Pam," Jack replied, "that's no worse than Stalin did."

"And don't forget the problems the French have had," Hugh added.

"The French?" asked Pam.

"Yes the President was using the intelligence services to spy on his political rivals."

"Not exactly in the murder and mayhem league though is it," Pam replied.

"Tell that to Greenpeace," chimed in Hugh, "on a smaller scale maybe but the same principle applies."

"You're right Hugh, I had forgotten all about that little caper," added Jack. "The sad thing is this guy Beg appears to have no cash we can remove, only his reputation but I would say that was a fair exchange given his misuse of power."

"But my goodness Jack, if that's true then it is a horrendous state of affairs," said Pam.

"But we have been given the power to do something about it."

"Yes Hugh, but what exactly, destroy or impoverish?" Jack asked.

"I say go for the jugular," Pam announced with conviction.

"But what will the consequence be I wonder. What do we know of Israeli politics?" Hugh said, sounding a little less confident than Pam.

"Remember the cautionary note from Aram, 'beware the law of unintended consequences'," cautioned Jack.

"What's to be worried about?" asked Pam, "so he gets found out and gets the boot. I bet they're queuing up in Jerusalem to take the job on. Maybe the next one will get the message."

"Pamela Mawgan, I never thought you could be such a hard-arse," Jack replied somewhat surprised.

"I feel like a Roman Emperor and I'm going to give the thumbs down to Mr Arial Beg, especially as he nearly killed my fella."

"So are we agreed, our first target and we are going for 'destroy'?"

"I'm not going to argue with that but what's worrying me is I feel no sense of drama about blowing the lid off the Israeli prime minister."

They sat peering at the screen whilst Hugh put the cursor on the menu item 'destroy' and immediately a message box appeared.

Confirm Destroy – Beg A. – Y/N

Without hesitation he pressed the 'Y' key. There was no 'bang', no explosion, no scream. Just a poignant moment of silence whilst the software whirred away. A few seconds later another message appeared.

Beg A. Destroyed – 19:52 17/12/06

Jack turned to Hugh, "Will they be able to track us down when the proverbial hits the fan?"

"They will have a job, my VPN is set to New York, via Mexico City. They may get there eventually but only if they deploy the state security system and they get multiple messages with the same pathway."

"So the next one you use a different pathway?"

"Yep, and we keep changing each time we use the software."

"I'll make some more tea," said Pam, somewhat deflated by the lack of occasion.

"What time is it in Washington?" Jack enquired, turning to Hugh.

"I guess they are five hours behind us so the Washington Post will get the story in good time for Monday morning."

"If the Guardian are quick off the mark they could have it in an early edition too."

Pam arrived with another tray of tea and biscuits. "My turn," she said, taking a seat at Hugh's elbow. "Can we do Mr Gordon Tobias Stewart now?"

Hugh returned to the list of names and clicked on 'Stewart G'. The screen changed to one displaying half a dozen folders each with an account number alongside the icon. Hugh selected the first account and went straight to the 'notes' file. He read aloud,

Commission payment account number one.

"What's in the next folder?" asked Pam?

"Hang on," said Jack, "how much is in the account?"

One click and Hugh responded, "Four million, two hundred and fifty thousand dollars."

"Blimey, that will buy you a nice holiday in the Caribbean,"

"Huh!" quipped Pam, "since when does the Prime Minister pay for his holidays. Come on what's in the next one?"

Hugh tried the next account and opened the notes file. Again just one note.

Solidarity fund

"Nothing much of interest it appears," added Pam, seemingly disappointed at the lack of detail. Hugh opened the statement file.

"Crikey, twelve million dollars."

"Solidarity fund, that smacks of some kind of political funding." Hugh observed.

"I guess the kind of political funding that's under the radar," Jack added.

"What about the next one,"

"Hang on Pam, give me a mo." Hugh brought up the third file and found a series of notes.

1. *Salisbury number one.*
2. *Transfer $1m to UBS A11200049675CH on 1/1/07*
3. *Transfer $1m to UBS A11200049675CH on 1/2/07*

"Doesn't ring any bells," said Jack, peering at the screen, "but we can guess that it's someone's numbered account in Switzerland."

"Don't suppose you can look it up for us Hugh?"

"No Jack, not today, maybe from my office facilities in Bristol but not here with this laptop."

"How much?" Pam asked. Hugh brought up the statement and they were mesmerised by the amount.

"Can that be right?" asked Jack,

"Surely not," said Pam.

"Guys and gals you are looking at one hundred and fifty million dollars."

"Wow, how does a guy like Stewart get that kind of money?"

"We'll have a look in more detail later but from what I can see the payments in and out are only detailed with a date, no commentary or explanation."

"That's not much help," said Jack.

"What's in the last account?" asked Pam, sounding desperate for something interesting. It didn't take long for Hugh to have the last of the accounts up on screen and together they peered at a long list of notes.

1. *Green – 1st payment due 1/6/94*
2. *Orange – 1ˢᵗ payment due 14/6/94*
3. *Green – 2ⁿᵈ payment due 1/6/95*
4. *Orange – 2ⁿᵈ payment due 14/6/95*
5. *Green – 3ʳᵈ payment due 1/6/96*
6. *Orange – 3ʳᵈ payment due 14/6/96*
7. *Green – 4ᵗʰ payment due 1/6/97*
8. *Orange – 4ᵗʰ payment due 14/6/97*
9. *Final payments 10/4/98*

"This is obviously an account that's been around for a while." Hugh noted.

"Yes, and no movements since the tenth of April in 1998, how much is in there?" said Jack.

"Not much, just look at the flows. There were two inputs in 1994 of ten million dollars then annual payments of one million to the two colour-coded recipients. There's an interest payment credited each year and it looks like that's all that's left after that final payment of two million dollars back in April 1998, nearly two million dollars."

"Well are we going to do anything about all this stinking polluted wealth that doesn't belong to him? I say we sink him and take the lot away." Pam was finding it hard to restrain her emotions. The evil of corruption in high office was something she felt so strongly about.

"What are you saying Pam, destroy him or just remove his hidden wealth?" Jack asked.

"Let's go the whole way shall we? He doesn't deserve any quarter."

"Might I step in here," Hugh interrupted, "there is a case for caution, let's just remove all his money and see what happens. I have a bad feeling about what we have done to Mr Beg. It's only Jack's adventure on the high seas that gives my conscience a break."

"All right," said Pam, anything to keep the peace.

"Here we go then." Hugh clicked on the 'Transfer to my account' button. The software worked away silently for half a minute then the text box appeared announcing that all the accounts had been transferred.

"Job done," Hugh said triumphantly.

"I think that will do for now," said Jack, "it's getting late and we had better think about what we are going to do tomorrow."

"I'm supposed to be at work in Bristol tomorrow but I'll call in sick in the morning and take a couple of days off, it's pretty quiet right now."

"Great, that means you can go to the supermarket and get some supplies."

"Jack," it was Pam, "I've just had a look upstairs and there's no bedding, at least no sheets or pillow cases."

"Ah, yes, I remember Auntie May saying something about that. She didn't have any bookings until New Year. Is that a problem?"

"Yes it is. Well it is for me. If you fancy sleeping under a scratchy old blanket then you're welcome."

CHAPTER 23

08.30 – Monday 18th December 2006
Rose Cottage, Helford Village, Cornwall

As DAWN BROKE OVER Helford River's placid waters the complete absence of man-made clatter somehow accentuated the calmness in that blessed little corner of Cornwall. The distant call of a lone seabird only added to the illusion that mankind had abandoned the entire estuary in favour of its native wildlife. The sky had cleared overnight and the temperature had dropped to just above zero. A light layer of mist hovered over the middle of the river where the waters were cooler, untouched by the warming effect of the tides on the river margins.

Hugh was up early and striding up the hill to Kestle Barton to find his car and assume the burden of duty shopper. His breath turned to steam in the cold morning air and he hummed an approximation of Paul Simon's 'April She Will Come'. His body may have been in mid winter but his soul was already embracing spring.

If the sounds of Helford were embellished by an absence of noise then the same could not be said of the smells. At low tide the rotting seaweed on the mud banks produced an acrid and disagreeable odour that wrinkled the nose and tested a man's appreciation of that beautiful wooded valley.

Jack was up and about, pottering around in just the jeans he had thrown on in the hurried escape from Lower Spargo the previous morning. The cold slate floor chilled his bare feet as he busied himself making a pot of tea. Pam was still sound asleep upstairs. The dulcet and reassuring tones of John Humphrys, the BBC host of the morning news and current affairs programme 'Today', emanated from the ancient transistor radio that sat on the equally ancient fridge. Suddenly Jack's attention was taken by the mention of the word 'Israel'. He turned up the volume and momentarily forgot about his tea making.

Breaking news in Jerusalem is just coming through from Reuters. We are monitoring the news from the Israeli capital following revelations in this morning's Jerusalem Post. We are getting unconfirmed reports that the Prime Minister, Arial Ehud Beg, has resigned. Details are still a little hazy but the Jerusalem Post is carrying a story indicating that Prime Minister Arial Beg paid a large sum of money to a Monique Leclerc. Leclerc is apparently the maiden name of the wife of the opposition leader Moshe Lavan.

If we can we'll bring you an update before the programme ends.

Jack returned to his tea making but kept an ear open for any updates. He could feel the adrenalin welling up inside him as the news hit home and he began to take on board the enormity of what they had done. It was the surprisingly rapid impact of their joint decision to, at one keystroke, destroy what at the time was simply a name in a list. Now he began to realise what Aram had meant when he said 'beware of the law of unforeseen consequences'.

Hugh came bouncing in the back door full of the Christmas spirit and in jolly mood. He carried bags of supplies and explained that he had to leave the car parked outside the garage, as there were more bags of groceries to come.

"Hugh, come over here, listen to the radio with me."

"Why, what's on?"

"It's the news programme, all hell has broken out in Israel apparently. The prime minister is rumoured to have resigned."

"Crikey, how can that be, the newspapers wouldn't have had time to get the story out until later today."

"Either the Guardian or the Washington Post, possibly both, have a link to the Jerusalem Post. It was them that broke the story."

"Of course, they are two hours ahead of us so they must have been chewing on it for at least …" he checked his watch, "four hours or so."

Pam appeared with sleepy eyes and tousled hair. "What's all the fuss about," she managed to mutter as Hugh began unloading the shopping and announcing each item purchased seeking confirmation that he had bought the right thing.

"Jeepers, Hugh, you've bought enough to feed the five thousand."

"Well, Pamela my dear, hungry minds have hungry bellies. I must say the shop in Manaccan is a real treasure trove and a bit like the Tardis. Small on the outside and vast on the inside."

"Sit down Pam there's a bit of a thing going on in Jerusalem you need to know about." Jack said, trying not to give away his angst about what they had done.

"Hang on let me grab my cup of tea. We need to light another fire it's blooming freezing down here."

"Sorry folks I forgot all about the night store heaters but I'll put them on now and stick the timer on override." Pam curled up in an armchair whilst Jack started making up the fire.

"The storage heaters will take a while to get going but we can at least get this baby alight."

"So what's the news then and can we turn the radio down a bit?" Hugh joined them and Jack began to answer Pam's question.

"Actually I've got one ear on the radio. We're on the news."

"What?"

"Well we are not exactly on the news but the impact of our decision last night is beginning to have some effect by the sound of it."

"You're kidding?"

"No I'm bloody serious, the Israeli prime minister has resigned. All hell's broken loose."

"Blimey, that was quick. How the hell did the news get around so fast?"

"We reckon that the Washington Post or maybe the Guardian ..."

"Maybe both, they do a lot of networking I seem to recall," Hugh interrupted.

"Anyway, maybe they have a link with the Jerusalem Post."

"Why the Jerusalem Post."

"They were the ones that apparently broke the story this morning."

"Hang on, it's the nine o'clock news."

This is turning out to be a Monday morning from hell for the Israeli Prime Minister who has resigned his post following revelations in the Jerusalem Post.

Mr Arial Beg will be making a statement at a news conference in two hours' time. The revelations concerned the payment of a large sum of money to the wife of the opposition party ZPL. The reasons for the payments are unclear but the fact that the evidence was so clear and uncontested has caused a rift amongst the coalition and opposition parties alike.

Our correspondent in Jerusalem reports that the military have indicated they will restore order if the coalition is unable to command the respect of the Knesset.

The three looked at each other. "We got him," said Jack, uncertain quite how triumphant he should sound.

"It's quite humbling really," said Hugh, "all we did was click the 'yes' key and bang, down he goes."

"Maybe it's Pam's turn now?" mused Jack.

"Actually," said Pam, "I want to balance the books a bit."

"The books?" asked Jack.

"Yes, wasn't there mention of 'disbursements' in the blurb about your friend Mikoyan, let's find out what sort of disbursements he's on about."

"Do you know that's a good idea, I forgot all about that. Let's take a look at that folder and see exactly what he means."

"While you are doing that I'll make us some breakfast."

Hugh returned to his makeshift office in the dining room and spent the next twenty minutes scribbling notes on a pad and clicking away on his laptop.

"Breakfast is on the kitchen table, come and get it," Pam called. Hugh didn't need a second call, he was hungry enough to eat the legs off a chair and soon found his place at the opposite end of the table to Jack.

"There's cereal, toast and those are five minute eggs in the bowl, grilled sausages and bacon on that plate, so help yourself, toast will be ready in a minute."

"Wow," said Hugh, "just what the doctor ordered."

"And the doctor cooked," quipped Pam. Her mind may have been tired but her sense of humour was intact and working well. There was little heed paid to the niceties of sophisticated table manners. The tension, drama and stress had given them all a healthy appetite and they felt familiar enough in each other's company to let those niceties slip a little. Tucking in was the order of the day.

Eventually Hugh's salivating returned to normal levels, enough to allow him to think about the work he had been doing on the question of disbursements.

"I must say Jack, your chum Aram really is a belter of a software designer, he could have a job with me any day."

"You should pay attention Hugh, first Aram was not my friend and secondly I doubt that he could write a line of code if his life depended on it. He paid others to do that."

"Well whoever it was they did a very neat little job on that SD card."

"You didn't buy any HP sauce Hugh that's close to criminal negligence."

"Ketchup should be good enough for any man, we can't cater for the obscure, not to say obscene, tastes of retired policemen you know."

Pam stopped chewing on her egg long enough to mutter, "Amen," before Jack rounded on them both.

"All right cut the crap and tell me what you know. How do we handle 'disbursements'?"

"Right now we don't have to do much. The cunning old devil has been doing some serious homework by the look of it. He's produced a file on just about every charity worthy of attention and listed them according to his view on how much good they do and how efficiently they spend their wealth."

"Any you recognise?" asked Jack.

"Sure, lots … and their rankings may surprise you. Some it seems collect money and never spend it, others appear to raise lots of money and spend most of it on themselves. He's devised an indexing process by the look of it. By logging on to the system with this SD card we have initiated a process that takes money from what he calls his 'personal account and sends it to the top ten charities. From now on, on the first day of each month $1m is transferred to each of those at the top of the list. The really clever bit is this. He's organised a server that is collecting online updates on all his data so everything runs according to the plan he set up when he started this caper and it keeps pace with any improvements or problems that the charities experience."

"But he said we could make disbursements."

"Yes Jack but we can only change the amounts, he decides where they go."

"And where do they go?" asked Pam.

"I'll show you the list, you can't print anything from the card because it will alter the checksum and that, as we know, will cause an error that will then trigger a wipe-out."

"When we have finished I think we should take a closer look at our Mr Gordon Stewart, he deserves to have his day spoilt just like Mr Beg," said Pam.

Jack got up from his seat, "Hang on, the ten o'clock news will be up in a minute, let's find out how things are going."

This is the ten o'clock news. Dramatic events in Jerusalem and the world's reaction to the rapid deterioration of the political scene in Israel.

General Meyer the Defence Minister, has declared the army to be in control of the government which collapsed earlier today following overnight revelations involving financial improprieties. The opposition parties are also involved and consequently the Knesset is in turmoil. General Meyer is well known for his right wing nationalist views and has been agitating for strikes against Iran's nuclear facilities.

The US President has expressed his concerns and the Secretary of State is currently meeting with the Israeli ambassador.

Jack turned the radio down a little and looked at the expressions on the faces of his co-conspirators. Hugh was showing signs of an inner fear gripping his intestines, Pam had her inscrutable expression on but Jack knew that this meant that she too was hiding a deep feeling of unease. The news was enough to make even Jack go weak at the knees but all three were so busy pretending that events were having no effect on them that none noticed the growing tension in the air.

"I'm going to take a walk," announced Jack, "I need to think a little."

"Is that safe?" asked Pam.

"Safe?"

"Yes, safe, you might be spotted, someone might recognise you."

"I think you're getting a little paranoid. Why would anyone in Helford be interested in me?"

Pam looked a little crest fallen. "Maybe you're right. The news on the radio made me feel like I had done something evil and they would all be looking for me. It's like I'm walking around with a great big spotlight shining on me."

"Come with me then, it will help shake that feeling off. It looks like a fine day out there. Let's walk up Orchard Hill. Hugh, you coming too?"

"Thanks Jack but I've already been up the hill once today so I'll just do a little more homework on our next target … our illustrious Prime Minister."

"That reminds me, when I come back I'll put my bike at the end of the garage and you can put the TR inside, out of sight."

"OK, see you in a while."

Pam and Jack set off along the creek but at Pam's suggestion they took the coastal footpath to the east and like an old married couple walked along arm in arm.

"You can get an inkling of why power can corrupt can't you?" said Pam at last.

"Mm … yes, I guess so."

"There are moments when I can feel myself buoyed by it and other times when it terrifies me. Can we really do what we did and remain anonymous?"

"Hugh seems to think it would take the combined resources of western intelligence to track us down to Auntie May's little hideaway." Pam didn't reply but she was somehow unconvinced.

"We need to be back home next week we've got to get ready for Christmas. We've got the kids coming, plus their girlfriends."

"And your Mum and Dad."

"Shame your brother couldn't make it too."

"I told him we would be up in the New Year."

"I'm supposed to collect the beef joint from Calenick Farm on Friday."

"We'll have this sorted by Friday I'm sure. If we can create the kind of mayhem in the UK that we have managed in Israel then we can hit the Men in Black where it hurts."

"How do you figure that?"

"If the executive are somehow financing their own version of MI5 'Black Ops' then they will need money and we can guess where that's coming from."

"Would the Prime Minister have all the funds then?"

"That's a good point, when we get back we'll get Hugh to do a search and see if there are any other prominent Brits on the list."

They continued on their walk, feeling better about themselves and a little happier about what they had done and were now about to do.

12.30 – Rose Cottage

"Ah, you're back. Good walk?"

"Excellent, thanks Hugh," said Pam. "It's a lovely day and God is in his heaven."

"You will be pleased to know I've been having fun looking at the list of charities and the statistics Mr Mikoyan has used to define his 'top ten'."

"Anyone we know?"

"Some names you would recognise and some I'm not sure you would. Near the top of the list is a charity based not far from here called 'Shelterbox'. I've never heard of it but it seems to be doing very well according to its place in the top ten; it's number three."

"I've heard of them," said Pam, "they have collection boxes in many of the pubs and shops. They have a warehouse in Helston, they're often on Spotlight, the south west news programme."

"I'm surprised you haven't heard about them Hugh, they do a lot of work all over the world helping people who are homeless after natural disasters, floods, hurricanes and the like."

"Well you Cornish folk have kept that one close to your chests," replied Hugh. "But what will surprise you is just how far down the list the RNLI is."

"What, the Lifeboats?"

"I don't believe you. They're a national institution, especially down here. I bet more people contribute to the lifeboats than anything else."

"I'm sure you're right Jack but the fact remains they have been too successful at raising money and according to Mikoyan's analysis are not spending enough of it. Apparently they are so rich they could probably afford to fund all your air ambulance helicopters you go on about."

"Don't get me started on that one."

"Now, what have we decided about our Mr Toby Stewart?"

"Pam and I have decided we need to take him down and find out if there are close associates of his that may be hiding more money. Our target is to remove all their illicit wealth and starve them of the wherewithal to support the Men in Black."

"You know I've thought about that and it's likely that these people, those you say support the executive's illegal army of spies, are independently wealthy so taking away one source of their ill gotten gains may not have an immediate effect."

"You have a point, that's why we hit the destroy button and then do the same to any other names on Aram's list that are close associates of Toby Stewart."

By early evening they had identified more than a dozen individuals who had used Aram Mikoyan's services to hide their illegal funds and all had joined Toby Stewart on the list of those who were dealt with via the 'destroy' button on Hugh's laptop. They calculated that it would be morning before any effects of their decisions were felt by the world outside.

With a log fire roaring and the night store heater on max Rose Cottage became a cosy corner on a night when the temperature outside was threatening to be below zero, something pretty rare in a village surrounded by the waters of Helford River.

"Let's see if the TV is working and catch up with the news," suggested Jack.

"Are you sure you want to do that?" said Pam. Jack ignored the question, switched on the TV and selected the News Channel just in time to catch news from their business correspondent.

... the markets took the news badly and stock exchanges across the globe are reporting falls of as much as ten per cent. This has had a knock-on effect on the price of oil and other commodities. The business world is bracing itself for a shock to the system not seen since 9-11.

"What's that all about?" said Pam.

"Shhh," Jack responded.

"Don't shush me, I don't understand."

"Hell's teeth, the collapse in Israel has had some kind of effect on the markets."

"But that can't be our fault, can it?"

"Not sure 'fault' is the correct word to use in this situation. We may well have been the catalyst but we certainly didn't commit any of the crimes that precipitated the crisis."

"Doesn't it give you a warm feeling inside," said Hugh, "just think we gave the bastard a thumbs down and the guano descended upon him in no small measure."

"I don't know about you two but I'm getting a bit wobbly about the whole thing. What will tomorrow bring? I'm scared to think about it," said Pam.

"Don't worry love, with a bit of luck the people behind the Men in Black will be locked up by this time tomorrow."

"You might be a trifle optimistic Jack, never underestimate the criminal mind, I should know, I see them all the time. CEOs who lie like a pay-day lender and finance officers who couldn't add up their weekly milk bill without feeling the need for mendacious modification."

The arguments continued over a makeshift dinner of ham and tomato sandwiches. There was no agreement about what the outcome of their revelations was likely to be. A large plate full of sandwiches arrived on the coffee table and they sat around the log fire in pensive mood.

"Shall we see what the News Channel is saying now?" Without waiting for agreement Jack switched the TV back on. The weather forecaster was busy explaining that the prospects of a white Christmas were becoming firmer with every passing day. The high-pressure system over the country was delivering fine days and cold nights but an Atlantic low was approaching and snow was definitely on the cards.

"Charming, everyone will be hitting the road at Christmas and there will be the normal chaos," moaned Hugh.

"How's Marjorie taking your forced exile?" Pam asked.

"She's perfectly happy provided I am back in time for the final Christmas shopping expedition to Cribbs Causeway Shopping Centre. It's becoming a regular Christmas ritual but to be honest I'd rather break a leg than have to fight my way through that lot again."

"Don't sound so hard done by Hugh, I drag Jack all the way to Exeter for ours. At least I will if I can get away from this beautiful village that's just a wee bit challenged in the retail therapy department."

"What's the plan Jack?"

"Look, it's back on again, he's talking about Israel," Jack said, immediately finding the excuse to turn the volume back up.

... The Defence Minister General Meyer has attempted to reassure the United States President that the Israeli Air Force is not making preparations

for war with Iran but Russian sources say that they have satellite evidence that fighter-bombers are being assembled ready for an attack and long range tanks have been delivered to bases in Sinai ready for a helicopter assault on Iranian nuclear facilities.

Meanwhile the market collapse continues to rock the world of finance and confidence in the markets is at an all time low. The gold price has risen to more than $1,000 an ounce and the Brent Crude price to $142 a barrel. Motorists across Europe have taken fright after the French Transport Minister forecast a shortage of petrol and diesel. The longest queues were in Rome where noisy lines of drivers honked their horns in protest and brought the Italian capital to a standstill.

The Israeli parliament meanwhile is in chaos after the senior members of both major parties and some coalition partners were implicated in a scandal stretching from the up market districts of Jerusalem, Tel Aviv and Jaffa to the ski slopes of France and Switzerland. More fuel was poured on this political inferno this afternoon when the head of the Israeli Intelligence announced that his department had intercepted a large number of attempted communications with overseas banking centres. He refused to give further information.

"So far so good eh!" said Jack as he turned down the volume.

"It's quite stunning how far the ripples of our earthquake have travelled, I can't help wonder 'what next'," said Pam.

"Does that worry you or encourage you? We may have our own earthquake to come."

"Should we stay here or find a new location?" said Hugh, "I can't guarantee that they won't track us down. I didn't expect this kind of outcome and when I joked about needing a cooperative effort by western intelligence services I didn't in my wildest dreams imagine circumstances where that might occur."

"You think they may be on to us?" Jack asked.

"I think we need to make plans, I mean it's not like before when we were up against armed criminals. Presumably the people likely to knock on the door will be forces of the state but if we destroy the data card they will have no evidence that we were in any way involved."

"Have we actually committed any crimes?" Pam said, in a voice that sounded a little less confident than before.

"Technically I guess we have because we have interfered with the banking system but given the way Mikoyan set the system up we could argue that he created an automated process that we inadvertently initiated. Anyway the 'public interest' defence comes into play as we can argue that we have been serving the interests of the public in outing the real criminals."

"I think our problem may not be with the forces of justice but with the so called Men in Black. If our efforts don't disrupt their activities then we could be a target."

They were startled by a vigorous banging on the front door. There was a moment of group panic whilst they considered the prospect that they had indeed been discovered but didn't know whether to run or not. A moment later a familiar face appeared at the window and a disembodied voice from outside cried, "Come on you lot it's bloody freezing out here."

They welcomed Dan in and there were handshakes all round, then Pam set about making yet another pot of tea and some more sandwiches.

"Good to see you mate, here, give me your coat and take a seat by the fire, we have just been discussing how to handle things."

"Things, what things? The last I heard you were running away from a bunch of make-believe cops but why decamp down here? All you had to do was call the local bobbies and they would have sorted things out," said Dan.

"I'm not sure I was going to be allowed that privilege. The two who came for me were intent on taking me with them. I didn't get the impression they were terribly bothered with niceties and certainly omitted what you and I know is very important. When arresting someone you have to caution them on the spot."

"And they didn't?"

"Nope."

"Bunch of amateurs."

"They were amateurs with very lumpy breast pockets."

"They were armed?"

"I reckon. I tend to take things like that seriously and hence not staying around for a bout of doorstep argy bargee." Pam arrived with a plate of sandwiches and a tray of steaming teacups.

"Thanks Pam, just what I needed, it's a three-day donkey ride getting to this forgotten corner of Cornwall."

"God's own country mate, don't forget that. There's something else you should know, you've got a leak."

"What do you mean?" Dan theatrically checked his fly zipper and they all laughed at his contrived misunderstanding.

"Not that kind of leak, you heedyet," scolded Jack in his dreadful Irish accent, more laughter. "The two ersatz detectives knew that I had been to the bank in Switzerland and they knew I had opened a safe deposit box. The only people that I have given that information to are sitting around this fire."

"Jack you must know that I have to report what I know to those further up the line."

"Then they either shared the information with a traitor or they are the traitor." Dan was silent, but he wasn't happy.

The four of them spent the next few hours chatting about the Aram Mikoyan data card and their exploits with the finances of the Israeli prime minister. Dan was a little shocked that the dramas being played out in the stock exchanges and commodity markets across the globe all began in the dining room of a four hundred year old cottage in a remote Cornish fishing village courtesy of three ordinary everyday folk.

When the discussion turned to their decision to 'destroy' the British prime minister and fourteen other highly placed individuals who were using Aram Mikoyan to hide their wealth, Dan asked to see the list. Pam duly obliged and he sat studying the names.

"Christ Jack! Do you know who these people are?"

"Some, we know four of them are in the cabinet, one is a civil servant working at number ten, five are knights of the realm and we think one is a judge."

"You've targeted the Prime Minister, his press officer, the Chancellor of the Exchequer, the Secretary of State for Education, the Home Secretary and the Attorney General. Of the knights listed here I only recognise a couple. One is a very scary character, William Salisbury, runs an organisation I believe you are familiar with Jack, National Security Services Incorporated."

"The guys who tried to scare me off when I started digging into Baroness Parker's death?"

"The very same."

"You may as well know Jack. It's Salisbury who is behind the Men in Black. He is very close to the government and we have managed to find and track a couple of his operatives. They led us back to a country estate west of London. It's owned by Salisbury through a series of cut-out corporations."

"Well in that case I am very happy that we have him on the list. The loss of all his secret and probably illegally obtained wealth will teach him a thing or two."

"He's a wily old bird, I wouldn't be sure that he put all his eggs in one basket. Mikoyan isn't the only financial demon on the planet."

With that thought delivered just in time to torment Jack through the night they adjourned to bed.

CHAPTER 24

02.30 – Tuesday 19th December 2006
The Prime Minister's Private Office

"FOR FUCK'S SAKE FREDDIE, you're supposed to be my fucking Press Officer. Why the hell didn't you warn me this was going to break before the bloody newspapers got hold of it?" Toby Stewart screwed the one page fax into a ball and tossed it into the fireless grate.

"Listen Toby we were damn lucky that the duty editor at The Guardian owes me a favour or we'd be dead meat already."

"Who else is running the story?"

"The Washington Post has it, but they are five hours behind so we have time."

"Time, what bloody time, what can we do in five hours?"

"Actually we don't have five hours. The Guardian people say they can give us two at the most. Can't we slap a 'D' Notice on them?"

"Sure, we can do that but I can't stop the Washington Post."

"The first thing I tried was to buy them off but the accounts I have access to are blocked and for some reason I can't get in to any of them."

"Do you think we can buy our way out of this? If so then get the money now, use my accounts." McLaren left for his office to try and find enough cash to pay off their tormentors. The Prime Minister padded across to the sideboard, his bare feet cosseted by inch-thick Wilton carpet. He took the heavy crystal stopper from a ship's decanter that had once adorned Nelson's table on the Victory and poured himself a good measure of the twenty-five year-old Macallan he kept for special occasions. The first one went straight down but the second he sipped slowly whilst thinking about a possible solution to their dilemma.

After a minute or so he picked up the cordless phone from his desk then went back to the armchair and punched in Sir William Salisbury's cell phone number. It rang and rang but no reply. He put the handset on the coffee table and waited, staring at the little plastic telephone statuette that sat upright in front of him. The little square face, with its indolent orange screen teased him as he sat willing it to light up. The warble of an incoming call signalled his success and he smiled. He knew that Bill Salisbury could not resist the temptation to find out why the hell the British Prime Minister tried to call him at two thirty in the morning.

"What is it Toby, please tell me there is something worthy of a sleepless night."

"Bill, we have a problem …"

It took just five minutes for Toby Stewart to spill the beans on the situation with The Guardian and the Washington Post and just one minute for Salisbury to formulate a game plan.

"This smells like bloody Mikoyan. I knew that bastard would leave a stink behind him. Never trust a Greek bearing gifts."

"Actually I think he was Armenian."

"Give me a moment and I'll call you back. Where's Freddie?"

"He's busy trying to find an account we can use to pay off anybody and everybody. He's tried to get into his own but they have been blocked."

It actually took five minutes for Salisbury to do what he had in mind then called back.

"Right Toby, I have given a story to the Mail and the Mirror. They are onside but we will need to pay them off down the line. I have reserve funds in The Caymans but I don't have Internet access."

"So what's the story?"

"The story they will run is that there is a loose cannon at large in the country. A disaffected ex policeman who was sacked for thieving money from a murder victim and has a grudge against the Prime Minister and his government. Police are doing their utmost to track him and his group down. Part of his plan is to flood the media with carefully prepared false evidence of wrong doing by the government. I think that will do for now, we may have to buff it up a bit in the morning but get Freddie onside and talk this thing off the front pages. If you can find any other stories we can put out there then do so. We just need to get the media talking about anything but you and your administration."

"Right. What about this character you are sticking the blame on. Who's your patsy?"

"The whole story is based on Mr Jack Mawgan, the guy you and Freddie used to head up your National Police Aviation Service. There's just enough truth in our version to keep the papers interested for quite a while. He's been a thorn in our side for too long and now we have a reason to put him away for good. I'll have my backroom boys make up some good looking evidence that he is behind all this and feed it into Scotland Yard."

"Anything I can do?"

"Yes, deny everything, you are a victim not a perpetrator."

"Got it."

"Try and get some sleep, you need to look at your Prime Ministerial best for the cameras in the morning."

The phone clicked before Toby could respond. He didn't feel much like going back to bed, too much adrenalin, too much angst and too much stress.

08.00 – Tuesday 19th December 2006
Office of the Editor in Chief, The
Guardian Newspaper, London

"You did what?" Archie Bollingsworth tore into his junior with the kind of gusto reserved for a headmaster about to thrash an errant third former. Having a senior staff member who was a close friend of the Prime Minister's Press Officer was a bonus that now came back to bite him in the backside. Archie didn't need a cane to do the damage for he had a tongue that was equal to the task. By the time he had finished with the overnight editor there wasn't, figuratively speaking, much flesh left on his shaking bones. What remained tottered from the room on legs that were barely up to the job.

When Archie discovered that the Mail and the Mirror were running counter claims to their own lead story as a 'spoiler', he needed to find the leaker as soon as possible. The errant employee was quick to confess once Archie had put him on the spot. He had dealt with the leak but now he had to deal with the fall-out. He faced a good old Fleet Street bout of newspaper fisticuffs – no holds barred.

08.10 – Tuesday 19th December 2006
MI5 HQ, Whitehall, London

"Dan, this is Justin, the balloon has gone up. The newspapers are all full of crap, The Guardian is carrying photocopies of what they say are bank statements relating to accounts belonging to the PM's private finances along with forms carrying his signature. We think they came from the broker Aram Mikoyan."

"You're right, the data Jack brought back with him links the PM to a series of illicit offshore accounts."

"There will come a time when you will have to justify that, but right now there are more important things we need to talk about."

"Like what?"

"Salisbury is working with the Prime Minister's approval if not his active support. We have been monitoring his calls and we know he is behind an attempt to derail the Guardian's story by running a series of counter claims in two other nationals."

"Things are getting serious then."

"The really bad news is that Salisbury is trying to make Jack Mawgan a scape goat for the whole damn mess and he has persuaded the Home Secretary to order a nationwide man-hunt. Worse still they've issued an 'armed and dangerous' warning."

"Fuck, do they know where he is?"

"They think he's with you." There was a pregnant pause which could only mean one thing, "wherever you are you need to get out of sight, and I mean seriously out of sight. If you are thinking of using the old west county haunts then don't, we have a leak. The leaker is under observation so we have him under control but he has pulled your file and knows all about you and Jack and he knows about your IT boffin too. Go underground and stay there until I call again."

"I'll have to turn my cell off when we finish. How will you call me?"

"Get yourself a pay-as-you-go and text me the number."

"Jeez Justin this isn't like the text-book, we're breaking just about every security rule in the book."

"Needs must, have you got your UHF scanner? Gotta go Dan, all hell is breaking loose."

08.15 – Tuesday 19th December 2006
Rose Cottage, Helford Village

"Time for a pow-wow Jack, get the others."

"Hang on I'm trying to watch the morning news but it's not quite what I expected." At that moment Jack's picture appeared on the screen…

Police are looking for ex-policeman Jack Mawgan in connection with his attempt to use the national newspapers to bring the government into disrepute. He is said to bear a grudge against the Prime Minister and they say he is armed and dangerous…

"What the hell…"

"That's what I want to talk to you about, I just had an update from Justin, there's trouble at t' mill."

Hugh was in the loo and Pam was coming down the stairs. Dan stood on the bottom step, allowed Pam to pass then yelled up at the closed bathroom door, "Hugh, we need to chat, in the dining room as soon as you have finished your … contemplations."

By the time Dan had filled them in about his call from Justin the mood had darkened. It was Hugh who spoke first, "Can I go home now, they don't know me do they?"

"Unfortunately they know all about you and I guess they know where you live."

"Does that mean I can't go home?"

"Not yet, we have to decide what to do." Jack said.

"Do about what?"

"The data card."

"Hang on," said Dan, "perhaps Justin was giving me a not-so-subtle warning. I'm just going out to the car to check something." Without more ado he left by the side door and returned a few minutes later with what looked like a two-way radio.

"Are you planning to call someone," asked Jack.

"No, it's a radio all right but primarily it's a scanner, Justin thought it might come in handy given that very soon there will be a veritable hoard of real and probably some not so real policemen coming this way." Dan fiddled with the buttons on the scanner and soon an assortment of messages began to come through along with the odd beep and a lot of 'shash'.

"Is that equipped for encryption?"

"Up to level 'B'."

"That'll do for the local police ... won't it?"

"Probably, the real ones anyway. If we start to hear unintelligible encrypted chatter then we know we are seriously in trouble, meanwhile we'll keep an ear open for PC Plod. I suggest we get on with things whilst we have time."

"What did you have in mind?" Pam asked.

"We have to use that stuff Mikoyan gave us to the max," Dan said, eager to get cracking.

"Hang on a minute, what happened in Israel is a bit of an eye-opener you have to admit, talk about the law of unintended consequences. Who knows what will happen if we go for all those others?"

"You soon changed your tune," carped Jack.

"Live and learn darling, live and learn."

"I reckon we have to go for the jugular. It may be the only chance we get," Dan replied.

"I think we ditch the card and make a run for it," she responded.

"I want Hugh to hit Control 'A' and then hit the 'destroy' button," urged Jack.

"Do you realise how much explosive material you will deposit on the world if you do that?" said Pam, "If you are worried about Israel then dumping all that stuff in one go will be like exploding an atom bomb. It will be better to somehow bleed it all out there gently, bit by bit."

"We're not going to have the time for that," Dan protested.

"But that's exactly what will happen if you do the lot," Pam pleaded, her voice raised in frustration.

"No, you're wrong," Jack said as reassuringly as he could, aware that tempers were becoming a little frayed, "if you do them all in one go then what will happen in reality is that a continuous stream of data will pour out of the computers at the Guardian and the Washington Post but they will have to deal with it bit by bit and I reckon their journalists are a lot better at sorting out who to do and when than we are. At the moment we have a fifty per cent success rate." There was a pause whilst that gem of an observation sank in.

"You're right," said Hugh at last, "it would in one fell swoop solve our dilemma."

"What particular dilemma are you talking about?" said Pam, her voice lowered but her angst intact.

"We don't want to be caught with the data card and we don't want to see all it has access to go to waste. We can't print it out or transmit to another device without endangering the software that controls its functionality. Mr Mikoyan was a very clever chap. I agree with Jack, lets dump it all, lock stock and barrel, on to the journalists Mikoyan trusted to receive it."

"Pam? What do you think of that idea?"

"It means that the journalists get to decide who to hit and when and not us. We won't have any control over anything."

"You're right Pam but it is the least worst option."

There was a sudden burst of unintelligible chatter on the scanner. The colour drained from Dan's face, his expression told it all.

"Is that your lot?" asked Jack.

"It's someone on a regular police frequency using Class A Encryption. It could be my lads but we know that the Men in Black have been using Class A encryption too."

"That means they're close then?"

"I guess we don't have much time, I had better get on with it," said Hugh.

"Hang on a minute. Pam, what do you say?" asked Jack.

"I'm going to abstain, my heart says no but my head says OK."

"Get on it Hugh," said Dan as another burst of unintelligible chatter added a new sense of urgency though none was required. Hugh set about his laptop and the others set about gathering their few possessions together in preparation for a quick getaway.

"Jack," called Hugh from his seat at the dining table, "what should I do with the card when the job is done. As long as they think it contains all that dangerous information people will kill for it."

"You're right, best destroy it as soon as you are happy that all the necessary commands have been sent to the server. Do you know how long that will take?"

"God knows, this line is not the best. Maybe half an hour or so, just to be sure." Dan arrived in time to hear the last comment.

"We don't have half an hour, I have a bad feeling that they are not far away."

"Hugh, hide your laptop somewhere and let it run,"

"But I can't leave it behind, it's my right hand."

"Your laptop or your life mate, it's decision time."

Hugh's expression changed as reality smacked home with a bang. "I'll put it in that side board, I think the cables will stretch that far."

No sooner had he hidden the whirring laptop that was now emptying its caustic commands to far away servers loaded with terrabytes of incriminating data than a concentrated burst of chatter came from the scanner.

"Close?" asked Jack.

"Very." Dan replied.

"Are we going to abandon Hugh's car and my bike and head off in your car?"

"Sounds like a plan."

"How come I have to leave all my stuff behind?"

"Don't worry Hugh, you'll want to come back for your laptop so you may as well leave the TR tucked up in the garage."

Suddenly there was movement outside the window and then a banging on the door.

"Open up, police." Dan turned to the leave by the rear windows but the darkly clad figures had the cottage surrounded. There was a huge crash as the front door burst open and two large men dressed in dark winter jackets came storming in the front door. The first carried a tool called an 'enforcer' used to batter down the door and the second was a more menacing character, short and stocky with heavy five o'clock shadow and a large automatic pistol that he waved at the astonished group of occupants. A taller, more distinguished looking man walked in behind them. He too carried a pistol but he was more discrete and held it down by his side. For a few seconds nobody spoke.

"Mr Mawgan, we meet at last, my name's Porter and these are my two colleagues, Bernard and Troy. You don't know me but I have reason to know you and I might say from my part it hasn't been a happy experience."

Without instruction Bernard and Troy began to cable-tie their hands behind their backs.

"Mr Barclay and Mr Martin I do believe?"

Dan made to speak but Bernard swiped him across the face with his weapon. Dan stumbled but remained on his feet, as blood dribbled down the side of his face from a cut on his temple.

"The disc gentlemen, the disc please." The three men stood defiantly silent but Jack decided it was time to speak up. His first words had barely left his lips when he too was pistol whipped and fell semi conscious to the floor. Bernie grabbed his wrists and dragged him back to his feet.

"Time for the duct tape Bernie, the rule, lady and gentlemen is speak when you are spoken to and not before." Strips of grey tape were placed across their lips. "Now, Mr Mawgan, the disc, where is it, simply nod if you wish to tell me?" Defiant silence once more. "Bernie, why don't you take the lady upstairs and amuse yourself with her whilst I have a chat with these three heroes." Bernie didn't speak but grabbed Pam by the arm and pushed her up the stairs ahead of him. Jack moved towards Porter but Troy produced his own pistol and jammed it painfully into Jack's ribs preventing him from getting too close.

Jack stood, head down, fighting the scene he imagined unfolding upstairs. The sweat rolled down his forehead but he remained stoically uncooperative.

The footsteps on the creaking floorboards indicated that Bernie had chosen the main bedroom right above their heads. The bed creaked and there were muffled sounds of a struggle. Suddenly there was a shot, then another, then silence. Jack leaped forward and was immediately bludgeoned to the floor. Porter and his sidekick stood spellbound as the footsteps on the creaky bedroom floor telegraphed their arrival at the top of the stairway. Porter and Bernie had their guns trained on the men sensing that Bernie's enjoyment had been cut short for some reason. Pam appeared on the stairs wearing only her underwear carrying Bernie's pistol like a pro. She let off a pair of shots and Porter went down in a silent heap, his pistol clattering across the stone floor. Troy span round and tried to fire at Pam but Hugh was nearby and threw himself at the attacker, spoiling his aim. He managed to fire one shot that disappeared into the cob wall just in front of Pam. He landed face-down with Hugh on his back but his gun still in his hand. By the time he had recovered enough to become a threat Pam was pointing her gun at his forehead.

Hugh rolled away and Dan helped him to his feet. Jack was already in the kitchen looking for a knife to cut their bonds.

"Don't for one minute imagine I won't use this," she waved her gun in Troy's face. "Your friend upstairs found out the hard way that I know exactly how it works. In fact he's nursing the worst vasectomy you're ever likely to see. If you want one too then I'm in just the mood."

Bernie could be heard moaning in the room above them. Troy was helped to his feet and Dan soon had him tie wrapped and duct taped. Jack recovered his weapon.

Within a few minutes order had been restored and Pam had been reunited with her clothes. Jack was administering first aid to Bernie. He had a wound in the left thigh and a second in the groin area. Jack wondered what on earth had happened and how Pam was able to turn the tables on such a hardened crook. She was all fired up and when she inspected the body of Damian Porter she was impressed by her own shooting ability, two chest shots and a quick death. When Jack appeared from upstairs she walked over to him and gave him a hefty kick in the shin and a thump in the ribs. "Just how far would you have allowed that creep to go before you gave up the bloody disc he was after?"

"I tried to intervene sweetheart but they knocked me out."

"What about you two?" she yelled at Dan and Hugh, "fine figures of men you turned out to be." With that she stormed outside tears streaming from her face. Dan and Hugh looked at each other and shrugged their shoulders. Jack had a face like thunder. Suddenly they were not so cheery.

Jack went outside to try and make peace with Pam.

"What now?" Hugh asked Dan who was stood over Porter and looking through his pockets whilst holding a handkerchief to his head wound.

When Jack returned, apparently unsuccessful in his attempt to calm Pam and make his peace Dan told him to think about his situation. He was a wanted man and he needed to get away whilst he still could.

"The cops have you plastered over the papers and the TV. You have to stay free as long as possible. We have to discredit those who are making the allegations against you. Once you are out of circulation they will all close ranks and all the stuff we sent to the papers will be called fake and forged."

"Look, Pam is in a bad way right now, she won't talk to me. I think she is in shock; you don't kill someone every day. She's a tough nut but right now she needs my support."

"OK, if she needs you then you must both go, take my car."

"Thanks Dan I'll see what she says." Jack went back outside but Pam was in a terrible state and still wouldn't talk to him.

"You will just have to go and you had better go now. We can hear the local bobbies on the scanner, one of your neighbours has called 999 and reported 'shots fired'. I'll tidy things up here and square things away with the locals."

"You need an ambulance for the bloke upstairs."

"Yes, yes, get going. They are unlikely to be looking for my car yet but get a new set of number plates as soon as, take this scanner, there is a Glock behind the radio, just push both knobs on the front at the same time and all will be revealed."

"I'll find a hideaway and give you a call, take care of Pam for me."

As Jack drove away they could hear the faint sound of sirens, he was leaving in the nick of time.

CHAPTER 25

17.00 – Tuesday 19th December 2006
Chief Constable's Office, Devon and Cornwall Police HQ
Middlemoor, Exeter

"Sir, Number Ten on line two."

"Thank you O'Donnell, close the door behind you but don't leave the building just yet."

"Yes Sir." ACC O'Donnell returned to his office knowing that he was in for a hell of a long day. He had better give his wife Anne a call and tell her to put dinner on hold.

"Chief Constable speaking, how can I be of help?"

"Hello Alex, Freddie McLaren here, what news from your patch?"

"News? Well I can report that the forensic boys are giving the crime scene a good going over but they have not found this mysterious disc that everyone is getting worked up about. They have located just one computer, a laptop belonging to the suspect Martin. It's been quarantined and sent up here for our I.T. boys to go over."

"No, I don't want it touched until it gets to the Home office. We need to be sure of what we are looking at."

"All right sir, I'll have it couriered up right away."

"Good, in the meantime, tear the place apart. I want that disc."

"I have one corpse and two suspects in custody, one of which is in Treliske Hospital with one testicle shot through and a flesh wound in his leg. They will be charged with assault and fire-arms offences in the morning. They all appear to be employees of National Security Services."

"Yes, I heard as much from Sir William Salisbury this afternoon. What about Mawgan and his associates?"

"The shootings were in self-defence apparently and Mawgan's wife was the one who turned one of her assailant's weapons against him then shot the man Porter as he attempted to shoot her. I'll send you copies of their statements on the fax this evening."

"Thank you but what of them, where are they?"

"Mawgan left the scene before my men arrived. We have an alert out for his arrest. His wife and the other two, Barclay and Martin have returned to the Mawgan home in Perranarworthal. Mrs Mawgan is being treated by a fellow GP and is under sedation. Mr Barclay has friends in Whitehall that have vouched for him and likewise Mr Martin. They are currently all at the Mawgan home and supervised by two of my detectives who are finalising their statements. They will be free to go about their business when that process is complete."

"I want that man Mawgan found and locked up, please Chief Constable."

"We'll do our best Mr McLaren." The telephone clicked before he could complete the sentence, he looked at the handset and said, "Prick" under his breath.

21.00 – Tuesday 19th December 2006
NSS Corp HQ, Cardinal House, Heathrow Airport

Sir William Salisbury was at his London office bemoaning the loss of his top man and two reliable operatives with co-conspirator Freddie McLaren.

"Damn, damn and damn. That bastard Mawgan is getting in my way yet again. We should have finished him off when we had the chance."

Freddie was a worried man, and he shared his worries with Sir William, one of the most powerful men in the country. Until that afternoon they had enough wealth and influence to deal with almost any contingency and a small private army of skilled operatives to ensure their will prevailed. With virtually no money available thanks to what they perceived was Jack Mawgan's manipulation of Aram Mikoyan's computer records and their reputations trashed by the newspapers they were very much on the back foot. Sir William's efforts to use spoilers in the newspapers that were not

264

carrying the exposé had faded due to lack of funds to back up the promise of substantial 'incentives'.

"I'll have to get back to Number Ten. Toby's panicking about the headlines in the Washington Post. Christ knows how they found out but they are running a story about the payments we made to those troublesome buggers in Ireland to get the Good Friday Agreement off the ground."

"Yes, ironic isn't it. I was a member of the Government at the time you may remember. The country would have paid ten times more to make that problem go away but I fear they are about to condemn us for paying a few millions into the pockets of the main players."

"Whatever … the shit is hitting the fan and I need to go and reassure our esteemed leader that there is a way out of this mess."

"Do you think there is a way out?" Freddie made no reply but the body language said it all. He gathered up his overcoat and scarf and departed for central London.

Sir William picked up the desk phone in his office and dialled the number of a senior member of his operational team.

"Raymond, I want you here for a briefing as soon as you can, bring four of your best men. We're going to avenge Damien's death."

23.00 – Tuesday 19th December 2006
Prime Minister's private office

"Have you seen the latest in the papers?" said the Prime Minister.

"No," replied a despondent and now not so confident Freddie McLaren, "what now?"

"The Guardian and the Washington Post say they have been chosen by a major player in the financial underworld to reveal all about the people he helped to avoid taxes and to facilitate the laundering of proceeds of criminal activity. They are saying they have the financial details on nearly two thousand of the world's most powerful men and women, elected officials, military brass, criminal masterminds and business leaders. They are planning to publish their account details showing where payments came from and the recipients of payments made from those accounts."

"Can we close them down?"

"I tried but the Commissioner won't have it and the Spooks told me to get lost. The Americans are involved now so it's gone too far for us to use our usual powers to suppress this kind of crap."

"The Irish thing is going to bury us, I think we need to talk to the lawyers, give the Attorney General a call will you? Ask him to join us for a breakfast meeting in the morning."

11.00 – Wednesday 20th December 2006
Church Cove, The Lizard, Cornwall

The first thing that ran through Jack's mind as he wound his way out of Helford Village earlier that fateful day was that everyone would be expecting him to make a bid for freedom and escape to the north, out of The Lizard peninsular. Jack had other ideas and with almost nothing in the way of resources he had to think fast. Hugh had tipped him off to the possibility of shopping in Manaccan Stores and he managed to get some cash-back too. His credit card would soon be hotter than a good tip on race day so he needed to make use of it whilst he could.

Pulling up in the little car park behind the churchyard at Landewednack he settled down to await developments and formulate a plan. The temperature was falling and the granite skies told of bad weather ahead. The forecasters talked of snow.

He had a bad feeling in the pit of his stomach. He was unable to get through to Pam before he left and was deeply troubled by the dark place she seemed to be in after the trauma of killing a man for the second time in her life. Some years ago they had been working on a project in Africa. Pam was attacked by a mad gunman but she had a pistol and Jack had taught her how to use it. She killed her attacker but didn't seem to suffer any lasting ill effects from the experience on that occasion. This time it was different. She took the events leading up to the shooting at Rose Cottage very badly and was clearly not impressed by the silence of the menfolk in the house who had stood by and allowed an evil oaf of a man to drag her upstairs for God knows what kind of dreadful experience … and for what? For a bunch of data on another lot of evil men. No wonder she was pissed off, thought Jack. He did try to say something but was cut short by Troy's beating. Why didn't he say something earlier, why didn't the other two say something? He was heartbroken that he hadn't been able to resolve things before going on the run. For her sake he had to prove his innocence. He had to prevail against these evil men.

Church Cove is a beautiful little corner of Cornwall that Jack had been introduced to as a lad. His father used to rent Angel Cottage opposite the church for a week in July. They would go fishing with the local serpentine turner Viv Bosustow. Viv kept a boat on the slipway down at the cove and when the tide was right they would manhandle her down into the narrow channel and set off on fishing adventures that used to excite him no end. He still had vivid memories of the sparkling mackerel flapping away in the bottom of the boat as Viv flicked them off the line.

As the day wore on the temperature fell below zero and the wind went around to the east driving small flakes of sleet right up the valley and shaking the few trees that were left after the great elms that surrounded the church were lost to disease back in the '80s. Jack had to run the engine to keep the car warm. Dan had left a winter jacket in the back of his car but even with that wrapped tightly around his body the cold gnawed at his innards. He knew that the tell tale exhaust smoke might draw attention but there was no sign of anyone out for a walk as the bad weather threatened. The balance of risk, he figured, was in his favour.

Darkness fell and the sleet turned to occasional snowflakes. By midnight it was snowing heavily and the easterly wind was taking the snow from the nearby pasture and building a drift that surrounded Jacks car. He realised the dangers of carbon monoxide poisoning and periodically left the comfort of the driver's seat to keep the exhaust pipes and the air intakes clear. He had taken the precaution of stocking up with high energy foods at Manaccan Stores so food wasn't an issue. Cartons of orange juice would also provide some liquid sustenance but the lack of something warm was telling on his spirit.

Fitful sleep in the back seat of the car was an unsatisfying experience and by dawn he was physically tired and mentally exhausted.

It was six o'clock in the morning. He turned on the radio to catch up with overnight events. There may be information that would help him escape the confines of Cornwall. He needed to track down the head of NSS, Sir William Salisbury, and make sure he paid a price for all the trouble he had put his family through.

The newsreader began with details of a virtual civil war in Israel and the threat of an opportunistic attack by Syrian forces in the region called the Golan Heights. Jack was stunned at what they had started by simply telling the world about the corrupt activities of just two politicians.

As the bulletin approached its final news items he heard mention of the word Cornwall …

… at least one person is believed to have died in a house fire this evening in the small Cornish town of Perranarworthal. The victim is believed to be Doctor Pamela Mawgan. Police and fire brigade experts are at the scene. Detective Inspector Andrew Mulligan told reporters that arson is suspected and they are looking for two men in dark clothing seen in the vicinity behaving suspiciously. A Land Rover Discovery was seen leaving the scene late last night.

"No, it can't be true." His heart began to pound and a flood of adrenalin fired up every sense in his body. He tried to drive away from his parking spot without thinking but the snowdrift was already too deep to get away easily. The cold-hearted dawn took on a new sadness as the tears rolled down his cheeks and the news hammered away at his heart like a builder's mallet. He was desperate to speak to someone. Could it really be true? Surely they couldn't have taken his darling Pam. He remembered his cell phone, it had been switched off to prevent the police tracking his movements but now he didn't care. He needed to talk to someone.

He switched it on but down in the Cove there was no signal. If he could make his way back to the heart of the village then maybe he could call Dan, anyone, someone who could tell him it wasn't true.

By careful weaving and expert use of the clutch Jack managed to ease his way out of the relatively level car park and on to the hill that led up to the village. The easterly wind that had brought such misery to that little corner of the countryside had scoured the snow from the road so with a little wheel slip he managed to get halfway up the hill where the thick hedges had sheltered the road from all but a thin layer of virgin snow. Arriving outside The Top House pub he checked his phone and found he had a signal at last. He called Dan's number, it was six thirty, Dan's answer machine cut in but he couldn't find the words he needed and after a minute or so the line went dead.

He sat with his head bent, his spirit broken. His handset rang out, it was Dan.

"Have you heard? It's Pam, they're saying she's dead. Tell me it's not true Dan, tell me it's not true." The silence at the other end of the line told its own story as Dan tried to find the right words.

"It's true Jack, I'm so sorry. I got the call first thing, Monique and I are heartbroken and can't find the words ..."

"They killed her didn't they? The bastards set fire to the house when they knew she was asleep inside."

"Yes I think you're right. The police were on to me first thing wanting to know how to contact you. I guess you had your phone switched off."

"Yes, I heard on the six o'clock news."

"You need to speak to Nat. He wasn't home last night and he blames himself for leaving his Mum alone. He's in a bit of a state too."

"Why Dan, why did they do it?"

"I can't answer that Jack, not for sure anyway. I can have a guess and I suspect you could too."

"Do you think it was Salisbury's men?"

"Given what we know I would have to say yes."

"I'm going after him Dan, he's going to pay for killing Pam."

"You're too late Jack, he flew out of the country last night and we believe he is in hiding in northern Cyprus. He has a house there apparently."

The sound of sobbing made Dan feel uncomfortable and he waited for his friend to compose himself. The sobbing eased and Dan judged Jack was paying attention.

"Jack, listen Jack, we need to get you a good lawyer and get the situation under control. Right now every policeman in the country is under orders to find you and bring you in. It will be better if we can present you at the Police Station with your lawyer. Where are you now?"

"I'm sitting in the car park in the middle of The Lizard village."

"What are the roads like down there?"

"Some drifting but not too bad by the look of things. They must have had the gritters out on the main road last night."

"Stay there and don't move, your car ... my car, is a bit too hot at the moment. I'll send Nat to pick you up and take you to the lawyers."

07.00 – Thursday 21st December 2006
The Lizard Village, Cornwall

Nat managed to get to the Lizard village in just twenty minutes as he and his brother Josh had been staying with Pam's parents at Cury Cross five miles away.

When he arrived he found Dan's car with the engine running and the driver's door wide open. There were footprints in the snow leading away across the village green and down towards the cove at Kynance. The snow was falling in fits and starts and the easterly wind was beginning to lose its sting. Fresh snow was making the footsteps less and less clear as he hurried along the pathway wrapping his scarf tightly around his throat and pulling his woollen hat firmly down on his head. The cliff edge was not far away but visibility was down to forty or fifty metres. He was trying not to think about what he may find when he reached the end of the pathway. He hoped and prayed that he would find his father in one piece and not lying at the bottom of the cliff.

The footsteps veered along the edge of the costal path and with a sigh of relief he could see a bench seat with a lone figure huddled at one end.

"Dad?"

"Hello son. Not such a fine day today." He was shivering and pale and probably hypothermic but he was trying to smile.

"When I saw the footprints leading to the cliff I began to think the worst."

"No son, I gave it some thought but I have been through the full cycle of emotions from revenge to suicide but in the end I came down in favour of you and Josh. The man who put this bench here did so because he lost a son at the age of nine." Nat read the inscription carved on the back rail. "It made me think about us, about our family and about what a good life we have had. That young lad didn't have such a chance so we need to be grateful for small mercies."

"We need each other Dad, we need you, don't leave us now."

"Don't worry son, we'll sort this mess out and then we'll do justice to your mother's memory."

"Come on Dad, let's get you back in the warm. You'll catch your death out here."

CHAPTER 26

17.00 – Sunday 24th December 2006
Editorial Offices, The Guardian Newspaper, London

ARCHIE BOLLINGSWORTH SAT AT his desk surrounded by the members of his editorial team. Nobody was excluded, they were all there; Business Editor, Financial Editor, European, Transport, Home Affairs, Legal, Culture, Middle East, Far East, North American, even the Sports Editor.

"Ladies and gentlemen, in a cruel and unexpected way Christmas has come early to the world of journalism. It has fallen to us to deal with enough criminal evidence to sink many of the world's most powerful and influential men and women. Unfortunately we are dealing with such widespread corruption that it is impossible to forecast what the fallout from publishing the data we have been given will be.

"The situation in Israel is dire and we suspect that it was precipitated by the first attempts by those in control of the data to use it for their own ends. They must have had the fright of their lives when they found that the result was a near calamitous situation close to civil war in Israel and all-out war in the Middle East.

"As we know only too well the same do-gooders tried to sink members of the UK government only for them to turn like a wounded animal on the press and run spoiler stories designed to denigrate anyone who didn't support them. Events of the last twenty-four hours are unprecedented in our history so if we have learnt one thing we have to take care and try to foresee the outcome of events should we decide to publish more data.

"I want to go round the table and catch up then we will decide our next move. Without wishing to overstate things the fate of our nation, and several others may depend on how we deal with this situation. With news of the resignation of the Attorney General I think we'll start with Legal."

The legal editor was a small man in his fifties, a successful barrister until he crossed a member of the establishment and found himself unable to get work.

"The Irish dimension has I'm afraid finally taken its toll on the office of the Attorney General. The incumbent has resigned forthwith and no successor has yet been appointed. He has refused to confirm or deny that his regime achieved the success called the Good Friday Agreement on the back of illegal payments to leading personalities involved. As his resignation comes just hours after the Prime Minister, three of his senior ministers, the leader of the opposition and four members of the shadow cabinet it would be an understatement to say that the situation is chaotic. The Speaker has seen fit to recall Parliament but he has insisted that prior to convening the sitting the new Prime Minister must be identified along with an agreed leader of the opposition."

"Is that going to happen?" asked Archie.

"Nobody knows but we are likely to have a decision by morning,"

"At the moment I can see us having the first ever sitting of Parliament on Christmas Day." There were a few muffled chuckles and comments at that news.

"Finance please," said Archie, bringing the banter to a halt. The Financial Editor was a well-built lady in her forties who had made her reputation in the stock market before swapping 'boredom' for what she saw as the exciting world of journalism.

"If the political scene is chaotic then you should come and see the text messages I've been getting. It seems that every mother's son wants to be a whistle blower and there are plenty of CEOs in the square mile who are not currently answering their phones. The insurance world seems to be watertight but the banks are being decimated by the rumours and the lack of information from the top. Share prices are still heading south and the FTSE is now down by 26.5%, a world record fall in just two days, twice the previous largest fall on October the 19th 1987 – Black Monday. Gold is through the roof at two thousand, three hundred dollars, another record. The instability in the market is palpable."

"Thank you Jenny, Business next." An elderly balding gentleman in a three-piece suit began speaking; his accent had an American twang to it.

"The simplest thing you can say about the current situation in the market place is to describe it as chaotic. Some of the big players with substantial government contracts are showing some nervousness as their relationship with the administration comes under scrutiny. This saga has a long way to run and it's very early days.

"One very curious effect of this crisis is that for some reason the main charities and a few smaller ones are out there spending like there is no tomorrow. They seem to be flush with funds and aid agencies in particular are buying up food supplies and even dabbling in the futures markets. The price of emergency aid products like blankets and tents is rising as a shortage of supply kicks in. The strange thing is we cannot see where all this money is coming from. We track the liquidity of the major charities on a routine basis so we would normally be able to forecast their expenditure but in the last few days their funds seem to have just materialised."

Archie sat back in his chair, his expression indicated he was thinking deeply.

"Maybe there are a bunch of anonymous benefactors out there trying to assuage their collective consciences." He had no sooner said the words than his face turned to a broad smile. The others sat bemused as their editor in chief stared into the distance wearing a broad grin. He started to chuckle, then to laugh then the laugh turned to a guffaw that nearly choked him. What on earth was going on, had he gone mad, was he ill?

"Sorry ladies and gentlemen I have just had a spiritual moment, a moment when it suddenly came to me what is happening here. I don't know for sure but my best guess is that the stream of accounting data we are getting through the Internet is coming from someone associated with Aram Mikoyan. Many of those we have information on are known to have contacts with him. Now that he is dead it looks as if he put all his information into a computer and willed it to us along with colleagues in America. I am willing to bet my pension that he is cascading all the funds belonging to those we have data on into the world's major charities."

"How could he do that from the grave?" asked Jenny in her naiveté.

"Jenny my dear, when you have unrestricted wealth and a plan you can do almost anything. I just can't believe that an old rogue like Mikoyan would see the light, turn one hundred and eighty degrees and give back to those he had spent so many years doing his best to steal from." He felt compelled to laugh out loud once more and this time one or two of his staff went along with him.

"OK, this is what we'll do ..."

Archie went on to plan his own campaign to wrest the world from the growing number of powerful and wealthy people who used their wealth to re-write the rules so that they could become ever more wealthy and ever more powerful. Using his skills and those of the Washington Post the two newspapers ran a programme that would last more than two years. They worked methodically through the long list of those whose corrupt activities were so carefully documented by the late Mr Aram Mikoyan.

During that time the political worlds of many countries went through a cathartic period where the local press was given the necessary information to bring about the necessary change. The experience in Israel had been a salutary lesson in how not to use powerful data on powerful people.

Nowhere was the effect more dramatic that at home in the UK. The nearly two dozen individuals who had been dealt a fatal blow were, for the main part, history within a matter of months. Parliament was controlled by Mr Speaker for the ten days it took for the ruling party to discover someone clean enough to take on the role of Prime Minister and a similar story could be told about the opposition politicians.

The following year the number of by-elections in the UK had steadily grown to an astonishing one hundred and twenty. One such by-election was scheduled to take place in the Truro constituency. The candidates included a man who had recently become a widower after a tragic fire at his home in Perranarworthal. He was supported during his campaign by his two sons and it was quite a surprise to the established world of politics but no surprise to those that knew him when he became The Honourable Jack Mawgan MP. "Sometimes in order to beat them you have to join them," he was heard to say during his acceptance speech.

His arrival in the Houses of Parliament signalled another important career change for Jack. Could a detective ever forget his policeman's skills, could the caring and loving medic survive in the cut and thrust of politics?

For Jack, one door closed and another opened. For the few that knew his capabilities and understood his motivation there was an air of expectation. Would politics in the post Mikoyan era be different? Would the flood of fresh blood into the British political system bring about a change to the way wealth was distributed in Britain's multicultural society?

One thing was certain Jack would never pass by when the opportunity to right wrongs came along.

EPILOGUE

May 2007

THE MAN WHO HAD orchestrated the death of Doctor Pamela Mawgan and created so much pain and sorrow was sipping gin and tonic on the veranda of his seaside home in northern Cyprus. He was at peace with himself and with the world and felt secure in this anachronistic corner of the globe where power apparently replaced the rule of law and extradition was not allowed.

Sir William Salisbury had always believed in the maxim one should never put all one's eggs in one basket. He may have lost millions thanks to the treachery of Aram Mikoyan but he still had access to the money he had salted away in Cypriot banks. Life was good; he had his freedom and all he could wish for in the shape of life's little luxuries. NSS Inc. was alive and well and living in dark corners wherever these were tolerated.

It had taken Nathan Mawgan just two months to research the lifestyle of the man who had killed his mother and to lay the plans for his demise. Dan Barclay was a willing tutor when it came to teaching Nathan how to use a high-powered rifle and Nat turned out to be a natural. Soon he was matching Dan with a six inch grouping at five hundred yards.

Hunting was a popular pastime on the island. Boar hunting was encouraged to minimise the risk of disease transmission to the domestic pig population.

Getting a licence to hunt on Cyprus like most things on that island was simply a matter of finding the right person and offering the right bribe. With licence in hand Nat found a group of UK sportsmen who were keen shots and avid hunters and persuaded them to join him for a week of boar hunting in the north of Cyprus. They too were furnished with the correct documentation and Nathan was able to call upon a special fund set up by family friends to pay the bills.

As the de facto leader of the group it was down to Nat, a natural woodsman and experienced outdoor sportsman to organise their daily activity. On the last day of their expedition he found himself in a much better location than he could possibly imagine. The edge of the woods turned out to be just four hundred yards from the rear of Salisbury's villa and had a clear view of the terrace and pool. He sent his three colleagues on a route around the back of the wood. They would work their way along the ridgeline towards the coast, driving the boar towards his chosen vantage point. His colleagues were unaware of his real motive for being up on that hill and had no suspicion that his focus at that moment was not on a boar but on a man.

It took half an hour of patient waiting before his target appeared. Salisbury, in red shorts and colourful shirt, was prodding the contents of his barbecue and holding a conversation with someone out of sight on the terrace.

He removed the covers from the telescopic sight and peered through the orange coloured optics. He felt the breeze on his left cheek and just as Dan had taught him he adjusted the scale, two clicks left. He was firing downhill so would need to compensate. He put the cross hairs on the target, took and deep breath, put his finger on the trigger and took the first pressure, flipped the safety off and quietly said to himself – "BANG".

The sudden rustling behind him signalled the arrival of his real prey. A group of boar emerged from the undergrowth darting this way and that. He changed from the prone position to kneeling in a jiffy and as soon as the large males leading the charge were in a safe zone he fired two snap shots and they both dropped to the floor. Two kills with just two shots. The thrill of the hunt was still pushing adrenalin round his body when he remembered the cold emotionless moment when he had peered through the gun sights at a human being. He doubted that he could ever kill a person but as a young man who had spent many months in some of the world's finest wildernesses he knew that killing for food was an essential skill and the only kind of killing he could tolerate.

The day ended in a local restaurant where they congratulated each other on a good week's sport. The day's haul had been exchanged for a fine dinner and copious amounts of wine although no one seemed to notice that Nat had actually consumed very little.

By the time the party broke up the others were well oiled and staggered off to bed in fine spirits. Nat stayed in his seat, checked his watch and took out his cell phone. He sent an SMS to an associate, sat back and waited.

Half an hour later a van pulled up outside, two men Nat had never seen before took a third man from the rear of the van and led him into the restaurant. His hands were tied behind his back and his mouth was gagged with a piece of tape. They sat him down at Nat's table and removed the tape. He had a look like thunder but was doing his best to remain cool. He was still wearing the same colourful shirt and red shorts.

"Who the hell are you?" he spat at Nat who smiled and said calmly, "I, Sir William, am the son of Doctor Pamela Mawgan. She was a fine woman and a brilliant mother but unfortunately for me she died in a fire that was set by two of your goons just before Christmas."

"I don't know what the hell you're talking about. I had nothing to do with it."

"Ah, so you do remember the incident then?" Salisbury remained silent but looked Nat straight in the eye.

"Earlier today I was looking at you through the sights of a high powered rifle. I was just above your villa, on the hill. We were hunting wild boar but that was a ploy. I wanted to see what it felt like to have the man who killed my mother at my mercy. I wanted to see what it felt like to make the decision to kill you or to let you live. Killing you would have been easy. You would have had an easy death. You don't deserve an easy death Mr Salisbury."

"Pah! You're just a damn schoolboy, what would you know?"

"Let me tell you something Mr Salisbury. You know all about power because you had the money to back it up. As of five minutes ago you no longer have any money, your family no longer has any money, you no longer have a home, your family will very likely disown you anyway when they find out about your stack of child pornography found by the police on your computer."

"But I don't have any such thing on my computer,"

"Well Mr Salisbury you do now. Your credit cards are no good, your bank accounts are closed and your cars have been impounded after drugs were found stashed in a secret compartment."

"I've never used drugs in all my life."

"By tomorrow your boat will be gone and when you finally leave prison you will be forced to wander the streets a friendless pauper despised by all. The newspapers will tell it all. And by the way, the hundred thousand Euros you keep in the wall safe along with your wife's jewellery has been confiscated. You see Mr Salisbury, you overstepped the mark, now I am the one with the money so I have the power. I have friends, good friends, friends in high … no, very high places, with influence and power and because this is a good cause they helped me to pay off your friends here in Cyprus. Now, to them you are a nobody so in the morning you will be going to prison and in Cyprus they don't treat paedophiles well I can assure you."

Salisbury moved as if to attack Nat. but the two heavies pushed him back in his seat.

"Take him to Police HQ, they're expecting him."

THE END

LIST OF CHARACTERS

Jack Mawgan – Ex Homicide Detective and now Registered Paramedic.

ACC Edward Hastings – Aviation Specialist at the Home Office.

ACC Norman Bennett – Former Unit Inspector at South Sussex ASU.

Aram Mikoyan – Armenian Oligarch of Russian descent.

Archie Bollingsworth – Editor in Chief at The Guardian Newspaper.

Ariadne Cooper-Smythe – Freddie McLaren's girlfriend, known to all as 'Harry'.

Arial Ehud Beg – Israeli Prime Minister.

Baroness Parker, (number nine) – Patron, East Yorkshire Air Ambulance (widow and previously head of MI6). Maiden name Helena Baker-Knowles.

Boris Mikoyan – Son of Aram Mikoyan.

Brian Curnow – West Briton journalist.

Bridget Wilson – Eleanor Bennett's sister.

Captain Diego Dellamorte – Captain of La Reine Bleu.

Captain Max Penworth – Home Office Aviation Advisor.

Claude Deschamps – European Sales Manager, WEA.

Clementine – Sir Gerald's mistress.

Damien Porter – Operations Director National Security Service Corp.

Dan Barclay – Still running his PI business in Exeter.

Darvesh Singh – Vehicle electronics expert.

David Montgomery – Chancellor of the Exchequer.

Derek Salisbury – One time CEO of Consultancy for Helicopter Operations and Administration (CHOPA).

Doctor Assad Helu – Lebanese business man and owner of the farm that Jack worked on in Morocco.

Dr Monique Barclay – Dan's wife. Now working at Devon & Exeter Royal Infirmary.

Dr Pamela Mawgan – Still a GP at Devoran but now full time.

Dr Skellie – Rogue government scientist who apparently committed suicide rather than face justice.

Eleanor Bennett – ACC Norman Bennett's wife.

Freddie McLaren – PM's Press Officer, advisor and custodian of almost limitless 'back-room' power.

General Meyer – Israeli Defence Minister.

George Parker – Baroness Parker's husband (d.1995).

Gerard van Damm – Owner of Scandes Trucking.

Gordon Mulligan – Aide to the Chancellor.

Haitham – Doctor Helu's chauffeur.

Hercule – Manager at Scandes Trucking.

Hugh Martin – Head of IT at accountants in Bristol.

Jack Blakeney – Home Secretary.

JoJo – Friend of Boris from The Netherlands.

Josephine Mallard – Home Secretary's advisor.

Julie Stewart – PM's wife.

Julio Emmiyan – Boris Mikoyan's cousin.

Justin Wood – Deputy Head MI5.

Lars Jontvedt – Friend of Boris from Denmark.

Maria – Crew member La Reine Bleu.

Marian Herd – Labour Health Secretary.

Marjorie Martin – Hugh's wife.

Marko – Helicopter Pilot La Reine Bleu.

Moshe Lavan – Israeli opposition leader.

Mr Jordan – National Security Services Corp.

Mr Smythe – National Security Services Corp.

NPAS – The Chief Pilot, Eric 'Lofty' Anderson, all five foot five of him; Ian 'Robbie' Robertson, Chief Training Pilot; Cliff Barman, Chief Engineer and Chief Inspector 'Dusty' Miller, the Unit Executive Officer.

Patricia Wellborn – Jack's replacement at the Cornwall AA.

Peter Falconer – Jack's replacement at Halfpenny Green.

Peter Norman – Air Ambulance Pilot.

Petre Iliescu – Romanian truck driver.

Rodney Parker – Runs a boatyard in St Just in Roseland, Baroness Parker's son.

Sandra Deschamps – Friend of Boris from France.

Sergeant Murray Burton – Rogue ASU agitator.

Shayetet 13 – Israeli Navy Special Forces Unit.

Sir Gerald Anthony Lummis KCB – (b1948-d2001) Patron of the helicopter community.

Sir Richard Shakespeare – Head of MI5.

Sir William Salisbury – President and CEO National Security Service Corp.

Sonja – Crew member La Reine Bleu.

The Gordini Brothers – Paid muscle at Scandes Trucking.

Toby Stewart – Prime Minister.

Trudy – Paramedic.

The Jack Mawgan Trilogy
Book 1
FOR THE PRICE OF A HAT

Synopsis

Jack Mawgan, a successful homicide detective, abandons his career to become a paramedic but his instincts for solving violent crime prove impossible to leave behind. In his first case in this new role a millionaire businessman from Glasgow is assassinated at his home in Cornwall. The killer's trail leads to an aristocratic crook and his henchman who both have much blood on their hands. Jack attends the murder scene in his new role as ambulance technician but it leads to a life threatening situation for him, his family and his friends that is only resolved after more murder and mayhem.

The Jack Mawgan Trilogy
Book 2
RENDER UNTO CAESAR

Synopsis

Jack Mawgan is about to fulfil his ambition to become a qualified paramedic when an incident involving a young Muslim found naked on a Cornish road in broad daylight draws him into the sinister world of 'Extraordinary Rendition'. This campaign was run by the US security services and involved their operatives in torture in their search for information about Al Qaeda's activities. Jack's involvement sets off a chain of events that leads him to the depths of the African interior in pursuit of a self-proclaimed jihadist fomenting rebellion and heavily involved in the drugs trade.